also by
ignácio de loyola brandão in english translation:

Zero
And Still the Earth
Teeth Under the Sun

anonymous celebrity

Originally published in Portuguese as *O Anônimo Célebre* by Global Editora, 2002

Library of Congress Cataloging-in-Publication Data

Brandão, Ignácio de Loyola, 1936-
[Anônimo célebre. English]
Anonymous celebrity / Ignácio de Loyola Brandão ; translated by Nelson H. Vieira.
-- 1st English translation.
  p. cm.
ISBN 978-1-56478-432-2 (pbk. : alk. paper)
1. Fame--Fiction. 2. Satire. I. Vieira, Nelson. II. Title.
PQ9698.12.R293A8613 2009
869.3--dc22

                    2009009290

Partially funded by grants from the National Endowment for the Arts, a federal agency; the Illinois Arts Council, a state agency; and by the University of Illinois at Urbana-Champaign.

Obra publicada com o apoio do Ministério da Cultura do Brasil/Fundação Biblioteca Nacional / Coordenadoria Geral do Livro e da Leitura.

The publication of this book was partly supported by the Ministry of Culture of Brazil, the National Library Foundation, and the General Coordination for the Book and Reading.

www.dalkeyarchive.com

Cover: design and composition by Danielle Dutton, illustration by Nicholas Motte
Printed on permanent/durable acid-free paper and bound in the
United States of America

anonymous celebrity
ignácio de loyola brandão

translated by nelson h. vieira

Dalkey Archive Press
Champaign and London

I'm not the owner of this image of me.
I'm not the owner of this image: —he is.
He is not me.
We converse in the garrets of our sentences
We put personal pronouns at intervals.
I am my own

Image,
Affonso Romano de Sant'Anna

Because the noblest purpose
is not to be ourselves, or better,
it is to be by being others,
to live in a plural way,
just as the universe is plural

Mr. Pirandello Is Wanted on the Telephone,
Antonio Tabucchi

I fought with a billy goat
but I don't know what happened:
I entered into him,
he entered into me,
and in that mix-up
I don't know if I was him
or if he was me.

The Poet of the Absurd, cordel story,
Orlando Tejo/Zé Limeira

THIS IS MY LAST
CHANCE TO
MAKE MYSELF
INTO A LEGEND.
OTHERWISE,
I'LL BE CONDEMNED TO SUFFER
THE EVERLASTING
TORMENT OF THE
ANONYMOUS.

It's delicious not to be ordinary. Not to be a common man.

Not to have good sense.

Not to be levelheaded, decent,

restrained.

And, therefore, stupid. Ignorant.

Not to be sensible (what a horrible word),* and therefore foolish.
Silly.

Not to be the same as everyone else. To separate oneself from
the masses (it rhymes with asses) who live a humdrum, morbid,
sickening daily life. You've all probably read how the extraordinary, the famous, the celebrated, the legendary all suffer. They're
so anxious! The price of fame is too high! It's not worth it! But that
all just comes from jealousy. Resentment.

Makes you want to laugh. Burst out laughing.

Sure, we suffer. But we suffer differently. We suffer with pleasure. People follow all our problems on the news—our depres-

---

* I know what you would say, Letícia, with that sarcastic grin—you always
smiled when you wanted to hurt me a little: Sensible? So who's talking about
good sense?

sions, headaches, our cheating and being cheated on, our sadness, unhappiness, sickness, pain.

People read the papers and are on our side. It's lovely.

Though at the same time, there's also the satisfaction that comes from seeing the famous, the celebrated, the idolized suffer—seeing them depressed, ruined, bankrupt, fucked up, decadent.

Yes, certain ordinary people want us to die out, want us out of the way. Even I feel that way sometimes, when I read about rivals of mine who have become more successful.

But I don't see a problem with any of that—the sympathy or hatred my celebrity causes.

I don't have any complexes. I'm not neurotic. I don't even go to a shrink. What matters is that everyone wants and idolizes me.

I don't insist that they love me, not even that they like me. It's not necessary. Just so long as they recognize and admire me.

I insist that you be envious, respectful, and jealous. I am what I am and you are nobody. Nothing. Worthless. Dust. Particles. Corpuscles. Specks.

How many millions of people like you have no one, absolutely no one to want them? Don't you think our old-fashioned ideas about loneliness and happiness ought to be revised a little?

Because no matter what you say, it's always the anonymous who suffer most.

It's practically impossible for a celebrity to go out into the street, to a bar, to have a peaceful meal in a restaurant, to go shopping, to take a walk in a mall (there's a mall that pays me just to walk around and be seen in it—can't remember the name), to go to the movies, to see a show, to go to the theater, without being recognized.

But surely it's worse to go out onto the street and have nobody recognize you—for no one to know who you are.

To have nobody staring at you with curiosity, nobody asking for your autograph or telephone number, nobody flirting with you, kissing you, nobody pointing at you, nobody envying and admiring you. Nobody following you, nobody photographing you with one of those disposable cameras they make for tourists.

It would be better never to have been born in the first place than to have to walk the streets unrecognized. (Is there even a difference?)

It's only the fact of being seen and known that makes me real, that makes me certain that I am, that I exist, that I am here.

It's wonderful to be seen, to be recognized. It's the mainspring of my life.

It's wonderful to be loved and hated—because, yes, there are people who detest me, despise me, people who'd even like to spit on me.

I wonder: has any celebrity ever really been spat on, really spat on—had a mouthful of phlegm emptied out on him?

What would that be like, do you think?

To feel all that rage splatter over my skin, seething, because of my success, my fame.

Still. Anyone who'd spit on me like that would be a worm, a larva, a microorganism.

An insect to be squashed.

BEING EVERYWHERE, BEING NOBODY

There's a crucial moment when a celebrity finds himself separated from the world of the anonymous.

The moment when you find your name inscribed on the same tablet as the other great legends of our time.

Lots of people have good, memorable names, of course, but they're still in an uncomfortable position—still vulnerable.

The crucial moment is when a newspaper reader or television viewer asks: Who's that? What does he do?

If no one knows the answer, you've been entered into the catalogue of the damned, along with the rest of the herd, those people who swarm over everything but mean less than nothing. You've become no more than one of those charming, smiling, amusing, talkative, well-dressed hangers-on who snap up invitations to every event, who become friends with everybody, but have no trade, profession, career, occupation, or specific function. They make appearances, that's all—fodder for the gossip columns.

The other day I overheard a chilling précis of this type of minor character: "Every court has its fool—kings had them once upon a time, and today the powerful still keep them around."

Modern clowns: they cheer us up, entertain us; they know how to drink, how to treat a lady, light a cigarette, laugh at a joke, dance all the steps from bolero to techno, snort cocaine; they're well informed, at ease with computers, subscribe to all the financial magazines, buy *Wallpaper*, *Arena*, and *Spruce*, read all the society and political columns (even though they have no views of their own); go on and on about the latest trends, know all the up-to-date slang.

Well-dressed, well-groomed, maybe gay, probably parasites; the women always chic, with tiny bodies, maybe fashion models, probably whores, maybe lesbians, probably asexual, still probably orgasmic when they get to appear in photographs, when they see themselves in magazines; usually tacky, behind the times, but always considering themselves indispensable at parties; interesting, good sports, accepted by everyone, circulating in every social circle. People who drop important names, who socialize with financiers and CEOs, theater directors and producers, promoters, executives, politicians, con-men, thieves, bank presidents, secretaries of state, ministers, cabinet chiefs (few people really know just how powerful a cabinet chief is).

A really famous person has to be careful not to mix, not to blend in. He should tolerate these court jesters, yes, but if he can, it's better to avoid fraternizing with them. They'll say you're their friends.

Still, we who play the game have reached an understanding, a gentleman's agreement, in which their deceit is accepted and embraced, and as such the truly famous will always applaud the audacity of these nonentities, admire their façade.

People in the know are able to distinguish, to separate real fame from the mere appearance of fame.

I want to be in the know. I intend to research, to delve into this lifestyle. These entanglements, this labyrinth separating hangers-on from a true celebrity.

I intend to do this, to acquire these skills, in order to better combat the machinations of my enemies, as well as to plot my own. To better trap my many enemies, that is, because in my new life they are legion, and they all work together: lying, cheating, fucking each other, and making my life difficult.

It's war. And war doesn't allow for any compromises, any passivity, conformity, or comfort—unless of course you're the self-destructive type and want to make sure you fail.

You have to plan your every move in your sleep and wake up in the morning still planning, because it never stops: there's always another day, needing another stratagem, day after day after day.

9

What's really deadly, a gradual suicide, a slow-acting poison, is the life I'm leading now. Just existing. Not yet a legend. I spend the day imagining, planning, mapping out what I intend to become.

Because I suffer like few human beings have ever suffered, secluded here in my room, my dressing room, Room 101—a shameful place, though spacious enough (a bit old, it's true: the walls are peeling), almost a suite, surrounded by the books and notebooks containing the details of my grand design, my plan to achieve what is, after all, my true destiny.

I would love it if the press would tell the world what a bastard I am. The gossip, the arguments, my name spoken at every table.

They could say that I'm a hick, a crude fucker, completely feral,
perverted, a pedophile, a crook,
a sadist, rustic, rude, a shit,
a rat, morbid, the Antichrist, the devil himself,
a faggot, a son-of-a-bitch, a pederast, a barbarian,
out of control.
Wouldn't bother me at all.

What breaks my heart, what leaves me sleepless, is that my fame is still being kept from me.

IS A DWARF-DOG AN ANIMAL?

The latest big success on television is this dwarf who, during a live talent show, pretends to be a dog and goes around on all fours, wearing a collar. There's a little house for him, and he comes out to bark at the amateur singers who compete on his program. His bark is the gong, as it were, that ends a given performance. If you sing well enough, the dwarf-dog stays quiet; to create suspense, though, sometimes he growls at the camera a little.

The public loves the animal, brings it hot dogs, little woolen clothes for the winter, flea remedies, colorful collars, embroidered cushions. Sometimes the show's announcer calls the dog over and asks him to stop barking. Then he teases the dog until he starts barking again, and the announcer begins to kick him and order him back to his doghouse. The public laughs and shouts: Go on doggy, go on home!

A woman once brought a little bitch to crossbreed with the dwarf; she wanted little dwarf-dogs, wanted to raise the exclusive specimens of a new race. The announcer made the dwarf-dog come out of his little house to sniff the bitch's tail and to try and breed with her—right there on stage. The audience yelled, Breed, breed, fornicate, fornicate! and the dwarf tried but couldn't. The crowd, hysterical and indignant, began to shout, Fuck the bitch already, fuck that dog! The director cut things short and went to commercials.

The dwarf, desperate, ran back into his house. The announcer called him, but nothing happened. Nothing, that is, until—beside himself—he grabbed his whip and began beating the roof of the little house until the tiny man-dog came out, trembling, at which point the announcer whipped him so violently that he bled. People complained to the Society for the Protection of Animals, but the Society said, We can't do anything, a dwarf isn't an animal. The

11

newspapers devoted pages and pages to the incident, and maga-zines dedicated their covers. The dwarf is making food commer-cials now. He's going to be rich. There are women lining up at his door. After all, little men do have big dicks.

I hate it when other people get so lucky!

MONSTER

Bette Davis being interviewed on a cable channel:

"Unless you are known as a monster, you'll never become a star."

The interview didn't have a date. TV documentaries are pretty unreliable. Bette was right, however, as I've just noted in my *Manual*. She knew. She understood our pain.

I think Bette Davis may already be dead.[*]

---

[*] Research: Yes, she's dead. I only just found out. I don't know when she died, the details escape me. I love to read news about famous dead people. Bette was born April 5, 1908, and her real name was Ruth Elizabeth Davis. She was obsessed with order and cleanliness and afraid of bee stings and being bitten by cats. Of course, I love *All About Eve*, directed by Joseph L. Mankiewicz. But I confess I like her in *The Little Foxes*, directed by William Wyler, even more. She gave a wonderful, fresh performance, even though she might have been less than pleased at having to play yet another bitter, cold, ruthless person. I disagree: those type of characters really fascinate me. And it's easy to play them. We're all bitter, cold, ruthless. Civilization forces us to repress these feelings. I've got Fagner on my CD player, singing "The Last Parrot's Perch." It's not the right background music for these thoughts, but what can you do. I'll get back to Mankiewicz later. If I don't forget.

MANUAL OF SHORTCOMINGS TO BE CORRECTED

I think of all the rules. The sacred rituals of modern life. I have moments of lucidity when I see that men like me must deviate from the norm, writing new rules by virtue of their behavior, new rules that end up becoming the major trends of their time. This is one way to make use of the media.

Without the media I'm nothing. We're nothing. I would be nothing. Without the media, I wouldn't be able to live. Not a single one of you out there in TV-Land, or else you faithful moviegoers (even though I've made so few films: having to wait around between my scenes irritates me; they still haven't invented a way to set up new shots quickly enough to keep me interested), would know anything about how I lived my life.

The public lives according to the norms set by celebrities, isn't that so? What celebrities do, how they act, and what they think becomes law, the testament of our times. I'm not exaggerating. The media is a survival manual, a design for living. It tells you everything you need to know:

What to wear.

What to eat.

Where to eat.

What to drink (the "drink" of the moment).

What wines go with what food.

The right entrée.

The right cheese, the right bread (bagels are popular these days).

In fact, bakeries are very hip right now, highly sought-after by columnists and photographers wanting to hobnob with the elite. This tradition was initiated in the Sumaré neighborhood of São Paulo, in the bakery next to the old TV Tupi building—the broadcasting network with the little Indian logo, the pioneer channel, the first station in Brazil. I would give anything to have been in that famous photo of the important TV Tupi personnel, all standing in that bakery. You can see Chatô, the entrepreneur (I need to reread his biography, the one by Fernando de Morais), Homero Silva, the announcer, and an unknown young woman— an unknown with a famous face; I could have been one of them, why not, when I was just starting out . . .

What's big at the moment are organic greens and vegetables, without agro-toxins, not transgenic.

I don't actually know what "transgenic" means. I just know that I have to express doubt or repulsion whenever I say it. It impresses people. Anyway:

Best collar.

Best cuffs.

Ideal length for sleeves.

Ideal cut for pants.

Fortunately, there are books to help supplement and refine what the media tells us. I thank Glória Kalil, Costanza Pascolato, and Fernando de Barros. I memorized their manuals, studied photos of society events to see how everyone dresses.

This season's colors.

Best type of shoe: High heel.

Best belts.

Best wallets.

Trendiest credit card.

What beach to frequent.

Best swimsuit—though you don't say "swimsuit," these days, you call it a "speedo," maybe, or what? "Swimwear"? Note to self: Research this.

Glasses. A pair for each occasion, of course.

The right hat for the right moment.

Music. Most popular CD. And then, least popular CD—a CD so unpopular I own the only copy in town. To "hook" a completely unknown album, Iranian maybe, or one by some regional singer from New England. An Irishman or Norwegian. In Norway, by the bye, they don't just hook good codfish—they're also making excellent films. Go out and buy *The Best 100 Films of All Time*, you'll see. The verb "to hook" is popular now. So is the word "acoustic."

Which DVD player to have in your Home Theater.

EVERYBODY THINKING ABOUT ME AT THE SAME TIME

"You know how it is: You're young, you're drunk, you're in bed, you have knives; shit happens!" Napoleon said that death is nothing, but to live defeated and without glory means to die every day.

I printed and framed a passage from Julien Green's book (*Si J'étais Vous* [If I Were You]): "You know as well as I that one of the major causes of boredom is the narrowness of our daily life. Every morning we wake up the same creatures . . . The thought that man must be eternally the same is one that, to those whose minds are ennobled by the practice of reflection, is really unbearable. To get out of one's own shell, to become someone different, are surely as intelligent aspirations as have ever entered the human brain?"

No other sensation in life can surpass the instant when you discover, are told, see that the whole country (why not the world?) has its eyes on you.

Everybody is thinking only about that one person, about the celebrity who inhabits their minds and desires, prayers and jealousies, passions and denials.

If this were to happen to me, it would be the ultimate, multiple, final orgasm.

To live after that would be painful.

Unnecessary.

THE DIVINE GIFT OF AGGRESSIVENESS

The well-known man must be temperamental.

Must impose his notability by being harsh, by being abusive, by making demonstrations of one's insanity, by indulging in unexpected and frightening behavior.

Must impose himself by rebelling against his boss—in my case, since I am a television star, against the writer, against mediocre colleagues. Must make his producer, cameraman, and director unbearably anxious by way of his temperament—must especially cause his director constant agony.

John Ford. I'm sure you recognize the name: one of the great pillars of American cinema. His biography was recently published. About the book, Amir Labaki states: "John Ford emerges from this narrative as a rude man, cruel director, absent husband, lapsed father, and insolent drunk." And the journalist Alexander Agabiti Fernandez says: "Patrick, the filmmaker's son, described him as an offensive father, but a good film director and a good American . . . He was a leader, did what was necessary for people to follow him and didn't hesitate to intimidate, to lambaste people. It's not difficult to understand the absence of close friends in his life, despite his being surrounded by people . . . He demoralized John Wayne during the filming of *Stagecoach*, 1939, one of the great classics of film, by saying that he walked like a queer." Just imagine, Wayne, the most virile man on screen! While filming *Mister Roberts*, 1955, he came to blows with Ford and the two never spoke to each other again.

That's how legends are made. I support my views with exemplary figures so people won't reject my reasoning.

It's important to threaten the photographers or reporters who might pursue you, wanting to know all about your personal life.

I attack them by swearing, shoving, hitting them, spitting in their faces.

To show my contempt.

After the outrage, reported with indignation, the public-relations person for the aggressor will hold a press conference "lamenting the event" and explaining that so-and-so behaved out of nervousness motivated by personal problems, and besides, the other guy had invaded his privacy.

The press, always groveling before celebrities, will want to know more about these personal motives. At this point, the tone of my announcement will change. My internal "manual" advises me to utilize as many odd and difficult words as possible.

Reporters have terrible vocabularies, you see. They don't know how to write. Their articles are infantile, their editorials primitive. Most journalists are hardly even literate. I ought to write my own editorial exposing them. And if they ask me to name names? I'll try and get away by rephrasing my attack: "*Some* journalists are barely literate." But what if they insist? We live in a time of exposés. The media would like us to believe that we live in an age of transparency; it's necessary, we've been told, to put the finger on every corrupt and incompetent worker in the nation.

I really need to hire myself a lawyer to teach me how to make defamatory remarks that aren't actionable.

Anyway, only antipathy, ferociousness, the threat of violence, and constant aggression can lead to respect and admiration.

People should approach celebrities with fear and anxiety clearly stamped on their faces.

Should come up to us like mangy dogs, only too happy to be kicked.

Plane trips are real resources. Onboard, one must play the lunatic, must insult the flight attendants, offend the other passengers, spit wildly, knock over other people's trays. Look what the media did to that carioca designer who flipped out, or that minor actor who ended up being tied down by his fellow passengers. They became stars.

Down deep, I know I should become a *real* lunatic, not just pretend to be one. I must live this experience, must truly adopt this unpredictable persona.

Observe my tactics:

If someone expects to be kicked, offer them your affection. Disarm and conquer. They'll love and defend you forever.

Today, a caress, no matter how small, is uncommon—an anachronism.

A good line for the magazines to use in their "Notable Quotes of the Week" sections.

MODERNITY

"Stop resisting," says my Consultant on Personal Well-Being. "Go to a fortune-teller. She'll give you peace, certainty. Provide you with direction."

LET IT BE KNOWN WHAT IT IS I'M PREPARING FOR

I've come up with some thoughts that will seem abnormal to so-called normal people, people who want a conventional life, daily existence without anything to upset them, people who like to float around in the infinite tedium of a life that's always the same as yesterday and identical to tomorrow.

I've given fame a lot of thought.

There's a hitch. You can be known, spoken of, famous for some indeterminate time—that's easy enough. Afterwards, though, it depends on you, your luck, your destiny. You can still be forgotten.

To be a legend, to be remembered in perpetuity, it's necessary to die young. The price of eternal fame is your life.

It's a ritual, like the Incas practiced. Sacrifice.

I was certain, at sixteen, that I wouldn't live past my twenties. Maybe I'd reach twenty-two, after having made one movie, a real melodrama. I imagined people wouldn't even pay attention to my work before then. Then: death. I dreamed about it!

An extraordinary accident, brutal, or a routine misfortune, inconceivable. A murder at some intersection, a stray bullet while gassing up my sports car, or maybe I'd choke on a fishbone (Norma Bengell almost died like that at the Cannes Film Festival in 1961), expire from an overdose during an orgy, fall into an alcoholic coma, contract a little anthrax (is anthrax likely?), fall from a great height, or be thrown into the volcano at Vesuvius (like the republican Silva Jardim).

The news of my demise would be widely broadcast. Because, in this society, the death of a young actor arouses curiosity, causes excitement, sells newspapers, gets good ratings. Who *was* this man?

Because such tragedies occur so swiftly, and so beggar the public imagination, the masses rush out to buy the daily newspapers, gorging themselves on the gory details, pillaging the newsstands of every last copy. Extra editions are printed. The magazines, however, hold back the news of the event, saving it for a special issue—which then promptly sells out as well.

What was his life like? So little is known. There is scant information, not one family photo, a barebones biography. This excites people all the more.

Mystery. Perplexity. Who was this kid? Why this widespread hysteria? The lives of the great. It's an enigma.

Then, somebody discovers an amateur film (remember Zapruder, the man who filmed Kennedy's assassination?), made just for fun by some kids from the slums, in which I appear shirtless, a naked torso. Watch the six and seven o'clock soaps. All the young actors have to take their shirts off, have to show off their abs. That's how they say it, isn't it? Abs. No talent, only "ripped abs." A television station buys the Super 8 film (not made anymore) and shows it on the air. 80% rise in the ratings. Repeat showings. 90%. Amazement all around. The little film develops a cult. Albums emerge with frame enlargements. Posters. Scenes from the film are reproduced in magazines. Semiotic scholars study the phenomenon. Plastic statuettes. Buttons. Pilgrimages to the cemetery. Marketing, merchandising, sponsors hoping to get tax breaks by investing in the phenomena (courtesy Rouanet's Law).

Friends of mine spring up from nowhere. All the people who never gave me a chance suddenly gain lucrative notoriety. Exploiters. Nonexistent girlfriends, the bride (fantasy of some neurotic nymphomaniac) I abandoned at the altar in some small backwoods town (small towns are pretty terrible, because—they tell me—of the monotony). Women adore this kind of detail, especially the lonely ones. Where's his father? Mother? Thousands of copies of the film are shown all over Brazil. Countless editions remastered for video. DVD.

An immense talent gone forever.

Few see through this nonsense.

The Brazilian James Dean, Jim Morrison, Rimbaud, Jimi Hendrix, Radiguet, Kurt Cobain, Ritchie Valens (my God, he had an enormous hit, "La Bamba," and only eight months of absolute fame), Michael Hutchence, Buddy Holly. Does anyone out there know how many years Scott Fitzgerald lasted as the God of American Literature? Nine years. Only nine!

Legends die young and thus are made eternal.

Janis Joplin died young, like the Brazilian poet Ana Cristina César. And why not mention the great Brazilian film director Glauber Rocha? And then there's always Che Guevara.

I didn't die prematurely. Therefore, my legend is already dead inside me.

You get only one chance. Or do you? Only the mysterious, the strange, the unusual can reconstruct my legend at this late date.

This is what I'm pursuing. I'm preparing myself for it by organizing this *Manual of Instructions*—a unique and original work of art.

CAREFUL, PLEASE

These scenes are fluid and quick.

They can dissolve. Volatile, changing, and fickle. Problems I still haven't been able to resolve. Being weightless, I don't know how to keep them down, to hold them steady in the same place.

Subtle and temperamental, portable (a pleasant attribute), they float around in all of us, somewhere or other.

LOVE IS SOLID, HAZY

My love. That kiss was unforgettable. There are moments that touch people forever. I've had several with you. Many have been like this: special, dear, and rare. Some can't be classified at all. They occupy a place I don't know how to describe. All I know is that the merest reminder of them causes a kind of hot-cold shiver, a trembling in my heart—the certainty of a love so sublime that it surpasses and transcends every and any attempt at classification. Today's kiss. The first touch of my fingers on your breast, inside the car, stopped halfway between two places in the deserted night, a moment so confusing for the both of us. Having slept by your side and upon awakening felt the warmth of your body next to mine. Having made love to you at dawn and afterwards to sleep again in your arms. Those are some of the moments I treasure and are saved in this special place in my memory that, besides the simple details of the fact, brings a kind of vivid sensation to the surface of my mind, and makes me believe—and very much so—that love exists. That it is solid and palpable. Also ethereal, hazy, a kind of wave, like mist on a mountain. It radiates from the heart, spreading itself over everything, rolling outwards towards the extremities, reaching the limits of the body, enveloping it totally. I'm at the edge of an abyss—in the best possible sense. Total detachment. Plenitude. Flight. The memory of these moments together brings tears to my eyes. Their beauty, purity, and tenderness. For a fleeting moment, dizziness and fear. Kisses. Letícia.

BEAUTY OF IMMORALITY

They put out the lights, turned off the electricity. Nobody can know—I was listening to Teixeirinha: "I kept our wedding band inside the old trunk, in the sorrowful trunk of unhappiness. I don't ever want to see that forgotten wedding band, the broken band of our happiness."

Oh, if they saw me crying, crying over such hackneyed nonsense. It would destroy me. Since they started rationing electricity, I'm afraid to walk around, to bang my knee against a piece of furniture in the dark, to hit my face against the sharp edge of a dresser, to bleed. William Holden fell and hit his head on his night table—he hemorrhaged and then died. He was drunk. He was an alcoholic. Being an alcoholic is one thing, being drunk is another.

Alcoholism confers status, you see, whereas a drunk is just someone who falls down in the street. I almost said gutter—a cliché. I don't drink. I hope nobody finds out! Part of my fame comes from always having been seen with a glass in my hand. It's tea, but it gives the impression that I have a vice, that I'm a man walking down the road to self-destruction. The public loves it. To know that the guy who has everything, money and fame, is sick, fucked in the head. It's dangerous, but they wish they could live like I do.

Alcoholics get compassion, they're news. The folks at home sit with their eyes glued to their boob tubes (I hate saying "boob tube"), looking for the signs of some addiction in their favorite stars. Everybody would love to get addicted to something, to be so fucked up, so rich, so seductive, to be somebody who doesn't have to give a damn about anything. The only thing is that most people are afraid, they need to live responsibly. So they control themselves. That's what has fucked up the world—control. This damn blockade that keeps life from being lived.

The other day, a newspaper called me up. Or a magazine. I don't know. One of those rags that costs a buck and sells like crazy. The public is a mangy dog nipping at our heels.

"Sir, can you make a statement?"

I always do, why not? One more piece of publicity.

"About what?"

"What's it like to be an alcoholic? It'll be important to the National Campaign for Solidarity."

The idiots on television adore social causes. Fake. All fake!

"I don't drink a drop."

"Everybody knows that you drink. You yourself said so to Hebe Camargo—it was a very moving statement. AA meetings all over the country were full of people confessing later that night. Your words have power. Help our campaign. You can save many people."

"I don't want to save anybody."

"It's a good cause, humane."

"Oh, shove humanity up your ass."

"What?"

"You deserve a kick in the balls, you know? Educational campaign my ass. Saving humanity! What lovely bullshit."

"Wait a minute . . . calm down, sir . . . celebrities have a certain responsibility towards the public . . ."

"Responsibility! I want to drink, I want to smoke, I want to drug myself stupid, eat fat, have high cholesterol, high blood pressure, a beer belly, I want to fuck, eat cunt, suck dick, die of cancer—I want the world to go fuck itself. Fuck you, mister—and fuck your magazine. I want to fuck all the girls who work in your office, and all the guys too. I want to get tuberculosis!"

"Good lord, you've really hit bottom! This is one hell of a binge! You do know I'm recording this, yes?"

"Record! Record! We live in the age of recordings. Of wiretaps. Send it to the goddamn senate, to the commission on ethics, to those idiots in Brasília. I want to see them revoke my rights, see if they can manage to revoke me entirely."

"Revoke you? Revoke what?"

"Revoke my fame."

"You have a pretty high opinion of yourself."

"If I'm not what I think I am—and what I think I am is one-hundred percent accurate, by the way—why are you bothering to interview me? Why come and ask me to save some drunks? Let them drink. Freedom for all addictions, I say, and for moral corruption, for the free ruination of our souls . . . For perversion! Hey, what a beautiful title for a prime-time soap. 'Ruins of the Soul.'"

"And what if I publish all this? I have it on tape!"

"Go ahead and publish it, it's the truth. And anyway, I'm going to say that I was licking your ass while you were busy taping all this."

"I . . . I've never met such a disgusting person. Absolutely disgusting. You're awful. They warned me."

"Hey, kiddo. Why not go fuck yourself."

"'Kiddo'? What year do you think this is? Who still talks like that?"

"Rude. You're rude!"

"I'm recording everything. I can sue you. For harassment."

"Go ahead, sue me. Sue me. Would you like me to eat your cunt out over the telephone? Stick the receiver in between your legs. Do you have money for a lawyer, you loser? I'll bribe the judges, I'll bribe all the judges, I'll bribe everybody. Senators bribe, entrepreneurs bribe, so I can bribe too."

"You're a monster!"

"Don't take that tone with me. You're loving every minute of this—you're going to play your little recording to everybody who'll listen. I want to hear it on the news! We could even burn ourselves a CD. It'll sell millions. The public loves to hear dirty stuff like this. I can say other things too, you know, really disgusting stuff, it'll make the hair around your pussy stand on end. This is going to make our CD sell like nobody's business, you know? And another thing!"

"What?"

"I want everybody to die of dengue!"

"They warned me. You're out of your mind."

"If I went out of my mind, the world did too."

"This is why everyone's afraid of you, why everybody hates you. They're furious with you. That's why everybody avoids you."

"You slut. You cow. Shit, everybody's afraid of everything—the world's already bursting with terrorists gearing up for holy war."

"Holy war? You don't know a thing about it. You're just some alienated fuckhead who spends his time contemplating his navel."

"Just leave me alone, you dike."

"You flaming, junky fag."

"You know what? I'm recording this too."

"So it's going to be one recording against another."

"It'd be nicer to have your cunt against my prick."

"I don't know why I don't hang up."

"Because you like it."

She hung up. She adored the interview.

If my PR guy saw me, he'd give me the Critic's Prize for that little performance. One more prize—I don't even have any shelves left to keep them on. Just a little room for my Oscar. I lay down, I'm tired. I put away my notebook. I snuff out my candle. Ideally, no one even saw me light it in order to read. I had my answers, all my vulgarity prepared beforehand. I wrote and rewrote it, the sentences are trim, perfect. For all occasions. If somebody telephones me, I'm not going to hem and haw. I'm becoming a stylist. A Father Vieira of vulgarity!

That newly-graduated journalist hates me. Or she loves me. I wonder what her name is. I'd like to put her on my mailing list. She'll come running when I invite her over.

PARTIES FOR CREATING IMAGES

My love. At that party you stood stock-still, neither drinking nor eating. Only staring. How you stare! It seems this is how you like to pass your time. I admired you for it. At those types of parties what people mostly do is devour the trays of food. Beautiful university girls, hired as servers, offer you champagne, holding the bottle by its base, a new protocol in the art of serving. You fascinated me. I mentioned you to my friend Francisca Botelho—the one who made the shiny gold ring. I'd never seen anybody observe others with such intensity. You'd stop in front of models, actors, artists, advertisers, writers, socialites, designers, drag queens, nobodies, journalists, stylists, watching them all "pose" for the cameras. Then I realized you knew all about the game of illusion and appearance. You knew those people weren't there for the pleasure of the party. The thrill came from exhibition, from parading themselves in the shop window. It came from lenses clicking, flashbulbs exploding. How horrendous the flash makes people look—the light flattens the face, bleaches the skin. And what about that magazine that forces women into a corner in an improvised studio—with a drape standing in for an infinite landscape behind them—and photographs them for the "Elegant Woman" section? You understood all those people standing in the "right pose," making the right gestures, the correct movements, everything rehearsed, the position of the head, hands holding their glasses or their canapés, the legs and feet planted just so. Everything studied, prepared. I imagine there's even such thing as a personal trainer who specializes in gesture. Oh, the happiness stamped all over their faces when they felt themselves held in a camera's lens. Those parties, we know, aren't staged to have fun, but rather to create images. There isn't, my love, a single natural gesture, a single slip, one misstep. Even the faux pas are intentional, because they are meant to be noticed. I have a stylist friend who hired herself a special Faux Pas Consultant. She's a

29

sociology and communications student—she comes up with the funniest, most ridiculous notions. A faux pas executed with wit makes the person in question "simpatico," human, "just like the rest of us," us being the mortal/normal ones, and the witnesses of said faux pas need this for their self-esteem. The faux pas mortalizes *him* or *her* who commits it. I just invented this word. A famous but distant and inaccessible person provokes rage, anger, and envy in an audience, resulting in negative karma, you see—bad vibes that spoil one's aura. This is not to be recommended, especially during eras like our own, when everybody lives with certain expectations as to what life owes them. It's also important to take care not to become known as a picturesque kind of figure, which feeds the anecdotal. You, you were approaching the party guests with a notebook, drawing them, you draw well, and you captured their gestures, attitudes, movements, tics, or, in the immobile, their stance. This is equally essential: to stand well. In a correct manner. I asked, Why is this man doing that? Who is he? And I think it was at that moment that I began to like you, to fall in love—you were a different sort of person in this world of sameness. I didn't just see you once, either, and just twice. It was many times, many times in the space of a year. It seemed like you attended every function, calmly taking notes with your beautiful hands. Later, when your fingers moved over my body, I appreciated their smoothness. The madness in your eyes, the intensity of our love. It took some time for me to see the passion you said you felt, see it in your eyes. But then it appeared—exploded. But the mystery, the curiosity was still in me: What does he do? I asked myself. Do I need to know? No. For the first time in my life, I was in love. I imagined that our love could knock down every barrier, could make the wall that hid you collapse. I would see my friends in unhappy relationships with domineering men, or else weak, insensitive men—narcissists, uncertain, restless. My friends weren't doing well. But me, I was content. Who were you? Who are you? Are you married? Ah, I knew that you had to be mar-

ried. A bit of a problem, but I let myself be taken in, let my love spill out—who can manage to hold it back when it really happens? And it made me feel good. It still does. Do you have other women too? Women you dream about? I never imagined that I could love a man like this, and I do love you. You seduce me, caress me—I give myself in bed with you like I never have to any other man. I'm sure I'm educating you to pleasure, and you are receptive too, showing things few men ever dare to reveal: gratitude, diligence . . . that you were my apprentice. I wonder whether or not it was that mysterious, insurmountable side to you that first seduced and enchanted me. Despite its sometimes bothering and depressing me. That I don't know what's really going on in your mind. A Kiss, Letícia.

THE RED DIGITS

They're pursuing me.

It's a fixation.

An obsession.

On the night table, always covered with papers, were many small notebooks, glasses of maté or ice-cold Coca-Cola, electric bills, hairclips, rings, bills, check stubs, appointment books, and heaps of our erotic love letters. There used to be two pictures of me there in plastic photo holders, but they must be empty by now.

I turned my face and saw them. The red digits.

They indicated what little time together we had left. I was sure I heard a slight click sometimes, when the seconds moved. Nonsense. I was so immersed in her, the hot smell of her mouth, her teeth shining in the shadows. My tongue touching those teeth.

But the digits were a prison. They commanded me: *Go, you have to go, enough for today.* How could I stand to look at them, remove my hand from that warm cunt, withdraw my tongue from that mouth, and go out and resume the responsibilities of my daily life?

I hurt her so many times, glancing up at those numbers, counting down the time we had left for the day.

Why did you love me, Letícia?

I loved you in order to save myself—for pleasure, passion, and a last chance to try and be someone else. No one knows how isolated I feel.

RESCUING THE ANONYMOUS FROM THE CAVERNS: WORLD TRADE CENTER

The photo was published in the majority of Brazilian newspapers in a full-page spread. When CNN and all the television channels of the world broadcast the scene, they froze it for a few seconds. Or minutes, hours, I don't know. For me time has infinite duration—I don't know how to measure it by normal parameters. Trying doesn't even interest me. From the World Trade Center buildings, minutes prior to their collapse—which would appear as a perfect and planned implosion—only grayish-blue and black vertical lines can be seen. Like a modernist painting—by whom? Which artist painted lines? Mondrian? No, not Mondrian, he painted squares, rectangles. Anyway, in the picture, the man is falling head first. His body straight, one of his legs bent. Did he jump? Slip? Did he faint and then fall? He probably lost consciousness because of the height, the smoke. He fell. He disappeared from the scene, from life, from the city. A million tons of rubble buried him soon after. Nobody knows his name. Impossible for his family to have him identified. He's an unknown who entered into history at the twenty-first century's first great moment of horror—the history of the world, the United States, communications, photography. Without anyone knowing who he is. And nobody will ever know. We'll only have suppositions, families who'll swear that he was theirs. But was he Brazilian, American, Latino, Chinese, Italian, Irish—what? He could have been anything, but now he's nothing. One among thousands, gone forever. And, while we're on the subject, what about the firemen who supposedly became such heroes that day—can you name a single one?

SO AS NOT TO BE EXCLUDED FROM LIFE

Always keep yourselves "plugged in." Jot down the latest things—now.

Make love with your own wife in public places, and be sure to invite a bevy of masturbating voyeurs to observe it. This has been the latest trend, ever since the publication of Catherine Millet's *The Sexual Life of Catherine M.*

I must take my wife, or companion, to a variety of sexual melees and report on what I do and how I do it, disclosing my hang-ups, quirks, and fantasies. I must feed the magazines and the innumerable gossip columnists who have their own bylines or spend hours on the radio, talking about famous people.

These columnists don't know, because their cultural education is minimal, dispensable (as much for the writers as for their readers), that the pioneers of this type of journalism were Louella Parsons and Hedda Hopper in the United States. They made the superstars eat from their hands, dance to their tunes. Then more than half a century went by, and nobody seemed to notice.

Since I'm normal, nothing exceptional, I have to hire myself a writer to make up fantasies, transforming me into a sexual object. Someone who makes love ten times a night, who fucks with a soft cock, according to oriental practice, who anyway has a thick and enormous prick, who comes up with odd new positions.

Gastronomy: tasting a skewered cricket or bat, cooked with garlic. A menu known as the "Outer Limits," an homage to the television program.

Purchasing a Japanese van with four-wheel drive with which to summer in the Bocaina Mountains.

Anybody who's really somebody is able to give good interviews about the best summer in his or her life. But Brazilian summers don't count. Nor do Argentine summers. Those are pretty tacky.

The Brazilian is curious, meddlesome, impertinent; he loves to stick his nose in everybody else's business. He wants to know everything—thus, success is guaranteed for the man who is willing to expose himself. Everybody saw those thousand people who went to pose naked for that American photographer in Ibirapuera Park. Those flabby, naked bodies that believed they were making art.

In the trendsetting magazine *Daslu*, I read that Riedel goblets heighten the aroma and taste of wines.

I'm in tune with my epoch. Or is the word "attuned"? If I were to say "up-to-date," I'd be banished.

When socializing, I need to be careful—do research and verify my facts. At dinner, the latest trend is to have a fashionable picnic: eliminate the entrée, main dish, and dessert—eat with the tips of your fingers—only a smattering of hors d'oeuvres, sipping vodka with apple juice as you go.

One no longer uses a "swear word." The politically correct synonym has become "adverb of intensity."

Tattoos confer status (though what they carve on you can't be too hip; I'll explain this paradox later).

I get extra points if I take along a bottle of Laurent-Perrier champagne.

I'm a man who's plugged in. I have to be, or else I'll be considered "out"—outside of the real world, outside of transactions, contracts, events, parties, relationships, opportunities—the opportunity to make a soap opera, for instance, or a film, commercial, or political campaign.

Outside of life, of living today's life.

Outside, even, of making love.

SELECTIONS FROM THE MENU

A famous person never ever orders his entrée from the menu. He always knows—is informed—that he will be offered a special item the chef has only just created, or created only for the privileged.

To have a menu in one's hands is to reveal that you're not somebody who counts.

You're a commonplace customer. Insignificant.

GALLERY OF CHARACTERS: FLITCRAFT (1)

The story of Flitcraft is one of the most extraordinary I've ever read. Perhaps it's not really all that sensational—it's hard for me to tell. All the strings of my body are so sensitive, taut, stretched to the limit, only waiting for the right touch to make them vibrate or snap. I know I can make this happen. I'm afraid. I don't know why. It's a real, physical fear—palpable. When we speak of others, or give advice, everything seems easy; but the moment we take the initiative in our own lives, all the colors change, become somber. Because we're dominated by a tragic, looming, dramatic feeling that's always with us—accompanying us everywhere, hemming us in. I am definitely catastrophic by nature. Certain people live happily, despite being unhappy, because they manage to laugh at their misfortunes: they transform their dramas, turning them around, using irony to reduce them to nothing. Myself, I know I'm walking down a blind alley with a wall facing me, and the entrance behind me now obstructed by another wall. Still, on the day I read the story of Flitcraft, I felt that a reprieve was actually still possible.

PAINTING ONE'S TOENAILS

Letícia. High-heeled sandals, very high; dresses that let you see her olive-skin belly, her suntanned skin, dotted here and there with tiny moles; an expression always oscillating from the enigmatic to the dubious, from the ingenuous to the clever, to the derisive, from the interrogative to the sarcastic. Her toenails painted with bright nail polish. How can one not be reminded of the title sequence from *Lolita*, 1962, directed by Stanley Kubrick? Sue Lyon's foot hovering onscreen, her toenails being painted, sensually, one by one—and those tufts of cotton stuck between her toes.

IT'S IMPORTANT TO HUMILIATE OTHERS

Meetings with an actor's entourage are boring and interminable, albeit necessary.

One rules over a gaggle of incompetents. Meetings have to be held, periodically, in order to keep them worrying.

In order to squash their self-esteem.

Run down their confidence. Drag down and otherwise undermine their sense of security. Do this two or three times a day.

Accuse them of not being passionate enough about their work, of not communicating well with each other, of not being team players who exchange ideas, of not planning things out, of not keeping an eye on expenses.

During these meetings, I formulate, organize, and structure future projects.

They accuse me in turn of not knowing how to listen.

It's not true. They're a bunch of parasites. There are some who keep talking to one another or flip through magazines even during the meeting, while important topics are being discussed. As a matter of fact, there is no discussion: *I* speak, *I* invent.

They say I shout, humiliate people, that I'm insensitive.

I could fire the whole bunch of them. I myself am sufficient council to direct the course of my own career.

If necessary, I can call an employment agency and hire some part-time help—use and then send them away.

On a chessboard, the pawns don't count. They're nothing. I can lose them, they won't be missed.

I prefer to play with the powerful pieces.

RESCUING THE ANONYMOUS: MARILYN IN KOREA

Marilyn Monroe married Joe DiMaggio in January, 1954. They went to Japan on their honeymoon. She flew to Korea before it was over, where she performed for American soldiers, singing songs like "Somebody Loves Me," "Do It Again," "Bye Bye Baby" and her signature tune—the classic "Diamonds Are a Girl's Best Friend." A UPI photo, now held by the Bettmann Archive, and published in almost all the Monroe biographies, shows MM on an improvised stage in front of thousands of soldiers, all sitting on the ground in a natural amphitheater on a sloping hill. There's a Greek atmosphere to the scene.* She's smiling, in a black dress, her shoulders uncovered, indifferent to the cold, as evidenced by the majority of the soldiers being bundled up, some even with fur jackets and earmuffs. Their faces are smiling and happy and even those who aren't smiling wear expressions of contentment, the happy pleasure of contemplating Marilyn. You can see there's a camera in the hands of every soldier. Amateur cinematographers are filming in 16mm. Thousands of anonymous souls, and each one made sure to keep a souvenir of that moment. It was recorded in their memories, and it was fixed on their film. Spread all throughout the United States, there must be thousands of picture frames or albums in places of honor on living-room walls or coffee tables, thousands forgotten at the bottom of boxes hidden away in closets, and each with a Marilyn—thousands and thousands of her. The soldiers must be grandfathers by now, and they probably still talk about the day when they were face-to-face with the goddess, a day more important than any mere victory. They probably even framed that official photograph from UPI to show their families and friends: I was there and so was she—

---

* See *Marilyn Monroe and the Camera* (1989), Schirmer Art Books, London and Munich, preface by Jane Russell and with an interview by Georges Belmont.

MM! It was a trophy each one took home from the war, gratified. And their faces have been preserved as well. But who are they? Nobody knows and nobody cares. If we were to examine each face, we could uncover a story, a family, a private world at that moment focused upon and illuminated by Marilyn. For many, it could well have been the greatest moment of their lives, recorded indelibly. How many might have changed their lives from that day on, casting aside old prejudices and settling on new goals, new directions for the future? The possibilities fascinate Lenira. She would like to sound these depths—locate the soldiers who are still alive, research their biographies. The lives of the anonymous who saw Marilyn Monroe one day in Korea. What did they think when she died eight years later? What did they say? Did they get autographs that day, get close, even touch the goddess? Do their stories about the day continue to circulate within their family circles, in the cities where they live? Lenira wants more pictures. She wants to make a documentary using all the extant photos and footage of that show. Locate each of the soldiers, identify where they're standing in the picture, and collect the photographs they took as spectators. To investigate the look of pleasure on the faces of the anonymous. And then there's the particular angle of each of their own images taken at the show—fragments of Marilyn never before seen, treasures kept secret by Americans who were swallowed up (some may have died in combat, so their photos would've been sent home to their families) by their day-to-day lives, without knowing that they were immortalized in the UPI photo, in the histories of cinema and photography, in the great book of stardom—footnotes in the mythology of a woman who changed the world.

THE FEAR HE HAS OF THE TRUTH

He: my scourge. Source of all my suffering.

I refuse to say his name. Let's be content to say "the Lead Actor." Or "LA." Admitting and accepting that he plays the leading role is already a concession, already a violation of my principles, my desires—is enough of a mortification, like I'm some backwoods penitent whipping his back.

He condemned me to *not be*.

Not being, I review my thoughts. I mean, I rethink them. I like sentences. My hatred is creative. Poetic. Someone could confuse me with a philosopher in the Sartre tradition. LA has no poetic thoughts. All he wants is to be on the covers of magazines.

LA—the bile in my mouth, the ulcer in my duodenum.

The cancer in my prostate, the cause of all my rancor.

He's afraid of me.

Even though he doesn't have the slightest idea I'm going to get rid of him.

I'm a threat to his career, his fame.

He knows it.

His world can come tumbling down: the truth lies with me.

Truth always prevails. I'm shivering. It's hard to explain.

One can expect very little from this world.

Very little.

If only I could explain. Life is confusing, inexplicable. Everything that reaches us is adulterated, impure.

Real feelings don't exist.

ELABORATING INTELLIGENT SENTENCES

Look at my face, look at the faces of celebrities past and present—are there some similarities between them all? Identical features, expressions, any kind of parallel? In the lines on our faces, the structure of our noses, eyes, eyebrows, chins, the shape of our mouths or ears—can we extrapolate those elements that are the mark of success, of triumph? If we put all these famous faces together and boiled them down to their fundamental elements, could we then—armed with the basic foundations of fame—select a man at random from a crowd of the anonymous and make him famous by giving him these features, by performing plastic surgery?

What makes certain people attract your eye in the street? Is it simple magnetism, a quality born within us, or is it a skill, something you can develop and hone? The other day, a set designer said that it was all kinetic energy transformed into potential energy. I didn't understand what he meant by this. I didn't say so, of course. I don't confess my deficiencies. Plus, I suspect that his sentence (that's a good word, it has rhythm; delicious to say: "Sentence") was meaningless.

People love (especially when they're near a columnist) to say anything that'll produce an effect (usually something they've thought about for days)—something that stays in the air. These worthless phrases get printed in magazines, in their "Overheard This Week" sections. For one minute they gain a kind of notoriety. My Bruising Declarations Consultant even developed a list of opinions for me to air in order to get me a spot in that very popular section. The more complicated and meaningless the thought, the more intelligent we sound. This week, my Consultant has come up with the following winner: "Extrinsic problems lead to passing fatalities, provided they are seen from the intrinsic, virtual side and, as a result, fortuitous!" Spread this around as much as you like. It will become true as you do so. Direct yourselves, please, to the section below, entitled "I Feel Like Messing with the Fuckers."

PODOPHILIA

Somebody caressing my feet.

Putting me to sleep. But also exciting me with their delicate fingers.

I would have given anything to have been in *Raise the Red Lantern*. That scene where the Chinese woman massages her lover's feet is quite memorable. One of the best depictions of pleasure to grace the cinema. Every person watches movies for his own reasons, of course—from his own point of view. I search for pleasure in films.

It was she who taught me this, during one of those afternoons we spent together, fleeing from work, from responsibility.

Pleasure. "It's what I concentrate on when you touch me," she would say to me, with half-closed eyes.

When she came, she gave out soothing, muffled, tender moans.

PEDOPHILIA

I don't know if I should broach this subject.

I don't even know if I can.

It involves the police, bad habits, public prejudices.

Temerity. Trembling.

I can be more than hated, you know. I can be cursed—and watch my career be destroyed forever, dumped in garbage.

The word "trash" glows on my monitor. Are you sure you want to send this subject to the trash? asks my computer. Oh, the courtesies that men put inside their machines in order to make them seem more human.

I could fuck up myself forever with this subject, condemn myself, be arrested, and get raped in prison—unless I lead a rebellion, of course, which seems like an easy enough thing to do. Or maybe I could escape through a tunnel—I've seen lots of movies about prison escapes. And fugitives make headlines for days and days.

More than ever, pedophiles are now being discovered lurking on the internet. Not to mention in middle-class condominiums. The other day, in Brasília (Jesus, that city bores me!), they arrested a government economist, married, with a good family background—at least according to the caption under his photo, which showed a chubby guy with a badly trimmed goatee, thick eyeglass frames, and thinning hair: the epitome of a pervert. The headline reinforced the image: *DEGENERATE PERVERT*. Nelson Rodrigues, the playwright, would've called him the scum of the earth.

This economist had an enormous collection of photos of naked adolescents, and juicy ones too: girls (just beginning to grow pubic hair) kissing each other, pubescent girls (oh boy!) licking each other, and even pictures of his fucking the girls. And now pedophile priests are coming out of the woodwork too, making the Pope downright depressed.

A new kind of sex-ed class needs to be taught in every school, centering on good taste and pleasure. Really, what terrible taste on the parts of those children (the newspaper insisted upon using the word "children") to sit around naked with a drooping pervert begging for a little liposuction of the crotch. To allow that tongue darkened from cheap cigarettes to explore their rosy little cunts.

I like the little girls I see in the halls of the studio dressed in miniskirts, on their way to the stage, being led by their mothers. The girls are so charming to the doting producers they meet, those old men with their dyed brown hair and Ray-Ban sunglasses—as though they were the aviators (that's right, "aviators," a dated word; not "captains," not "pilots") flying the DC-3s that first did the São

44

Paulo-to-Rio run, dying to "stick it to," that was the expression, not "have sex with," but anyway to make love to their flight attendants (not "stewardesses"). I need a Learjet!

Anyway. Careful!

Sex? Only the safe kind, thanks!

NERVOUS CUNT

My love.
Each passing day,
I feel my love for you growing.
It's good to see you. Good to look at you.
When I think of you,
I feel a warmth
beginning in my lovely cunt,
ascending in waves
until my whole body is boiling.
And it becomes nervous and very hot down there,
very wet, thinking of
and waiting for your mouth, your finger, and your cock.
I keep on saving up this desire
until again the opportunity comes
to discharge all the yearning, all the physical love
I feel for you.
When I see you,
when I take in your scent,
when I kiss and touch you. Letícia.

THE MONSTROUS BANALITY OF DAILY LIFE

Daily life is appalling—its mediocrity is utterly exasperating—it's made up of nothing but a string of dull, useless moments—a maximization (a word I picked up from the icons on my computer's desktop) of the ridiculousness of the human condition—unbearable—depressing—an empire of triviality—banality—day after day filled with traps—as many landmines as there are in Vietnam (the part where there was a war)—treacherous—tasteless—I tremble when I think of shitting—pissing—belching—farting—brushing my teeth—snoring—catching myself licking a spoon—spitting—coughing up phlegm—caught in my underwear—shaving—pulling the hairs out of my ears—putting on my socks—wearing flip-flops—smelling the socks that stink because of my rotting rubber shoes—picking a flower—taking a pill—bringing down my fever—letting on that I'm constipated—losing track of time—yawning—cleaning the caked-up secretions from my bleary eyes—picking my nose—scraping the dirt from under my fingernails—smelling my sneakers to see if they stink too—filled with the terrible feeling that I might be a common man—the kind who sands his feet—who does sit-ups—who hesitates when picking out a CD—who's afraid of that unlit hallway in his building—who does (beginner's) crossword puzzles—who reads horoscopes and believes them—buys bananas at the market—boils eggs—buys bologna—kale—asks for half a kilo at the bakery—eats a warm salami sandwich—crosses the street flustered because he's afraid of getting run over—who scratches his balls—snorts—drinks the coffee that's dripped into his saucer—dries his shoes on a radiator—puts his cold feet on the heater grate—removes wax from his ears with a cotton swab—wets the tip of a pen to see if it'll still write—licks the cover of a yogurt container—blows his nose on his fingers—if only we could eliminate the daily stuff, leaving only the grand moments in our lives—to live only the basic, necessary, important instants—for the others, the ordinary and the timid, their ideal for us is that we keep ourselves frozen in such grand moments forever—it's what the public expects—desires—nobody wants to know that his idol is the same as he is—the public is the sum total of nobodies—the flock that accepts life on the level of a larva—of an amoeba—but each man worries how that larval mass sees him—or anyway, great men like myself worry about it—and what is a great man, really, if not the astounding simplicity that is yours truly?

MODERNITY

"I find their addresses. It's so easy. I have all the information at my fingertips, after all—I have access to the station's files, and promoters, socialites, professors, reporters, and civil servants always need ways to get in touch with the stars." My assistant has an old copy of *See São Paulo* in his hands. What's he up to?

"It's with fame and beauty that I achieve my objectives"

The actress Luana Piovani, quoted in all the weekly magazines.

My Networking with Other Famous People Consultant couldn't get me Luana Piovani's telephone number, no matter how much I asked. I wanted to call her, congratulate her, send flowers, honor her wisdom, tell her she knows this world of ours, this world of cutthroat competition. Here she has provided a wonderful précis of the philosophy of someone who hates being anonymous, who wants to break through the stifling barrier of anonymity that life imposes on us from birth. If Luana were to come to my dressing room, she would see that I've typed and framed her classic, poetic, and definitive declaration. No thesis, essay, treatise, or book will ever be able to achieve such a perfect synthesis as the above. Luana Piovani. Your words are a prayer. Amen.

THE MAKING-OF OF MYSELF

Lex Mercatoria. Before, I didn't know how. Now I've learned. Observing, conversing, reading, reflecting, comparing, seeing how others act, consulting biographies—hundreds of them—watching all the films and soap operas I could find and going to plays and looking at paintings. Watching, alert to people's expectations, seeing what makes success, finding out what success actually is, picking up on what the public likes to see—this is what I had to learn. I admit, I have an Image Consultant. She makes discreet suggestions. She's my Holy Ghost.

I will develop a *Manual on Celebrity Behavior.* To shelve alongside the *Manual of Media Necessities.* These complement each other. I know, it's like giving away a treasure map. It took weeks, months, and years to plot my course. *Lex non scripta.* I almost grew old hunched over my newspapers, magazines, websites—wearing my eyes out watching television. I spent decades telephoning, inquiring, interviewing people, all to reach this moment, this moment when I'm finally ready to be reborn. This is how it should be. It's all going according to plan.

Now, there's little left for me to do to reach the very top. I will have to take his place, of course—that fucker, Mr. Leading Actor. Lenira agrees: It's not enough to replace him, he needs to be killed, taken out of the picture entirely. Having reached this decisive moment, however, I feel it will do no harm to reveal how I came to be. An actor prepares. He must be better prepared than someone who simply worries about being chic, than someone who just wants fame. I spent years humbly submitting myself to my education. Now I'm almost ready. I want to pass along the knowledge that I uncovered. To be generous is to grow. Was it Buddha himself or just the Dali Lama who said that? The bookstores are stacked with books by the Dali Lama—all the man seems to do is write and write. Yes, giving you this treasure map is my great magnanimous gesture for the sake of humanity—a guide to the art of being famous. I am composing the Holy Book of Fame. The Kama Sutra of Idolatry. The Garden of Delights, the Bible, the Koran, the Torah, the Constitution, the Rules of the Game, *Corpus Juris, Lex Legum*.

THE IDOL BROUGHT A GIFT BASKET

LA is the enemy.

If I do as the Americans do, preferring acronyms and not saying his name, it isn't because I've become globalized, a servant to the United States.

My motive is something else entirely. Soon you'll all know. My thoughts are scattered—I can't muster sufficient hatred at the moment to concentrate on them, to make them solid, to allow me to work, to tell you.

Letícia is making me blind—the terrible thing I've done to her. I will include her in my *Notebook of Cruelty*. I think about her all the time. Here's a good sentence, very touching: If I were on the seven o'clock soap, I would make the female audience (why don't they come up with a shorter word for the people out in the audience?) watch me on the screen with love in their eyes.

When the character he plays does good deeds and is rewarded with the caresses of a co-star, an actor has had his needs taken care of—he sees himself as contented. He can walk down the street, wave, smile and be smiled at, accept a free beer in a bar, and be embraced by all. I hate beer myself, and when they offer one to me, it's usually the cheapest kind they've got. The other day a Bengal woman came up and hugged and kissed me—I felt poisoned by her saliva on my cheek. Fans come up and slap our backs with gooey familiarity. The public is a terror—they all deserve a good smack.

It would be so lovely if we could live our whole lives in character. It's painful to leave them behind at the end of the day, all alone inside the studio, locked up in our dressing rooms. Haven't you ever thought about the loneliness of the characters abandoned in the empty studio when it's shut down for the day, when the lights go out and the doors are locked, when the scenery returns to being nothing more than wood, chalk, cardboard, and plastic?

To shut down for the day. An ordinary expression. Makes it sound like we work in some corporate office, with time cards to punch, a Christmas bonus, a gift basket of staple foods, vacation time, occasional promotions, a country headquarters with croquet and silly morale-building games. The despicable things that make normal people happy.

The other day, the hateful LA, rotten and abominable, arrived with a gift basket for the cast and crew. The whole studio loved it. They love everything he does, the filthy energumen (there, I found a word almost as bad as he is).

The basket was filled with Japanese condoms that had been fitted out with all sorts of extras—nubs, protrusions, scrapers—Vaseline, Chinese powders, Viagra, Vasomax, pornographic magazines, and collections of erotic art from the fifteenth to the twenty-first centuries. Contemporary shots show nothing but cunts, wide open like gorges—like the caverns so beloved by eco-tourists. It's delicious to lose oneself in them.

Ah, Letícia, Letícia—never again will you lie on top of me, spinning like an out-of-control merry-go-round, as in *Strangers on a Train*. The final scene. Go see it. You'll know what I mean.

NOT BEING IDENTIFIED, LETHAL INJECTION

There's a moment when you begin to emerge from the world of darkness that shelters the invisible, the anonymous. It's not enough to have your name in the credits, it's important for people to know who you are, what your name signifies.

It's horrible when the viewers ask, And who is this Mr. X?

This is the stage of non-recognition, of being a no-name—a thing so useless that it doesn't deserve to be recognized.

Or worse: to remain entirely unidentified.

The history of photo-journalism is replete with the unidentified. If only they knew how much it hurts. If journalists had any soul, if they were human, if their hearts contained so much as an iota of compassion—no matter how tiny—they would do their best to identify everybody who's in every photo they take. Which makes me think too of anonymous journalists and photographers—professionals who, by being denied identification themselves, anonymize their unintentional collaborators. I like this word: Anonymize.

The expression "unidentified" is a real killer. It deserves a trial, a sentence, the highest punishment possible. If I were on a jury judging a journalist who'd captioned his photos "unidentified," I would vote for the death penalty immediately.

Lethal injection.

Like that terrorist from Oklahoma, McVeigh.

The term itself is impressive. "Lethal injection." Poison in your veins.

To remain unidentified is synonymous with lethal injection.

I take this injection every day—every day I open the newspaper and don't find my name.

I FEEL LIKE MESSING WITH THE FUCKERS

". . . they called for women with sculpted bodies
to give pleasure to men, women, and even couples . . ."

I go to the studio. A woman (white) on the stage there has a good voice. Really good. And, she looks good too. If I were the host of the show, I'd give her the prize right away. Afterwards, I'd try to fuck her. Well, you have to be a son of a bitch in this game. Of course a white woman, even a knockout, will always fall far short of having real talent, a real voice, a voice full of blood and rage—like Nega Gizza's, for instance, who put out this amazing rap song called "Prostituta." The white woman is still rehearsing. Big firm breasts—she's eighteen-years-old and she's already stuffed with silicone. Of course, it's the thing to do.

> "Yesterday I saw an announcement in the newspaper
> On TV, outdoors, broadcast digitally to every receiver
> Asking for women with sculpted bodies
> To give pleasure to men, women, and even couples
> But actually what I want is to be an artist
> Give autographs, interviews
> Be a cover girl
> I want to be seen
> Really beautiful on television
> And ride in limos, not the backs of police cars."

A lot of noise. My thoughts are sent scattering.

There's a girl throwing up just a few feet away from me. Scum. Nervous, tense, all fucked up. They're here every Saturday. Auditioning. They kill themselves just to get here, to the barren hinterlands of fame (I'll come back and come up with a better way of

putting it, later)—the dreamers, the zealots, the ingenuous inno-
cents who believe that they have a chance, that they can still make
it. Amateurs.

Rock, funk, *pagode*, *axé*, rap, reggae, hip hop, old sambas. The
longer the program takes, the more nervous the groups backstage
get. They are overwhelmed with fear of the dwarf-dog's bark, the
bark that will destroy their dreams and make them shit in their
pants from terror. There were once some people who tried to bribe
the dwarf-dog, without knowing he wasn't the real judge—it's the
host who decides, who sends a sign to the doghouse in code. And
then the dwarf is obliged to wag his little tail, the scum. Yes, a
pretty blonde with tits sticking out like bottles of vodka, long and
hard, gave herself to the dwarf, and he promised very earnestly
not to bark. These simpletons circulate through the corridors of
the studio, waiting to be discovered. They believe that agents are
standing right offstage with contracts in their hands.

On Saturdays, the idiots are out in force. The ratings skyrocket.
Many future contestants watch avidly, their eyes on tonight's victims, seeing how they make out, rooting for them to be disqualified, trying to glean some insight on how to improve their own
chances. Eighteen-year-old girls who are out to ape the success of
past stars settle in the lounges and green rooms offstage. They rehearse the songs they'll sing in two or three hours. Some older
ones (still trying to make a career of their folly) take refuge in the
tried-and-true methods of the old crooners, those dinosaurs who
could memorize long endless lyrics and sing as though they meant
what they were saying. A dead art. These cretins don't even sing
Roberto Carlos songs anymore, they think the lyrics are too long.
And yes, there are also the introverted ones, the withdrawn, the
timid—certain failures. I'm the only introvert who can function in
this atmosphere. I made myself a character—I assumed a role.

There are the frightened, the restless, the anxious, the nervous.

And then there are the pretentious, the arrogant, the megalomaniacal. A small mulatto woman sobbing in a corner. Either way, when the time comes, they tremble, fart, sweat, won't speak to anyone, look at everyone with suspicion. They know that what the jury wants, what the public wants, is to fuck with them, humiliate them, grind them into dust.

I stop one of them on his way to the stage.

"Careful! You see that guy in the front row? He's paid to get the crowd going, start them applauding or booing. And? He's completely corrupt."

"Corrupt? What do you mean?"

"You need to split your winnings with him. Otherwise, he'll boo you, and you won't stand a chance. Make sure he knows you won't put up a fight."

"Split my winnings?"

"Half for him, half for you. They'll pay you in cash, with his half already taken out."

"Nobody told me anything about this."

"Of course they didn't tell you. Wise up. All first-timers have to pay."

"First-timers? I'll bet you got disqualified and now you hang around making trouble."

"Go ahead, you'll see. Afterwards, you'll tell me you were sorry you didn't listen."

"It's not like they pay all that well in the first place. Why would they take half? I was thinking of putting a down payment on a house for my mother."

"Fuck, a house for your mother! Where are you from, anyway?"

"Why?"

"You have tiny dreams, mister."

"I want to be a singer."

"You're not going to be anything at all."

"Why?"

"Failure is stamped all over your face. You'll win the prize, then fill your nose with powder!"

I know just by looking. This idiot will never be anything, never be anyone. He is nothing. His face is faint, fading from my memory even as I look at him. His eyes are dull, his mouth is thin and drawn. His teeth are small. He quivers like a frightened rodent.

"Powder?"

"White powder!"

"White powder?"

"Cocaine, buddy! The real stuff."

"I'm a religious man. I belong to the Church of the Resuscitation. No drugs allowed."

"You think the pastor doesn't snort the stuff? You need a lot of powder in your nose to fight the devil, you know. How else can you come up with those long sermons?"

"God doesn't approve of substance abuse."

"God bores me silly."

"Don't blaspheme!"

I destroyed the guy. He went away scared, confused, insecure, sad. He'd thought that television was paradise—that everything would be lovely, with lots of dough for everyone. The little blonde with thick lips, the one who vomited, passes by, says she sings ballads, she's going to do musicals when she gets big. I wanted to feel her muscular thighs. I love a muscular thigh. I always wanted to date one of those women who work out and have a buff body. This one wears leather pants, very tight—you can see the furrows of her ass and her cunt. Musicals! They've all already been done. And now Broadway and Hollywood are distributing prepackaged entertainment to emerging nations. Like Brazil. If this one starts singing and dancing, though, Betty Grable, Ann Miller, Eleanor Powell, Mitzi Gaynor, and Ginger Rogers are all going to turn over in their graves, wondering what the hell they suffered for. I'd like to see this suburbanite sing "For Me and My Gal," "Over the Rainbow," "Put the Blame on Mame," "Ain't Misbehavin'," "I'm Looking over a Four Leaf Clover," "Perhaps," or "Pagan Love Song." Why doesn't this poor thing just go out and become the godmother of a new school of samba music, wearing a golden ankle bracelet given to her by a neighborhood drug dealer?

RAISE THE PLACARD: APPLAUSE

Clap clap

RESCUING THE ANONYMOUS: THE HORSES OF VENICE

There are four of them and right now they're inside the Basilica, in the Marciano Museum. Taken from the façade, where the passage of time was corroding them, they've been substituted with perfect replicas, products of modern technology. Nobody knows who devised and sculpted the original horses in bronze. An artist from the island of Chios, near Smirna, facing the Island of Lesbos, was certainly assisted by a group of apprentices, seeing as the work would have required an oven and a foundry for him to create such marvelous animals, looking like they're about to stampede. Who was this man? What else did he accomplish? What other works of art came from his atelier and became eternal, while he himself remains unknown? Was he a loner, did he have a family, lovers? Was he gay, hetero, promiscuous, temperamental, timid, depressed, crazy? A pervert or an exemplary employee in a shop, taking in commissions? 2,300 years ago, his animals were transported from Chios to Byzantium and placed at the doors of the Hippodrome, the busiest place in the city. Byzantium became Constantinople, though today it's Istanbul. Thousands of people passed by the horses without ever knowing who'd created them. The Fourth Crusade saw the horses plundered and carried to Venice in 1205. Twenty-three centuries have passed since those horses were made. Twenty-three hundred years. One hundred and twenty-four thousand and two hundred weeks. Eight hundred and thirty-nine thousand and five hundred days—according to modern-day standards of time. The bronze horses (though they were gilded, and the gold leaf has remained unscathed) continue to be seen and admired, but how many of these admirers think about the artist who gave the animals their brazen, eternal forms? The artist is an unknown, responsible for a work of art that has become famous. Therefore, he is an anonymous celebrity.

I'VE NEVER HAD SEX

"You're out of your mind! You want me to say I'm a virgin? You might as well get yourself committed."

"You're going to go out and tell everyone that you've never had sex?"

"Absolutely not!"

"Yes, you are! In all the newspapers! On TV! On the radio! In magazines! What a reaction we'll get! What a scare we'll cause! Incredulity! Shock! Astonishment! An unheard-of revelation for a star!"

"Impossible. Out of the question. I have a reputation."

"You didn't fuck anybody. Ever. Ergo—"

"I don't have the guts. I can't go through with this."

"You'll get media coverage like we've never seen before in Brazil."

"But at what price?"

"Look, haven't you ever read that interview Maria Della Costa gave? 'I'm tired of being beautiful,' she said. The whole country was amazed."

"That's prehistoric. When was this? The '40s? How about I say, 'I'm tired of fucking so many women'?"

"That sounds arrogant! Besides, everybody's already saying that you fuck anything on two legs. To confess that you've never had sex with anyone ever—now *that* will get their attention!"

"I have to think about this. It's a strange idea."

"Exactly. Everybody's going to want a piece of this. We'll make headlines. This is front-page material. Religious programs will invite you to speak. Priests and pastors will talk you up during mass, exorcisms, revivals. A man who kept his chastity. Who fights for it. An anachronism. New congregations, pastors, and religious sects will make you their hero . . . You can't even imagine the number of conservative companies who'll want to sponsor a soap opera or a miniseries with you as the star. You'll go on TV. Women's programs. Radio. Everybody will talk about you and nothing but you for weeks."

"I don't know. I have to consult Lenira."

"Leave that Japanese cunt out of this."

"You don't think people'll laugh at me?"

"Have you even considered how many women are going to show up offering themselves to you once we go public?"

"You think so?"

"You think it's easy to make news, these days? How long's it been since you got so much as a sentence to yourself in the paper? By the way, did you read Zézé di Camargo's statement in *Isto É*? Here it is, October 17. The 'Overheard' Section. 'We document everything.' 'The popular artist is of value only in terms of pure numbers—of the size of his audience. He doesn't have the privilege of absenting himself from media attention, like Caetano Veloso, for instance, who is valued as an intellectual.' Take this as dogma. Gospel. A Papal bull."

"I just don't know. It seems risky. But I guess I have nothing to lose. What will Letícia say, though? She'll flash that ironic smile of hers that always humiliates me. 'Don't be ridiculous,' she'll say. Do you think she'll ever come back to me? Bind herself to me again? I don't like the sound of that word, but it's true: Letícia binds and unbinds. Speaking of which, I saw a photograph in the daily paper of Francisca Botelho, the jewelry designer. She makes these scapulars that are all the rage, apparently. Everyone who's plugged in is wearing them now. I should probably pick one up, and maybe give it to Letícia. I think I'd like to see her with a scapular hanging around her neck."

ALWAYS KEEP YOURSELF "PLUGGED IN"

Have I explained the concept of being plugged in? Plugged as in connected, tuned in, accustomed to what's current, modern, up-to-date (though "up-to-date" is quite antiquated)—in on and even above all the ongoing trends, peering over them, standing on the tips of my toes (not that I can admit this last bit to anyone).

There are daily lessons to be had. I study *Vanity Fair, GQ,* and *Vogue.* I see Julia Roberts wearing Gucci twice, and then Calvin Klein. She's in four out of five international magazines. Brad Pitt wears Prada. Guy Ritchie and Madonna choose Dolce & Gabbana. Toni Braxton (who the hell is Toni Braxton—is this a new name that's somehow escaped me?) wears Richard Tyler. Serena and David Linley show up in Ralph Lauren. Lauren du Pont, barefoot, in Luca Luca.

Pay attention to Miu Miu, Krizia, Roberto Cavalli, Anna Molinari. Mention Mimi McMakin, the American designer.

To have an exotic, vibrant, difficult-to-pronounce name excites the media all the more. Like Ariana von Hohenlohe. Sounds nice and sophisticated. I worry that my name is much too simple.

One must hire a personal guru to help one deal with stress, must have a good shiatsu massage once and a while. In London, rickshaws pulled by university students, parked by the doors of theaters and restaurants, make short trips for a pound. Very chic!

This summer, masculine shoes with square heels.

I'm feeling down. I just discovered a new word, invented by the Americans, right before the planes destroyed the towers. They use it now in the captions under the photographs:

"Non-celeb."

Non-celebrity.

If I ever find that designation under my name, the game's over. I'll be dead.

THE EIGHTH SENSE

A daily exercise I engage in is to study photos of cocktail parties and celebrations with a magnifying glass. I cut out the most important, appealing shots. I notice there are people who are in every social column, who appear at every function. They're my models, my prototypes. Or should I say archetypes? I paste these photos in albums that I evaluate. A regimen passed on by a demanding teacher: me.

The project, elements of. I'm preparing myself for posterity. If Lenira executes the plan correctly, if she manages to corral the LA, if we manage to install me in his place—this is what the poor dear wants, after all . . . he's so tired, the LA, so sickly—I'll have to assume the role of high-rank celebrity efficiently and with a minimum of preparation time. This is a role one must live in daily life. (Live or play? I'll figure this out for myself, in time.)

As Paulinho da Viola sings in "Stoplight," "I go on running to grab my place in the future." I also study the photos to see how famous people are meant to be photographed. *Faces, Chic, Vogue*, columns by César Giobbi, Mônica Bergamo, Joyce Pascowitch, Hildegard Angel, and reports by Amaury Jr.—these are my reference tools.

They show, for example, the best position to be seen holding a glass in one's hand: keep your body slightly tilted backwards, with an attitude that seems bored, indifferent to the camera.

Indifferent despite the fact that celebrities develop an eighth sense: they always know where the camera is. And yet they know how to behave as though it weren't there.

There's a symbiosis with the camera: a relationship between soul, flesh, and glass.

A slightly perpendicular manner of holding oneself enhances the fit of one's clothes and makes one look entirely controlled. This is the stance of someone who knows how to make his presence felt, who is interested in what you have to tell him without being servile, who never lets his guard down, who has excellent posture.

Never letting your guard down is essential. When the camera comes in close and the famous sense it's coming with its fourth eye (nothing to do with the third eye, celebrated by Lobsang Rampa back in the '70s)—the eye that modern folk develop thanks to constant exposure to the media—they begin to speak with theatrical gestures, to laugh (laughing is essential, unless you want to play the sullen type, like Buster Keaton), wrinkle their forehead, listen attentively, then look up distracted, as if they were searching for something in the void above them.

I continue my exercises in front of the mirror—this studio of mine was a good idea of the architect's; at first I didn't want it. I rehearse my behavior here before going out, whether it's to a party, dinner, autograph session, film première or shoot. Now I can begin to circulate.

There are more parties than ever, for everything. Like the '50s, filled with glamour. During the '60s and the '70s, apparently, Brazil was too rich or just confused—lots of bustling about and making useless plans. I don't like to hear about that decade, it just depresses me. Then, during the '80s, people withdrew, out of fear of showing off their jewels, dresses, cars (now they think that tinted windows solve everything—they've become careless). There was a lot of violence, robberies, kidnappings, murders.

My Consultant on the Subject of Violence made the following comment: Last year in São Paulo, there were 273 kidnappings. In one year, in Brazil, 717 new shantytowns appeared. Now, however, even with the escalation (who remembers that this term first came into use during the Vietnam War?) of violence—even with the blackouts, which happen more and more often with the power plants folding—everything's gone back to being glitzy, "in," hot: all the international brands can be purchased right here in São Paulo.

Our parties are staged in monumental venues, and they all have corporate sponsors taking care of the buffets, drinks, decorations, flowers, sound system, power, lighting, special effects, rear-projection screens, waitstaff and bodyguards (it's not done, or safe, to receive guests without having bodyguards at the door: they represent authority), and the other, less obvious, but no less numerous security people, all in dark suits, communicating with one another via radio.

What one sees on the walls and on the ceiling are corporate logos, projected by special spotlights, all part of the special lighting. DJs are hired (sometimes from abroad), and they're stars too, charging a pretty penny, and their mission is naturally to keep people on the dance floor, to make sure no one can have a conversation, to make everyone excited, to complement the effect of the Red Bull and Ecstasy that seep through the bars, bathrooms, hallways, walls. (Who sponsors the drugs?) We're living *La Dolce Vita* forty years after Fellini's film. But that's how it is, everything is a little behind the times in Brazil. We don't have any Fellinis around, it's true—but we do have paparazzi, and subjects eager to have their pictures taken while pretending they hate photographers, the rich and/or the nouveau riche, the sluts with their plastic surgery, the whores, the fat-ass starlets, the studs, the plastic faces, the faggots, the orgies, the drugs. And that's where the violence is: pent up in resentment and envy. Sure, it's true that no weary Brazilian intellectual has killed himself like Steiner does in Fellini's film—you'll see, we don't have any intellectuals at all; or else we have no reason to be weary; or else it's just that no one has the courage to kill himself. And where are our noble, decadent, existential revelers? Nowhere to be found. But beyond these quibbles, no difference at all.

Getting invited to these parties is another art entirely. It's up to my various consultants to get my name on their lists—and these lists are very well structured and maintained.

To have one's name in on all the promoters' mailing lists is proof that one isn't anonymous. You count. You're one of the items necessary for the success of a coming event.

RESCUING THE ANONYMOUS
FROM THEIR DARK CAVERNS

Lenira gave me the idea. She made a good start, but doesn't have the time to continue the project. She knows that the subject fascinates me, so she's handing over all her research, papers, books, notes, photographs, magazines, recordings.

I study the history of the anonymous.

The anonymous of the world.

A difficult task. To coax them toward the light, to soothe their pain and suffering.

I have organized I don't know how many stories from this material, which continues to accumulate. It occupies my early mornings, when I don't have to be at the studio.

I'm composing a *Manual of the Anonymous*, you see.

It's a battle everyone should take up. Make it your personal crusade. A war.

There's an enormous sense of well-being, great happiness, to be had from the knowledge that one isn't himself a despicable, despised, anonymous soul.

I DON'T NEED SYMPATHY

The pain is light, but percussive. I forget about it, then it comes back to sting me.

One moment it's the sting of a bee, more or less ignorable, and then blinds me like an exposed nerve. It never lets me rest, lets me get accustomed to it. It's unbearable.

"Why bother ruminating over your problems," asks Letícia, "it's not as though you'll do anything about them." She knows what she's talking about. And once again the pain fades out, only to come drumming back again.

No, it doesn't matter where the pain is coming from. It circulates through my entire body, presses down on my chest, makes my stomach do flips, closes my throat. It prevents me from breathing and swallowing, it presses down on my eyes and weakens my legs to the point that I have to sit down or else fall.

It's a problem when we're taping. I have to stop the scene and they think I forgot my lines. No, it's nothing like that. Just the amnesia caused by agony. It wears me out, causes sleepiness when I least expect it. Like that afternoon when we saw *Mahabharata*, the film by Peter Brook (1989, based on Jean Claude Carrière's text), which she fought so hard to see. She harassed video stores, looked through international catalogs, searched all over the internet. Finally she had to use my credit card; hers had been stolen one night while she was stopped at an intersection.

Seeing me fall asleep during the first scenes of *Mahabharata*, she was terribly disappointed. Tears ran down her face.

4:00 P.M. 4:00 P.M. 4:00 P.M. 4:00 P.M.

This pain causes constant uneasiness. I can't find a single place that feels comfortable to me—I'm not comfortable in the world. Not on a chair, sofa, bed, carpet.

I lose all notion of time passing—not that time has ever been of much importance to me.

You must be wondering, Why should we care? What a lot of whining. Such self-pity.

No, I don't want your sympathy, that would only make me anxious. You all can go to hell. Not one of you can know how much I hurt, can know the first thing about this pain, which I myself provoke and about which, therefore, I shouldn't complain.

I'm responsible for my own actions.

Time. Sometimes I remember those red digits shining in the shadows, especially on rainy days, when the room got dark. I remember that storm, the storm that raged when I had to get out, get back. I became a caged lion, angry, hateful.

I feel like I don't belong anywhere. I'm just floating, sluggishly, buoyed up by my pain.

"Do you know what you remind me of?" she asked.

"No."

"A non-place."

"And what's a non-place?"

"In this instance, I mean that cubicle, that non-place you call a dressing room. That small, stuffed, hidden room you so adore, where you flee, waiting for your call to the soundstage, to go out and stand-in, or whatever it is you do there, whatever it is you refuse to tell me about, and which I think I no longer have the slightest chance of understanding. I don't know why you still haven't left me. Anyway, that dressing room is a non-place, my love. And why, by the way, haven't I ever seen a single scene of yours on television?"

"A non-place? You were there only once!"

HE EVEN DOES TAMPON COMMERCIALS

I found out that I'm eight months older than LA, our Lead Actor—and this only because I happened to be reading one of those popular magazines that really irritate me, the ones written expressly for the illiterate (short pieces, big print, simple words, lots of slang), read only by cretins. You've noticed I still can't bear to say his name. There are words that, according to some superstitions, mustn't ever be pronounced, like the names of the devil or certain diseases.

Eight months. Therefore, I existed before he did.

LA is an imitation.

A usurper who's built up an impregnable barrier around him.

He believes himself to be a precious jewel exhibited in a museum, kept in a bell jar, protected by lasers that will set off thousands of alarms if tripped. Do you remember the film *Topkapi*? Who directed that? I can't remember anything today. I'm getting old. Or maybe it's just that it's a really old movie? I wonder who I think I'm talking to. Regardless, he is secure. There is something that prevents me from unmasking him. But unmasking him is what he deserves. What needs to be done? To expose him to the ridicule of his public. To make plain that he's a farce.

Still, I must acknowledge his intelligence, his astuteness. He refuses to face me, to submit to a confrontation, to go to the press, to stand beside me so the public can decide for itself. Which is which? Who is the more genuine?

He pretends not to receive my letters. Faxes. E-mails. Notes. The law protects him. He has money, fame, he's in the news every day, he contributes to good causes, makes donations to political campaigns. He complies with the necessary and ongoing ritualized obligations and genuflections before the public that God knows I would gladly take upon myself so long as it was proof of my not being anonymous. He makes appearances at parochial debutante balls, shows his face at graduations, makes his presence felt at millionaires' parties—those that require a little celebrity in the mix, according to the promoters—an intellectual, a funny guy, an eccentric, an exotic type, someone elegant, a whore, a drag queen, a corrupt politician, somebody involved in a scandal, gays of all kinds, one or two representatives from traditional society, DJs, and a famous person. All the better if a socialite who'd been considered elegant back in the '50s can be included too—this will make the party more prestigious, and make sure some of the bottom-feeding novices are kept from crowding the ranks. I'd would love to have the money some of these neophytes have, even if I just owned a popular pastry shop or something similarly anonymous. Or if I were the one out of thousands of sugarcane grinders who came up with the idea of selling iced sugar-cane juice. Straight-up with lime or pineapple. I saw a report on TV about a man who became a millionaire selling little time-saving gadgets to street vendors. He owns a three-story house and the magazines had a spread on him. Almost as much as the Corrupt Official, whose banking records the courts still can't manage to subpoena.

LA dances with women who have bad breath at parties for the elderly (no, the expression now is "ideally aged"); he supports demonstrations by lesbians, recites poetry at labor union halls in the industrial suburbs of São Paulo, and once almost took part in the siege of a local farm with a crown of landless protestors—but he was saved at the last minute by being called in to re-tape a scene because an actress had been hospitalized because of an overdose while he was away and had to be replaced.

He takes part in ecological demonstrations (the latest straightjacket we've been tied into by the cognoscenti), even though he hasn't the least idea what he's doing, what he's fighting for—doesn't have a single thought in his head. He signs petitions calling for investigation of governmental corruption, supports feminist causes, delivers Christmas gifts out in the shantytowns, signs petitions in favor of gay marriage, prays at large open-air masses and dances with charismatic priests, is called upon to do commercials in favor of various causes. I've read that our Lead Actor is the last word in credibility for the consumer public. He sells everything. So much so that he was the first man to lend his name and face to a tampon ad, which got him a hell of a lot of press. He knows what he's doing. He'll use and risk anything and everything in order to make a splash.

THE BEAUTIFUL AND ALL-ENCOMPASSING ART OF WAR

I look at the grill that covers the air-conditioner. It won't filter out anthrax, you know. If some came creeping in here, I could gather some samples and send them to LA in an envelope. So many fan letters—he'd never suspect, and they'd never find out who the culprit was. But no, I would just end up killing off some assistant from his entourage—not that I'd feel a lick of remorse. In a war like this, assistants are like civilians: expendable. Anyway, it's a ridiculous proposition: my air-conditioning doesn't even bring in uninfected air, let alone air filled with spores. They're closing down my wing of the studio, where my dressing room is. One of these days, they'll start knocking it down. They're going to build cable television facilities here, to be linked to the existing network. Lenira told me so the day before yesterday, as she was opening the door to let me in. It was 5:30. I got back on time.

My battle continues. The ground is mined, and the woods are full of guerrillas. I need to develop my strategies. Need to read classic books about war by Sun Tzu or Clausewitz. Those two are enough. Books that nobody reads anymore—except of course the few individuals still interested in surviving.

These texts provide one with resources for getting by in cities like São Paulo, cities that exist in a permanent state of war—cities filled with snipers, armed assailants, gangs, fugitives from prison, kidnappers, muggers waiting by every ATM, rapists, etc. But my own war is something else entirely. Subtle, perverse, replete with rules, norms, prejudices, betrayals, subterfuges, mannerisms, hypocrisies, dirty tricks. I've given it a lot of thought. I've been thinking it all through, the last few weeks.

I smoothed out the rough edges in my design. My plan has to be clear and concise. Before continuing, I decided to convey the fundamental principles of my war.

Among the five pernicious dangers for a leader, according to Sun Tzu in *The Art of War*, is "over-solicitude for his men, which exposes him to worry and trouble. If, however, you are indulgent, but unable to make your authority felt; kind-hearted, but unable to enforce your commands; and incapable, moreover, of quelling disorder: then your soldiers must be liked to spoilt children; they are useless for any practical purpose."

Whatever that means.

If the stuff actually exists.

And faith in what?

In the shitty place the world's turned into?

Who can guarantee for me that my television isn't about to implode, that there isn't anthrax in the air and that someone isn't about to launch a load of missiles right at Brazil?

My heart is broken. It's nonsense, a cliché, but I couldn't help myself. We think of so many foolish things, only we usually don't say them, we keep them to ourselves. If everyone were to start saying everything that came into their minds . . .

RESCUING THE ANONYMOUS:
THE JEWISH HAIRDRESSER

He died as a Jewish hairdresser. Nothing else is known about him; to learn what little else there is, you have to slog through page upon tiresome page, picking through the thick volumes that record the official proceedings of an old, interminable trial. The Jewish hairdresser was murdered. Did he have a family, children? Anyone to carry on his forgotten name? Did he have relatives or were they all dead? Anyway, a life was eliminated. Just like that. A man disappeared from the history of the world, or the history of Europe, and we don't even know his name. Nevertheless, he grew up, chose a profession, had dreams, desires, fears, grew disillusioned, fell in love. Then he melted away.

Between October 1962 and May 1963, in the German city of Koblenz, the trial of two hardcore Nazis was held: SS-Hauptsturmfuhrer Heuser and his "accomplice" (our word) Franz Stark. The latter, decorated with the medal of the Blood Order, was Hitler's close companion, having participated in the Beer Hall Putsch in Munich. Facing the court, filled with pride, Stark confessed, amidst other crimes, to having murdered the hairdresser assigned to Wilhelm Kube, General-Commissar for White Russia, and Commander of an Einsatzgruppe responsible for the death of thirty-five thousand Jews. Stark murdered him because he became "furious at seeing a Jew without the star that identified his 'race' daring to work on the hair of pure German women." This is a summary of the transcript one can find in the book, The Industry of Horror, *by Joseph Wulf, Le Cercle du Nouveau Livre D'Histoire, Paris, 1970. White Russia was located between Hungary, the Ukraine, and Lithuania. The hairdresser was another anonymous soul, exemplar of everything that occurred in Germany during the Third Reich.*

EVERY ACTOR HAS THREE LIVES

"You interest me. You play with people," Lenira said to me.

That's when it started. I'm not ashamed to say so. We celebrities can't be shy, can't have false modesty. If I don't have pride in myself, don't love myself, don't praise myself, who will? People seeing that I believe so much in myself will also believe. I am a seducer of women, a walking turn-on. That's what Lenira told me during a premiere, and in front of a bunch of witnesses too. I was in the lobby of the movie theater, my body tilted slightly backwards, with a bored look on my face (good for photographs), when she came up to me. She knows how good she looks. She knows what kind of effect she has on men. Everybody was observing us.

"You look just like him. Everyone says so. Do they ever confuse the two of you?"

"It's my curse. I live in perfect damnation."

I like the word "damnation"—it's sonorous, dramatic, Faulknerian.

"And you're an actor too? Doesn't that make things rather complicated?"

She said LA's name. The unspeakable.

"Of course it does. It's enough to make me want to kill myself."

"Really?"

"Once I even turned on the gas and put my head in the oven. But I hadn't paid the bill. I was broke."

"Why?"

"I don't have a chance. All because of *him*. Casting people always turn me down, saying, 'We already have one, we don't need another.' Agony. In the good old days, at cocktail parties and such, the paparazzi would take pictures of me, and the next day I would see my face in the papers with his name underneath. Remember? Remember when they used to marvel at how he could be at every single event? He was in one place, I in another. I was he."

"So why persist? Your slot's already been taken. Give it up."

"That's my tragedy. I was born into a world where my place had already been taken."

"Don't be so dramatic."

"When I see myself in the magazines, I know I'm me. Not him. I know what it's like to be an anonymous celebrity."

"What on earth does that mean?"

"I have no idea. I love being enigmatic. Don't worry. I'm going to end it all—I'm sick of this pain."

"Too bad."

"But what's the use of living when he'll always be out there to prevent me from being myself?"

"It's quite the unique affliction."

"Affliction"! I think she's being ironic. How does one decipher the face of a Japanese woman? She's probably not even Japanese—maybe she's the daughter of Japanese immigrants?

"It's horrible."

"It doesn't have to be. Why not take his place?"

"The Lead Actor's place? What do you mean?"

"I've been his technical assistant for years. He's lazy, indolent, he doesn't like to budge an inch. A rare disease. He just likes to stay in bed and fuck."

She said "fuck" so naturally, it excited me.

"I don't understand."

"It's not necessary to understand everything I say. Don't disappear. Stop tormenting yourself. Prepare."

"I *am* prepared—I know how to act."

"You do? On TV or in real life?"

"In real life?"

"An actor has three lives: the real one, his character's, and the lived one, the one you assume in order to have the opportunity to act in the first place, the role you play in front of the public and the press, the role of being famous, the role of being a celebrity."

"You have no idea how well I know the part. I've been preparing for years, I know everything."

"What's the point of knowing if you don't do anything about it?"

She stood there looking at me, perplexed. This woman could show me the way. What did she mean by "take his place"? Changing places with someone is a familiar trope in the movies, it's been used for a hundred years, on television too. To murder someone, to occupy their place. *Purple Noon* (*Plein Soleil*, René Clément, 1960), for instance. The first appearance of Mr. Ripley in films. Patricia Highsmith. And there was a soap opera on television, *The Other*. Now they're talking about clones. I looked at Lenira, intrigued. Everybody says that she, the Lead Actor's faithful assistant, is dangerous.

"You mean, I should swap places with him?"

"No, idiot. You ought to live the life he isn't using. Live the life he'd rather lie in bed than enjoy. You should *be* him, in public."

"And remain anonymous as myself?"

That night was the beginning. It's been such a long time since that meeting. A lot of time, little time, no time. As I've said, time doesn't exist for me. Not in the way you see it, measure it, refer to it. Everything has its time. But I invert this old chestnut: Every time has its thing. But what thing?

If the gossip columnists had even a patina of culture (my own level of cultivation is also a patina, only a sliver, I admit it); if the TV critics forgot their Dominican battles over the ratings for just a moment, they would have known about Julian Barbour's thesis about a timeless universe. Barbour reasoned in *The End of Time*—and I agree, as my sense of time is one without movement—that time is such a mystery that it ought to be left to philosophers and not physicists. Time appears to exist since our brain leads us to believe in movement and registers images in such a way as to convey the idea of linear movement. However, there is no such thing as movement. We are made up of a quantity of "nows." Barbour emphasizes that our body passes through billions of changes in only a second. Billions of hemoglobin are formed and destroyed. Down deep, we are different people at each instant and that is part of our consciousness. Each now comes with a range of experiential possibilities, and it can't be said that one experience comes right after another. That's the problem with the hand of time, there seems to be a chronology, an impression so consistent that we believe in the line of the flow of time. A story can be arranged in order for it to seem chronological. However, some changes in this structure wouldn't give the same impression of continuity. I place the "Time" dossier in my filing cabinet.

PILLOW TALK ON LONELY NIGHTS

Lenira forgot her cell phone, so I called Letícia, late. I knew she wouldn't be sleeping yet, she tends to lie around listening to music before she retires, hugging two pillows, one against her chest and the other between her legs. "The one lying next to my heart is you. I miss your warmth, your mouth," she usually says. On this night, she was crying. "What happened?" I asked, somewhat relieved. The way she usually answers the phone—coldly monosyllabic, sharp, giving me the impression I shouldn't have called—is worse. "I'm watching *Anna and the King of Siam*," she said, "and I always cry when I watch movies about impossible love. You know what I'm talking about," she added, twisting the knife. When she feels hurt, she wants to punish me. She ends our conversation harshly, when I say I'm sorry, giving me a curt "that's okay" instead of our customary kiss into the receiver.

TREMBLING, AS THOUGH HER BODY
WERE GOING TO EXPLODE

When I tried to bring my mouth to her left breast, she grabbed me, delicately. "It hurts, there's a little lump. Best not to squeeze."

The first time we slept together, and I, anxious, tried to go down on her, to bring my mouth to the place between her legs, still hidden by her minimal, yellow panties, she stopped me. "I never let that happen the first time," she told me later. "It's something that's very intimate." As always, there was a CD playing. We never made love without music.

I let my hands clasp hers, her fingers tightly glued to mine, for an instant. I noticed her toes were twisted over one another. I put my hand on her thigh, caressing it gently. She uncrossed her legs at once.

I was startled by her brusque movement, and my mouth went dry. I picked up a mint, offered it to her, but she didn't even seem to notice, she wasn't looking at me. I kept my hand on her knees, on her olive skin—smooth, not rough. For a few moments, I forgot about my hand, then I woke up and began to move it up towards her pussy, thinking about the word, pussy, pussy, pussy, the most delicious word.

I was excited, but didn't have a hard-on. She was calm.

It was a new experience for me.

My hand reached the magical intersection, and I felt her pubic hairs beneath her panties. I searched with my fingers until I got to the spot. I knew there was a spot, but I didn't know what it was. Men think they know, but they need to be taught, always taught— every step of the way.

I figured out that I shouldn't pull too much on her hairs down there, since it would hurt. I slowed down and noticed that Letícia, with an imperceptible movement, was making my task easy for me.

I stuck my forefinger between her skin and the elastic of her panties, and continued. I felt it get wet, and I began to get excited. The pleasure of having my finger there overtook me completely. I kept going.

Slow, gentle, so tranquil that I almost fell asleep. (Once—I shouldn't tell you this—I fell asleep when she had my dick in her mouth; maybe because it was so relaxing, because I can completely abandon myself to her, with her.) From time to time, she, with her legs open, would adjust the placement of my finger, putting it on the right spot.

Letícia bent backwards, supporting herself on her blue pillows, moaning. I stuck my finger deeper, smelling the sweet fragrance that emanated from her and began to make me a little deranged. I wanted to tear her panties off, grab her flooded pussy. I was happy—it was the greatest joy I'd ever felt.

She raised her legs, panting, sucking in air, breathing in the smell of the cologne I used and her own fragrance and the mint I still had in my mouth. I groaned and thought I was going to die. She had an enormous smile on her face, and her eyes were shining—I could see them in the dark.

Then she let herself go, grabbed my hand forcefully, locked her legs, closed her eyes. She had a small mole near her nose. She began to tremble all over. I knew it was a good thing. She was letting out the pleasure that was still inside her, that had taken over her body.

AUCTIONING OFF THE CONDOM I USED

I've discovered via the internet that celebrities are now auctioning off their intimate apparel. Years before this, however, in a São Paulo nightclub, an actress did a striptease and put her panties up for auction. A masterstroke.

Then an impresario auctioned off the sandals and bikini of a leading patroness of the percussion section of a samba school— she was really hot. It was a benefit auction and the winner went to receive the pieces of clothing from the lady herself on Faustão's TV program, watched by forty million people. Genius! The guy who organized it all really knew how to do things! His statement about the success of the event circulated in all the weekly magazines: "I put them up for auction because we all know what a boon this woman is to men everywhere." It was the quote of the month, the year, the decade, the millennium.

Another fellow, a man in advertising, got himself a bikini from one of those nameless girls who parade around half nude on Airton Picolo's trashy Saturday-night program. He paid what's known as an "undisclosed" sum, and framed the bikini on the wall of his office. Smiling widely enough in his happiness that you could see his badly made false teeth, he stated: "I intend in the fullness of time to find and then dress a deserving girl with this famous article of clothing. When we're alone, I'll imitate Airton Picolo, and she'll be my muse—it's going to be amazing. I'll fuck her ten times that night! The only problem is, how will we get the papers to document this last bit for posterity?"

What do I own that I could auction off? Something sufficiently intimate? Underwear, a toothbrush, talc I use for my sweaty feet, the condom I used when I fucked Mariangela, the co-ed? She was in the hall, nervous; I called her, she came, let me fuck her, and then calmed down. It was a good deed, on my part. I helped her feel better. I'll tell the newspapers all about it, in time. What a pleasure.

I MUST ALLOW FOR A THOROUGH INVESTIGATION OF MY PERSONAL LIFE

My house.

I've been thinking about it for a year. I dream about it.

Consulting home-design magazines, newspaper reports, advice columnists. My dreams always followed the strict rules of the season.

Which neighborhood should I choose, whether a condo is superior, how a modern house is put together—clean, empty, minimal—which are the trendiest colors, which architects should be used, which decorators. If I hire designers from off the approved list of current industry darlings ("darling," a popular word at the moment), my house will never get a feature spread.

Is there such thing as an anonymous house?

A house nobody knows. That they've only seen from the outside.

Might as well live in a shantytown, hotel, campsite.

The public wants to go inside the houses, naturally. Stick their noses into the pots and pans. That way, they feel like they're being intimate with you—honored guests.

Opening my house up to reporters, I'm seen as generous, magnanimous. The readers have to thank me, of course—and they will learn from me, copy me, imitate, admire. They're going to dream I received them personally, that they were in my presence. They saw my bed, my dining room, my kitchen, my pool, my squash court (it's time to take up some new sports), my sauna.

If in one of the pictures they can make out a pair of my briefs, or even some mysterious panties, the readers' pleasure will be quite orgasmic, believe me—they're going to think they've achieved a real sort of intimacy with me.

Everything is fake, of course. Designers bring the panties, briefs, condoms.

On this point, he, the damned one, my arch-enemy, is savvy.

His house. How many times has it already appeared in magazines? How many times has he staged a massive and newsworthy redecoration? Every year his house is different. He's clever—I can't underestimate my enemy.

No, the Lead Actor has experience.

The names of my architects, decorators, artists, and photographers are annotated in a special notebook.

I know which paintings must be hung on my walls, which sculptures, installations, photographs must be purchased.

Yes, installations. They're all the rage at the moment. The other day I read a piece about a dinner at this actress's house. A very pretty and delicious blonde, gracefully sculpted by the silicone in her breasts, buttocks, thighs, and calves. Hell, her tits, her ass. What do I want? To seem educated, refined? Anachronistic words.

Anyway, everybody at the actress's dinner tripped over an installation that had been set up in the middle of the room. Nobody understood, they all thought the house was being renovated because there were rocks, barbed wires, crumpled bags, cans of paint, and paintbrushes in the dining room. They all said that the actress really ought to have had the work finished before inviting people over.

The artist was in attendance. He was offended.

He's a designer, in a sense. All of his pieces are signed.

To sign is to raise the price. To create a brand.

STRANGERS ON A TRAIN

I recuperated just in time.

All the destructive power I've been turning against myself must be channeled instead towards a proper outlet. I must direct it toward the Lead Actor, that damned usurper.

Calm down. I have to be calm. They say revenge is a dish best served cold. Though that would make it a vichyssoise, one of the most exquisite soups I know. When served ice cold, it's nectar. Nectar.

I give up. Today is not my day to come up with a plan.

A plan, like in *Strangers on a Train* (1951), by Hitchcock, in which Robert Walker proposes a perfect crime. And it almost was perfect. But plans can never be perfect because men are imperfect, unpredictable, unknowable. Robert Walker was an alcoholic and died at thirty-six from being given a tranquilizer when he'd been drinking. In truth, what killed him was losing the love of his life, Jennifer Jones, to David Selznick, the producer. The pain of losing his love.

I know all about this kind of pain, ever since Letícia told me, via e-mail, on a Monday morning, "Let's break up! I want to break up!" It was harsh, ruthless. But there was no other way, I was the one being ruthless, really. But then we started up all over again.

That e-mail was terrifying. She's always breaking up with me, however. Then it starts again.

She wanted to break up. She told me so, she was determined.

Terminate. Determinate.

De-terminate.

GADGETS, GADGETS

Lurdete (she would do well to change her name—how can anyone be successful in this business calling herself Lurdete? But she says it's a pet name, that it has sentimental value), my Image Consultant, parked her "bunker-mobile" in front of the supermarket. She called to me when she saw I was coming out with bags of sugarmints, cream-filled cookies, Quaker oatmeal, guaraná syrup from the Amazon, potato chips, chocolate, and wearing my flip-flops too (I have a pair in each primary color).

Lurdete nicknamed her car the "bunker-mobile." All the Image Consultants in São Paulo have the same model. It's a job for women: they do well, they're quick, organized, have the right contacts, know all about diplomacy, persuasion. The bunker-mobile is a traveling kitchenette. In the trunk she keeps all the necessities for her social, personal, professional, and spiritual life, she tells me. She repeats this a lot, in fact, as though she needs to convince herself. Lurdete never goes home—sometimes she spends the night going from one apartment to another, hopping from one boyfriend to another. She and the other Image women invented the bunker-mobile—with room for carrying spare sneakers for exercise classes, deodorant, towels, bikinis, underpants, bras, different pairs of shoes, jeans, t-shirts, perfume, glasses, fruit—banana, apple, kiwi—power bars, sunscreen, face creams, bottles of mineral water, band-aids, cough-drops, vitamins, toothpaste, thermoses of soup or consommé, teas, a first-aid kit, kneepads for in-line skates, gum, coconut milk (it's in style), little crackers.

Seeing me come out of the supermarket, she shouted, "Come here, *now!*"

"What's up?"

"Here's the list I was suppose to make. I had to do some real research."

"List?"

"If there's something missing, let me know, I'll take care of it! You're going to have to spend a lot—these companies won't allow you to keep the products you advertise. They sell so much anyways that they don't even need to promote their own stuff. And you have to buy all of it right away because improved models will come out almost overnight, and you don't want to fall behind."

"I'm sorry, what list are you talking about?"

"Read it. Bye-bye. I've got a meeting, a conference call, right now in the car."

Lurdete, in her scribbled script (almost nobody knows how to write by hand anymore) had written, along with a litany of specifications and brand names:

Carry a cell phone at all times.

Also a pager.

Laptop with wireless.

PDA.

Digital tuner.

Don't ever be disconnected from the world.

Things never stop happening. There might be a press conference, a meeting at an agency that's selling a product, auditioning for a commercial, looking for someone to make an appearance at a dance, a graduation, a business convention.

Don't be disconnected. Keep yourself plugged in!

RESCUING THE ANONYMOUS: GRACILIANO

It's raining. On the morning of June 29, 1936. Graciliano Ramos, "physically humiliated," thin, bald, and with deep bags under his eyes (as Denis de Moraes recounts in his biography, Old Graça*) left Ilha Grande just outside Rio, after eleven days of ignominy. He was being sent back to Rio de Janeiro. After a conversation with the Director, he said his good-byes to two criminals, Cubano and Gaúcho. Then, "one of the soldiers escorting him, out of pity for his lamentable state, took him away on horseback to the pier, under an intermittent, light rain." This nameless soldier joins our gallery of the anonymous. He felt pity at seeing one of the greatest writers in the history of Brazilian literature in such a deplorable state. Let's be clear: He didn't have the slightest idea who Graciliano was. All he knew was that this man was one of the many detainees who filled the island prison to capacity. Perhaps he knew how to differentiate the criminals, murderers, and thieves from the political activists who were there due to their convictions. Later on, would he ever have read* Prison Memoirs *and recognize his gesture from Graciliano's description? Would he have been touched? Did some transformation occur within him at this revelation—did he come to some decision to change his life? Did he long for something better? Or was he merely one of the thousands of illiterate and dispossessed souls who saw the police force as their only way to make a decent living? In any event, this one showed compassion, a sense of humanity. It's a significant detail in Graciliano's biography. Somebody from the other side, among his enemies, extended a hand to him. A kind gesture. Anonymous. A person who perhaps deserved to be remembered for his kindness, but who has been completely forgotten. We know nothing about this soldier who carried a weakling on his horse. Note the two criminals, Cubano and Gaúcho—their names were revealed and they have been remembered, just like the thieves who were nailed up to either side of Christ. Anonymously named, if I may put it that way. We have their names, but no other information: why were they there on the island, what do we know about their lives? Nothing.*

ALWAYS KEEP YOURSELF "PLUGGED IN"

Memorandum. Words currently in fashion: Anxiety, depression, schizophrenia, bipolar, hallucination. I listen a lot: bipolar. Bipolar. I am the greatest of this country's stars, even though so far this is only my own opinion. Some papers persist in criticizing me, saying I always play the same role. I must point out, however, that they always come up with the same criticism.

It's cool to be fanatical about old TV series now, to discuss them, quote them. *CHiPs, Bonanza, I Love Lucy, Kojak, Get Smart* (cult status!), *Wonder Woman,* and the divine *Bewitched,* with Elizabeth Montgomery (she just died not long ago, of cancer) and Agnes Moorehead (or am I confusing her with Jo Van Fleet, the mother from *East of Eden*?). And also *I Dream of Jeannie, The Waltons,* and *Lost in Space.* Everyone remembers Dr. Smith (Jonathan Harris). That's what I need. A role that will launch me into posterity. One is enough.

Financial news in the papers from not too long ago: a list of the salaries for actors in a popular TV series in the United States. Kelsey Grammer is the highest paid actor in American television: $1.6 million per episode of the series *Frasier.* Ray Romano receives $800,000 per episode of *Everybody Loves Raymond.* Drew Carey gets $750,000 per episode. Or something like that.

It's of no real interest to the general public, though the papers adore publishing these figures, and do it pretty regularly. This is all just a passing thought, a personal memorandum—I am collecting information to have at hand when the time comes for renegotiating my contract. To shove the above in my agent's face, so that he'll negotiate better. Of course, if there in the States they pay a million dollars, here in Brazil they'll want to pay about twenty thousand reais, at best. Around eight thousand dollars. Depending upon the going exchange rate, of course. How's the dollar doing right now? Not very good. Remember, darling, this is Brazil—things are different here, and anyway, do you think those hacks really make so much money? Ridiculous. They lie like crazy!

THE SEXUAL LIFE OF KANT

Now I find I can understand one of Letícia's peculiar statements, made on a certain rainy afternoon when lightning and thunder tore the city apart, and I started getting stir-crazy, like a prisoner in solitary, plotting ways to escape. Letícia was irritated and didn't understand my restlessness. Why do you have to go back? Can't you ever relax? Forget everything else? Once, just one time, for me? In the meantime, the digital clock read

4:00 P.M. 4:00 P.M.

The gigantic numerals, illuminating the bedroom, were my prison. And yet I never broke that damn clock, I didn't even cover its face or pull its plug out. I could never forget that I had to return to my dressing room. I never stayed with her for so much as an entire afternoon.

"You're almost as bad as Kant," she said.

"The philosopher?"

She read quite a bit. Not trash, either. Like *The Professor and the Madman*, by Simon Winchester, a fascinating account of murder and insanity. Insanity is always fascinating.

"You're exactly the same as he was."

"I don't know the first thing about philosophy!"

"I'm not talking about his philosophy. I'm talking about his mania."

"Mania?"

"I bet you sleep with your stomach up in the air."

"What?"

"The same as Kant. Do you bundle yourself up in blankets every night, regardless of the temperature?"

"We've slept together. You've seen me sleep."

"Hardly. And you don't ever sleep anyway. You just stare at the clock."

"Where are you going with this?"

"Kant never relaxed."

"Are you making fun of me?"

"I only want to laugh. To laugh, my love. To laugh a lot. All the time. And to give you the pleasure Kant didn't have. I'm sure you won't say no."

And she did laugh. What comforts/frightens me is to know that Kant's life was insipid, tedious, monotonous, filled with tiny little restrictions and rules, was replete with systematic norms, established habits, routines adhered to with minute precision. She'd been reading Jean-Baptiste Botul's book on Kant. That's what started all this. Botul had invented a fake sexual life for the philosopher. A literary sensation. Then it was discovered that the book was a fake, Botul doesn't exist, the revelations about Kant were invented. It was a trap set up with the intention of debunking academics, but not one of them reacted.

People refuse to admit they know nothing, because there's always some new thing that can be discovered. Thus, the absence of opinions. This leads me to believe, more than ever, that my own strategy is bound to succeed.

DANGEROUS, ALBEIT BANAL, MISTAKES

There aren't many people out there who really seem to have understood or studied the role the media plays in current world culture—not in its bare essentialities. For the majority, everything roles along intuitively—few of them really think the situation through.

I will give you a précis. The media needs news; consultants, personal assistants, and press agents can fabricate and provide it, but never according to a careful battle plan. Only advertising agencies plan their output with real precision, these days.

The media shapes my soul, my tastes, my words, my thoughts, my attitudes. It is the basis for my *Manual*, which must be continually revised.

Changes in behavior and expectations are swift. This is facilitated by means of contemporary technology—the internet, that is. It's so easy for news sites to pull an item down and paste a new one in its place.

Color of the moment: Blue-indigo.

Delete. The new color is violet green.

Delete. The new color is canary white.

Delete. The color is cyclamen.

Delete. The color is Renoir-beige.

Somewhere, somebody is having a good time, knowing that nobody will bother to call up Renoir's paintings to look for beige there, to learn if this color exists. They aren't colors anyway. They are words, used to create an effect.

I save my updated color file and shut off the computer.

It was canary white, last I checked.

What's it going to be next?

Where do these color names come from, anyway?

But it's necessary to have a catalog of them handy. So as to be able to request the proper fabrics, ceramics, and paints from factories. There are a thousand combinations, all put together by computer. Names are invented for the new colors, the old colors get re-baptized. The human imagination is fertile.

The world invents and reinvents itself.

A car ad shows a definite preference for boreal silver. Now it is the color of the moment for automobiles. Poetic. Poetry is good for sales. The executives like poetry when it serves to mask marketing strategies.

I know all there is to know about good selling practices. It's all in my *Manual*. A goldmine, really. Until I finally understood that there are rules, codes hidden throughout the news, in commercials and on billboards, I was lost, anxious, without direction.

I used to worry obsessively about it: if I suddenly become famous, which will of course happen to me sooner or later, it's virtually assured when one doesn't have talent, doesn't have any skills, how is one supposed to act? After success arrives, it's important to nourish it—to behave oneself according to the necessities and norms of fame; that is, to be aware of the merciless oscillations of the market.

A celebrity must be continually reinventing himself, according to the changing trends of the market.

It is forbidden to commit the banal mistakes common to normal folk. Just one can poison you forever. Example: At this moment I'm listening to Elba Ramalho sing "Cajuína." I adore this song—it really gets to me, takes me back, restores me, leaves me peaceful. Because I never spend a single moment of my life in silence, constantly monitoring the media filled with uneasiness over the possibility of my being condemned to anonymity, to have some tranquil music to fill the gaps is particularly helpful.

Nevertheless, listening to a song like "Cajuína" is something I do in secret. I don't know if I'm allowed to listen to Elba, though I must—I don't know, for instance, if she's on the weekly list of those who RISE or those who FALL (published on Sundays).

I know the song is by Caetano Veloso and is on one of his CDs too. Caetano is always on the RISE list. Listening to Caetano bestows prestige, increases my value, earns me mileage (everything is measured in mileage nowadays) in intellectual spheres. I make appearances praising him in the literary supplements, in the fan magazines.

There are thousands of fan magazines out there reaching completely isolated publics, directed at various insular tribes outside the mainstream.

My God, I almost said "alternative." A word that's already worn out.

If something has been worn out, it must be deleted. Canceled.

I have to be careful. And so, I listen only to certain songs, watch certain movies, and read certain books late at night—behind closed doors and barred windows—in order not to expose myself. This secret side of mine has its compensations, mind you; we all have to have secrets, all need our little refuge. I adore Alcione Nazaré, Jair Rodrigues, Miltinho, Vinicius, Reginaldo Rossi—high society detests him—I own a bunch of old records by Libertad Lamarque, Pedro Vargas, Bienvenido Granda, Trini Lopez, Connie Francis, Sidney Magal, Carlos Galhardo, Erasmo Carlos, Catarina Valente, Isaura Garcia, Nelson Gonçalves, Martinha, and so forth.

DID I HURT YOU, MY LOVE?

One time or another, with her moving restlessly under me, twisting herself around, a perfect acrobat, always finding a way for me to penetrate her more deeply, my dick gliding into her divine wetness, goddess of sex making love with a prosaic mortal, yes, one time or another, a more abrupt movement, a moan, and then her despairing question: "Did I hurt you, my love?"

Oh, how she pronounced "my love"!

With what we may describe as a discerning gentleness.

No, you never hurt me. Never in those sheets, becoming stained beneath us, you've never caused me any pain with your pussy, your hands, your flashy, colored nails.

Your tenderness is entire.

TO SCULPT THE IDEAL MAN

Yes, but there was always something wrong with me, a change that needed to be made in my character, my way of being.

She wanted me transformed. She wanted me to be another person.

Perhaps she had invented a man in her head and wanted to mold me into that image. But if I don't even know who I am, how can I be what others want?

Perhaps it was there and then that everything began to fall apart. She was stubborn, insistent. She wanted me to be how she'd dreamed I would be.

IN THE BATHROOM WITH A CELL PHONE

I telephone the rental agency: I want a limousine. To welcome the American director who's telephoned me, and who I need to take out to dinner. The American said, "Pick me up in a silver limousine, please." Pretty cheesy, I thought, but it's best not to argue, there's the possibility of making a film, you know, maybe with a big star. (Who will it be? Sandra Bullock, Nicole Kidman, Melanie Griffith, Sharon Stone, Irene Jacob, Courtney Love, Cameron Diaz, Maggie Cheung, Alicia Silverstone, Angelina Jolie, Anna Geislerova, Meryl Streep?*)

The guy at the agency answered in his choked voice:

"Helloooooooooo. Whoooooo is it?"

I found it strange. Then I heard a familiar sound. Like a tiny fart.

The guy: "Whoooooo izzzzzz it?"

"It's me."

I said my name. He wasn't impressed.

I heard another sound, a dissonant fart. Loud this time. Of course it was.

"Oh, it's you, sir. Whaaaat do you want?"

"A limousine."

I heard the log of shit drop into the water—clump, clump, piss flowing, *pissssss*. What a son of a bitch! He was taking my order while taking a shit. The fucker takes his cell phone into the bathroom. What if telephones develop a sense of smell someday? He farted again, a prolonged one. He did it on purpose.

---

* I would love to be able to make a film with Vera Miles, Tippi Hedren, Anne Baxter, Gianna Maria Canale, Barbara Steele, Annie Girardot, Dora Doll, Anna Maria Ferrero, Liv Ullmann, Jean Peters, Ruth Roman, and even Madonna (I find her type of interpretation to be interesting). But it's an impossible dream because I don't know if she is Argentine or Spanish, where she lives, who's her agent, it would be like making a film with Mia Maestro, the beautiful star and marvelous dancer from *Tango* by Carlos Saura.

"Jesus, how fucking coarse. Sitting on the toilet—shitting and doing business."

"Business goes on as usual, friend! When do you want the limousine? Will you come and get it? Should we bring it round, as usual? Do you need a chauffeur?"

I warned him:

"Don't come here with a car full of shit, you bastard!"

The other day, in a restaurant, there were four guys at a table, along with four very beautiful women. The only trouble being they didn't even look at me, which really got on my nerves. The four men ate their entrées, their desserts, had coffee, liqueur, lit stinking cigars, and didn't stop talking on their cell phones for one minute of their meal.

If I were the wife of one of these guys I'd cheat on him in a second. I'd stick the cell phone in my pussy and order myself a real man.

RESCUING THE ANONYMOUS: OLYMPIA

In 1862, a singer left a cabaret in Paris in the early morning and, for a brief instant, had the opportunity to eternalize herself. The episode lasted minutes. When it ended, however, she'd entered into anonymity—she lost her chance at history. Perhaps she lacked curiosity or audacity. Maybe she was tired from working, saturated with experience for the day, unwilling to take on anything new. Or, perhaps her destiny was to remain unknown. We aren't in control of our fates: we are designated, selected: the dice with our numbers on them fall from spinning plastic cylinders, like they use in the lottery drawings on TV. There's some implacable factor that isolates, eliminates, or elevates us—trifles with us. On that morning, Manet and a friend, Antonin Proust, were walking along the Boulevard Malesherbes when they saw a young woman leaving a cabaret. The show must have ended and she was walking quickly. Toward home or another bar. Singers and dancers did two or three shows a night in order to survive. She was a striking beauty and Manet approached her, asking whether or not she wanted to pose for him. A common request. Painters behaved then like fashion photographers do today—thriving on nudes, but usually behaving. The singer must have looked at the two of them, convinced she was facing one more act of sexual harassment after a long evening of similar propositions, rather than an artistic proposal. Or else she knew about the tediousness of posing as a model, earning a pittance for the work. She refused, and at that instant she crossed the border forever, her passport stamped: unknown. That same year, as Otto Friedrich relates in his book, Olympia: Paris in the Age of Manet, *Manet was taking a walk on the Ile de la Cité, "when he caught sight of a remarkable looking girl, young, sturdy, vibrant, full of life and spirit" and became dazzled by "her original look and her determined manner." The young woman was called Victorine-Louise Laurent, and unlike the other woman, accepted his proposal. After using her as his model in several paintings, Manet painted* Olympia, *causing an explosive scandal at the* Salon de Paris *of 1865. The painting was described as indecent, ridiculous, repugnant, fascinating, and powerful. Manet never managed to sell it. Today,* Olympia *is considered one of the national treasures of France—a kind of Mona Lisa because of the polemic it unleashed (did she make love with the painter?), and due to the disparate interpretations of her expression. "Since one had to look upward [at the painting], one almost inevitably became awed, hypnotized, transfixed," Friedrich stresses. In this way, two simple encounters, more or less identical, transformed two women entirely. The singer of the cabaret disappeared forever, her name effaced, making research impossible. She could never have imagined that the blond, tall, handsome young man in front of her was neither a nocturnal predator nor a painter in search of illicit adventure. Or maybe he was those things, but so what? He represented the link that would have made the transition, taking her from an ephemeral and obscure life into eternity. She refused. Upon accepting the same offer, Victorine-Louise saw herself captured in an instant of immortal beauty. She was immortalized one hundred and fifty years ago. In light of this, I'm continuously thinking—making plans, calculations, assessments; waiting for my own proposal to come along. I must be prepared. There has to be a way to make sure one has a fighting chance of preventing himself from plunging into the shadows once and for all.*

GALLERY OF CHARACTERS: FLITCRAFT (2)

I was in a doctor's office. I'd been taken there by Lavinia. Or would it have been Camila, my second wife? She was worried about how lethargic I was. But no, it's LA who's lethargic—making him useless for days. It's like a virus. He's more or less catatonic. In the waiting room, I reached for a paperback that was on the table in the center of the room, left behind by some patient. You never see books in doctors' offices, only old magazines. It was *The Maltese Falcon* by Dashiell Hammett. (So many sets of double letters in one name. It's a nice effect. I'm going to consult the numerologist and duplicate some of the letters in my own name.) It was a crumpled, yellowed copy, like from a secondhand bookstore. I stole the book and got to the bit about Flitcraft that very night. I had just finished reading, and found myself sobbing (a rarity). I went out into the street, I walked around, and I accidentally witnessed a murder. Four men were killing another man. I distanced myself, as the *Survival Manual for São Paulo*—sold at gas stations—recommends. I walked the rest of the night. In the morning, far from home, I decided to go back. I still didn't have Flitcraft's determination. I didn't continue reading; that character was enough for me. He was the one I wanted to play, the rest of my life. I wanted to live that man's life, to inhabit his adventure. Flitcraft acted, he made the decisive gesture. To be.

In the (excellent) film by John Huston (*The Maltese Falcon*, 1941; the director was thirty-five when he made it), the Flitcraft story was cut. It has nothing to do with the plot, it's just something Sam Spade tells Brigid O'Shaughnessy, and it doesn't even have an ending. It's one of those times when it seems the author came up with a story he liked, and left it in his ongoing novel in order not to lose it, like a memo to himself to follow it up at a later date. Faulkner did the same thing in *A Fable*: there's a chapter that has nothing to do with the rest of the book. He tells the story of a marvelous and invincible racing horse, though it only has three feet. A diversion—an insight he wanted to store away, but the import of it is not immediately apparent.

I memorized those pages of *The Maltese Falcon*, and for some time it was an obsession for me, the topic of all my conversations. As though I were testing the information out, experimenting with it, rolling it around in my mouth, the better to capture the meaning of the parable, to tease out all its implications. To know, for instance, if it was directed at me. (Who was the anonymous soul who forgot the novel in the waiting room?)

I forced people to listen to me, becoming quite a bore. At parties people would avoid me—they were sick of Flitcraft. I called soap-opera screenwriters accustomed and they weren't interested. Flitcraft's peculiar depth was only inside my head—the story had been meant for me and only me. It was a code set up between life and myself. There, that's a good quote for the magazines. I'll have my assistant type it up.

MODERNITY

"Things in your head will become clearer, clean, receptive. You'll learn what you can and cannot accomplish—you'll know which forces reign over your destiny. You'll attract positive vibrations in the shells, cards, numbers, tea leaves, bones, crystals."

AVOID BEING LISTED SECOND IN PHOTO CAPTIONS

I understand my Image Consultant. Situations progress in stages. Stage one is to locate someone who's already a favorite target for photographers. These are the people who editors separate out of the crowd during the first cut, by virtue of their faces, their fame.

You have to know what the photographers are up to. You have to get close to them. You have to know what kind of lens they're using, so you can sneak inside the frame. This is why I took a photography course, in order to know my enemy, to know their methods, their criteria. Some photographers like wide angles, others focus their frame on one or two people, one or two faces.

One must study photographers, keep them in the corner of one's eye, track their movement.

Artist X conversing with actor Y at W's opening.

Guga surrounded by actors.

During the first stage, as detailed above, the first name would be that of the most famous person in the shot, followed by secondary celebrities. I would be Y.

This prime-time star is having a good time listening to stories told by Y, X, Z, W.

The Minister of Economy, actor Y, model Gisele Bündchen, and the popular DJ Z.

At the Abit Awards, in the first row, the theater director X; his wife, the dancer W; and Y, who is beginning to get noticed for his role in a popular prime-time drama.

You'll notice that my name is oscillating between second, third, fourth place. Eventually I will muscle my way into second place. The objective is to be in the lead. So, I have to gain points.

Each piece of news, each photo, each cover gives points. Miles. I think I already mentioned the mileage thing. Or no?

A cover. Ah, how a cover elevates prestige.

Satisfaction begins only when one makes it into first place.

The *actor Y here exchanges secrets with the very beautiful Maria Fernanda Candido at the opening night of a popular play. Maria Fernanda is considered to be one of the most sensitive and intelligent actresses of the new generation.*

Actor Y, fresh from a popular miniseries, takes part in the Champion Charity Bridge Tournament.

Actor Y.

Actor Y.

Actor Y.

Actor Y.

What a pleasure to see one's name in the papers and magazines! It's as good as sex. Multiple orgasms.

Still, it can take years to reach pole position in the captions. Until then, one has to be prepared to be unidentified, unquoted. Especially if one is sharing a photo with three or more heavy-hitters.

How terrible. *Unidentified.*

At Carmen Mayrink Veiga's celebrity dinner, X, W, Z, and an unidentified person surround the host.

God but it hurts.

It hurts a lot.

Enough to make one cry. I think it's worse than outright omission.

Thus, until one has reached the second stage, until one begins to be reasonably identified, reasonably famous, one mustn't approach groups containing three or four top names.

There's another word I dread, in this context. "Friend."

W and his friend at the premiere of a hot new film, etc.

It's enough to turn one's stomach.

One day, I almost assaulted an editor because I saw I'd become "*an admirer.*"

W and an admirer.

Also, I felt real anguish on the day when I unexpectedly saw myself marked with an X, a real X, an X instead of a name. A book on fifty years of Brazilian television. There I am, surrounded by the great and the good . . .

All of them identified. Their names spelled right. But me? An X. They didn't even bother to type out "unidentified."

Mister X. Like in an old thriller serial.

X. X. X. X. X. X. X.

It hurt me. Deeply.

An X was used to crucify Saint Andrew, the patron saint of Scotland.

If I could have relied on seeing justice done, here in Brazil, I would have sued.

Instead I spent three days stuck in bed with an allergic reaction that swelled my lips and eyelids shut, that made me gassy, colicky.

IDLE CONVERSATIONS

A strong new trend in architecture. Designate the maid's room with a secondary, social function. The hell with the maids anyhow (they're always women, underpaid, it hardly matters how they feel about it, they'll do as they're told). Their rooms can be turned into libraries, studios, breakfast nooks, studies, ateliers. You can even take down the wall, depending on your floor plan, and connect the room to your entertainment space to make a home theater.

(Damn it, I don't understand anything. Why should I have to read about the economy, with projections of the Gross National Product being 0.5% less for the third trimester and 0.3% less for the fourth trimester? What interest can this possibly hold for me? The economists say that the drop is going to last and the expectations depend greatly on generating movement. Son of a bitch! Honestly! Maybe they'll ask about this during the roundtable at noon. I'm going to respond that I adored it when we had high inflation—my savings account yielded 20%!)

I wanted to see Letícia wearing Giancarlo Paoli sandals, or others by Cesare Paciotti, Pollini, Julie Dee, or Sergio Rossi. Thin high heels, very high, with extremely elegant straps, open toed, in wild colors. Giving an incredible shape to her legs.

Speaking of Letícia, she just telephoned:

"The Orishas are coming to play in São Paulo."

"The ones from Bahia?"

"Orishas, not orixás—those are African gods. You don't know anything, do you?"

"My Music Consultant isn't here. So what's the deal with these orishas?"

"They're Cubans. They're coming to the Jazz Fest. They do rap."

"Cuban rap?"

"I have tickets. Do you want to go?"

"If Lenira lets me."

"Lenira? What does she have to do with this? Who does she think she is?"

"It's up to her."

"I don't get it."

"Look, I don't get it either. That's why I'm reading Michael Bruckner."

"Bruckner? What does that have to do with anything?"

"He talks about the dictatorship of happiness. The ideology of the last century that was passed on to this one. It's the greatest industry of our times."

"You're a real joy, some days. Why are you telling me these things? To upset me? Because I talk to you so much about pleasure, happiness, enjoyment?"

Pleasure. She always talks about pleasure. She closes her eyes while we make love and concentrates on pleasure.

"Everything you do is superficial. Bruckner, happiness. You get it all from the papers, from magazines. You don't know how to speak about any topic with depth. But I'll tell you what. I think you'll like it, since I read it in an interview somewhere—right up your alley. 'One needs courage to be happy.' And you, my friend, don't have any!"

RESCUING THE ANONYMOUS:
THE DEATH OF MARION CRANE

Marli Renfro is a part of one of the classic scenes of cinema. The shower scene in Psycho, *1960, is quite traumatic. Seen again and again by millions of spectators, on TV, in revivals, and on home video. Enlargements printed over and again in books and magazines. It's in all the anthologies. One of the most perfect sequences devised by Alfred Hitchcock. Shivers, stomach cramps, and screams from the audience accompanied the murder of Marion Crane (Janet Leigh). It scared people to death. And, yet, who's ever heard of Marli Renfro? Nobody, only those within a fairly restricted circle of technicians and friends, and—who knows?—her husband, children, relatives. In the motel run by Norman Bates (Tony Perkins), Marion is stabbed to death by Norman's mother. Who isn't his mother, but Norman himself, who had killed his mother long before and taken her place. Exchange of personalities, identities. Marli Renfro, a twenty-three-year-old dancer, had a body identical to Janet Leigh's. She was brought in by Hitchcock to lend fragments of her naked body to the shower scene. What we really see is Marli, but the spectator sees Janet Leigh (Marion). She got to be Marion just long enough to die. Her name isn't in the credits. She never had a photo taken of her on set, never had a photo of her with a caption listing her name published in the papers. Marli was the studio's and Hitch's secret. Marli both was and wasn't. She was never in another film. She disappeared. The story was told by the American screenwriter Stephen Rebello in a book published thirty years after making the film,* The Making of Psycho. *Until then, Marli remained in the shadows, her name trapped among the ranks of the unknown. Eventually, a small opening was made for her. A crack in the shutters. Enough for her name to get through.*

THE COMPLETE CIRCLE OF LOVE

I miss you so much. Whenever I think of you, I feel a warmth running through my body. It's a strange sensation. As if I had a fever. I want to feel you on my skin. It feels like a piece of me is missing. Every time you go away, you take away a small piece of me with you. I want to see you by my side, feel you near me. Each second we aren't together is a waste. Oh, I love you so much. I love to smell your scent. I love to exchange glances with you. I love to lean furtively against you in public. I love it when your lip swells from too much kissing. I love to feel your dick getting hard in my hand. I love to run my hand over your chest, run my fingers through your body hair. To move my face towards yours until I feel the warmth of your breath on me. To hook my foot around yours. To have our fingers entwine. It makes me feel connected to you. It makes me feel our love completing a circuit between us. From my mouth to my toes, passing through your fingers. Everything I feel, I pass on to you, and again you pass it on to me. Nothing is wasted, everything returns, everything circulates between my body and yours. I love you. Letícia.

ALWAYS KEEP YOURSELF "PLUGGED IN"

The newspapers announce the following: Pink champagne is in now. Selling out all over town. It gives color to the Carioca summer.

Envy, jealousy . . . Calm down. This is a life lesson (cliché).

In the seventies, Elizângela recorded some big hits, like "Close to You." Afterwards, she was forgotten as a singer, although not as an actress. Beautiful woman. Now, the DJs love her, she's being played and played in all the hippest nightclubs of Rio de Janeiro. That's what I want to be: a cult figure. I repeat: a cult figure, that's more than enough. You do one great thing, then sit back and wait. Eventually, they discover you—the elect.

Trends. New "in" words: ethnic, sitcom, funk,

pit-bull, pit-boy, dreadlocks, dizzy spell,

drum'n'bass, buddy list.

I need a Consultant on the Languages of Various Tribes to teach me how to use these words, to help me define them. So as not to appear ridiculous. So as to use the right word in the right place, for each appropriate clique. Imagine using anachronisms like "peace and love," "dude," "love conquers all," "pimp," "get with it," "what's your thing," etc., in conversation nowadays? My Language Consultant will keep my conversation modern, make me a proper hipster (and what exactly is a "hipster," anyway? I find it a peculiar word, meaningless. Like everything else). The problem is to know the lifespan of each term. The impermanence of language. And of fame. Everything is going fast—they're born and they die. Words are soon consumed. Is there such a thing as a chronometer for linguistics? Is this even linguistics?

ORAL, ANAL, TANTRIC SEX—POMPOARISM

We've been drinking cans of Red Bull, which is one of the major sponsors for the talk show tonight, and taking lots of ecstasy. They say ecstasy gives you a hard-on, but I don't feel a thing. Was it ecstasy they gave me? Or maybe it was MDMA. Maybe the 2C-B known as "synergy" or "nexus" (same as the Henry Miller book).

Lenira, the Japanese woman, just passed by the make-up room. Winked at me. What's she doing here? Since she works as an assistant to my arch-enemy, she must have come to spy on me. People haven't been seeing LA lately—his publicist announced that he was traveling, But according to inside information, the whispering of veiled voices (that's quite good: "veiled voices," nice and mysterious), he's actually quite sick. Terminal cancer, AIDS, tuberculosis, multiple sclerosis—maybe shingles? Famous people only come down with epic, drastic, dramatic maladies. Far as I'm concerned, however, he can just die!

If only I could fuck this make-up artist. It would be a quickie, looking in the mirror, lit by its lights. She'd leaned her thighs against my legs, on purpose, as she applied some base to my cheeks. Ugly left knee—it has a bone sticking out, or malformed. But small defects excite me.

I asked to be made up in my dressing room, and they said they were sorry, couldn't be done. Half of the make-up people are out due to the bus strike, they said. And the ones hanging around don't give a damn—you'll have to go to them. I hadn't even heard about the strike. Things like that don't interest me; I have nothing to learn from them. When my car picks me up, I shut the tinted windows—I don't like to look at the city, ugly and fucked up, full of pot holes. São Paulo looks like a mouth full of cavities. I am taken directly to the studio. The hostess tonight is Andrea Flores, a "voluptuous dirty blonde," according to the magazines. Brazilians will always celebrate great blondes. Natural or dyed. They tend to date soccer players, mainly the black ones, or else male models, race-car drivers, television producers, advertisers, impresarios, ranchers, horse tamers from the festival at Barretos, executives, or restaurant owners. They display their pussies in the magazines, charge a price to show up and make your party more exciting. They lend their names to brands of lingerie.

My nose is dry, a sign of nervousness. I feel a little shy about having to debate sex in front of an auditorium full of people, with other spectators taking part via e-mail, fax, or telephone. Sometimes I'm old-fashioned. Really, the subject isn't so interesting. Besides, they won't really care about what I have to say. There really aren't too many straight people left in this business. Not that I'd go around saying this in public.

It's more fun to be a spectator, I think. A very queer reporter once invaded a couples bar around here that plays swing music. Each woman in there was trying to swap her husband away for the night, and each husband was waiting around to fuck some other guy's wife. All of them wearing five thousand dollar watches and multiple chains on their hairy and/or flaccid chests. Bait for muggers waiting at intersections.

Andrea's program (she guarantees that she's going to hypnotize the entire city with tonight's show) attracts a real crowd—they're not going to fit on the set. The producers will have to divide them into blocks. I'm introduced to the other guests: the psychologist, the sexologist, the dwarf-dog (also covered in neck chains), the oriental guru specializing in the suppression of desire, the anthropologist who's going to elucidate the sexual prowess of Brazilians, the cartoonist who's developed a way to come without getting hard, the sex-symbol who first had an orgasm at the age of thirty-five, the newly out-of-the-closet actor (one of these days I need to fuck a guy, just to see), the ditto for the lesbian (now *she* fascinates me), the virgin, the black (is this the right word now?), the Indian, the patroness of the samba school who slept with her entire entourage within a two-year period, the transsexual, the fourteen-year-old boy (whose presence was authorized by the Magistrate for Minors), the arrogant deputy (who's promised to tell all about sexual practices in the legislature), the corrupt impresario (currently under investigation by the Attorney General) who intends to reveal how easily money gets him laid, the butler of the nymphomaniac socialite, the priest, the pastor, the guy who's still a virgin at forty-three (it's his formula for longevity), the woman who's a specialist in pompoarism, a kind of tantric sex (she said she's going to teach us all how to exercise the pubic-vagina muscles, whatever the hell that means), the multiple-orgasm specialist, and the plastic surgeon who's already made more than a thousand silicon prostheses to augment penises. Popular singers, hillbilly dancers, and so forth filled out our ranks, warming the audience up. They were signing autographs for cleaning ladies, cooks, bar folk. We could fill a stadium with all the people who've come to the show.

The producer gives us all pieces of paper.

"Your briefing. This way you'll be able to 'mentalize' the questions before they're asked. I'm dying to hear what you've got to say. Thank you for your participation."

The woman can barely string two words together. It hurts my ears to listen to her mangle the language. We participants read, concentrating. Receptionists, whose job it is to take the calls phoned in from the people watching at home, stare up at us from the orchestra pit, giving us all funny looks—though they're accustomed to this circus, their eyes are curious, tonight. I wonder which one of them gives the best blow-job?

Andrea greets us one by one, thanking us. She's using a strong perfume—sweet, nauseating. Her lipstick glistens, and the roots of her hair show she once was a brunette.

"I don't even want to think about it, they almost cancelled the program wanting to debate the first war of the new century and I don't even want to think about a war that isn't even ours, nothing to do with sex, yes it's a war but I fought to keep the agenda we'd decided on and, you know, on top of that the sponsor gave us five hours for this show, so let's make it a hit, they've been making calls since yesterday, thank you for having come, thanks, you're all respectable and serious people, you have opinions and depth, the program is going to be controversial all right but it's important to bring sex to the masses and vice versa, really we're doing them a great service, unfortunately our main attraction wasn't able to be here, she had problems at her office, it was Doctor Regina Navarro Lins, author of the excellent book *Conversations on the Veranda*, which as you know concerns Brazilian sexuality, good here's today's memo."

Does she always speak without pauses, everything running together?

Another piece of paper. The memorandum details, topic by topic, segment by segment, what issues are going to be addressed. David O. Selznick, the American producer (I've just finished reading his biography), directed his studio—controlled the scriptwriters, directors, photographers, and editors—via tyrannical memos. He was an enlightened despot. How to be tyrannical, obeyed, feared? How to acquire or develop these essential gifts?

I take note of how the program is run. In my dressing room later, I will put it into the *Manual of Media Necessities*. This is how the program was structured:

> **Preliminaries. 6 minutes.**
> **Caresses. 5 minutes.**
> **Male and female erogenous zones. 7 minutes.**
> **Methods of stimulation. 9 minutes.**
> **Massages. 10 minutes. (Professionals will give demonstrations.)**

The breasts. 6 minutes. (Introduction of women who have implants.)

Women who fake orgasms. 8 minutes.

Premature ejaculation. 4 minutes.

Behavior of the penis and the vagina. 9 minutes.

Oral sex. 11 minutes.

Anal sex. 11 minutes.

The G-spot. 9 minutes.

Masturbation. 11 minutes.

Contraceptives, pills, condoms, diaphragms, IUDs. 4 minutes.

Impotence. 8 minutes.

Viagra/Vasomax. 4 minutes.

Chinese techniques to maintain an erection. 11 minutes.

Male homosexuality. 9 minutes.

Lesbianism. 9 minutes.

Virginity. 4 minutes.

Chastity. 3 minutes.

Various miscellaneous perversions. 15 minutes.

Sadism. 10 minutes.

Masochism. 10 minutes. (Demonstrations by enthusiasts.)

Testimonies to accompany each segment.

Production Note: We tried to bring the preserved penis of the insatiable Russian monk Rasputin—thirty-two centimeters long, unseen by the public since 1968—from Europe, but were denied permission by the owner (a Parisian woman). Unfortunately, too, Columbia University wouldn't lend us Napoleon's shriveled member, 2.5 cm. These would have been phenomenal additions to the program.

Sex is discussed every afternoon, on every network. Every night we watch lingerie fashion shows, commercials for sex shops, discussions about fucking, transsexuality, male and female hookers, faithfulness and unfaithfulness (shall we see how long your husband can resist the advances of another woman?), the other woman, the other man, the woman who discovered her husband was gay, S&M dungeons.

The show starts. I'm in one of the corners, almost out of sight of the cameras. I don't like it one bit. "Right now, ladies and gentlemen, we're going to talk about sex in a way never before attempted on television—that is, frankly. As a way to orient, clarify, educate, to lose one's inhibitions, to help make our society better adjusted, with everyone balanced, filled with energy and harmony," Andrea Flores informed the audience.

I'd rather be seated in the middle. Now that priest is going to get all the attention. How annoying. But the priest demanded he be in a central position, and since he's apparently the spiritual advisor for the network's Board of Directors, he has clout. He has adherents around the world. He wants to establish a religion based on sexual attraction. Nobody knows how it works quite yet, but the newspapers are already starting to talk about it.

This is a small cable TV network. It's owned by a disgraced Senator. He never shows himself, but he invests a lot of money. He wants to use the network to help his political comeback. The other day, a newspaper published a small note to this effect (immediately refuted after they were threatened by his lawyer). One of my consultants cut it out and kindly pasted it in my *Manual of Useful Information to Be Kept for Opportune Moments*.

We've been on the air for three hours now. I'm hungry. I keep on drinking warm mineral water. They serve disgusting coffee. My mouth has a bitter taste. I didn't get the chance to say very much. They don't really ask me questions. They prefer the more sensational participants—the young women with breast implants show their chests, the men who have prosthetic dicks drop their pants. That's what the public likes. Obscenity. I can make up a lot of good stories—all you really have to do is lie; there's not one person here telling the truth—but no one asks me. Not while there are other people here with their legs wide open for the camera, happy as can be.

The production crew tells us to keep on going. The show will never end.

"We're going to extend it . . . we have more than three hundred e-mails . . . telephone calls . . . from housewives . . . professors . . . bank employees . . . prostitutes . . . geologists . . . publicists . . ."

The other networks are biting their tongues with envy . . .

Not even the reality shows ever pulled in this kind of audience . . .

people want intimacy . . . they want to go into people's homes . . . they want to see famous people taking a shit . . . fucking . . . getting waxed . . . eating . . . throwing up . . . .

we're living in beautiful times . . . times of liberty . . . there's nothing more to hide . . . everything is allowed . . .

the Ministry of Communications is calling, incensed . . . nuns . . . schoolboys . . . drag queens . . .

and even after all of this, we still haven't gotten to sadomasochism yet . . .

sadism . . . bestiality . . . various odd positions . . . common fallacies . . . I say, what about fellatio? (what's fellatio, asks the producer, clipboard and memo in hand) . . .

foot-jobs . . . orgasm provoked by stroking with hair . . . frigid women . . . asexual men . . .

"And you, what do you think?"

Me. They're asking me. This question is for me. I'm terrified. I don't know what they were talking about, I wasn't paying attention. I was thinking about Lenira, about the disappearance of Mr. Lead Actor. I can't resign myself to only being his double. I can't keep on waiting around for a soap opera needing two identical actors. At the very least, I have to switch networks, but they don't let me go—they're afraid I'll compete with LA, they know I'm the more talented one. Everybody who meets me thinks I'm the other guy. I feel anonymous even to myself.

"What do I think?"

"Yes, with your experience, what can you tell us?"

"My experience?"

"Yes. You've been married four times. You've had romantic affairs with some of the most beautiful women in Brazil."

"Oh, come now . . ."

"Don't play modest. I know that's part of your charm, but this isn't the time. What's your philosophy on the subject? The concept?"

Concept. Everything is a concept to them. People who don't even know what the word means. The other day, the candy-vendor with the cart at the intersection outside my building came up to my car and started yammering about a new confectionary concept he'd come up with. Now I just keep the windows rolled up. What a farce.

"Let me think. Please repeat the question."

"A conscientious, thoughtful man. We're talking about penis-size. Women often say it's not the size but rather how it's used. Others, however, feel that thickness is paramount. What's the average penis-length in Brazil, would you guess? Is a good size penis a substitute for tenderness? How big is yours, by the way?"

Did I imagine that last bit? But I can't ask her to repeat the question a second time.

"Do I have to answer?"

"That's why we're here. Our ratings are through the roof, you know. It's a new peak for the network. Millions are watching. You can't disappoint them."

She should have said "prick" rather than "penis." Maybe she wanted to say it. She looks like she wants to sit on a prick right this instant.

. . . it looks like every television set in São Paulo is tuned to our little station. People are opening up . . .

it's like a giant confessional . . .

a therapist's couch . . .

. . . people are calling up crying . . .

we're doing an enormous service for the people . . .

this is what television is for, education . . .

we're providing some guidance . . .

Andrea Fontes is feeling really charged up, as if celestial clarions were playing in the background whenever she speaks. Sex, the future, salvation through pleasure, total liberation, absolute surrender. She's on fire, she's forgotten she's on television, forgotten that we're her guests. And me? I'm still trying to figure out how to answer the question. I'd never really thought about size before, even though they say it's what men talk about most. Why not talk about the relative merits of wide, narrow, dry, and/or wet pussies? What about the size of my tongue? I'm dizzy. I can't tell if I've just spoken aloud, if I've kept silent, if I'm going to speak. The receptionists are working constantly, there's an unending stream of calls, they're chattering away, excited; if I were at home, I'd be calling here too, talking dirty into the ears of those sexy girls.

Andrea won't let me alone.

"So? What are you going to tell us?"

"You want to see? Do I have to show it to you?"

"I'm sorry, what?"

"I can show my dick. Why not?"

"Please! I never imagined! Have some respect . . ."

I'm sure now she wants me to show it.

"Talk, talk, talk. Let's get down to brass tacks."

"Go to commercial," she orders. She raises her hand and snaps her fingers, as Flávio Cavalcanti used to do, and quickly looks at me. No, no. She wants me. Of course. The voluptuous Andrea Fontes just gave me an inviting look. She wants to fuck me. Of course she does. She looked right at my crotch. She knows it's there. She wants it. She's licking her lips.

The lights go out.

What happened?

Is the show finally over?

I never even answered my question. The cameras are moving away. Where did the other guests go?

"Sir . . . they're waiting."

"Waiting?"

"To take you back. It's over."

Everybody's gone. The tables in the cafeteria are empty. My plate's full, but I'm not hungry. The best live program that's ever been produced on sex is being rerun on the television—

the priest talking about colossal holy water basins,

the pastor confessing he always wanted to be a girl,

the sexologist teaching us how best to lick a cunt,

the drag queen shaking her ass, telling us that these movements help a penis enter more smoothly and deeply,

but the camera doesn't show me, I've been forgotten—

I'm ashamed to think that Letícia might have seen the show. She, so delicate in bed, so loving, she who knows and worries so much about pleasure. Until meeting her, I'd only penetrated women, I didn't make love. Anyway, that's what she told me.

Before Letícia, I used to have a momentary pleasure that disappeared as soon as I stood to leave. With Letícia I learned how to take the pleasure with me, keeping it warm inside me.

For hours and days, she lives in my sleep and in my dreams. I always dream about her, sleeping or awake.

My little motorized car slowly winds its way through the studio's endless, labyrinthine corridors. My dressing room, number 101, is located in sector 9, lot 38, third floor.

I know this route by heart. I've kept the same room for decades. They wouldn't dare to give it to anyone else, out of respect for me.

My dressing room is at the far end of this wing of the studio complex. They're renovating everything. Soon we'll be in a new, ten-story building, they say.

For the time being, it smells of mildew and humidity.

The corridors are dark since the blackouts began, the rationing. Damn economy. Why so many blackouts? Who came up with the word "blackout"?

My dressing room is a refuge, with my boxes, files, notebooks, photos.

My home, my life.

I wonder if the sex program was actually any good?

Haven't people gotten tired of the topic yet?

Aren't they saturated by sex?

We talk about it so much . . .

And yet you don't say a thing, Letícia complains.

RESCUING THE ANONYMOUS: KAFKA'S NURSE

Destiny showed its cruel side once again to a young eighteen-year-old Swiss girl, living in Italy. It denied her an important role in the history of literature. Though it's hard to imagine literature recovering from the blow it would have been served had Franz Kafka managed to marry her, continuing a romance that's been memorialized in the brief lines of a letter. Between September 22 and October 13, 1913, Kafka entered a sanatorium in Riva, recuperating from a bout of depression. More than the doctors, Kafka's cure can be attributed to the young girl with whom he fell deeply in love. In a letter dated January 2, 1914—sent to Felice, the eternally celebrated fiancée—he described the woman: ". . . quite unformed but remarkable and, despite a morbid streak, a very real person with great depth." A short romance, ten days long. However, one can imagine what it must have been like for the always-tormented Kafka. In The Nightmare of Reason: A Life of Franz Kafka, *Ernst Pawel states that "The affair, probably platonic (he later speculated that it might have cost him a chance to sleep with an interesting and interested Russian lady), lasted only ten days; the girl exacted a promise of total discretion and barred all further contact, including correspondence." Kafka: "To have her smile at me in the boat. That was more beautiful than anything. Always the wish to die, and the still-just-hanging-on, that alone is love." The girl entered and left the scene without anybody knowing, except for her and Kafka (and now of course some Kafka scholars, who say her name was Gerti Wasner—but what kind of fame is that?) . . . Would she have changed Kafka's life? The interesting Russian lady has also slipped through the sieve of history. A fleeting extra.*

THE LIGHT THAT MOISTENS MY PUSSY

I will never forget.

Whenever I try to sit down and think, Letícia's voice resounds in my head, it echoes in my cavernous skull:

"I want so much for you to wake up by my side. In order to see how the light comes over the bed until it reaches my pussy. The light caresses me, as though it were your fingers. You have a glorious hand—it goes between my legs and warms me. I feel myself protected, excited. I make your hands wet, I make my thighs wet, thinking of your body. I cry out of happiness. I cry easily. The sun's light, passing between the slats of my old wooden shutters reminds me of you. It reminds me that you are never here in the morning. Will you marry me?"

How many times has she asked me to marry her?

Her eyes shining.

Oh, how I loved that woman!

Even though she'd said, "You don't know how to love. You're too insensitive. Hard as a rock."

She liked soft, poetic words like "glorious."

LIST OF ESSENTIAL CONSULTANTS TO THE FAMOUS

Short meeting in the morning on the subject of consultants and other employees. I adore having meetings at four in the morning. I feel active, full of energy then. It's a holistic attitude. I'm using this word a lot, "holistic." I don't exactly know what it means, but it has a nice ring to it. Howard Hughes had meetings with his advisors at unusual times and in unusual places: on his feet, taking a leak at three in the morning in a suburban bathroom. Here in São Paulo, I've read that the owner of the Panco corporation (breads, biscuits, spaghetti) has his most important meetings at five in the morning. Today, my Consultant Consultant presented me with the list of all the consultants I'll need to hire, to fill in the gaps in my education, in my preparedness.

"Do I really need all these people? We're going to have to rent an entire apartment just for them!"

"They don't need to be around all the time—or not all of them. Most work on an informal basis. They'll observe you and grade you. Or not. It's all a gimmick anyhow. You know that."

"But what happens when I actually need them? What if it's urgent?"

"Call a video conference. They're all equipped. Anyone who isn't is going hungry, nowadays."

"I like to see people face-to-face. I mean, in person. To yell at them, if need be. To threaten them. It relaxes me."

"Yell through the video link."

"That's no fun. I want to smell their fear. Feel them sweating. Fear is a physical thing. Organic. You need to be with someone in person to know how scared they are."

"Oh, please. What do you know about fear? You're a cold, controlled kind of person. I envy it. You're a rational man."

"Don't be a sycophant. I hate ass-kissers. And how often am I supposed to confer with these vultures?"

"Once a month."

"Once a month? I have to go thirty days without advice?"

"You could call them once a week, but they get paid by the meeting."

"Let me see this list of thieves who are going to live at my expense. They should work for free. It's an honor just to associate with me. Won't they get more and better clients because of me? Doesn't working for me give them status? My name opens doors. They can show off about how close we are, about how I rely on them—they're just a band of exhibitionists anyway. All right, give me the damn list—if I'm going to get furious, I want to start right away."

Secretary.

Agent.

Lawyer.

Press Agent. So far, nothing out of the ordinary.

Consultants on Hair and Make-up. They'll hang my photo in their salon and bill me every time someone asks them if they know me.

Cultural Consultant. Explains current events, news, literature, criticism, essays.

Consultant on Terminology. Deciphers the neologisms that come up each day in the press, generated by the various "tribes" that make up present-day society.

On Tribes. Each season, cliques are formed that speak their own language. They need to be kept track of.

On Images. Vetoes unflattering poses, angles. Guides photographers.

On Art. She'll point out good paintings and sculptures, will research their market values, give good advice about investments. Collects tips for me from the dealers: look into Jac Leirner, José Rezende, Ernesto Neto, Maria Bonomi, Alfredo Aquino, Waltercio Caldas, Siron Franco.

On Style. Two good names to know: Emanuela Carvalho and Helena Montanarini. Gloria Kalil is extremely expensive.

On Fitness.

Shopping Consultant. To help me buy the right brands.

On Food.

On Dressing. A long-distance butler.

On Music.

On Health.

On Voice. That is, diction, pitch, and intonation.

On the Stars. Which means astrology here, not celebrities. May also dabble in numerology and the tarot. By the way, I'm thinking of dropping the "de" from my name. It's cumbersome. And maybe it will leave a numerically auspicious number of letters behind.

On Mental Health.

On Autographs. He can even sign them for me, long-distance.

On Sponsorship. He'll lobby for support, both private and governmental. He'll write grants, draw up budgets, convince businesses to finance me.

On Merchandising. To help get product placement deals into my shows and movies and thus to get me free samples, from diet drugs to sound systems and watches to clothing for appearances at premieres, parties, weddings, graduations, balls, interviews, etc. (and which I certainly don't intend to return).

On Baseball Caps. Yes, of course. With company logos on them. To wear at interviews or sporting events. Even though I loathe them, I condescend to appear at horse races (the Jockey Club has a good restaurant, the Charlô—they offer me free lunches. A man like me can eat a whole year without paying, and on top of that they thank you. Only problem is that the waiters and customers expect autographs). Caps are very, very déclassé, but since they make me money, I make an exception on this one little point of style.

Correspondence Consultant. To answer my letters for me.

On Nutrition and Endocrinology. They set and balance my diets. Not at all the same as the Consultant on Food.

On Culinary Matters. To organize my exclusive recipes and distribute them to the press and to various women's programs—early morning or late evening shows. From time to time, maybe even publish a cookbook with my name on it. Very different from the Consultant on Nutrition.

Newspaper Columnist. It's a good idea to have a newspaper column published in my name. It'll offer sentimental advice, self-help pointers, will advocate cultivating one's own personality; will tell "secrets" about the acting profession, and spread nice lies about the beautiful solidarity that exists between a cast and crew on set, or between stars and their fans, or stars and journalists.

Miscellaneous Consultants. For example, someone in charge of taking me to soccer games where I'll be heard uttering sage opinions about the game. I'll come prepared with pre-memorized texts like: *This team lacks spirit. That team, however, has it in spades.* Or, *That team is playing very carefully; it needs to play more openly.* When the time comes to vote for the best player of the year, I'll just call out the first name that comes to mind and add: *Say what you like, for me he carried the entire team.* I can also go to tennis games, polo, and beach volleyball. I especially favor women's volleyball, since the tight and tiny uniforms give what I will call a sensual definition to their thighs and buttocks.

Financial Consultant. Who takes it upon himself to falsify data on my income tax and sock away money in bank accounts on certain islands. She'll work with investors or brokers to pick me stocks and bonds, like so: $$$$$$$$$$$$$$$$.

Consultant on Lying. Specifically about my life. Someone who composes lies about me to be divulged to the media. Completely different than a press agent. For instance: I was a street kid and only learned to read when I was sixteen. At eighteen, at night, I performed at intersections doing acrobatics with lit torches, collecting money from interested or sympathetic drivers. One night, hungry and hurt by her refusal, I shoved one of my torches into a whore's face. My father never acknowledged my paternity. They say the great Portuguese novelist Eça de Queirós—whose novel *The Maias* was turned into a miniseries—was a bastard too. Comparing me to Eça is a great idea! A literary giant. I should probably read one of his books.

And then **Drivers**. I'm going to need three, working in shifts, given the intensity of my life. The night driver will suffer the most—he'll have to carry me when I fall down dead drunk or faint from mixing Red Bull and ecstasy—I'm less and less in control. Though I quit the heavy drugs a long time ago. I'm clean.

Bodyguards. From specialized agencies. Two at the minimum. Not only to protect me from potential muggings and kidnappings, but also to contain the excitement of my fans. Note to self: Arm the car. Maybe do a commercial for an arms manufacturer, get them to cover the cost. This way, prospective attackers will take one look at me and know there's no use trying. A lot of recent robberies have been very motivated by the sight of expensive watches, and for this reason I haven't worn any of my ninety-three time pieces of late, which include brands such as Bulgari, Montblanc, Tag Heuer, Patek Philippe, H. Stern, Jaeger-LeCoultre, Cartier, Girard Perregaux, Panerai, and Calvin Klein. I always say I use an old pocket watch, if anyone asks: an Omega that belonged to my grandfather. Nobody knows I never knew the guy.

Special suppliers. Since this memo is personal, internal, from me to myself, more or less, I can admit that this is a euphemism for drug dealers. Narcotics Consultants. Necessary, indispensable. There are various categories, from your simple and inoffensive pot deal (a transaction between lowlifes—poor folk who are just starting out and get jumpy after so much as jaywalking), all the way up to the machinations of the decadent veterans who need their supplies in order to survive—that is, crack, coke, heroin (I'm still going to try heroin, but I have this terrible fear of needles).

Phalanx of delivery boys. For urgent services such as express correspondence, getting me money from the bank, collecting and delivering contracts, picking up my dry cleaning, buying me clothes off the rack.

And, finally, the supreme being, my **Life Consultant**. To redefine my professional objectives, to continually reassess and readjust them.

(Why do I do this to myself? I'm generous—take note. No one goes hungry here.)

Clap clap clap clap clap clap clap clap clap clap clap clap clap clap clap clap clap clap clap clap clap clap clap clap clap clap clap clap clap clap clap clap clap clap clap clap clap clap clap clap clap clap clap clap clap clap clap clap clap clap clap clap clap clap
I'm applauding myself quietly. I deserve it.

MY SISTER'S BEAUTIFUL ASS

I was listening, in the dark, again and again, to my vinyl copy of dialogue highlights from Zeffirelli's adaptation of *Romeo and Juliet*, with music by Nino Rota in the background. I never get tired of listening to the whispering, murmuring voices of Olivia Hussey and Leonard Whiting. That's when my slut of a sister came looking for me.

I said, "I'm not going to help you. Absolutely not!"

The slut has a phenomenal ass, let it be said. It can move by itself. My sister's ass always made men crazy. A woman like her can have a career, get promotion after promotion, if she lets the boss fuck her in the ass.

But the bitch doesn't give her ass to anyone. She told me: "It's very humiliating!" I respect this decision—my mother put this "humiliation" idea in her head. My mother was a real idiot who bored the hell out of my father his whole life by talking about honesty and dignity.

My father worked in an agricultural company owned by the government. He was the one who made decisions about purchasing new equipment. Businesses would offer him little "incentives" that would easily have paid for a vacation to Europe several times over, but my mother said that if he accepted these, she would leave him and take us children with her. Of course, she was bluffing—she had nowhere to go—but my fool of a father believed her. The only time he had the guts to take one of those bribes, he immediately lost it all in a card game. My father gambled, had terrible debts; his life was a living hell, and he never let my mother know. She would have eaten his liver if she'd known. To put it mildly, I never understood their relationship.

What I like, you know, is to fuck women. They come to the dressing room and offer themselves up. I'll transcribe this week's list. Out of spite, really. Principally for Maria Gertrude, who everyone thinks is a virgin and innocent—a romantic, religious, but who fucks like she's got Saint Vitus's Dance and who screamed so much one night when she came that she made an entire motel shut up and listen. Yes, motel. Of course I don't take these whores to my home. Maria Silvia likes to snort coke, take ecstasy. She spends days and nights raving. See below (men are supposed to show a little solidarity, supposed to share info with one another):

Maria Gertrude. Phone: (11) 2139-8756-44. If you bring some coke, you'll find out what she can accomplish with her tongue in your ass.

Cremilce Matias. Phone: (21) 8765-6731-73. Terrible name, but she swivels her body around slowly with your dick inside her, twisting your orgasm out from deep down.

Eduarda Frasão. Phone: (11) 6759-8673-92. Phenomenal thighs. Nickname: "Dudu." Granddaughter of the former Secretary of Security, I don't know which state.

Silvania Cleo. Phone: (31) 4653-8794-35. Beautiful eyes. You can come in her mouth. She has the name of a very nice little town in the interior.

Milena Seidt. Phone: (41) 2223-3344-27. Descendent of Czechoslovakians, she told me she has the same name as one of Kafka's girlfriends. Who? Like a good girl from Curitiba, she fucks the whole night long without stopping, leaving your dick completely raw.

Carla Carlota Carlina. Phone: (16) 5678-9745-19. She lives in Rio and she'll make you pay for her plane ticket. Call early in the morning, that's the time she likes best. I don't know her real name, but her pussy is real enough (if somewhat wide).

Those of you who don't live in São Paulo, feel free when calling to use the long-distance carrier of your choice. However, if a telephone company pays me to say so, I will be sure to tell you they are the very best.

Don't show this list to just anyone. I could get sued. Whores are crazy about suing famous people.

If I give out names and telephone numbers, it's because these particular ladies managed to piss me off. They did the job, but afterwards they told me they'd only slept with me because of who I am, which looks very good on their CVs. If it weren't for that, if it weren't for my fame, they wouldn't have bothered, because, after all, I'm not particularly attractive, nor am I good in bed.

I don't know what I did to deserve such pettiness on their parts. I even suggested some of their names when small parts came up in the popular soap *The Essence of a Soul*. Of course, without fucking me, they wouldn't even have gotten this much.

You don't get something for nothing. Even my own sister, if she wants to get a part in a miniseries—and I'm going to be in one soon, right after my plans come to fruition—will have to give up that delicious piece of ass. Not a drop of silicone on or in her. Pure meat.

RESCUING THE ANONYMOUS: HEMINGWAY'S FRIENDS

*In the book that Anthony Burgess wrote about Hemingway (*Ernest Hemingway and his World, *1978), there's a photo of Ernest, thirteen or fourteen years old—thus the picture had to be taken between 1912 and 1913—seated among friends at a campsite. The caption reads, "anonymous friends." That is, none of the writer's friends has been identified: the three friends appear in the photo with their faces hidden by caps, so almost nothing can be seen of their physiognomy. Are they close friends or merely incidental acquaintances that Ernest met at the campsite and later forgot? It's not clear if the photo belongs to the Hemingway archives, to the collection of one of the nameless friends, or was found by some family member. Growing up, did those three boys eventually realize that the Ernest Hemingway had been their companion on that day? Did each one of them keep a copy of this photo as a memento? Were the others already friends with one another or did they meet that one day and separate, each one going back to a separate place—never thinking to stay in touch, never remembering that vacation as something remarkable? Or is there a letter from one to the other lying undiscovered somewhere in the world, referring to the young Hemingway, then still undiscovered and unpublished? The obscurity of the three friends goes deeper. Do you think they would have cared to meet Hemingway, a celebrated writer who changed American literature, as adults? Would they have been interested? Would they have been scandalized? Very early on, Hemingway began generating as much publicity about himself as possible—creating a role. Few writers of the period were so in tune with the media; he knew how to make news. Was he just an intuitive promoter or did he plan everything out down to the last bit of drunken bravado? Regardless, he was in the papers more or less consistently until the day of his death in Ketchum, when he* *put the barrel of a rifle into his mouth and blew his brains out. So, what happened to those "friends" during their lives? They studied, worked? Did one of them grow up to be someone important in his community? Or did they all disappear forever into the gray mediocrity of daily life? Without knowing it, they had all been selected by fate—they crossed paths for a brief instant with a famous man. But this same fate denied them recognition. They have neither names nor faces in the biography of the famous writer who went on to receive the Nobel Prize. Like barnacles on ships, unknowns are always clinging to our photos of the great and the good. It's too bad Lenira didn't think her idea through to its logical end. Why not do research on these anonymous souls, the unidentified "friends" always hiding in our historical documents? Actually, she doesn't have the money for this project. Literature doesn't get sponsors from the business world. Only music, cinema, sometimes the theater. Visible things. Things that give your product visibility. The word "visibility" is in.*

ALWAYS KEEP YOURSELF "PLUGGED IN"

Further excerpts from the *Manual of Media Necessities*.

It takes a lot of money to dress as the media likes to see and present us. If we're not just so, they leave us by the wayside.

Bermudas by Moschino Mare, Dockers, Ermenegildo Zegna, Thomas Burberry.

My Sports Consultant and/or Personal Trainer must immediately teach me about hacky sack, this game that one plays with a little cloth ball. Could this herald the comeback of the stocking ball? Apparently the little ball is decorated. Or rather, it has a design on it. It's more or less impossible to have a trend these days that hasn't been co-opted by designers.

With a designer hacky sack, one can also play footbag, which has two variations: freestyle, and then with a footbag net.

The perfume *Allure* by Chanel. For men. Hasn't arrived in Brazil yet. Will it get here soon in a pirated version?

After a day in the ocean, the body needs a massage with Body Kouros, the relaxing spray by Yves Saint Laurent.

Stress, migraine, skin diseases, poor digestion, insomnia. According to Ayurveda, these are problems that occur when the three forces—Vata, Pitta, and Kapha—that control one's physical and mental processes are not in sync. No medicine will have any effect unless one's life habits are changed.

I can't see the sea from my window, but I can smell it. Letícia used to say, Every two weeks I need to go to the seashore to smell the salt air, to dive into the ocean, to let go of all the heaviness the city leaves on my skin and leaves inside me, sapping my strength— to get rid of all that bad energy. Letícia's skin often smelled of salt water. Something about it excited me. Why was it she didn't like to do sit-ups? Was it something related to this "bad energy"? Maybe something to do with her chakras?

HOW TO BE HAPPY

My past.

Nobody knows anything about it. And they'll never know.

I need to pick out the past that'll do me the most good. I'm thinking of going the mysterious route, maybe letting out the occasional, contradictory clue (which excites the public). Things like this enchant people, make the public think you represent a kind of adventurousness, that you've lived life to its limits. There's a certain inclination toward transgression and violence inside everyone, contained by what's called the civilizing process.* Or simply by fear.

People who lack this suffocating fear learn to recognize that civilizing norms are castrating. Politesse stifles us from birth. The majority of people live with a constant dread of transgression; they shelter themselves under the tent of the big circus of suspicion, proclaiming: Look, I'm polite, well-behaved; I'm considerate of my fellow man! What frauds.

There's only one way to be happy:

to lose it

to lose control

to rebel

to embrace the chaotic

to push everything around you into anarchy.

Nonetheless, for many people (and I mean many—many, many, and many more still), those who've lived their entire lives bound hand and foot to civilized norms, principles, and ethics, anything that smacks of a little chaos brings discomfort, allergies, migraines, uneasiness, suffering.

---

* Civility is the process of making civil and bland individuals' customs and habits, according to Jean Starobinski in *Blessings in Disguise: or, The Morality of Evil.*

The result is a pacified life,
odorless, colorless, insipid, lukewarm, regulated,
antiseptic, sterilized, pasteurized,
without any scares, without any shocks, without any pleasure,

pleasure
pleasure
pleasure
pleasure
pleasure

(Isn't that right, Letícia?)

Pleasure

MY WIFE'S TWISTED FACE

There are moments that mark our lives. They happen, and then we're stuck with them forever. And they're not even significant in themselves. This one from October 1991 must have some meaningful detail because it keeps coming back to me. Sometimes I think it was a dream. It wasn't. I remember, we were listening to a CD of gypsy music—lots of violins. It was our wedding anniversary.

I'd been bound to that woman for twelve years at that point—today makes twenty-three. I can't abandon her—though only I know why. When they ask me why I don't divorce her, I say it's an intimate matter, private. Perhaps it might be easier to tell the truth: I can't leave a crippled woman who's being slowly devoured by a tumor.

Really, there's a part of me that simply oozes integrity, and ideally I'd like as many people as possible to know about it, I'd like to see it publicized. Lavínia never goes out. She doesn't want to. She's ashamed. Pain pulls her facial muscles into a terrible, twisted shape. There are times when she seems like something out of a horror movie.

On that particular October of 1991 (what day was it?), she was irritated with me.

"Look, what harm does he do?" she asked. "He doesn't bother you. He does what he does, he fills a certain slot. You never even see him. What more do you want?"

"He's an impostor."

"Because he looks like you?"

"Which of us is the real one?"

"Real one what?"

"Which one of us should occupy that 'slot'?"

"Whose fault is it if he looks like you?"

"He's destroyed me."

"Ingratitude."

"I'm anonymous to him. Because of him."

"So what? Live and let live."

"Television, acting, is my life."

"There are other networks. Hundreds."

"Only one produces good soap operas, soaps that are distributed around the world. Do you know what they told me when I went for a screen test?"

"How many years ago was that?"

"It's not important. They told me, 'What do we need with two of you? Your face is already very well situated, you're receiving one of the highest salaries, adored by millions. We don't need a second. We don't even need you as a stand-in! We've got four stand-ins on standby as it stands already. Look, he has a common face, there's no shortage of look-alikes. That's the secret of his success—he looks pretty much like everybody.'"

"Just drop it."

"Ever since that afternoon, I've been one of the walking dead. It was like someone telling me I shouldn't have been born. That I was a mistake. That I am not me."

"Do something else. Just . . . pick another trade."

"What else can I do? I only know how to act."

"What do you mean act? The closest you've ever come was taking that magic course. Magic. Given by a radio actor who couldn't adapt to television after the war. At the time I thought you were just taking up a new hobby."

"You never understood me, Lavínia. You never wanted to understand me. You never encouraged me, never supported me."

"Oh! And who pays for this house?"

"With your disability checks? You call that a life?"

"You spend everything you make on magazines, books, albums. What's left for food?"

"Wait and see! Wait until the day I replace him, the usurper. Or, not replace, but reclaim my birthright. My rightful place."

"Yes, rightful. You sure do love that word. And 'usurper.'"

"You'll see. I'll pay for this house, the beach house, and our country place too. We're going to visit the casino in Punta Del Este, and we'll do nothing but dance the tango, which you love so much, in Buenos Aires—I know some incredible steps . . ."

"And you keep watching that film by that Spaniard, what's it called? Quite beautiful but boring. No story at all."

"By Saura. Carlos Saura. It's fantastic, I'll have you know. He was married to Chaplin's daughter! In Europe, people marry Chaplin's daughter, and Rossellini and Ingrid Bergman's daughter, and De Laurentiis's son, they marry Monica Bellucci . . . they marry Grace Kelly . . . and what about us, here? Who do we marry here? Not a name in the bunch. What good is Brazil? Everything here is second rate."

"Saint Expeditus,* give me patience! What have I done to deserve this?"

---

* Note: I open my notebook. Ancient, made of paper. I should follow Lurdete's advice and abandon paper for a laptop. Anyway: Today, October 12—latest trend: Famous people are renting out their voices for voice-mail messages. You can call up and hear LA, the bastard (may he come down with a little cancer of the throat), instructing you to leave your name, number, and a brief message. I'd love to get this gig. Not exactly prime time, but I hear it pays well!

FLOWERS GROW IN THE UNMADE BED

I don't know, Letícia, if this letter will reach you.

That is, reach you inside. Inside yourself.

Though, to be honest, I suspect that none of my correspondence ever gets past the studio's front gate. I imagine that some anonymous nobody who works here (a voyeur) keeps them. Or perhaps there's nothing prurient about it. Maybe he's just an amateur collector, someone who's saving up a stockpile of celebrity correspondence, knowing how much my letters will be worth someday. This would explain why you never reply to my letters, would explain why even when I do get a letter from you, they never contain answers to any of the questions I've asked. Our love might be confined to some drawer, closet, shoebox. Or maybe it's just been thrown away. It hurts.

But let's be realistic. It's hard to feel like our petty concerns mean all that much. Think of the airplanes that dove into the gigantic ribs of the Twin Towers in the United States. It's said that the twenty-first century began right there and then—that the world would never be the same.

I felt like throwing up. That footage gave me a migraine.

But, guess what? The world is the same. Humanity continues to be the same. That is, fucked up. The world only changes because of the wars we fight within us, my love, not because of massacres and explosions.

The wars we fight within it, and then the wars we never fight. The wars I never fought.

Maybe this letter will get through. It doesn't really matter.

I'm only writing it so I can include some poetry I found in a blue-covered book by Neide Archanjo called *As Marinhas* (The Seascapes). The publisher has an interesting name: Ibis Libris. You know, texts come to me occasionally, unexpected, unasked for—but fortuitous, one way or another. Always showing up just when I need them most.

There's always someone out there who's already put what we feel into words, has already said what we ourselves haven't managed to express.

> Yesterday
> deep in the night
> in the unmade bed
> your astonishing image
> plunged a sweet dagger
> into my body
> where desire was being reborn.
>
> Nobody was watching us
> even the sleep
> that had been staring at you
> was suddenly looking away.
>
> Yesterday
> deep in the night
> in the unmade bed
> flowers were born
> flowers were born

P. S. Flowers warmed and illuminated by the sun's rays coming in in the morning between the slats of your shutters, my love!

Hey, how are you doing?

I'm moving on—but

what about you? Everything okay?

Everything's okay here, I'm

moving on, rushing on

to take my place

in the future.

Red Light, by Paulinho da Viola

THE ENGIMA OF BRAZILIAN TELEVISION

If someone were to kill me.

If I were shot down by a girlfriend,

by the husband of one of my lovers,

by a neurotic fan,

by an American serial killer on vacation in Brazil,

in a drug deal gone wrong or by a mugger,

by one of the thousands of stray bullets that fly through this city,

by one of the thousands of motorcycles that career over our sidewalks,

by a jealous show-business colleague—

If I were to die in a flood, was struck down by lightning, or was crushed by a tree toppling in a gale wind,

was killed by a nurse giving me the wrong dosage of my medicine, or by spoiled food.

It would be a tragedy, of course, and get reported on in the media, which would find nourishment in the news of my demise for days on end. Voracious headlines would chew up my short life, outlining it in detail, and then regurgitate the remains to be devoured with pleasure by the public.

No, better if I died for reasons unknown. For one thing, the news would last longer—the case would be reexamined over and over again by curious folk with a penchant for seeing enigmas and conspiracies behind everything. They'd demand an autopsy, an exhumation.

Yes, it should be something that will cause a little doubt. Something that, years from now, might cause someone to make a documentary about my death like the one I just saw about Kurt Cobain's suicide,* which implied that Courtney Love (so beautiful, and such a good actress—I adored that film about Larry Flint and *Hustler*

---

* *Kurt & Courtney* (1998), directed by Nick Broomfield.

magazine) had actually murdered the man. Her own father believes his daughter was more a gold-digger than a fame-digger. And Cobain was tormented by his fame and his money, they say. It's a shame, really, that he checked out when he did—at least for Courtney's sake. She could have matured into the Yoko Ono of today's rock. But who will be my Yoko, my Courtney? Lenira, perhaps. She's driving me to kill LA—keeps telling me he's not going to die just yet, that he's never going to die. I'm worried that I'll never get the chance to take his place unless I execute him. How cold and indifferent I am when talking about his death. He hardly seems human to me. Merely an impediment. With LA alive, I will never be him, and therefore never be me. Intolerable. There's no other solution. I can't stand the pressure of waiting any longer. It's been eating me alive for too long. I have to think this through . . . what can I lose, after all, if I have nothing? With LA alive, I'm hardly human myself. I would be capable of murder, I think. Apparently there were a number of other mysterious deaths following Cobain's. Who knows how many people might have to disappear in LA's wake, compounding a mystery that will generate headlines for years to come? What more could I ask?

To be this new century's great enigma, that's what would be my crowning achievement.

I wouldn't mind dying myself, if I could be sure that this would be the result.

IMPIETY

You must be cold, a machine, bereft of emotions.

You must yank out your feelings and cast them aside, put them out with the trash.

You must free yourself from all impediments.

You must not be moved by tears, pain, or the sadness of others.

Their pain belongs to them. It isn't mine. It can't get to me, mustn't slow me down.

Somebody else's pain is a straitjacket. They want to put shackles on you. Want to lock you in a cell. Want to drill you open and put their unhappiness inside you.

When the film *Apocalypse Now* premiered in Brazil, Glauber Rocha—an angry young filmmaker who was perhaps over-fond of drugs—said that Marlon Brando was "a narcissistic actor, egotist, romantic, coarse, pretentious, petulant like all ignoramuses, and, as such, pathetic, sublime, but invariably reactionary." Now Coppola's added sequences that had been eliminated at the time of the initial release— he's made the movie longer and retitled it *Apocalypse Now Redux*. I don't understand this "redux." He can't mean "reduced," surely?

Anyway, "reactionary" is a quality I don't concern myself with. I know nothing about politics. I'm not interested. I don't mingle with those types. I keep my opinions to myself.

I hope no one ever presses me on the above statement.

It's enough to know I'm cold. The politics of apathy. No one knows how much work this takes. They don't know the effort I make to repress myself. It borders on self-mutilation.

The public doesn't care for weakness. They turn on the weak.

(Unless they feel sorry for them. Sometimes they love an underdog. Stand by him. How to know?)

I have to be an actor every minute of every day. On set and off. The role I play in real life is by far the more difficult to maintain. You probably guessed that.

THE FEAR SHE FELT

Whenever I take a little rest while making love, slow down for a moment, which I do when I feel like I may come too soon, Letícia gets worried: "Is something wrong? Are you not feeling well? Is everything okay? Did I hurt you? Do you want to stop?" Afraid I might die inside her. Who knows why. It was quite moving, really—her frightened eyes, her nervous laugh sprouting childlike and contagious from her mouth when I'd say, "No, no, everything's fine, I just don't want to come yet, I want to stay inside you as long as possible." Sometimes she'd become sarcastic then, would start making demands, which naturally was no help in terms of my keeping my concentration She might as well have been stroking my chest with a crochet needle. "As long as possible? As though you'd ever stay the night, or even an entire afternoon with me. No, you'd rather be in the studio, taking care of your 'responsibilities.'" Responsibilities. She would accentuate the word. To aggravate me. I think down deep she really wanted to lose me. Or she wanted to force me to leave her. Responsibility. An odious word. And I'm odious too. But isn't that what the public admires? Lenira, Lenira, why does it have to be at four o'clock in the afternoon? Why won't you give me more time?

WORDS FOR THE AGES

Oh, how quickly the actions we take—the words, thoughts, gestures, and concepts we're responsible for at every moment—vanish into the air. Expressions are casually wasted in conversation that might, in the right hands, define our lives entirely. The other day, lunching with executives from Mexican television, I said something that astonished them: "With every new day, the mountains devour another volcano and choke on its lava." One of them opened his PalmPilot and asked me to repeat this. "That's very touching," he said, "it reflects the condition of modern man—why, this is one of the most beautiful moments I've ever spent in Brazil. What an epiphany. This country is enchanting." Sure. When he takes a bullet in the mouth, shot down by some thug, we'll see just how enchanting he finds it.

THE BREATH OF AIR COMING OUT OF YOUR MOUTH

My love.

I feel strange, airborne, enraged, hurt, jealous, confused, euphoric, like a blind alley. What should I do with myself? I don't recognize myself. Even my girlfriends say they hardly recognize me.

Today when we were together, something was different.

The silence, the touching, the kisses, the absence of laughter. As though we were trespassing. As though the room felt invaded by the presence of our bodies.

But, even so, even silent, even without gladness, I'm impressed by the intensity, the tenderness, the warmth and the love so obvious in our gestures, our kisses, our touching.

When we're together, when you let your guard down. You make me feel so good. And now I have to go. I'm going to travel. Going to find work somewhere else. You know what the situation is like here—no one is hiring. But how am I going to survive so many weeks and months—I don't even know how long I'll be away—without seeing you? Being tortured by my fantasies?

I'm miserable.

The only thing that makes me feel better is to breathe in the air coming out of your mouth, to feel you resting close to my heart. It warms me, completes me, feeds me, and gives me peace.

I'm not exaggerating in the least. Or only in the first paragraph.

I love you. Letícia.

It does me a lot of good to reread this letter.

I reread all of them. Though I tend to get the dates mixed up.

MODERNITY

"The one and only real problem is solvable. That is, scheduling. May I make you an appointment? You need not have the least doubt."

My Guru for Personal Well Being is very anxious, insistent. Yes, I said *guru*. Guru is now more "current" a word than consultant. My guru swears to me that clairvoyants, witches, numerologists, cabalists, and tarot-readers are fundamental, key elements in today's lifestyle. If you're not prejudiced, there's a good number of medicine men with websites, easy to contact and well-informed . . . politicians and crowned heads rely on their advice.

"We have our choice. They have offices spread throughout the city, and believe me, they're all very hip. Of course, some are more expensive than others—depends on the neighborhood. But there are good and honest practitioners in the suburbs, too, and they're slightly cheaper—I can give you some names. You know, a publicist friend of mine doesn't so much as comb his hair without getting a consultation. Shall we go? Trust me, this is what it takes to be plugged in, to be in tune with your times. [*My goodness, he said "in tune." It's been quite a while since anyone's used that expression.*] Readers of coffee grains, tea leaves, graphomancers who can tell your fortune by examining the doodles you make while talking on the telephone (save everything you write!), nephomancers who can read the formation of the clouds the afternoon of your appointment, austromancers who can interpret the sound of the wind, copromancers who can hear your fate in the noises coming from your intestines, see it in the sculptural formations of your shit, or smell it in the particular odors contained in a fart—and then others who can do the same with the color of your urine, the length of time you were laid up with the flu last year, the designs left on your plate after you've been playing with your food, the color of the tartar that forms on your teeth, and the typos they find in your business correspondence."

Yes. Wise and sensitive men can penetrate the deepest recesses of my mind, see my past, contemplate my future, and work spells to block malevolence, perversity, pettiness, nefarious designs on my person, and general scorn.

Anonymity is a result of all the ill-will inflicted on me by the jealous nonentities who populate this world.

"We need to prepare ourselves accordingly."

"Isn't it enough for me to memorize my lines and act?"

"Those days are gone."

"Sometimes I ask myself if it's worth the trouble. I'm not going to make it. I'll never take his place. Better for me to resign myself to being a duplicate. What's the point of my killing myself for supporting roles—when there aren't any to be had? Going to graduations, barbecues, political rallies. Is it doing me any good?"

"Things have changed. It's not like the old days, the days of the method, the days when you paid attention to your script and tried to muster a little feeling. The future is now . . . please pay attention . . . Modernity has arrived. Actors transcend the studio, the stage, the recording studio or movie set. Your performance is also your life. You know this already. But maybe you haven't figured out that your performance in day-to-day life is actually *more* important than what you do on television. Yes, that's an actor's masterpiece. To create an image, to smooth out the rough edges of his real life. That's what audiences will love you for. That's what you'll be remembered for, when you're gone."

"You know what? Go fuck yourself!"

"Listen. Do you know what the public wants?"

"I . . . well, no one knows for sure."

"Nonsense. Women want to see shirtless models showing off their abs. They want to be turned on. They want to see men covered in sweat, lying in bed with some unknown, blank, silicone actresses—they want sculpted bodies, they don't give a shit about performance. They want men so stupid they can't even memorize dialogue. They don't care. The dialogue can all be taped and looped in. What matters is that there are bodies to look at."

I think he's jealous. He's an ugly man, resentful, with a face like a prune. Intelligent, sure, but if I were a woman I wouldn't fuck him. Then again—who *do* women fuck? My Cultural Consultant talks like a high school teacher. I feel like I'm sitting in the last row, whispering to my friends, as always. The only class back then that interested me, that I was really crazy about, was history, since it was filled with so many outsize characters, so many great and petulant celebrities: Julius Cesar, Nero, Alexander the Great, Hannibal, Genghis Khan, Nebuchadnezzar, Tutankhamen, Nefertiti, the Sun King, Ulysses, Socrates, Philip the Fifth of Macedon, John Wilkes Booth, the Venerable Bede, Petrarch. Or Mesha, King of Moab, who found himself besieged by the powerful army of the Israelites. He offered his eldest son in sacrifice, putting him on a bonfire. The gods responded and the siege was lifted. His prayers heard, Mesha massacred seven thousand Israelites as a sign of gratitude. And then there was Cambyses, who had a corrupt judge flayed alive and used the skin to upholster the chair on which the new appointees would sit. Today, here in Brazil, Cambyses could upholster an entire stadium's worth of seats with that kind of leather. I found these cruelties quite enchanting. I filled a notebook with them. I think I still have it. It must be on one of these shelves. After all, only cruelty will ensure my success, my ascension to a place where nothing can harm me, cause me pain. I should track down my old notebook of atrocities and turn it into a *Manual*. Cruelty combats stress. It does wonders for your self-esteem.

"Hey! Are you listening to me?"

"Yes, yes. What were we talking about?"

"About fashion."

"Fashion? What's that got to do with me?"

"You must stop following trends and start dictating them yourself, for one thing."

"Me? Are you crazy?"

"Start wearing whatever you want, whatever you find beautiful, comfortable, convenient. Whatever suits you."

"What?"

"And if you happened to favor a certain imprint's clothes or shoes, stop throwing money away—send *them* your bill."

"I'm not a mannequin. I want my face in the papers, want to be interviewed and photographed. Today, now."

"That will come in time. You need to be patient."

"How am I supposed to know what kind of trend the public is ready for? I don't want to look silly."

"What's important is that you wear what *you* like. It doesn't have to be beautiful for the public, for journalists. If you wear it, and it's photographed, everybody's going to wear it. What you wear has market value, because *you* have market value."

"I can't make something ugly into something beautiful just because I wear it."

"There's no such thing as beauty. There's no such thing as good taste. Only taste itself. And your taste will become the public's taste. Your charisma can turn anything into gold. If you say something is beautiful, it will become so. And your decision will be validated by the cash you get for wearing whatever it is you want, whatever it is they need to sell."

"Taste? I hardly know which socks to put on every morning."

"Don't worry about it. We have people who'll choose for you. They know exactly what you like. They'll pick out each outfit, down to the handkerchief."

"Clothes . . . clothes . . . Christ, I thought you told me that women want to see actors baring their chests, shirtless. That's why they give contracts to professional models, guys who have experience on the runway. Gorgeous and witless. And anyway, nobody uses handkerchiefs anymore."

"They will if you do. Your image will be composed down to every last detail. One look for dinner, one for cocktails, one for art openings, one for premieres."

"I thought you said what mattered was my own taste."

"Look, if some famous cretin wears underpants around his neck one day, the next morning it'll be in all the magazines that the new thing to do is wear underwear around your neck. Even if they're already used, soiled, secondhand underpants. Sharon Stone wore underpants as shorts and the world copied her. Celebrities choose a path and the world follows. We'll discuss this phenomenon in greater depth, next session."

BEING ALIVE, WHILE DYING

And what if I were to offer you another life?

The possibility of dying, while still being alive?

Japanese Lenira. Trying to save me.

How long has it been since she made this offer?

I didn't have my current job yet. This job that seems like it'll never end.

I'd like to have a little more free time. I'd like to do other things— not have so many pressures, obligations, commitments, ties.

And then, later, in the same brusque and abrupt manner, cold as only she knew how to be, Lenira made her offer in reverse: How would you like to keep on living, while seeing yourself die?

ONLY FAILURE MEANS SUCCESS IN BRAZIL

I put on my Oliver Peoples glasses and ask myself:

Why bother? Why put yourself through all this trouble?

After all, in Brazil, failure is success!

True success is hell. Talent is a curse. If you have talent and use it right, if you know what to do with it, you are condemned.

However, he who fails is loved, is free, is embraced.

This country loves victims. It joins failures in solidarity: lifts them from the mire and sits them cozily in its lap.

The scene reminds me of the *Pietà*.

Joaquim Ferreira dos Santos, the writer, is someone I feel could understand me—if he knew I existed. I see he's on my side, for example, when he takes time to comment in *Jornal do Brasil* on two facts with real-world historical repercussions: the eviction of Xaiane from the *Big Brother* House because of her having the most beautiful body on the show. And this year during the Rio Carnival parade, the marvelous Empress Leopoldine samba school, with its always-impeccable presentation, was booed: "Brazil doesn't excuse talent or beauty, and when it sees these qualities being brought into play, will punish those who have indulged in them for having dared to rise above the herd. The punishment for these unfortunate, successful people will be demotion or simple exclusion from their fields . . . Brazil, so fond of failures, won't tolerate success. It jeered at success on the avenues during the Carnival parade . . . begging, for the love of God, that the judges not consecrate such great beauty with yet another title . . . Brazil doesn't deserve Brazil, as Elis Regina used to sing. And she too was criticized for being so great a technician and, consequently, cold."

RESCUING THE ANONYMOUS:
THE DANCERS OF *THE RITE OF SPRING*

A fundamental night for modernity. May 29, 1913. Théâtre des Champs-Élysées, Paris. Music by Stravinsky and choreography by Nijinsky. An appalled astonishment took hold of the audience, divided as it was between avant-garde intellectuals, anxious to applaud the new, and a snobbish and dressed-to-the-nines elite that booed, stomped their feet, and proceeded to cause one of the greatest scandals ever to grace the history of the ballet. Even if they hadn't already been famous, Stravinsky and Nijinsky would have made history that night. People still talk about it even today. But what's usually glossed over is that there were forty dancers on stage that night. Only one was given any prominence—one Maria Piltz, *who played the lead role of the sacrificial virgin. There are never any references made to the rest of the troupe. We know nothing of their lives and careers and what that night might have meant to them. Were they sensitive enough to understand what was going on, aware of their role at this all-important cultural moment? Or did they let themselves feel crushed and defeated by all the booing and shouting? Did some of them quit after that night, traumatized? Did those, who bravely carried on, tremble at the possibility of that night repeating itself whenever they stepped on stage? Did they abandon the avant-garde, or did they develop a taste for shock, experimentation, innovation? What did they think about, how did they proceed? Regardless, they've remained anonymous—perhaps dumbfounded, perhaps amused. Unknown partners in a* cri de coeur *let out by history—a cry provoked by art, and which marked the beginning of a new and thenceforth rapidly evolving era. Imagine having contributed to the transformation of art, of culture as an entirety, and nobody so much as noting down your name. I would tear myself to pieces.*

PEOPLE WHO LOVE EACH OTHER
DON'T STAY TOGETHER

Letícia looks at me, her eyes flashing. I know that look. I'm afraid.
She immediately puts me on the defensive.

"Why don't you just come with me?"

"I can't. I can't leave everything behind."

"What do you have here? Tell me!"

"A life . . . a career . . ."

"Comfort, routine, boredom, conformity."

"A future, a career. It's about to happen. Just you wait!"

"What's going to happen? I've been waiting for two years. It's all
talk."

"All right then. I like it here, it's safe. There's nothing here to be
afraid of."

Her look changed. Its intensity lessened. I saw she was afraid.
She can't see inside my head, can't understand me. In my mind,
I see everything coming out right, I know that everything will be
taken care of.

"If I went," I say, "what would I do?"

"Live."

"I am living."

"That's what you think."

"It's what I know."

"You don't love me?"

"Stop it."

"I'd just like to understand. Why can't two people who love each
other actually be together?"

And now she's crying. It's torture for me. I lose my tact. I can't
stand a crying woman. And Letícia's crying is so deep. She cries
meaningfully, like an abandoned child; but she knows I don't have
an answer for her. I can't leave. I look around at my dressing room.

I can't leave this place where I keep what I was and what I am and what I'm preparing to be. When I'm up against the wall, when someone is forcing me to make a choice, I lose myself entirely. It's unbearable.

"This is the last time I'm coming here," she said.

"You hardly ever came here anyway."

"We've already broken up and started over again dozens of times. I can't take it anymore."

"I never understood why you fell in love with me."

"You were the one who started it, that night you declared your undying love for me. That goddamn night. And I thought—said—shouted: This isn't going to be easy. And I was right. But I let myself be carried away."

"We both got carried away. But I never promised anything. You know that."

"You can't love that wife of yours. It's compassion. Pity. Routine! Your marriage doesn't even exist."

She doesn't know that Lavinia is paralyzed, that the tumor is going to kill her. And then Letícia turns her back and walks out, leaving the door open. Dressing Room 101. She walks slowly down the corridor, slightly bowlegged. She's gained a bit of weight—because of anxiety? But I really like her like this—a little more substantial. I'm never going to caress those smooth thighs of hers again. Why does she frighten me so much? Is it her frankness? The way she leaves me exposed, leaves me without a clear idea of what role I'm supposed to play?

Why don't I give in once and for all—let everything else fall by the wayside to be with her?

But would everything else let me go?

My life is a succession of nevers. All losses and no gains, like the lottery—a game against impossible odds. But I tell myself, "If you stop playing, you'll never win."

WHAT TURNS ON LENIRA

I like to brush up against men in bookstores, hidden by the shelves. Everything is much easier with the big mega-stores. I pretend to be idly flipping through a slang dictionary. At random I open to the word "crab" and ask the fellow next to me:

"Hey, did you know that the word 'crab' also means 'vagina' in Acre?"

The word "vagina," said so suddenly, startles men. They become intimidated, lose confidence. I look seriously at his face:

"And a 'shaft'? Do you know what a 'shaft' is in the Northeast?"

He hasn't managed to compose himself yet, so doesn't answer. I toy with him:

"It means a small ass. Isn't our language strange?"

I turn a few pages and ask again:

"Sir, I hope you don't think I'm some sort of baggage for saying these things aloud. Do you?"

"Baggage?"

I don't tell him what it means. I finish:

"And what about a 'stem-in-the-croup,' do you know what that means?"

I smile, close the dictionary, put it on the shelf, and walk away. I observe the man from afar. He grabs the dictionary and discovers that "harlot" means "whore," that "stem" means "prick," and that "croup" means "anus." He immediately looks around, trying to find me, and then starts stalking around, looking for me, all excited. I stay in another section and soon see him approaching.

Men are quite predictable. He's surprised to see me with a book on quantum physics. I've put on my thick-lens glasses. The lenses are just plain glass, no prescription. The frames are the same as the ones used in that soap opera about Italian immigrants, a big hit. Seeing the book's title, he hesitates, perplexed. They always hesitate at this stage of my little game. Now I pretend not to notice him, pretend I just happen to be looking for a book shelved right behind him, at hip-level. I kneel down in such a way that my head is about parallel to his dick. From time to time I throw my hair back in order for him to see the tattoo on my neck and to let my hair lightly brush against his prick. Hard, naturally.

Then I turn around slowly and face it. I lean in and give it a quick little kiss on the tip, over his pants, then I rise and go to a corner of the room, out of sight. By now they've figured out that I know the store by heart, that I've studied its geography, like theater directors study the space available on their stages.

Again I appear indifferent, as though nothing has happened. If he approaches me again (and he will, they always do), full of himself, confident (this is how they all act), I seem inaccessible. No chance. I suddenly have an interest in philosophy. I read aloud: "Seeing all delight is appetite, and appetite presupposeth a farther end, there can be no contentment but in proceeding...

FELICITY, therefore (by which we mean continual delight), consisteth not in having prospered, but in prospering."

I pass my tongue over my lips (men always find this arousing, for some reason) and scratch my breast a little, lightly opening my blouse so my playmate can see my hard nipples. I let him get real close, I stick my hand through the side-slit of my skirt (specifically chosen for the occasion), caressing my thighs. I open my dress until he almost sees my cunt. Almost.

If he has the courage to reach out, I give a little cry—as though I were coming—and I shout: Fuck!

Then I leave, I go straight to the middle of the store, near the cash registers, some place full of people. I walk around there for a bit, and then walk out the front doors without looking back.

He may come after me, but they never catch me in time—the chauffeur is waiting for me, and I disappear. Maybe the man writes down the license plate number, maybe he tries to track me down, but plates are registered to my boss, the actor, who has enough clout to keep his plate numbers from being given out.

Do you think my men go home and masturbate after these run-ins with me?

I know I do. And I think of them, alone, caressing their cocks.

---

* Hobbes, *The Elements of Law, Natural and Politic* (1640).

Without monumental egos art is no better than housework

The above statement occurred to me today when I bolted my dressing room door and later realized the lock was jammed. I was imprisoned for hours waiting for the locksmiths who finally had to knock the door down to let me out. They were all pretty nervous at how I'd react. Silly of them, really—I like being by myself. I got a lot of reading done while I was waiting. I plunged, fascinated, into Marina Picasso's memoir, *Picasso, My Grandfather*. She tells us that Picasso needed blood to sign his paintings, and that he felt he always needed to destroy something in order to create—especially if he thought this something might be standing in his way. Marina's relationship with her grandfather was, she says, made up of broken promises, abuse of power, disdain, and miscommunication. Two of his wives killed themselves after Picasso himself died: Jacqueline Roque and Marie-Thérèse Walter. Olga, another wife, died of cancer. Pablo's grandson Pablito killed himself by drinking a bottle of disinfectant. For years Marina lived in poverty. All this information on Picasso has taught me a big lesson. It's the work of art that survives and will go on to enchant the world—not the man who created it. A few days ago I tore a page out of a weekly magazine supplement that comes with my newspaper because it was there that I found my lovely little axiom hidden in an article that quoted a 1946 letter Lewis Mumford (one of the great critics of modern architecture) wrote to the poet John Fletcher about Frank Lloyd Wright: ". . . one of the greatest architectural geniuses of our time; not merely that, but of any time . . . He has more imagination in his little finger than the most of his contemporaries have in their whole organism . . . But this great genius has equally great weaknesses . . . His greatest weakness is a monstrous ego; though he talks of democracy, he has the manners and beliefs of a Renascence prince: at heart, he is a despot. His despotism is so all-embracing that he resents the very existence of his clients . . . arrogant, violent, despotic, high-handed, and yet, with an occasional gleam of self-criticism or the occasional act of self-transcendence that redeems him . . ." I expanded on this and gave the results to my assistant to distribute to the press. She was moved by my axiom's brilliance and lucidity—especially how I've related art and life. Now Lenira is going to use my little formulation in her thesis. Yes, she's working away on her thesis, but when is she going to move forward on our body-swapping project? When will I be free of the Lead Actor? The idea of killing him is too pleasant to put off for much longer.

SELECTING THE SETTING

My ex-wife (my first—let's keep things clear) wants to schedule a meeting. She needs to talk to me. Nothing about money, apparently—she already gets plenty: it's one of the highest-paying alimony arrangements in Brazil, and I've never once fallen behind on the payments. Not because I'm generous, mind you, but because I don't want to go to jail. Not paying alimony is one of the few things in this country that will always land you in prison—the mysterious hand of justice. I was lucky with my other exes. The second and the fourth get along well, so much so that they've even opened a boutique together on Oscar Freire Street (very chic). I haven't seen the fifth since we split up. She danced flamenco—excellently. Letícia also enjoys flamenco: she has classes twice a week. Sometimes I think of waiting for her outside the door of her dance studio. And then the second one . . . I'm drawing a blank. How is that possible?

Anyway, I asked Lavinia, my first, who was requesting an audience, to give me two days grace before meeting her. Not because I was busy. I'm not. It's a matter of selecting the right setting for our get-together. Where best to meet her? It needs to be a place where we can be spotted together. It's good for my image to show that I'm on good terms with my ex-wives, even though I'd like to see some of them dead. The public mistakes this for generosity.

I must be seen in an appropriate setting, appropriate and impressive, given that I'm seldom seen in public at all. I can't think straight—there are these goddamn helicopters filling the sky. Why did they bother inventing helicopters? Why is the traffic up there so congested? What do they want? Where do these people go? What's the rush? How am I supposed to get anything done in all this noise?

I need a good location for our meeting.

Everything in life is a set.

(All this seems misplaced. Just my intuition!)

ODIOUS LUCIDITY

How long has it been since Letícia visited my dressing room? How long has it been since I stopped counting the days? There's no point in knowing.

I divide time up as I like. According to my needs.

Moments are not concurrent but synchronous. Two can occur simultaneously. Three at once. There's no point in explaining this to someone who can't think outside pedestrian conceptions of time. For me, therefore, these moments now, waiting, exist parallel to the time of final preparation leading me to the fatal moment Lenira has guaranteed will come.

From that moment on, however, there will be only one kind of time. Mine.

Yes, "fatal moment." Lenira used this expression. She's intelligent, you know—wrote a dissertation about anonyms, beautiful, brings tears to the eyes. Quite possibly the first time an academic thesis has had this effect. And yet, despite her having a Ph.D., Lenira uses clichés like "fatal moment." Sounds like the title of a soap opera. A melodrama. You wouldn't bother seeing it unless there was a cheap matinee.

Nevertheless. It will indeed be a fatal moment for *him*, the hated Lead Actor.

Letícia was disappointed with my dressing room/studio, even though she admired the obvious organizational skill with which it had been assembled: my meticulously catalogued books, clippings, diskettes, periodicals, photographs, documents, notebooks. She wanted to know where all my materials had come from. I lied to her: They're part of my work, I said.

I couldn't tell her the truth.

I couldn't stand having Letícia think less of me.

She's the only powerful, the only real thing I have in life. Or had. Or will have again.

She makes me uncomfortable. She is clear and precise. Her ideas have breadth. She talks a lot about relationships, about love and sex. And I don't know how to respond. I remember Cássia Eller saying something in an interview once that struck me as particularly apposite about my situation: "I don't know how to put myself forward, I don't know how to talk, I don't know how to resolve anything with words. I'm horrible at explaining things! On stage, I don't have to say a thing! And I don't even try. I get all mixed up forming sentences. I'm very timid, that's probably why I'm so intense on stage. It's a way of compensating for the difficulty I have in expressing myself in life, in my day-to-day life."[*]

"How can you work in such a tiny little cubicle?" Letícia asked, seeing it for the first time.

"I work."

"They could at least make you a little more comfortable. And all those terrible corridors. All gray!"

"I really don't spend all that much time here."

It's a lie, but I'm ashamed. My dressing room really is painfully small.

"You have talent. You deserve better. I saw two of your performances on television. You're good."

"Good! Good won't cut it so long as that guy is out there, standing in my way."

"What guy?"

"The Lead Actor. I look exactly like him. You must have noticed."

"I don't see it."

"I was cursed from birth. How can I have a career? He's too good."

"He's fifth rate! What kind of competition is he, anyway? A man who wears silk neckerchiefs? Who lets himself be photographed in the bathtub?"

---

[*] Singer Cássia Eller, interviewed by Deborah de Paula Souza for *Marie Claire*. I've filed the clipping in the folder labeled "Personal Mythology."

"He has a reputation."

"He's a mediocrity. The network's desperate. Everybody knows he's not going to last very much longer."

"He fucked up my career."

"He doesn't even really look like you . . . He's on his way out, anyway . . . He's going down the drain."

"We have the same face!"

"You're exaggerating. You always put yourself down. Don't blame him. Just go out and do what you want to do."

Letícia doesn't understand that I need the Lead Actor as much as the network. I can't strike out on my own. No one is allowed to know how often I stand in for him. The public has no idea how often the voices they hear or faces they see are anonymous men or women filling in for their famous sound- or look-alikes. And then there are the voices on TV commercials, or the ones that announce the time, that call out the departures in airports. All stand-ins: stand-ins for voices of authority.

I'm tempted to explain the plan to her. How the stand-in will take the place of the stood-in-for. I don't want to lie to Letícia. It's not easy to hide things from someone who loves you.

"This is a powerful network," I say.

"Who are you kidding?"

"It sustains itself, it has an audience."

"Do you really believe that? This network is eating you up. You're believing its own propaganda. It's going to consume you. Don't you get it? What are you afraid of? Leave! I saw the short films you made before you came here. They were good!"

"Drop it."

"Everybody knows the truth about this network. How it survives."

"What have you heard?"

"That they're giving away commercial time. That the network is leaching funding from the government instead of taking in ad money. That they only produce state and federally sponsored programs. There are no profits. The board members sell shares in the network to pay grocery bills, car repairs, vacations, hotel rooms, decorators. I think they don't even pay for doctors, dentists, their children's schools. Their wives go shopping, rent designer clothes and don't return them, have their hair done for free, and buy up paintings from art galleries, all by giving away worthless bits of the network. The executives live their lives on credit. Get out, my love. There's no future for this place. Nothing is real here anymore."

I hate it when she tells me the truth. She exudes the odious stench of lucidity. It bothers me. It bothers me, but it's also good for me. Letícia is right, she sees everything, knows everything. She knows how the world works. Maybe because she works in publicity. And she called me "my love." The ground quakes when she calls me that. How did I ever have the courage, at that party, to approach her and tell her I loved her? It felt wonderful. I don't know how she managed to love me back, though. She loves me more each day, difficult though that is to believe. She worries about me, wants to rescue me from this place—but she doesn't know that what I have here isn't an ending point, but a beginning. My finale will be on a far grander scale.

"And what's that on the door? 'M. M.'? Does it stand for Marilyn Monroe or the chocolates?"

"It was M. M.'s dressing room before they gave it to me."

"So, he's gone. Put your own name up there."

"It's not important."

"Put your name up there."

"What difference does it make?"

"You won't be anonymous."

"I really can't be bothered just now . . ."

My name will be put up, all right, but not here—on another dressing room door, at another network. As soon as the fatal moment occurs, and I take his place.

"What are you mumbling about? Who's going to take what place? I don't understand you. Is this the plot of some new soap opera? A movie, maybe? A miniseries?"

Incredible. And yet, Letícia doesn't even see that LA looks like me. I wish I could explain, but this is one story I can't allow to get out.

Or does she suspect something? Does she already understand? Has she given up on me?

The public can't tell the difference between when I'm me and when I'm him.

When I'm him (and I've been him a lot—more and more often, in fact, as his mysterious disappearances continue), I'm not me.

I stop being me.

I'm an anonymous being inside him.

Only I know the difference.

ALWAYS KEEP YOURSELF "PLUGGED IN"

Summertime and the *Manual of Media Necessities.*

Magazines: the Spanish and German editions of *GQ*, the Brazilian edition of *Playboy*.

A strange new publication has also been recommended to me. It arrived today and was promptly entered into my files: *Technikart.*

In-flight magazines offer the following reminder: The summer is the ideal time to indulge your kinks!

This year, take care of (his or her) feet. Massaging, kissing, toe-sucking, caressing, scratching, nibbling. Women's toenails are to be painted. Each nail a different color. Ah, Letícia always took special care of her feet. But I could never touch her feet—she was too ticklish. I like to remember that.

Sneakers: Air Presto, from the brand whose logo sort of resembles a half-moon. You know the one.

I have to hire a golf trainer. Buy a Maglite so as to be prepared for blackouts, emergencies, nightfall.

Listen to Astrud Gilberto's *Look to the Rainbow.*

Acquire an Esarati 400 Blackhawk: an electric motorbike for short runs. Ideal for driving from my dressing room to the studio in time for taping.

Tinted glasses. Calvin Klein, Giorgio Armani, DKNY, Polaroid Eyewear. Square, triangular, round lenses, inspired by sports. Like scuba goggles, or ones for cycling, swimming, diving. Yellow lenses, greenish-brown, lilac, blue, olive green, gray. Shaded or not.

YOU INSIDE ME, AT THE MOMENT I'M SLEEPING BUT VIGILANT

My love. I've already told you, several times, about the sensations I experience when I'm sleeping—or at a certain stage in my sleep. That is, I seem to be sleeping, but inside, a part of me is aware, and my mind and senses are racing at a thousand miles per hour. Generally I've noticed that I tend to enter this state in the early morning. I'm conscious but not awake. At those moments I always feel your hands on my skin. I manage to control my desire and I intentionally prolong this ghostly touching in my mind. Around four this morning, I entered into this state—half-asleep, half-awake—and began to feel exactly what I would have felt if you had been lying by my side. I felt the heat emanating from your body, I even felt its size, its weight in the bed, by my side. When I leaned up against your phantom body, I felt the same electricity on my skin that I felt when I put my hand on your chest for the first time, long ago, standing with you on that shaded avenue. The sensation was so strong that it woke me up; I couldn't fall back asleep again, and just lay awake in bed until it was time to get up, all the time wanting to go back, to rewind the tape in order to keep on feeling that you were with me, to keep on feeling that shock, that electricity, that relief I always feel when I have your body next to mine. I was so very sure you were there, last night, in my bed—until I woke up. I almost called you to ask if you'd snuck into my bed in the night and then snuck away again before I could wake up. Or perhaps you visited me in your dreams. Telepathically. When I finally got up to have breakfast, I saw the hydrangea you gave me, and it was wilted, wilted, wilted. I hope everything is all right. I worry about you. I hope you're happy, calm—that you have everything you want. When I got home later that day, there was a telephone message from you. I want to believe this all means something. I want to believe you slept with me today (last night). Letícia.

NOTEBOOK OF CRUELTIES

I finally found my old notebooks. Reading them, they nourish me, give me newfound purpose. These monsters from history make the perfect models for me. Almost mirrors. In Assyria, for instance, I read that war prisoners were massacred due to the impossibility of feeding them. They knelt down in front of their conquerors, who proceeded to split their craniums open with clubs and afterwards cut their mutilated heads off. The king, if he had time, used to preside over these activities personally. Captured noblemen, however, received special treatment. They had their noses cut off as well as their ears, hands, and feet, and were then hurled from the highest towers available. Their children were decapitated, skinned alive, and/or roasted over a slow fire. It's important to be strong, merciless. Victory can only be achieved through strength.[*]

---

[*] Memo: If I seem rather heartless in the above passage, please keep in mind that I'm trying to set down new precepts for myself to follow—to implant them in my mind as deeply as possible. Cruelty must become nothing less than dogma. Its law must always be present within me.

MANUAL OF SHORTCOMINGS TO BE CORRECTED

A migraine like an explosion blossomed in my head from doing the reading that was assigned to me this week by my Cultural Consultant—I spent all day and all night on it, and I'm still no closer to making sense of the subject.

It's about this philosopher Sloterdijk (is that how you spell it?) and the false conscience of the Enlightenment (Jesus fucking Christ), involving the anthropogenic, apparently, and passing through the physiological base to morality (goddamn it), and the publicity and imbecilic pressure of the media, with enormous reflex action following from the intellectual fields and the mummification of academic culture (Lord above). Sloterdijk says that the era of children having a good or bad conscience has already passed.

"What does it all mean?" I asked my Consultant.

"Don't worry about what it means. Just talk about it as often as possible. Speak, speak! Repeat what you've read. Confuse people!"

"What's the use of quoting this person if I don't even know who he is or what the hell he's talking about? What if I run into someone who presses me on the subject?"

My consultants are all accustomed to my outbursts. They aren't bothered. They're professionals.

"Just worry about enunciating. Reporters and columnists don't know a thing about it either. They'll only remember that you brought it up, they're not going to argue or ask you to elaborate. They'll bill you as an intellectual, a star with real substance, someone who takes part in the great philosophical debates of our time. That's a good image to cultivate, and your image is all you really need to understand."

"But I understand a lot more than that. For instance, to quote Linda Evangelista, 'We don't wake up for less than ten thousand dollars a day.'"

"And who is this Linda Evangelista, if may I ask?"

"What do you mean, who is she? What kind of stuff do you read, anyway?"

"Some things escape even me. Certain elements of contemporary culture."

"I don't believe it. You're usually an encyclopedia . . ."

"It's impossible to digest all the information available today. It's torrential! No one man can take it all in."

("Torrential"? Shit, he said "torrential"?)

"Then why are you recommending that I absorb this gibberish?"

"I didn't! I recommended you mention it. That's all. Throw in some stuff about this evangelical thing too, it sounds like it has potential."

"Evangelista! A model. A millionaire, forty-three years old. Dozens of *Vogue* covers—and I mean all the *Vogue*s, from the American to the Australian. And do you know what her manager told her when she was seventeen?"

"I must have missed it."

"He said, 'Enjoy all this now—you've only got three years left in this business!' What fucking nerve. He got off easy—a lucky bastard. His name's disappeared from the history of fashion and media. He became just another anonymous imbecile."

"I'm deeply moved by this story. The question is, however, whether you believe it. Do you consider this story to be indicative of one of the great world-historical issues of our time?"

"I don't know. You tell me. Go ahead. What are the great issues of our time? What moves people? What matters to them?"

He stared me down. I froze. You know my limitations. He does too. If he'd actually trotted out the great issues of our times, I wouldn't have been able to stay awake—well, he's boring as hell. He knows I think he's boring, but he earns his money honestly, trying to give me guidance. An old professor, kicked out of the university because he didn't know how to perform for his students, didn't know how to make them give a damn.

"Breast implants. Designer pocketbooks," he said.

"I don't understand."

"Liposuction."

"These are important issues?"

"Think. Go deeper. Think. The small lapels on sport coats. Theodor Adorno and James Bond. That shower designed by Philippe Starck. Silk cloaks with fringes embroidered with beads. Separate bathrooms for men and women. *Bridget Jones's Diary.* Harry Potter. The Sisleÿa Global Anti-Age Cream . . ."

"Sisleÿa?"

"By Sisley. The most expensive cosmetic in the world. The first batch to hit the market in Brazil caused street brawls to break out in Rio de Janeiro. Think. The revolutionary textiles, created in Dartmouth, that contain bacteria that consume sweat, semen, piss, shit, and dead cells, all the while giving off deodorant and cleaning themselves. Professor Laura Kipnis's thesis maintains that pornography, in the right context, has a liberating effect. Think. Remote controls: one for the DVD player, one for the VHS player, one for the stereo system, one for the radio, for the karaoke machine, for raising or lowering lights, opening doors. Five-meter-wide beds for jumping and doing somersaults, one-hundred-eighty-meter-square bedrooms."

"I'm fucked!"

"The young girls at raves who raise their skirts and sit on their partners' laps, copulating during the dances, our modern version of the Roman orgies."

"And I've never gone to a rave! What a waste. I was always afraid of the gangs who hang out at those things. You're only pretending you don't know about all of modern life—you know everything. Always alert, always observant!"

"Now, with shows like *Big Brother* to contend with, a new era has arrived."

"A new era? And what does that mean?"

"No one knows yet. It's new."

And then there's the war. American soldiers tossing bombs around in a desolate country—without trees, arid, colorless. He didn't say anything about the war. I wonder what he thinks of me, really. Of my tiny TV set, fourteen inches, black and white, playing its favorite rerun, an American film, a catastrophic super-production.

Two airplanes penetrating the towers of the World Trade Center in New York, and then the towers toppling down.

What catches my attention this time is the dust and the thousands of pieces of paper flying around: paper and more paper, almost blotting out the sky, as though there was a celebration going on, all the office workers tossing torn pieces of paper out of their windows, into the street.

The sound is lousy on that thing. It's time for the production department to send me a new TV: big, thirty-eight inches, flat screen, color.

The one I've got now can be donated to the homeless people living underneath the viaduct on the other side of the studio.

RESCUING THE ANONYMOUS:
THE RUSSIAN ARISTOCRACY

Thousands of people: the elite of the Russian aristocracy. Princes, counts, dukes, the high officials of the imperial army, the privileged caste. Dandies and sophisticated women in all the splendor of their jewelry, French perfumes, and imported gowns (or else those designed and made by the haute couture of the period). In this photograph, later published in Paris Match, *you can see a little bit of this golden world, the cream of Russian society, 1914. The caption tells us that the Counts Tolstoy and Orlov are present, as are the Princes Volonski and Dolgoroukov. In the background, all lined up, is a legion of impeccably dressed butlers and waiters designed to ensure the successful operation of the Ball of the Colored Wigs, in the palace of the Countess Shuvalov, in the month of February, in Saint Petersburg, or Petrograd, or, later, Leningrad (when the majority of these people were probably dead or exiled), and then Saint Petersburg again. The photo gives us a good presentation of what was then considered to be the very best society had to offer—admittedly according to somewhat disputable criteria, but this is not the place to discuss the class struggle in any detail. My point is this: at that moment in time, when the photograph was taken, none of the people captured by it were what you could call "unknown." Each one was known, each would have appeared in pre-Revolutionary Russia's Who's Who. The beautiful, the elegant, the powerful, the despised, the admired, the envied, the rich, the brilliant, all shining in their splendor. They were the talk of the town—their every sentence caused a stir, their every party, tea, reception, dinner, ball, salon, musical soirée, duel. A curious detail: The majority of the officers in uniform have their jaws sticking out in what's called a prognathous position. One could put this down to the primitive lens distorting the image, perhaps. Even so, why aren't the women prognathous as well? Could this have been a characteristic* of the arrogant brass of that period? Almost all of them have a small black beard, well trimmed. The prognathous position gives them a petulant air, a superior look, mixing disdain with ennui. And yet, they're having a good time. The majority had already finished dinner. Champagne glasses are on all the tables. In the front, to the right, there's a young woman, twenty or more years old, with a distant and melancholy air, remote from the festivities around her, indifferent to the excitement. Absorbed in something, unaware, concentrating. Was she only like this for a brief moment while the camera's magnesium flash was going off, or had she really tuned out, was she lost in some intimate train of thought? What was she thinking about? Who was she? That unidentified young woman stands out in the photograph, clashing with the harmony of its other elements. She is a break in the atmosphere, she is disrupting the scene, calling undue attention to herself. We cannot help but zoom in on her. Nevertheless, her name is not in the caption. Today, almost a century later, her name has disappeared entirely. No one knows who she is. And yet, there she is, perpetuated in the photograph, discovered in some museum in Russia, preserved in the archives of Paris Match. Is it from a family album? All we know is that she was a member of the nobility that even now survives here and there throughout the world, preserving remnants of the bygone days preceding so many years of socialism. Or does one say communism? Anyway, from a different era in the history of the Soviet Union. I mean, Russia. Or do I have that backwards? I'd better consult an atlas.

TO RECOGNIZE A STAR

At the beginning of the '50s (I'm paraphrasing what Eli Wallach said in a documentary on James Dean I saw on cable the other day), *we decided that a young beginner who was rehearsing with us—we'd never heard of him before; he was coming out of the Actor's Studio—always full of theories and questions, always delaying rehearsals, was going to become a star. Just because of the number of demands he made, we knew he had the stuff—that he absolutely was going to be a star.*

If I had my own video store, I would play and replay these documentaries, take notes on everything, revise and extend my *Manuals*, correct behavior, bring it more in line with the mannerisms of the great.

Stars make demands. As many as possible. As foolish as possible.

The more absurd, exotic, and irritating the demand, the more you command respect, admiration.

THE FRAUD HE REPRESENTS

If I could prove that he was a clone, a copy of me, perhaps that would destroy him in the eyes of his idolizing public. The newspapers call it "idolatry." An odious word. How can they love/admire a fraud?

He is I.

I am he.

I am the one.

Not he.

A LIFE IN PHOTOGRAPHS:
ONE PER DAY

I envy Cláudio Claro, who started out as a fashion model and became a promoter, an impresario, who was always fucking gorgeous women left and right, preaching bisexuality to the masses, and is now directing his third motion picture and may be in line for an Oscar nomination. He told Marilia Gabriela (she always manages to squeeze every single secret out of people—why hasn't she called me yet? My gurus/consultants all need a kick in the ass) that ever since he was twenty, he can review his life through pictures, because every minute of his existence has been captured on film. Isn't that fantastic? Cameras have followed him virtually every day of his life. He must be forty-two by now. The Botox makes it difficult to estimate.

I need to buy those pants with seven pockets. They're top of the line. The "cosmopolitan" is the drink of the moment in Miami: lime juice, Absolut Citron, Triple Sec, and cranberry juice. In Miami, dozens of Ferretti yachts are anchored, the latest in boating, priced between three and five million dollars. I'll feel like more of a man on one of those boats—more confident, more virile, more domineering, more aggressive, more handsome: indomitable. And modern.

Nothing new on the *Party Crashers* website. Not one bit of information I don't already have. It's been months since something new has turned up, some new game plan, a different angle, a foolproof scheme for getting into parties uninvited, major parties, parties with repercussions, or else ways of getting legitimate invitations despite not being on anyone's list. Attention: A new, all-purpose and forgery-proof ID card is now being used in certain foreign countries to help citizen-consumers avoid identity theft. How can I keep up with all the latest technology?

Today I've also come across this revelatory statement made by a hairdresser from São Paulo: *The more fashionable you are, the more your hair has to be out of fashion.* Mullets are in, now, in Brazil.

Long, straight hair or a mullet looks like the spiny-rayed fish called striped mullet found in Brazilian waters.

For more information, consult <u>www.mulletsgalore.com</u>.

HOW TO GET INTO PARTIES DESPITE BEING A NOBODY

My Mailing-List Consultant was supposedly working with my Consultant for Sought-After Invitations. I called a meeting. I was annoyed.

"So many parties! The magazines talk about them left and right, and yet I can't help but notice that I'm not getting any invitations. What's happening? How am I going to go to them all?"

"All?"

"All! I don't care if it's for the grand opening of a lunch counter in the suburbs! Where are my invitations?"

"We're working on it. It's not easy."

"Working? I don't care whether or not you're working. I want to see results. Bring me your reports, let me see your battle plan. Show me the rough road I have yet to travel."

I have to be careful—I still find myself using expressions I've picked up from people who are not at all hip, not the least bit plugged in. Still, after a half hour of haranguing, they show me their little book of strategies:

1. Bribe a promoter. If she takes your money, all is well. If not, regale her with flowers, presents, bonbons, greeting cards, telephone calls, dinners, lunches, trips, hotel accommodations.

2. Have sex with a secretary willing to put your name on one or two of the invitation mailing lists. Easier than strategy #1.

3. Get seen at as many non-invitation-only events as possible. Introduce yourself, carry different sets of business cards for different targets. Tell people you're a manager, a fundraiser for cultural events, a lobbyist, a consultant, a financial advisor—you can put whatever you want on a business card.

3a. Make sure the card is well printed, and tasteful. Hire a good designer. Or else make one by hand—originality occasionally pays off.

4. Send champagne to an actor who is making his debut in a new play. Visit him backstage. Get his telephone number by promising him anything he likes.

5. Go to fashion shows and sit in the wrong place. Pretend there's been a mix-up, that you were given the same seat number as your interlocutor, start a conversation with him or her, be gracious, offer your card, take theirs in turn. Don't be very expansive. Show that you're not a bore, that you're easygoing, act like you're slightly out of place, look intimidated. Women like that type. (Not all of them: Be careful.)

6. Take out a loan and buy clothes during a liquidation sale at the fancy boutique. Or else find an old-fashioned tailor who can duplicate their designs. You'll see that the profession still exists if you trawl the side streets and bad neighborhoods long enough.

7. Go to restaurants. Stand near a celebrity and read a prepared text out loud. Pretend you're well-read. Recite some good sentences by a great author in a loud voice. Attract attention.

8. Order a strange drink from the bar, preferably when you're standing near a reporter. Give him the recipe (you must memorize it in advance). When the journalist asks for your name, keep a low-profile: "Don't bother, it's my pleasure." Find out if the journalist goes to the same bar regularly, then show up again by chance.

9. Be persistent with promoters, managers, impresarios. Get their numbers. Telephone, telephone, telephone.

10. That is, be tiresome, a pest. One day, just to get rid of you, someone will give you an invitation.

11. Comb the social columns. Select events you'd like to attend. Show up and pretend you've lost your invitation. Give your name. Be visibly disappointed when the bouncer can't find you on his list. Say: I came from Rio de Janeiro, from Salvador, Bahia, Aracaju, New Hamburg, just for this party. Pretend to be devastated, smoke

cigarette after cigarette. The doorman will end up taking pity on you. Be patient. Also, try to bribe security men, bouncers, etc.

12. Take out a loan, throw a dinner for all the promoters you can track down, the big as well as the insignificant. Be extremely nice, affable, intelligent, discreet when necessary. Somebody will be won over and your name will get on their mailing list.

13. Find a forger who can make you a legitimate-looking invitation of your own.

14. Invitation scalpers. There are all kinds. Like bootleggers or drug dealers.

ALL THE FORMS

"Form after form,
he took on all forms.
His own form
is found everywhere."

Rig Veda, Grhyasutra 1–6

NAVIGATIONAL CHARTS SHOULD BE DISTRIBUTED AT PARTIES

My Image Consultant looks upset. He sits down in front of me, on the set. I've been given a fifty-minute break. My next scene will be with Fernanda Montenegro, who's late—she just arrived last night from the United States, exhausted, returning from a premiere in New York. We respect Fernanda enough here in the studio that I really don't mind the delay. It's not a question of being temperamental. She never put on airs. She appreciates professionalism and encourages her co-workers to do the same. All she wants is to play opposite someone who knows his lines.

"She improves every scene we shoot, just being on-set," the director said once. I keep observing her method. I want to learn, copy, steal her techniques. People like me need to be sponges. I have a drama teacher who gives me classes three times a week, and likes to use "the method"—which was popularized at the Actor's Studio, and is deeply indebted to Stanislavski. It was first used by the leftist theatrical groups, back when everything was political.

I envy Fernanda. She's never won an Oscar, but she's received fantastic national and international media attention, and was on David Letterman once. In fact, this delay is downright helpful—I'll have more time now to work out how to control my nervousness about facing her, working with her. We have a difficult scene together, and she's a heavyweight—she could demolish me. She wouldn't mean to—she even confessed, back when we started shooting, that she actually likes to play opposite me (I should have taped her statement, like a diploma, publicized it in all the newspapers)—but she could make me look like a fool just by virtue of her superior talent, her superior celebrity.

Our lines are complex, too. The scene begins with a moment of rage and hatred—easy enough for me to play: this is my permanent state of mind, after all—but then progresses towards prolonged weeping and finally a tranquil exhaustion. Now, if I somehow managed to outdo Fernanda, the crew would kneel at my feet. As yet, they have no faith in me whatever. They don't believe in me. I wanted to use this extra time to go over my lines, but I see that my Image Consultant is sulking.

"What was the point of bringing you to that party yesterday?" he asked.

"The point? Everybody saw me!"

"Saw you? Nobody saw you. Nobody who matters. You don't even know how to position yourself correctly."

"I circulated everywhere."

"It's not just a matter of circulating. There are tricks to this business."

"There are?"

"When you're talking to somebody, don't fix your eyes on your interlocutor."

"Interlocutor. That word again."

"Only talk to people who count. Whoever is most important."

"Intelligent people, you mean?"

"I could care less about intelligence. I mean people the photographers are going to seek out. Beautiful people, eccentric people, newsworthy people. People who might lead to another invitation, who might lead to a spot on a television program, a new party, a week at the castle of Mr. So and So, a modeling contract, and so forth."

"I'm not a model!"

"So what? Actors are sought-after commodities. They generate media. Do you know how much an actor gets paid to march down the runway modeling some outfit? So stay alert at parties—keep your eyes on the important people. Relationships are investments. Careful with the ones who are way down on the totem pole. Stay away! Pretend they have AIDS. Pretend they have leprosy. They're deadly. Give them a wide berth."

"Photographers already seek me out, whether or not I'm with someone more famous . . ."

"They take one photo of you, and that's it. It never makes it into their spreads. If you don't keep climbing the social ladder, they'll abandon you entirely. The idea is to be seen walking down the right path. Every party has its own navigational charts—you need to keep them to hand in order to avoid the rocks, to keep to the shipping lanes. Pay attention to the photographers: see where they congregate. Give out a kiss here, a smile there, a hug. Self-assurance, simulated indifference, studied naturalness. What's the point of all our rehearsal time if you don't use these routines when they count most? Now you know why I suggested you practice in front of that mirror."

"I did everything right. Everything!"

"You kept chasing after some little whore who only goes to parties to find a john. Pay her already, don't sweet-talk her."

"I'll have you know I've never had to pay for a fuck in my life!"

"Am I not getting through to you? Allow me to repeat: Be ever vigilant while talking to the lesser celebrities and party-goers. Your eyes must be like those of a cobra, ready to spring. Watch the door, check for the major celebrities, models, singers. Look and see if they're looking back, look and see if there's a center of attention in the room. Let your eyes wander. Be the cobra. Be the hunter. Don't just stare limply at the person you're talking to."

"They'll think I'm rude."

"To hell with manners. Nobody bothers with them anymore. If you want polite society, go hang out at the museum. Nobody thinks about anything at these parties—there's not a single thought circulating in the entire crowd, believe me. Certainly nobody gives a damn about anyone else's feelings. They're all there for one reason, same as you: To be seen. To be the one who makes everyone curious because of the way they dress or walk. Or the one who surprises everyone by showing up with some outrageous partner. New lovers are always a big help. Sleep with somebody important's wife and casually let the information slip out during a conversation. Or else manufacture a scandal: get caught getting a blow-job in the bathroom. Or be spectacularly betrayed. Or betray someone else spectacularly. Or even let it be known you've started getting it up the ass."

"The only one here who's going to get it up the ass is you, my friend."

"Such anger. Did I say something wrong?"

"What's wrong with you? I'm supposed to start sleeping with men just to get some publicity?"

"Oh, you're not as heterosexual as all that. You can't fool me."

"I'll have you know I've got women lined up outside my dressing room!"

"Lined up, eh? Well, that's good to know. It's hard to read people nowadays. The gender police really need to get organized . . . but honestly, are you sure you like women? I wouldn't have guessed. Are you really so attached to the idea?"

"I'm neither attached nor unattached. I am what I am. Why turn myself into something else?"

"Nobody is what they are."

"Don't start with that shrink bullshit. Nobody thinks I'm gay. Period."

"I wouldn't have thought you were a homophobe, either."

"Nonsense. I don't have a bigoted bone in my body. I'm the most open-minded person I know."

"What a waste. You're closing yourself off to some wonderful possibilities."

"Look. I'm not gay. I'm not."

"But don't you see that gay is 'in'?"

"It is?"

"Haven't you noticed that women always go after gay men?"

"Really?"

"Gay men are well-loved. They insinuate themselves into female society with ease. They're kind, improbable, funny."

"And what if my son hears that I'm gay?"

"Your son?"

"Lavinia's son. My son with Lavinia."

"Your son? Since when do you have a son, goddammit?"

"He's sixteen."

"And who's Lavinia? No one has a name like 'Lavinia.' You're making this up to scare me, right?"

AN IMPENETRABLE MYSTERY:
WHAT IS SHE HIDING?

She intimidates me. She's expansive—she laughs, talks a lot, but I'm a man of few words, despite my sense of humor, despite my ready irony (usually only wielded in self defense). Everything she does is seductive. Even the rage she shows when her car's CD player refuses to read a particular disc. (Music is vital to her. It's her second skin.) Yes, even her petty rage at this electronic ill-will.

That's how Letícia infiltrated my head and my heart. As an idea. It took almost two years of contemplation, from a distance. Two years of imagining her, of reconstructing her from the memory of a glance. Afterwards, I had no defenses left. I found myself fascinated by everything she said, and by the way she said it: by her interests, her opinions, her viewpoints. She was so different from all the other women I knew. (Though I was a little taken aback to find out that she's the sort of person who skips to the end of books when she likes the first few pages.)

There's an indefinable, *je ne sais quoi* about her—impenetrable, hidden, unattainable.

I know her so well, and yet her reactions still surprise me. There's a mystery in her that I can't get to the bottom of. I'm not complaining: without mystery, relationships would be monotonous, predictable.

She started to get inside me. She crawled under my skin and inserted herself into my nerves and muscles. I can feel her inside me when I move. All the cells of my body have been taken over, claimed by Letícia. They depend on her, live for her.

One person is the other. And vice versa.

NEW TRENDS CAN BE STARTED
AT THE SPEED OF SOUND

Some choice quotations to be inserted occasionally, casually, at a dinner, cocktail party, premiere, or at the theater, in the orchestra seats, during a debate, if there are reporters in earshot, or else at the movies (so people will turn and look at you):

"Just think, rhythm and blues, or R&B, which preceded rock music, is now making a comeback, influencing certain new styles of drum'n'bass!" I got this from *Jornal do Brasil*. I don't understand a word, but it always seems to leave my interlocutor rather impressed.

I've also memorized a line written by my dear friend, the late writer and critic Paulo Francis (the advantage of dead friends is of course that they aren't likely to turn up and deny that they knew you). I feel it perfectly characterizes modern-day Brazil. He wrote: "Our century has both greatness and tragedy. Only our daily lives are crummy." How I miss Paulo. No one could ever replace him.

Then, for my dressing room, I had bronze plaques made, inscribed with words of wisdom from Gianni Ratto, the actor. "He who was born talented is finished," says one. Ratto must have known my work, and LA's too.

Here's another: "Actors are people who take every advantage of their profession in order to live forever, to make themselves immortal. A true actor is timeless."

I could steal these lovely sentiments, pass them off as part of my own legacy. But I'm honest and I respect Gianni Ratto. Yes, respect is one quality that I possess in abundance. I'm telling you this, because if I didn't point out my good qualities, people wouldn't notice them.

Gianni made the above statement to the papers in June of 2001. (What year is it now?)

Still, the weekly magazines only print the most ridiculous nonsense—the kind of quote that impoverishes the world, that constricts us, hems us in, as though we were wearing a particularly tight skirt. Maybe it's time to fire my Consultant on Intelligent Declarations—what good is he, if no one's interested in wit? Maybe it would be better to cook up the most banal and idiotic axioms imaginable*—they'd get published without the least effort on my part, and no one would ever know that I was having a good laugh at their expense.

Now what's the point of all this, again?

---

* Memo: I've just been reading. I came across some words that have since become anathema. They've been banished from civilized speech: they can't be said, can't be heard. They indicate that one is no longer up to date, i.e., cyber, rent boy, nerd, daddy-o. They'll keep fresh in the freezer, perhaps. And one day be unfrozen.

I'VE ALWAYS PRACTICED IN LIFE WHAT I PLAY ON TV

My life experiences facilitate my profession. I've done everything and that's an advantage few actors can really claim. I know what it's like to have a father who lost everything gambling, I know how to balance tires, I replace burst pipes, I've done backstitches and hems. The Italian cuff was born when the Duke of Windsor, walking through muddy terrain, doubled the hem of his pants; he started a trend. I spend hours every night trying to think of little things I could do that might then go on to be copied and adopted permanently into our mode of dress. (I still haven't been able to find a Consultant on Altering the Verities of World Fashion.) I know how to weigh vegetables, with a discrete finger on the scale to raise the price. In short, I've really lived. Kids today making a start in television don't know a damn thing. They have no experience, have never had to fight for anything, have never had to prove anything, have never failed or succeeded, have never holed up somewhere and spent a week doing nothing but fuck, have never been impotent. Sure, they've humiliated themselves on reality television, took baths in front of the cameras, wept when they lost their spots on the show. But so what? Most of them had already spent years modeling, walking up and down the runways, posing for cameras—the camera was the breath of life for them. They're barely people. Actors need a good taste of human life in order to play a roll. For instance:

Cook. Sailor. Boxer. Handyman. Graphic designer. (*I adored my time in that ad agency, working in the art department—me, who can't even draw a little cat.*) Horse trainer (*I had to go to Barretos, stay a whole week, endure the rodeo and the miserable heat*). DJ. Consultant for Sponsorship Strategies. Soccer player (washed up). Locksmith. Director of Events and Promotions. Mailman. Poet. Stockbroker. Doctor. Newspaper archivist (*I adored my time on the* paper; I was the guy who got to tamper with all the documents and misquote birth and death dates).

Dog breeder. Taxi driver (*I bought a map and learned the whole city; São Paulo is so damn big and chaotic—do you know how many "A" streets there are? Two hundred*). Waiter. Computer programmer. Robber baron. Baker (*I used to fart into the bread dough before putting it in the oven; the union protested—it didn't understand art*). Reporter. Copyboy. Country-store clerk. Doped-up motorcycle racer. Television director. Gas station attendant (*I knew how to mix water into the gasoline in just the right proportions to make sure that a customer's motor would still start*). Bank teller. Web-designer. Projectionist. Printer. Fast-food cook. Car washer. Funeral agent (*I learned from José Mojica—great guy*).

Financial consultant. Bookbinder. License-plate maker. Title designer for film posters. Hotel receptionist (*not too many lines—usually they just want you to describe the room and hand over the key*). Pimp. Janitor. Landscape painter.

Florist. Parking attendant (*I helped rob a bunch of cars*). Plumber. Picture framer.

Bus conductor (*I pocketed the fare money*). Croupier.

Church-tower clock repairman (*I have a horrible fear of heights, like Jimmy Stewart in* Vertigo, *but when we shot the scene, it was on a set—everything was at ground-level*). Milkman. Window washer.

Pizza delivery man (*at the beginning of my career, I appeared in more than twenty porno movies; I'd deliver pizzas and get to fuck all the girls in each house I visited; they'd suck my dick instead of giving me a tip. I'm not ashamed of those films, by the way, and no one's ever dared try and blackmail me because of them. If they tried, I'd just have them all made public—obscenity confers status*).

Hot-dog vendor. Hero of the beach (*I'd wrap a handkerchief around my cock and wear a diminutive Speedo on top—all the women in range would just lie on their towels and stare at my crotch*). Shoe Salesman. Politician. Magician.

I can be anything. Pretending is easy. It's a lot of fun to hold down a job you know you aren't stuck in.

No matter what I do, I'm always an actor at heart. I adore being an actor.

(I've just jotted down some new notes in my *Manual of Short-comings to Be Corrected*.)

Considering how many jobs I've held, how many roles I've played, I still possess a rather notable degree of humility, wouldn't you say? After all, I'd play the role of a street sweeper without the least compunction, certain that my career would only benefit. I mention this because I just read in the paper that the ill-fated LA has turned down the role of cesspool cleaner because he considered it to be beneath him. "I," he said, "who have played in Shakespeare, Brecht, Beckett, Osborne, Arthur Miller and Jorge Andrade, Ibsen, Gianfrancesco Guarnieri, and Strindberg, cannot play a cesspool cleaner. Besides, there are no more cesspools left in Brazil—our sanitary systems have been functioning properly and efficiently since the pioneer sanitarian Oswaldo Cruz implemented them."

No cesspools left? He's mistaken.

He doesn't know what goes on in my head.

But he's going to find out.

ANOTHER ROUND OF APPLAUSE, PLEASE

Clap clap clap clap clap clap clap clap clap clap clap clap clap clap clap clap clap clap clap clap clap clap clap clap clap clap clap clap clap clap clap clap clap clap clap clap clap clap clap clap clap clap clap clap clap clap clap clap clap clap clap clap clap clap clap clap clap clap clap clap clap clap

Thank you, thank you, thank you very much

PLEASURE: THE ONLY RESPONSIBILITY

My hand runs over each curve—the only thing it can't touch are her feet, since she's too ticklish. My fingers try to be gentle, insinuating. They want to please her. "When I'm in love," she says, "my skin becomes smooth and soft. There isn't a better skin treatment in the world for a woman than to be in love."

And then: "The only thing we owe to one another is pleasure. It's our responsibility. This is what I want to give, and it's what I want most out of our affair."

My old doubts nag at me. How can she love me? Why? A guy with no charm, awkward. Nothing special as a conversationalist. I don't dance, I don't know anything about music, I've never learned by heart the lyrics of a song, and as for discussions of films or politics, I don't have an idea in my head—if somebody disputes some canned pronouncement I've made, it can take me days to think up a good rejoinder.

But she gives me pleasure, always. She seems to have been born for it. She is calm, focused, free. She half-closes her eyes when I touch her, giving out muted cries from down deep in her chest, as though joy were pushing out every last drop of air in her lungs. She is patient, always smiling. She chips away at my numbness, my petrified insides.

"Let yourself go," she tells me. "Relax!"

"I am relaxed."

Though I'm not, and I can't hide it from her. I always think I can fake it, but she's too perceptive, too knowledgeable. She knows too much about men and women.

I feel like she's pressuring me now. I resent it, and then, confused, catch a glimpse of just how twisted up I am inside. I want to give in, not offer any resistance, but I'm not capable. How long has it been since I've let myself really relax with another person? Is it impossible? When did I become such a terrible person? I'm going to lose her—nobody is so heroic as to be able to stand me for very long.

"Relaxed? You're trembling!"

"It's desire."

"Desire? That's a strange kind of desire!"

"I want to fuck."

The word "fuck" just sounds silly, sometimes.

In the beginning, she didn't like to talk dirty. She hated words like screw or fuck.

"Look how tense you are! Relax!"

But she's patient. Happy to be with me, for some reason. She laughs a lot, I feel it softening me up inside.

"Is this what you call love? I almost don't recognize it. What's going to come of all this? Do you really think we have a future?"

RESCUING THE ANONYMOUS:
IPANEMA VS. COPACABANA

In December of 1945 a historic if ridiculous soccer match took place in Rio de Janeiro, when Ipanema and Copacabana came face to face. The players weren't "the bronze he-men, the athletes who'd already faced each other on the sand time and time again," reported Ruy Castro in an article for O Estado de São Paulo *on May 20, 2000. They were writers and artists, rounded up by the wealthy poet and industrialist Augusto Frederico Schmidt, owner of a single soccer ball. Among the various celebrities who played that day were Di Cavalcanti (goalie), Rubem Braga, José Pedrosa, Orígenes Lessa, Moacir Werneck de Castro, Newton Freitas, Paulo Mendes Campos, Fernando Sabino, Vinícius de Morais, Carlos Thiré, and Carlos Echenique. Braga, Sabino, and Mendes Campos wrote newspaper articles about this game, which was as historic an event to the arts community as the game Brazil lost to Uruguay in 1950—or the other one we lost to France in 1998—or the one we lost to Honduras in 2001—or the one with Sweden we won in 1958 (World Cup)—or likewise the one in 1970 when we beat Italy (World Cup)—were to the sports world. (If there's an error in the above citations, please take my ignorance into account—the only soccer field I can remember at this point is Maracanã Stadium, where Frank Sinatra sang for one hundred and fifty thousand people. Can you imagine the sound of that many people applauding at once?) In any event, the newspapers finally make reference to a certain doctor who was the last man picked for one of the teams: a bald man with glasses, very good with the ball, quite likely the best on the field. Later, the playwright Maria Clara Machado thought she recognized this unknown person as her uncle Lucas, brother of the writer Aníbal Machado, but opinions still differ, and doubts persist. Thus, this doctor who should have entered into the history of the arts (as well as of soccer), immortalized in poetic texts by three of the best writers Brazil has ever known, has instead been walled away in obscurity, condemned to be unknown, unidentified. That's the way it went in golden-age Brazil, Ruy Castro explains.*

THE ADORABLE ARROGANCE OF JULIA ROBERTS

I read an article recently by Milly Lacombe that included the following interesting observation: 'What couldn't be explained was the joking tone manifested by the A-List cast during the interview. Julia Roberts came into the room ready to answer all the questions put to her as derisively as possible, even poking fun at the accents of the foreign correspondents. "I don't know why she acted that way— maybe someone asked her something she felt was inappropriate," said her *America's Sweethearts* (2001) costar John Cusack, trying to explain her behavior away. Apparently, however, unsettling one of the greatest stars of our age is a task demanding neither effort nor dedication. Julia Roberts is, as has been widely reported, the most arrogant and dissimulating actress in Hollywood, always ready to criticize reporters who arrive to an interview unprepared.' I cut out and save the news item in my files. The Julia Roberts folder.

Articles like this have probably appeared the whole world over by now. Julia can do whatever she wants. And everybody still adores her. Everybody throws themselves at her feet. The press idolizes her; reporters never get upset, indignant; they never say, "I'll never interview that woman again!" Of course not. They'll always interview her. They'll always run after her like a pack of drooling hounds. How else will they fill their columns? How else sell their papers? But Julia Roberts won't ever see me. She'll never even know I exist—because it's true, I don't. It's not even funny to consider the possibility of her falling in love with me during the Cannes Film Festival, for example. Though granted this passes through my mind at each and every film festival I attend. Berlin, San Francisco, Venice, New York, and wherever movie stars are paraded around before crowds.

What am I supposed to do with all *my* arrogance? No one will take it from me. Shall I vent it on the rats that run free here in the abandoned hallways with their terrible squeals, frightening away the starlets who otherwise would be lining up outside my door?

ONE BLESSING PER DAY

"Hello? Is this Carlos Heitor Cony, the writer?"

"No. Though I have a similar name. Carlos Artur Coty."

"Coty? Like the perfume?"

"What perfume?"

"Or the ex-President of France?"

"What President?"

"Mister, are you a writer?"

"I write poems. Every Brazilian is a poet, my friend!"

"But you're not a professional?"

"Professional?"

"A professional poet. Do you get paid for writing?"

"Paid? I run a telecommunications networking company, PABX, for the home or small businesses. Do you need one? Is your house very big?"

"Big? Of course it's big. But I don't need any telephone shit."

"Oh, go fuck yourself."

"*You* fuck *yourself!*"

Goddamn secretaries gave me the wrong number. I'll call someone else on the list.

"Bernardo Massar?"

"Yes. Who is it?"

I give my name. He gets emotional. Well, naturally.

"I don't believe it! What can I do for you? I don't believe it!"

We've begun badly. His deferential tone doesn't appeal to me. I don't even know if I want to work with the guy now. But they told me he was good.

"I need a good writer. I see here you've won all the critics' prizes. You're writing scripts for TV Globo. You must be pretty good."

"What would you need me for?"

"To write a daily newspaper column about me."

"Daily?"

"I want somebody with imagination like yours to invent a good piece of news about yours truly, each and every day."

"What for?"

"For sending to radio stations, TV news programs, to all the printed media."

"'Printed media'? You talk funny."

"Some people say a prayer every day. They ask for one blessing. Me, I need one juicy piece of news every day. Doesn't matter where it appears—TV, radio, newspapers, whatever. Just so long as people see it."

"I'm sure you don't need a writer for that. Incredible things must happen to you all the time."

"Sure they happen . . . But I still want you to use your imagination. Pad out my list of incredible things. We won't even have to meet. You can work from home. Send me what you come up with via e-mail. Easy money."

"My imagination? What sort of thing would you want me to invent?"

"Anything and everything that comes into your head that might get me good media coverage. A dinner with a starlet, incognito attendance at some Fashion Week show, a walk through the old center of the city, disappearing for a few days without anybody knowing where I am, then being seen drinking margaritas on a beach on the south coast . . ."

"Disappearing?"

"Disappearances are great, they make people really curious. Or how about that I get seen shopping at the Higienópolis Mall . . . No, that won't work, it's free advertising. We'll only run that one if they pay up. You do know I get paid for appearing in certain places, don't you? So, anyway, I want any kind of news you can dream up, anything that a newspaper might run. Pro or con, it doesn't matter."

"Con?"

"Looking bad is very good. No one likes an angel. I don't want to come off like a goody-goody. I want to be seen as unpredictable, mean, unlikable—but charismatic."

"I have to do all that as well? What about your press agent?"

"Busy. Look, my staff more than pulls its weight. Some of my people have got thousands of news stories in circulation right now. I just want someone who can give me a personal touch."

"Well, let's meet, come up with a plan."

"Do you have artist biographies, books on cinema, magazines? You'll need to learn the style. What about foreign newspapers? How are you on film history?"

"I can look into it, do research. What exactly are we going to do with this material?"

"I told you. Create news. Construct situations. Though we'll have to keep it our little secret. Writers and journalists are busybodies, indiscreet—as I'm sure you know. We can also recycle long-forgotten stories about Marlon Brando, Frank Sinatra, Kirk Douglas, James Dean, Fred Astaire, Brad Pitt, Anthony Hopkins, Bruce Willis, Michael Douglas, Peter Coyote, Antonio Banderas, Ralph Fiennes . . . and what about John Gilbert . . . his unhappy love affair with Greta Garbo was a hit—it became history. What, you don't know who he is? How old are you? Look, tragedies last longer than happiness, as far as the newspapers are concerned . . ."

"I think Ruy Castro or Sérgio Augusto—or here in São Paulo maybe Rubens Ewald, Jr.—would be of more use to you. They're great writers, have good senses of humor, know everything there is to know about the press, are good at legwork, have a network of contacts, and so forth. Movies aren't really my specialty. Nor is television, which I find to be a lesser art—full of stupid little people, mediocrities. Just lots of young girls shaking their asses."

He was put off by my radicalism. Scared. He thinks that forging bits of celebrity news is somehow immoral. Perhaps it is. He's not going to do it. It's a shame—he could have earned a nice chunk of change. Writers have imaginations, I hear. They would do a good job in this racket. Writing good fiction while using a real-life character, and getting paid for it. He's thrown away the chance of a lifetime.

How would it have been any different than writing a novel? And unlike most of the names in a novel, mine means something. He could have really believed in the life he was putting down on paper.

I would have liked to play this character with my name.

Writers! Aren't they all supposed to be dying of hunger?

Bernardo Massar didn't even thank me for my excessive generosity.

MODERNITY

"I made you appointments with two astrologers—you're going to adore them. One of them, the woman, has writers and television anchors and politicians and union leaders and bankers as clients. Have you seen the profits the banks made this year? Astounding! She charges two hundred dollars a consultation. The other one, the man, charges five. But it's worth it. Every penny. Just look at that list of clients! Nothing but successful people!"

Letícia began to distance herself from me before we'd been together seven months. Seven months or three years. I'm not sure, offhand. "I'm not prepared to love someone this way," she said. "I never was. I don't know why I persisted. My life has become complete chaos. This isn't love. Love is about going for walks holding hands, your being nearby when I want to give you a kiss, when I need you to give me a hug, to be next to me when I wake up, to make love in the morning, pick out a movie together, to go on trips, to eat codfish balls at the corner bar, do a little dancing, hurry home, sit around listening to music. Love is picking out useful little presents for each other."

She was tired of living alone—alone, but with me. She was hurt, having me and not having me at the same time. "How can you be so close to me and yet never within reach?"

She hated that we didn't have a future. She was committed to a relationship that could never evolve. She lived her days and nights wrapped in a numbing pain that would lull her to sleep and then wake her up in tears.

Very determined, she said, "It's over. It's no use! I don't even know who I am, what I want—my life is disorganized, without direction." Down deep, for me, the break had begun on the day I discovered that my picture had disappeared from her room and that she'd taken down the love notes I'd written her from the corkboard she'd hung in the hall outside her bedroom.

Nevertheless—and this confused me—she would suddenly show herself to be loving, committed, dedicated. She used to say things to me that made me feel unbearably tender, that nourished me and almost made me feel like a human being: "I've never met anyone so seductive," or, "I've never had better sex with anyone." And I'd become tactless, abrupt, uncontrolled, all at once.

Letícia would respond coldly on the telephone the next time we spoke, and I'd feel bad for having telephoned. I'd complain she was being unkind to me, and she would reply, "Love is also made of pain."

Then she'd break it off. Again. She would beg: "Leave me alone, I hate you. For what you're doing to me."

Then we'd reunite. It would last about a month. "Will you marry me?"

She'd break it off again. And then we would be back together. Two weeks this time.

"Why don't you leave your job?" she asked me. "It's torture. It's crushing you. You're better than this—you need to free yourself. And what about your wife? Does she know about us?"

We'd split and reunite. Over and over. A seesaw.

Then, I did an unforgivable thing.

I sent an e-mail. Ending it.

A love like ours, struck down by electronic mail.

It was undignified.

She deserved better.

But I did it. I got it over with. You may hate me for this, you who have managed to penetrate my thoughts. But believe me, you'll never be able to have as much contempt for me as I do for myself.

What I did was villainous.

That's the best word I can come up with, under the circumstances.

FUCKING THE SUN ON KUROSAWA'S CRANE

"Greta Garbo's father was allergic to work and an alcoholic to boot. Beat that."

Simple. I love movies.

"Luchino Visconti's mother was very beautiful, and his father, a nobleman, used to put on make-up and chase after young boys in the theater!"

One of these days, one of us won't be able to come up with a good story to tell, and our tie will be broken. Till then, stalemate. We collect anecdotes about the fathers and mothers of the famous. It's hard to imagine there's ever been a more despicable subsection of the human race. Just think about the overwhelming parental ambitions and pressures that they bring to bear on their children, propelling them relentlessly towards fame, stardom, neuroses, depression, and suicide. Lenira and I have a lot in common—she's good for me. Little by little, we're going to chip away at the odious image of maternal-paternal love that's poisoned modern life! We know it's a lie. We will purge the culture of Father's and Mother's Days—those advertisers' orgies, those feeding frenzies.

We went into Stage 9, the big one—they sutured together three already large stages to make it—and the most modern, equipped with all the latest technology. The door is locked by keypad—the code is 938. The light indicated that no one was taping, inside. We were listening to Liszt's *Hungarian Rhapsody No. 2 in C-sharp minor* on Lenira's miniscule walkman. She was wearing one earphone, I the other.

"We've been hit by storms for four days now," I said.

"Very appropriate. Since they were filming that series about Roberto Baal, the pirate, right here on this stage. He sailed the equator—stormy waters. Roberto Baal, also known as Jean-François de La Roque de Roberval."

How does she know such things?

"I read all the scripts. I got them off an assistant who was flirting with me."

"Yeah? And did this flirting lead to anything?"

"He didn't want to. He just wanted to look at me so he could jerk off. We climbed onto the pirate-ship set. I showed him my ass and he came. Quickly."

I never know when Lenira is telling the truth. She loves to make sure I know she's desirable—that the whole world is after her. Every day she tells me about some new fantasy of hers, some new fetish she's cooked up. She writes everything down with her laptop. She holds herself in very high esteem. I'm jealous.

Inside, workers are striking the pirate set in order to put together a seaport in ruins for a Venezuelan series about Simon Bolívar. The director and some technicians are standing around exchanging ideas, consulting storyboard sheets spread out on the floor. They speak an unintelligible and rapid Spanish. Lenira fondles the ugliest Chinese dog I've ever seen, all jowl, who's asleep tied to the foot of the director's chair. A Chinese dog! Can you believe it? Some people cultivate the strangest affectations.

Renting Brazilian soundstages, equipment, and technical know-how to Latin American television has been very lucrative, despite the downturn in the economy. It all began with a group of Mexicans in the mid-'90s. Their crews would show up with directors, screenwriters, blueprints for sets, and actors and then go back home with everything shot and cut and ready to be broadcast. Of course, the projects they brought with them were always evaluated and revised by Brazilian technicians—the scenery, at times, was virtually unrecognizable when compared to the original plans. And, of course, any programs the studio put together for the Mexicans were ripe for recycling for local use as soon as our tenants went home. International studio rentals are nothing new. In the

'60s, Germans filmed westerns in Cinecittà, Rome. In the '70s, American, English, Yugoslavian, and Japanese films were all shot on stages where Italian luminaries like Fellini, Visconti, and De Sicca had once worked. Not to mention Elizabeth Taylor.

"What's the deal with Elizabeth Taylor, anyway? Was her mother to blame?"

"How did you know I was thinking about Liz?"

"You're talking to yourself."

"I was thinking of her in *Cleopatra*. Now it's out on DVD. That's the movie she was working on when she fell in love with Richard Burton. The filming was delayed over and over again. The two of them made the movie go over-budget. That's power! To be able to delay a production costing millions of dollars. The whole world was talking about them. Reading about them. They generated some of the most spectacular news of the '60s. Today, if an actor is late, they just fire them—they kill their character off and move on."

"That was Old Hollywood! Things were different then. Do you wish you could have been Richard Burton?"

"I've thought about it. On account of Liz Taylor's violet eyes. She was married to Eddie Fisher at the time. The world press had a lot of fun pointing out that he was a cuckold. Burton was married to Sybil Williams. Everybody took her side against Elizabeth."

"Liz! How intimidating she must have been as a rival. Cleopatra. Talk about prehistoric. That film was made way before you were born. I saw it at the Telecine—it's a piece of shit. A big production for old people."

"It'll find its cult. Historical kitsch."

"So, your dream is to become a cult figure. Mine is to fuck a lot!"

Different pronunciations and accents in the halls, in the tree-lined passageways between the soundstages, dressing rooms, studio restaurant, and staff cafeteria—where they sell you food sold by the kilo. I hear *LL*s turned into *J*s. Or *LH*s. Casta becomes Castor, or vice versa. One goes from Mexico to Colombia, from Peru to Paraguay just crossing from one room to another. Blonde Argentine women blend with olive-skinned Indians with slanted, almond eyes, which prompts Lenira to ask if maybe one of her ancestors hadn't circulated throughout the Americas. Also, we're seeing a lot of Brazilian soap operas being sold to other markets after being dubbed in Spanish. Unemployed actors show up in Brazil to do the voice work—it's a new market.

"Are you talking to yourself?"

"I was thinking. Dialectically."

"Dialectically?"

"A vestige of my undergraduate days!"

Greetings here and there. Olá, what's up, buenos dias, oiga tchê. Motherfuckers. I know why they're being so polite. They think I'm him. The Lead Actor, that son of a bitch. The world loves him. One day I'll blackmail the studio—I represent their greatest secret. It's like a scene from a spy movie—I climb inside armored cars with tinted windows and everyone thinks it's him. Lenira helps smooth over any discrepancies.

Me, in his place. Nobody notices the difference, though sometimes they do pick up on the fact that the quality of LA's performance has mysteriously risen. One afternoon the great actor Paulo Autran grabbed me by the arm—yes, grabbed me. He who was always known to be so refined, so cultured, so respectful.

What's going on? he asked.

What do you mean what's going on? (I turned his question right back onto him! I am a master of little rhetorical tricks like this.)

What are you trying to pull?

Jesus, calm down. What do you mean, pull?

Watch your mouth.

What am I supposed to have done?

211

There are days when you're different. It's like you're on the attack, all of a sudden. Why aren't you always like this? I love a challenge. But then there are days when you don't even know your lines. When you throw tantrums.

Oh, Antônio Fagundes came into the men's room while I was in there. You know how it is—men don't like to piss alongside one another: It put me in a bad mood.

I don't get you. You're a mystery. Do you do coke, by any chance? Shoot up?

"Hey! You can't go around making accusations like that. Do I look like I'm some junkie? I just happen to be a damn good actor, thank you very much."

There are days when I'm afraid of you while we're filming. You seem possessed.

I do become possessed, as a matter of fact. I really do. My body is taken over by a Greek god.

A Greek god! Don't be so pretentious. However much you might bring to mind a golden-age Marlon Brando, (the wild one!), the magnificence of a Barrymore, the dignity of a Robert de Niro, the sheer power of a Raul Cortez . . .

The old flatterer. I should've had those words cast in bronze and hung up in my dressing room. My diplomas, my consecration. My Oscar. It's a pity no one heard him say any of that. Performances without audiences don't count. They have value for me, of course, but that won't help me get space in any of the columns. Can't send this out as a press release. It was a private conversation during a break. Still, it will always remain in my thoughts, my memory.

They don't know I stand in for LA. Nobody knows. Nobody except Lenira and myself. Not even Lavinia, my wife. That's why she doesn't understand my hatred of LA, why she can't see the cancer that's eating me away.

He has to disappear. Forever.

So only one will exist. Me.

I go over it again and again. I can't murder him—I'm a rational man, not a murderer. But I have to do it—murder is something all actors are called upon to play at least once. It's a must for a good role. If done tastefully.

When he's gone, the competence of the acting in our soap operas will suddenly rise to unimagined heights. All at once.

When LA is so drugged out that he can barely stand on his own two feet—I swear he lives on a diet of pure heroin—Lenira hides him in a closet and calls me. I come out of hiding. That's my life—he's hidden and I come out, or else he's out and I have to hide. They even go so far as to lock me up in my dressing room—Room 101, sector 9, third floor. Autran and Fagundes, you know, they're wonderful actors, very kind, very sensitive—they know right away when "his" performance improves. How much more can I take? Isn't the pain of losing Letícia enough? And what about Lavinia's paralysis, crippled in a wheelchair, looking at me with that mortified expression, enslaving me with pity so that I can never leave her?

I wave to people. I wear a look of withering ennui, to keep them in their place, so they'll respect the hierarchy. We arrive at the rear of Stage 9—colossal Stage 9, used for staging battles, outdoor festivals, city squares, pirate battles, golf courses (everybody plays golf these days). A crane is propped up in a corner, a relic from the early days of the studio. Some corrupt journalist spread the story around that it was the same crane that had been used to film some of the battle scenes in *Ran*. Everyone was really impressed. It got the nickname "Kurosawa's crane." Nearby is the rear-projection screen. They're testing out a variety of colorful landscapes, mountains, lagoons, oceans, abysses, plateaus, valleys, beaches, swamps, rainforests. Each piece of scenery lasts for a few minutes, then the rear projection director murmurs something on the PA and the scenery changes. Finally, one of them, a cloudless sky, is allowed to stay. The luminous screen gives out a blue transparency that the real sky never has. The men here can produce an absolute, formal reality—more intense than what life actually gives us. A lighting technician chats with the director of projection.

"Let's shoot the exteriors here. It'll look nicer."

"We don't have many tapes of the Pampas on file. This is the best we've got. Is it what you wanted? Does it look right?"

"I've never been down there."

"Eh, it all looks the same. Nobody's going to notice."

"That's what you think. There are people out there who adore catching us out. They go over everything with a fine-tooth comb and then send complaints in to the network."

"If you're worried about it, just use a sunny day with occasional clouds. We've got tons of those."

The lighting tech talks like the (beautiful) weather-girls they have on TV. Clouds appear to the right, on the screen. Wisps move toward the projected sun.

"Five-thirty in the afternoon. Right?"

The tapes are filed by the day and hour of the original recording, and then by season. You can track the sun's course for every day and hour of the year in the studio's files.

"Correct."

"We can't make any mistakes. The geography association has had its eyes on us lately. Ever since some idiot had the sun rise in the west."

"You just said nobody notices anything."

"The public are imbeciles. I'm talking about experts!"

"There are some birds in the background."

"Leave it alone, everybody loves birds."

"What if they're not Mexican birds?"

"You can't tell."

"And what if the animal rights people want to make sure the birds were treated right?"

"Birds are animals?"

They change the reel. Twilight appears filmed from high up on the mountain of Atalaia, in Arraial do Cabo. The strong and sugar-coated colors recall to mind *Duel in the Sun* (1946, directed by King Vidor), with Jennifer Jones and Gregory Peck. He was brave to play a cynical villain, working against his image as the perennial good guy at a time when everything in Hollywood was stereotyped and a career could be demolished by a single poorly chosen role. *Duel in the Sun* was produced seventeen years before *Cleopatra* (1963, directed by Joseph L. Mankiewicz). Lenira is going to laugh. She adores laughing at me. Like Letícia does, time to time. Did I already tell you about Selznick and Jennifer Jones? It's too bad Walker didn't live to see Selznick's decline. All the great movies are tied to some tragic love story.

When I think of Letícia, I feel like I'm going to go the same way as Walker. She said, "I'm not going to hang around and be at your beck and call." I could hardly insist. Someday I'll just be a bit of mist clinging to her heart—my face dissolving, half-erased in her memory. I don't think I'd be able to stand seeing her with another man. And what if one day she wrote to me to say that she'd begun to take an interest in younger men? Guys who'll send her flowers, give her bracelets, earrings, rings, things she likes. One afternoon I asked her if she was going out with somebody else. "You're in no position to demand fidelity," she told me. Letícia certainly does expect *me* to be faithful, but it's no use—I can't, and thus condemn myself to unhappiness. How can I get away from Lavinia? I can't divorce her. We don't even know how much time she has left. She's already lost the use of her legs. We can't find a single doctor willing to show a little optimism.

"In Ipanema you sometimes used to get a crowd of hippies standing on a hill applauding the sunset. Brazil was once an amusing country, don't you think? So happy!"

"Hippies? My mother was a hippy."

"A Japanese hippy?"

"My mother isn't Japanese."

"Let's take some acid. In her honor."

"Jesus. You spend your whole life tripping . . ."

We sit down on the old crane. Me where the camera's supposed to go, she on the director's seat. I play with the control panel and get the crane to rise. Yes, a Japanese crane: powerful, a museum piece. Got a lot of news coverage in its day, when the studio first started using it. When the first shows appeared that included location shooting—the end, they said, of the "claustrophobic era" of Brazilian television, where everything was filmed at eye-level in interiors (thousands of identical living rooms, kitchens, bathrooms, offices). Then the crane—for projects demanding great depth, a horizon. Of course, these things happen for a reason—television technology was improving. Larger screens and better resolution means you need to give your audience bigger and prettier pictures to look at. Kurosawa had never been within a thousand miles of our crane, of course. Everyone found out it had been assembled right here, domestically, in the studio's workshop. Brazilians are nuts about copying things, and of course making little improvements along the way. Little white lies don't hurt anybody—it's called marketing. Would the papers have cared if it wasn't "Kurosawa's crane" that the studio acquired? In the 1950s, hundreds of Italians suddenly showed up at Vera Cruz Studios in São Paulo, all saying they'd been Rossellini's assistants. Imposters. They wouldn't have been able to pick him out of a line-up, let alone tell you something about the father of neo-realism.

The studio played up the Kurosawa story as much as possible. The story was planted, obviously—the writer who spread the story around had been paid off. Legions of cinephiles, led by tourist guides, showed up to look over the fabled equipment. And they were paying for the privilege. Though most of these interlopers weren't really here to see the crane; they wanted to catch a glimpse of some real-live stars, and often wandered away from the tour group to look for our dressing rooms. I'm told that I was the most sought after celebrity on the lot, in those days. Or, rather, LA was. The autograph-hounds wouldn't know which one they were getting anyway—the only real giveaway is LA's suffocating aura of stupidity. Anyway, it isn't like anyone around here really knows who Kurosawa is. People just started calling it "Ku's crane," abbreviating the great man's name into some private gibberish.

You can control the speed at which the cart holding the crane moves forward, at the same time as controlling the lateral movements of the camera on top. Emma Shapplin is singing "A Darkness in the Sky" on our earphones.

"We're on top of the world," I say.

"You're so serious," Lenira says. "No fun. Let me see you smile. You're almost handsome when you laugh. I like to see your little teeth. Don't look at me like that. I never know how to read your eyes."

The sun on the screen in front of us sets, and I am able to match the movement of the crane with the false sun's, coordinating them so well that we neither of us seem to move. A red color, violent, turns the flat sky into lacquer. Since we're facing the sun, parallel to it, the light's intensity on the cyclorama is blinding, more intense than staring at the real sun. There are no imperfections in this sun. Our technicians eliminate them. It is a uniform, smoldering brightness. The technicians tell me that the reality they remove with filters and effects only improves the image. Nature lacks intention. It cannot compete.

I stop our descent and bring us back up to the clouds. The sky protects us, the cyclorama closes itself around us. We are level with the clouds.

"This is a weird place for a meeting," I say. "We're surrounded by people and alone in the sky all at once. Why did you want to see me?"

"Because we're coming to the time. The fatal moment."

"Fatal?"

"In a little while, he's not going to be able to function anymore. You know who I mean. He can barely stand up. He won't recover."

"You mean, it's time for the substitution?"

I'm trembling. The fatal moment. It's been on my mind one way or the other since that afternoon when I first showed up for a screen test and they said: "No way. You're exactly like our lead. The spitting image!" And they laughed. I lost a year recovering from that disappointment. My life ruined by a mirror.

Now I can finally take his place. But no matter how much you want something, if you've been waiting and waiting for it, you still get scared when it looks like you might finally get it. Like that day when Letícia said, "Come have dinner with me." I asked, "Where?" She replied: "My place." The emotion, the anticipation, the desire were so intense that they paralyzed me. She went straight to her CD player and put some Cuban music, Rafael González, I think . . . no, no it's not Rafael . . . it's Ruben. I wasn't familiar with Cuban music at the time—she had dozens of CDs, all piled haphazardly on a low table. "They're completely out of order," she said, " I don't like other people to touch them, but they always do—friends come over, they want to listen to something and then they don't put it back in the right place." We sat on her white sofa, in front of an enormous painting of blue flowers. She touched me—and I saw that the maid was peeking at us from the kitchen. Letícia noticed too: "Let's go to my bedroom." She took off her clothes very slowly, and then she took off mine as well, unbuttoning me unhurriedly, smelling my skin, her eyes closed. "Your skin gives me such a charge." She always liked my skin.

"We're flying."

Lenira, happy. Sometimes she acts like a twelve-year-old girl. Not ten, not thirteen. Exactly twelve.

"Flying . . . flying . . ."

I'm euphoric now, fear forgotten. Yes, the fatal moment is finally coming. Lenira has everything planned out, though she hasn't let me in on it as yet. She loves mysteries. LA represents money for the network—he's always in demand for commercials, has a thousand contracts. He's affable too, apparently: a good person. I don't get close to him, I don't want to learn to like him. What keeps me alive is hate. Hate is my energy. Have you ever seen *Gilda* (1946, directed by Charles Vidor)? I understand Ballin Mundson (played by Mr. George Macready) and his ideas about hate. And yet, LA can't be allowed to die without a successor—a lot of people would lose their jobs, their income, their status, their power. Lenira even uses his credit card. He will die and no one will know. I will become him. Despite my already being him. Yes, instead of being virtually anonymous, I will disappear entirely. Instead of leading a double life, I'll stop existing. What do I care? I'll be nameless, but out on the streets, famous, celebrated. And he'll become nothing—a body, buried anonymously, under no stone.

"Flying, flying . . ."

"Like airplanes."

"Helicopters."

"Gliders."

"Balloons."

"Without wings."

"Men can fly after all."

"And we're not crazy."

"We're angels . . . angels without wings . . ."

"Like in that Wim Wenders movie?"

Hammering sounds come up from the Venezuelan scenery. An electric saw, sharp, monotonous. I would have preferred a little silence for floating. Lenira turns up the volume on her walkman; we're listening to Brahms among the clouds. *Aimez-vous Brahms?* Françoise Sagan asked. She's a distant memory, now. So famous at eighteen, the whole world was talking about her. Is it too late for me? Myths are made early.

The crane reaches its maximum height. I make it describe a circle inside the recesses of the cyclorama. Enveloped by the twilight, we don't look left or right, we know the limits of our landscape, we don't want to destroy the illusion. We don't even look behind us, at the darkness. The air-conditioning vents above us make us shiver. I feel like kissing her. I try and she avoids me with a malicious smile.

"This sun doesn't give off any heat."

"The world should be kept swaddled in air-conditioning every day of the year. Nature is an inconvenience."

"I'd like to lay down on one of these clouds. Naked . . . showing my body to everyone down on earth. They'd like that, don't you think?"

"Spinning, spinning."

"I could wrap myself in the clouds."

"It would be wonderful to live up here. On the outside of the world. I've had enough of life on the ground. It's too late to save it."

Lenira stretches out her arms. I see the little hairs she bleaches. They turn me on. Does she shave her crotch? Letícia has a few hairs, but she's horrified by them. She gets uncomfortable if she goes too long without waxing.

"Let's go into the sun."

"We can touch it, anyway."

"Only us."

"Maybe we'll find a way in . . ."

"To penetrate the sun. Fucking can't really compete."

The clarity is blinding. We move towards the incandescent ball.

"Let's come inside the sun."

"Let's come together . . ."

Inside the light. We are the light. There is nothing left except from light.

"Hey! What the fuck do you think you're doing up there?"

"*Que estan haciendo arriba, cuernos?*"

The technicians are yelling at us. Sons of bitches.

I would have liked to enter that cold sun.

To mingle its coldness with the coldness I carry inside myself.

FORGIVE ME FOR NOT WAITING FOREVER

My love.

So we're back together again. But in the meantime I've been hav-ing second thoughts.

It's been at least a year since I made my decision. I haven't acted on it. I tried and tried, but it didn't stick.

How many times have we broken up? How many times have we gotten back together? How many times have I told my body to get out of the habit of making love to you every day?

Desire is irrational. It doesn't take orders. Even so, I keep persist-ing. I think, after reading your message, that you're going through the same thing I've been going through. You want to have something you can't have.

All of a sudden, you're feeling in concentrated form what I've been dealing with diluted throughout this past year. Desperately. Painfully.

Sometimes with a horrible certainty.

What good is the horizon if I'm in some dark alley? I'm not plagia-rizing Manuel Bandeira, I'm just adapting his poem to better express my loneliness. After all, he wrote for everybody.

I only hope this all will pass.

We have to know how to choose. We have to make decisions. We have to forge ahead. We have to move on.

The world turns. Movement is part of life.

Time, unfortunately, doesn't stop. It doesn't pay to stand still. For-give me for not being able to wait for you forever. Kisses. Letícia.

ALWAYS KEEP YOURSELF "PLUGGED IN"

"Synergy" is in. "Holistic" is on its way out. "Empathy" is in. "Hip" is hip again. Cell phone jargon: WAP (Wireless Application Protocol). Need to figure out how to work all these words into my conversations.

Words don't last very long, my Cultural Consultant assures me. How fucking tiresome. I lose my patience sometimes, no matter how much I adore my career. Scripts are arriving all the time, texts I need to memorize. So many things to read, to keep track of. I must always be alert. The Campana Brothers are the current "in" designers.

I can't make any slip-ups.

The use of a single incorrect expression can mark you as an outsider, old hat, the walking dead.

"Ready," my Terminologist tells me, is strictly a vestige of 1970 sociology. Don't use it too much. And if you must use it, don't enunciate.

That's how he talks. Enunciate, don't enunciate.

Magazines to which my Consultants on Vapid Culture subscribe: *Esquire, Vanity Fair, Visionaire, GQ, V, Nova, Glamour, Première,* and *W.* It's good to be seen with the American edition of *National Geographic* under your arm. *Cahiers du Cinéma, Le Point, Le Monde, La Republica.* It's a good idea to mix in a tabloid newspaper. Just so people don't get the idea you're too much of an intellectual. Or maybe fan magazine? Some print-outs of text from the Web?

Anyway, something representing the margins of society.

DECORATED WITH BRAND NAMES

There are three of them, all standing in front of me. Grinning.

"We scored some great contracts. And hip! Your troubles are over. You're well-dressed, -shoed, -fed, and washed through the end of the year. If you don't mind restricting yourself to certain brands of toilet paper, we've even got your shit taken care of. But you're going to have to commit to the whole program. Package deal. We've already taken the liberty of hiring you a Consultant on Organizational Diagrams to plot out your year by brand."

"One more son of a bitch eating at my expense?"

"You'll love paying up. Look how beautiful the program is. We'll start with the first month."

Day 1 will be Versace.

Day 2 Fórum.

Day 3 is for Ellus.

Day 4 is for Zoomp.

Day 5 has been reserved for Ricardo Almeida.

Day 6 for Richards.

Day 7 for Armani.

Day 8 TNG.

Day 9 was chosen by Calvin Klein.

Day 10 was awarded to DKNY, after extensive bidding.

Day 11 to VR.

Day 12 to Dior.

13 we left open, due to the rampant superstition in the industry. We'll hold a lottery when the time comes. (Ermenegildo Zegna won.)

14 belongs to Gianfranco Ferré.

15 to Stone Island. (Letícia doesn't approve.)

16 to Hermès.

17 was saved for Jean-Paul Gaultier.

18 for Windsor.

19 for René Lezard.

Toni Gard petitioned for and was awarded 20.

21 went to Hugo Boss. (Letícia hates these clothes—we had a terrible fight over them.)

22 to Romeo Gigli. (Caetano Veloso wears Gigli—very, very nice.)

23 is now and must always be for Kenzo.

24 Tommy Hilfiger.

25 CP Company.

26 Strell Sun. (They've got a good beat.)

27—we're almost out of days, but we still managed to squeeze Prada in.

28, Dolce & Gabbana. (I like their stuff, and that's good enough for me.)

29, Gucci.

30, Ralph Lauren.

And 31, getting in the final word: Helmut Lang.

"Not every month has 31 days," I pointed out.

"Lang didn't want to shell out our asking price."

"And then there's the stand-by list!" one of them pointed out. "Schneiders, Joop, Jeans, Patrick Hellman, Artigiano, Cerruti, Baumier, Lanvin . . ."

"When you travel you're going to have to use Montblanc suitcases."

"We're selling spots for caps, eyeglasses, ties, belts, watches, bracelets, necklaces, tie-pins, stockings, cell phones, handkerchiefs (you're going to have to pretend you blow your nose at least nine times a day), rings (Natan, the jewelry store, is *very* interested). Each centimeter of your body is worth some money. Underwear, condoms (you're going to have to show the brand to the woman, so she knows which you're endorsing, and you're going to commit to fucking four per day—no more buying condoms from bathroom vending machines for you!), toothbrushes (you'll have to brush your teeth in a public restroom—it can be at a mall—once a day, so they can be seen), eye drops (again, make sure to put them in somewhere crowded), cigarette lighters (leave one behind from time to time, forget it with someone—people are crazy about stealing cigarette lighters, so let them), pens (Montblanc, again, is head of the list, here). How do you feel about piercings? Probably not, you seem pretty square."

"Square? Your mother's cunt was pretty square, I hear. The only one she ever fucked was your father—if that. How am I supposed to remember all this nonsense?"

"Post-its. We'll wallpaper your room with them. They also want a piece of the action."

"I'm going to have to get a bigger closet. How about we use the maid's room?"

THE SILENT THERAPIST

Letícia had insisted so many times, so often demanded, pleaded. So I finally gave in and went to therapy. Four sessions.

"Did you like it?"

"No!"

"I knew it. You're resisting the treatment. Tell me about it. How did it go?"

"I went there and the guy said: You can tell me anything you want. I said: Ask me something and I'll tell you. He said: No, you need to start. I said: Where should I begin? He said: The beginning. I said: Guide me. He said: Look, you're the one who came to see me—just open up. I laughed. I said: I came here to learn how to open up! He said: Good, so start talking. What a fucker. He wouldn't budge an inch. Aren't you going to ask me anything? I asked him. He said no. If you don't, I told him, then, we're just going to sit here staring at each other. So, stare away, he said. I can take it. And he looked at me. And I looked at him. He didn't blink. He didn't look away. He kept on staring at me. I didn't back down. I stared right back. If I've ever hated anybody, it was that afternoon. My eyes burned and stung. Analysts are charlatans. If I just want to talk bullshit, I'll talk to a cab driver, they love to chat, and they're easier to get along with. So, after almost an hour of this staring match, the analyst checked his clock, like a chess player timing a move, and said: Time's up. I recommend that you come back tomorrow. I said: What's wrong with you? Why would I come back? Never, absolutely not. And when I went back the next day, it was the same. They guy should just hand out dirty magazines for his patients to leaf through while he stares us down. It would be a more productive use of my time."

"You never made any progress? Not any of the times you went back?"

"How could there be any progress under those circumstances? That motherfucker can rot in hell."

"What a waste. And you paid him to stare at you. You paid for the privilege of sitting in silence."

"I stopped payment on the check."

RESCUING THE ANONYMOUS: THE GIRLS

Four young women surround the journalist, art critic, and writer Luís Martins. They look like nightclub showgirls, hip-swinging starlets, extras, dancers; the kind that would pose half-naked in the "artistic tableaux" that used to be staged in the '40s and '50s between variety acts (they would have been wholly naked, but the censors had more power then). The caption only gives us two names: Luís Martins's—he's at ease, smugly satisfied to be among such beautiful women—and Grande Otelo, the comedian, who's looking at him with a roguish air. The photo was published in our daily paper, O Estado de S. Paulo, *on May 27, 2000. No information as to where or when the photo was taken, or under what circumstances. Perhaps in the wings of a São Paulo theater where Otelo had been performing? Were the women only there because they were curious to meet the famous men, or did they work in the same theater? Photo captions, and the names they omit, create a special subgenre of historical personage—the anonymous celebrity—and these four must be added to my list.*

The photo belonged to Martins, who died in 1981; now his entire archive is the property of the Center for Luis Martins Studies at the library of the Museum of Modern Art in São Paulo. Otelo and Martins are famous, of course: their names are part of the history of the theater, the press, and the arts. Martins, who left behind thirty-six published books, wrote in the neighborhood of ten thousand articles for O Estado de S. Paulo, *and left at least one enduring classic of Brazilian literature—*Noturno da Lapa. *He lived with Tarsila do Amaral, the famous modernist painter, and she painted his portrait. Afterwards, he was married to Ana Maria Martins, an excellent short-story writer from São Paulo. He eventually abandoned criticism, considering it inefficacious, innocuous.*

The four young women have been eternalized. This photograph is part of the history of a life, Martins's, and also of an institution, that of the Museum of Modern Art. No names. Only someone who'd been around at the time could be able to identify them.

Luís Martins died at seventy-four. In the photograph he appears about forty, at the most. Therefore, hypothetically, the picture was taken thirty-four years before he died, around 1947. And if he was thirty-five and not forty—because in the old days, people aged faster, seemed older and more mature—then the picture might have been taken thirty-nine years ago: 1942. It's difficult to say. Research in the periodicals archives might tell us there was a Grande Otelo show during either of these years. Nevertheless, if our four girls are just showgirls, used to pad out stage shows, we might never be able to identify them, as their kind weren't given any billing in the programs of the day. And then, depending on the venue—be it a nightclub or a small theater*—there might not even have been programs.

Did one or all of the girls see the photograph appear in 2000? Did they clip it out and paste it in their photo albums? Did they have any idea at the time that the man they were posing with was so important, or did they only like his looks—handsome, well-groomed? Would they recognize his name, now?

Young girls between the ages of twenty-two and twenty-four in the '40s. Today they'd be in their eighties. I think. Numbers aren't my thing.

Are any of them still alive?

---

*   Don't think you can guess my age because I happen to know these details about how theaters were run back then. I read about them. They were small venues with fifty or so seats, a few decent acts, and lots of beautiful women.

CHERRIES MADE FROM COLORED PAPAYA

"What are you doing?" I asked. Over the phone.

"Listening to music. Whenever I'm alone, I listen to music."

"What are you listening to now?"

"The soundtrack from *Mahabharata*. Do you know it?"

"What do you mean, do I know it? We once used to lie in bed together listening to it over and over again. You'd put it on repeat. "

"You're so affected. So artificial. How can I believe you ever loved me? 'Once used to.' How Continental."

"What? It's the imperfect tense."

"The imperfect tense? Jesus, you're unbearable. My cunt dries up when I hear talk like that."

I pretended not to hear her. I don't hear anything when I don't want to.

The maid called out: "Will you have your cream of avocado now?"

"What did I tell you?" I bellowed back.

"Excuse me?"

"Call me 'sir'! Don't get personal with me!"

"Yes, sir."

I eat a bowl of the aforementioned dish every day. It boosts my energy, re-invigorates my sexual appetite.

"How did you whip it today?" I asked the maid.

"With a little bit of lime. It's a beautiful color. And it's a tasty avocado too, organically grown, and local. Not from Japan."

"If you only knew how delicious and appetizing Japanese fruits can be."

I'm referring to Lenira, of course. Not that the maid knows a thing about it.

Sweet Lenira. An Arabic name for a Japanese woman.

I think her mother was Lebanese.

I don't know, you can never get anything out of Lenira.

Delightful, tight—the skin of a perfect Japanese woman, brought up in the shade of cherry trees. She always exudes a light, sweaty odor that makes me wonder what kind of orgy she's coming back from.

Cherry trees! Lenira was born in Marilia. Nothing there but huge, decadent coffee plantations. Lenira never saw a fresh cherry in her life. Just the kind they put in the sweet cocktails she drinks (or used to drink) in the late afternoon.

She used to drink so many that she would throw up and get a terrible headache. She didn't know that the cherries in candy bars are made from colored papaya.

Lovable Lenira and her collection of little fetishes.

DAILY LIFE:
REPETITION, REPETITION, REPETITION*

Worry about the income tax—rebates—medical receipts—schools—ordering new checks—balancing the checkbook—eating out—phone bill—electricity—cable—gas—inflation—bad credit—shopping—payment in three, five, or ten installments—mortgages—magazine subscriptions—broken-down appliances—buying lightbulbs—stocking the refrigerator—clogged drains—burned-out fuses—waiting for the bus—making sure to buy commuter passes—ordering pizza for delivery—food prices—sales on appliances shirts shoes stockings underwear yogurt bath-soap hand-soap toothpaste condoms fruit seltzer soda—taxi fare—cheapest tickets to the seashore—turning off all the lights before leaving the house—knowing where your septic tank is located—changing the lightbulbs—calling tech support on account of the television stove refrigerator microwave freezer sound-system video-player—reading instruction manuals (without understanding a thing)—assembling furniture at home because do-it-yourself is cheaper—finding underwear at the bottom of the drawer—sewing a loose button on a shirt—answering the phone—playing the lottery dominoes sports Powerball—checking the weekly results—eating a fried turnover at the open-air market—ordering fresh greens from the grocer—smelling a fish to see if it's fresh—vomiting in an elevator—removing the hairs stuck in your hairbrush—beating dust out of the carpet—gagging on a chicken bone—worrying about the heavy rain causing your clogged gutters to overflow—putting your pillow on the windowsill to catch some sun—staying alert every minute of every day in order to survive—

---

* Research: Here's what Nietzsche had to say about daily life: "It really causes me to feel such . . . nausea and repugnance . . . it doesn't seem more real, but spectral." Letter to his friend Erwin Rohde, December 21, 1871, quoted by Rüdiger Safranski in *Nietzsche: A Philosophical Biography*.

If a person has to take care of these minutia, how can he possibly achieve his potential, how can he turn himself into a legend?

Routine daily life is a prison—it overloads, it debilitates—we walk suffocated by the sun—breathing in dust and smoke—nauseated by the smell of people's sweat—fearful of the din—tripping over potholes—stepping into dog shit—bumping into the idiots in our way—being pushed back—trying not to be mugged—

How can we be creative while wasting every minute of our lives solving the problems that normal people face every day?

TO BECOME EVIL

I wonder what I can do to really make people hate me. Eartha Kitt sings a song called "I Want to Be Evil." And yes, I want to be bad. Bad enough that, once and a while, everybody—every newspaper, television, and radio in every home—abominates me. So they don't believe I'm capable of being an artist. Yes, I want to be seen as something nauseating, repulsive—I want to strike an attitude, commit an abhorrent act, make a resoundingly offensive statement. I want to do something indecent, prove myself a coward. That's the way to go down in history. The public loves the people they hate—that's a fact. The most hated men in history become myths. Everybody's afraid of them, secretly wants to be them. I'd love to see normal people be uneasy when I approach. Good men are inevitably forgotten. Saints are monotonous. They don't get you excited. Don't represent danger, don't make you want to break out of your suffocating life and have an adventure. The good are mollusks who live glued to a wall, leaving an inoffensive slime behind them as they slide to the ground. They are no threat to anyone, and thus always will be forgotten.

A DOOR THROUGH WHICH TO KNOW THE WORLD

Why do we always have to hide the most important things? Richard Stengel writes: "Social stability depends upon a certain degree of dissimulation." (I read this in a magazine, as you probably guessed.) I don't know who Stengel is, but I know that personal stability also depends on dissimulation. We conserve, clandestinely, what really touches us, matters to us—what drives us, what makes us feel alive. "If only I could get at what you're actually thinking," Lavinia once said—my ex-wife, the first one, the one I married in church, with a big reception for our friends; God, how loathsome. We even sent out invitations—can you believe that? Terribly bourgeois. When I said "I do" in that church, I was hating myself for having given in to doing things the way everyone else in the world thinks they ought to be done.

FAKING IT IN THE KITCHEN

I don't know how to cook. A big flaw, since a bunch of weekly papers like to bring a celebrity into their "kitchen" and show him wearing an apron and standing in front of all kinds of seasonings, pots, pans, oils (just like a movie set). They take pictures of him fiddling with the pots (probably empty), until, in the final spread, the finished dish appears, as if by magic, beautiful and perfect and splendidly decorated. Of course, the person who actually puts the dish together is some anonymous cook who's been hired by the paper and probably is paid by the hour or maybe even not at all, since they ought to be thankful for having the honor of cooking for so great a celebrity. Normal people are very susceptible to flattery, if there's a chance of their impressing a star. Anyway, the photographed dish is offered to the readers along with a recipe—people just adore getting an inside line on how we distant and inaccessible celebrities do things in our daily lives, adore knowing we go to the kitchen, get our hands dirty at the stove. Which is nonsense. Some of the women are so artificial at this point, buried under so many layers of make-up, that if they were to stand over a hot burner, their faces would probably melt right off, pancake, blush, mascara and all the other free junk they get paid to plaster on their faces oozing off into the frying pan.

Celebrities are our royalty. The highest caste. They don't pay for anything. Everything is provided.

GALLERY OF CHARACTERS: FLITCRAFT (3)

Flitcraft knew why he did what he did.

Like we all do, really. Even if things aren't quite so clear. Even if our functions aren't encoded in our names, like his.

Flit: a light movement, rapid flight, change of address, departure, leave-taking, emigration.

Craft: art, ability, skill, cunning, guile, artifice.

Hammett picked a nicely symbolic name for his character.

Flitcraft is smart enough to know how to emigrate away from his own self.

He has the ability to change.

TO SALVAGE A HEART

"It's so wonderful not to have to see you anymore!" she told me on the telephone.

But her voice lacked its usual firmness. Letícia is beautiful, honest, determined. Strong. Her voice never used to waver.

She'd been resisting me so much. Spending weekends by herself. Going to the movies alone. Having dinner with nobody by her side. Attending concerts with an empty seat next to her. Alone in bed, imagining trips she could take, knowing that I wouldn't be accompanying her.

Being with me was a death sentence. A living torment. I carry unhappiness with me wherever I go. Nothing I touch can ever prosper. "Why bother complaining about your problems?" she would ask me again and again. "You never solve any, you're incapable of making decisions." The only thing left for her to do, to salvage her heart, was to refuse to see me, to not answer my calls, to lie and say my letters had never been delivered. Being cruel to me when I'd telephone, her voice tremulous on the line.

It makes sense. I can't even stand to spend time with myself. How can I blame her for sending me away? I always represented suffering to her, in spite of all the love there was and is between us. I'm not a person to her, but a doubt. Nagging. Impenetrable. There's no hope whatsoever for us.

Yet, I—I who cultivate only filth and depravity—have kept a file full of our moments together safe and uncorrupted in my memory. Beautiful.

It's a pity she's never going to read this. It's a pity she can't read my mind.

RESCUING THE ANONYMOUS:
KEROUAC'S GIRLFRIENDS

*The pioneers of the Beat Generation—Jack Kerouac, Allen Ginsberg, Gregory Corso, and Peter Orlovsky—met in Mexico City in October of 1956. Kerouac had published one book to date (*The Town and the City*), had written others (Visions of Cody, Doctor Sax, Mexico City Blues), including* On The Road, *which had already been sitting around for five years and wouldn't be published until 1957.*

In Mexico City, the four read poems at the university, drank, got high, climbed the Pyramid of the Sun at Teotihuacan, took in the gardens of Xochimilco, got bored, and finally decided to go home. Ennui (Baudelaire's spleen) was a characteristic of the beatniks, instigated by the nausea (the Sartrean variety) provoked in them by American society.

To fight said ennui, they'd taken to the road, traveled all over America, crossed into Mexico, all without any definite goal. In search of some new bar or new drug, an audience, another displaced person like themselves, a good jam session, a poet living by the sea. They wrote a great deal, fulminating against the prosaic daily life of industrial society, against the American way of life. Yes, only a truly enormous kind of ennui could generate the energy they possessed to produce so much text, consume so much alcohol, experiment with as many drugs as they could find.

They waited, as Kerouac said, for "God to show his face." Isn't that what they all hope for? The freaks, the punks, the homeless—the miserable Brazilians, the anonymous, the fucked-up, lost, lonely, starving—suffocated by the economy, politics, ideologies, consumerism, globalization, fashion, trends, the media, brand names, the all-important and imperishable primacy of celebrity?

Finally, though, the Beats managed to thumb a ride with an extremely boring American who talked shit to them nonstop. It was unbearable. They traveled almost four thousand miles with him, split between the front seat and the back. "Sheer torture," Kerouac declared. On a frozen November morning, he was left on a street corner in New York City. Which corner? He was chilled to the bone and completely broke. Ginsberg took him to the home of two female friends. One of them took a liking to Kerouac, let him stay in her apartment for a while, until he was in shape to leave. He intended to spend Christmas with his family in Rocky Mount, North Carolina.

What would Kerouac have done if Ginsberg's friend hadn't taken him in? If she'd been out when they came by? Or in bed with a man or a woman? Or been drunk or high? She wouldn't have answered the doorbell. Who was this anonymous woman who sheltered him, anyway? Her name, physical description. Blonde, olive-skinned, black, a redhead—tall, short? What did she do? Was she a student, waitress, shop girl, bank teller, secretary, model, poet? Did she go to bed with Kerouac? He doesn't refer to the episode in his letters. What has she been up to in all the years since? How old was this anonymous woman at the time? Is she still alive? Will she have read the biography written by Ann Charters (Kerouac: A Biography, 1973)? Did she marry, have kids, grandchildren? Did she become mystical, rebellious, successful, an alcoholic? A moment of Beat (and world) literary history passed over this anonymous woman—an involuntary character in Kerouac's life story. Destiny cruelly threw her a line, pulling her out of the mud hole of anonymity where she'd spent her life, only to drop her in another, having been grazed by greatness. Waiting and waiting to be recognized in a photo, to regain her face and voice in the pages of history.

And what about that driver asshole who talked so much? We don't even know the make or color of his car.

ALWAYS KEEP YOURSELF "PLUGGED IN"

The new trend is to exhibit art in shop windows at shopping malls. Sculptures, installations, small paintings mixed in with clothing, gadgets, appliances, etc. In some cases, it's a little difficult to tell the art from the commerce.

Body modifications. Lip piercing. Numbers engraved on the arm (*branding*), all kinds of intentional scars, made by stilettos, penknives, nails, pins. "The pain is short and intense, but the statement lasts a lifetime," said *Time.*

Ecodesign: Ivy climbing the sunset sides of houses, with deciduous vegetation (need to look "deciduous" up), zenithal lighting, soluble paintings in water, troughs to catch rain. Landscaped gardens using recycled water, a pool with chic clay stones (used by the German Dr. Gernot Minke).

Another trend in decoration: Religious and esoteric objects, images of Ganesh and Shiva, crystal prisms, wind chimes, Catholic saints. Throw everything out that can't help get rid of your bad vibes. Feng shui ought to determine the arrangement of your books and CDs. Japanese floral arrangements—closed flower buds and a small fountain. Rattan is back. But rattan inlayed with little designs. And postmodern brand names (anyway, I think they're postmodern—I have to remember to sign up for that class on distinguishing the modern and the postmodern, and possibly ultramodern as well . . . I lose track) like *Pod.* Like the stuff designed by Kaname Okajima.

SNUGGLED INTO ONE ANOTHER

It happened. And when it happened it was wonderful, unbearably beautiful. It happened. And while it was happening, we were so happy that nothing else mattered.

It happened. And while it happened those moments were unique, insuperable.

One inside the other. Clasped together.

Every part of one of us adapted to the other with perfection. Arms in the right position, shoulders perfect, belly at belly, toes intertwined.

One day we said, We're like the coasts of Africa and Brazil—the same outline, two pieces of a puzzle.

We were united from the tips of our fingers to our mutual gaze.

Because our eyes were locked together as well, the same as our fingers and tongues.

It wasn't even necessary to penetrate her.

Even though there were days when we had barely settled down before I was inside you.

People don't know how to live certain moments. Don't know how to make them count. Don't know how to be satisfied with them. To be content.

They want plans, futures, programs. They want to prolong or repeat a moment that is by its nature unique. Fleeting, swift, ephemeral, and therefore painfully joyous. To repeat it would make it quotidian, normal, concrete, binding. It massacres passion, beauty, love.

FLITCRAFT: THE EXPLANATION

Flitcraft, a businessman, considered to be a good husband and father, left his office one day at lunchtime. He was never seen again. Five years later, Flitcraft's wife looked for a detective (Sam Spade, played by Humphrey Bogart in the film version), saying that somebody had seen her husband in another city.

Under contract, Sam went to look for Flitcraft. He found him, too. They spoke. Not even for a moment did the runaway resort to subterfuge or try to hide from Spade. He simply told him that he had gone away, having left his family well supported. Which was true—his business affairs had all been in order when he disappeared.

Spade couldn't figure out what the fugitive's motives were, at first. Flitcraft had left a family, house, business, city behind—a solidly established life, and around seventy thousand dollars. (Today, worth around three or four million.) The new Flitcraft had a new family, a new house, a new business. Anyway, there was no real crime involved, and the first Mrs. Flitcraft didn't want to create any kind of scandal, so she became reconciled to the situation, asked for a divorce, and end of story.

But what had happened to Flitcraft that made him disappear? Dashiell Hammett tells us that, on that afternoon when he went out for lunch, Flitcraft passed by a building that was under construction. A scaffold, or something like that, fell eight or ten stories and smashed into the sidewalk. It fell nearby without hitting our hero. Flitcraft was startled. Well, he was terrified. Traumatized.

Hammett explains: "He felt like somebody had taken the lid off life and let him look at the works." Flitcraft had been an upstanding person, an honest citizen, a decent family man, a good husband. This is the way it was because he felt better when he was in tune with his surroundings, with life "a clean orderly sane responsible affair." But the unexpected happened, because life isn't under our control, no matter how we would like it to be. There's nothing we can do about it.

The falling scaffold cancelled out all of Flitcraft's notions about life. It swept away his certainties, reduced them to doubts. He could have died for no reason at all.

Life changes in seconds, independent of our will, desire, determination. Perhaps there was already some little burgeoning speck of discontent in Flitcraft's life, some hidden mass of dissatisfaction under the surface of his methodical, systematized life.

The scaffolding affected him more profoundly by missing him than it would have by crushing him there and then. Flitcraft didn't even bother to go home. He decided on a new life. Sure, his new life may have been more or less identical to the one he was leaving behind, but he had to fight to put it together, had to do everything all over again, and this might have been the attraction. To destroy and reconstruct.

The crucial thing was not to go home. If he had, life would have been the same. A defeat. To leave it behind, to rid himself of the past, abandon it, to wipe out the familiarity of its situations, gestures, and words demanded great strength. Even though it had taken the accident, and its warning, to set him off.

GODDAMMIT! 24 HOURS WITH A FAN?

The network forces all its stars to go on TV and promote all sorts of crap on women's talk shows if we have a free morning. Those shows don't really attract big audiences, but they sell dozens of new products every day—nobody even knows where they all come from. Vitamins, impotence cures, salves for herniated disks, hemorrhoids, and bursitis, remedies for high blood pressure, depression, gastritis, muscle pains, obesity, anorexia, bad breath, gas, sinusitis, mycosis, inflammation of the testicles, yeast infections, hangnails, ingrown toenails, parasites, rheumatism, indigestion, erysipelas, impetigo, shingles. Being a shill earns me next to nothing, but the network rakes it in.

This week, however, my duty is to spend twenty-four hours with a fan who won a day with me thanks to a contest that was held for the studio audience of one of these talk shows—bussed in to applaud our cheerful celebrity endorsements.

I have no choice. It's part of my contract.

She's going to be positioned in my home so as to best witness my waking up, stretching, pretending to smoke my first cigarette (everyone thinks I'm so unhealthy, so contemptuous of health trends, and I have to keep the myth alive), getting up, brushing my teeth, taking a shit, having breakfast, going to the studio, memorizing my lines, putting on my make-up. Maybe she'll even watch me having a quickie behind the scenery with some needy starlet, make-up artist, or costumer—once I even had a cleaning lady; there are some really hot lower-class girls around if you know where to look. I hope she likes the idea. That would be exciting.

She'll stand there with her mouth wide open watching me perform, taking a little break, yelling at some fellow actor who's not setting the right comedic or dramatic tone, yelling at the lighting people, slamming the door in some reporter's face.

She's going to watch me running to the bar, having a shot of scotch, then a dark beer, then some grappa, port wine, a few shots of the Havana firewater (the sugarcane booze from Minas that costs around seventy-five dollars per bottle). Then I'm going to bring her to my dressing room: Room 101. Two contiguous rooms, as the building plans say, well-appointed (All Sig Bergamin or Chicô Gouvêa designs).

She won't forget this day in a hurry.

I'll be a cherished memory until she dies. And yes, it's a sweet and comforting thought to know that one will always live in someone's thoughts. I ask only that this damn fortunate fan be happy with what she'll receive and not insist on inviting me to her graduation, or to be the best man at a wedding with warm beer, lupine seeds, bits of meat on a bamboo spit, cold mayonnaise salad, and fried salty cakes.

So you dream about being an actor, renowned, famous, wearing dark sunglasses, giving interviews, posing by your penthouse swimming pool?

That's not the way it works anymore. You'll know you're really famous the day you receive an e-mail questionnaire from a glossy magazine. I've just finished mine. It'll be read on the internet and published simultaneously in thirteen international magazines—English, French, Chinese, Japanese, Pakistani, German, Italian, Czechoslovakian, Polish, Castilian, Spanish, Basque, and of course one in Continental Portuguese. They want to exhaust the world's interest in me, all at once.

Please answer the following, to the best of your ability:
1. *What was your nickname in school?*
2. *Is there anyone you feel you owe an apology to? Who is it, and what would you say?*
3. *If you could write only one letter before you die, to whom would you write?*
4. *Describe the worst haircut you ever got.*
5. *Are you unfaithful to your spouse?*

6. *Which book have you just finished reading?*

7. *What's your favorite word?*

8. *Do you lie? How often?*

9. *Gossip?*

10. *What's your favorite color?*

11. *Favorite time of day?*

12. *State your opinion of Professor Alfonso Bovero.*

13. *Who is the woman with the most beautiful breasts in Brazil?*

14. *The most beautiful ass?*

15. *The sexiest legs?*

16. *Do you pray? What's your favorite prayer?*

17. *Do you masturbate? How often?*

18. *Do you spit a lot? (Like those soccer players seem to always be spitting somewhere or other whenever there's a close-up on TV during a game.)*

19. *Is there anything in the world you find utterly ridiculous and inexplicable?*

20. *What do you consider the best place to make love to a woman?*

21. *Do you have a preference for a particular orifice, when making love?*

22. *Define elegance.*

23. *Define style.*

24. *Give us an example of something you find completely vulgar.*

25. *Do you have any nervous tics?*

26. *List some of your most prominent obsessions.*

27. *Recommend five restaurants.*

28. *Recommend ten bars you frequent regularly.*

29. *Who makes the best sandwiches in the city?*

30. *Which soft drink is always in your fridge?* (We'll get sponsorship money from the company you endorse here and fund a cultural project you'll have the honor of directing.)

31. *Which medical clinic do you frequent?* (You'll get free care and priority service in case of an emergency for this one.)

32. *What insurance company/ies do you use? (Idem, ibid.)*

33. *Name your five favorite health spas. (Ditto.)*

34. *Which hotels do you stay in, both at home and abroad? (Etc.)*

35. *Which airlines? (And so forth.)*

36. *Which beaches?*

37. *A favorite shop?*

38. *What do you believe in?*

39. *What don't you believe in?*

40. *Would you be capable of committing suicide?*

41. *What do you think about the violence in our streets?*

42. *Do you support police strikes?*

43. *Would you give land to a landless person? Home to a homeless person?*

44. *What is solitude?*

45. *What's your favorite toothpaste?*

46. *Do you cut your own nails?*

47. *Would you assist your wife in childbirth?*

48. *Would you hate your child if it was born ugly?*

49. *Have you ever dressed in drag?*

50. *Do you flush the toilet when you go to the bathroom in the middle of the night?*

51. *How many words do you know? Try and count.*

52. *Are you limiting your electricity use as is your civic duty?*

53. *Do you do crossword puzzles? If so, which level: difficult, medium, or beginner?*

54. *Do you eat bologna sandwiches?*

55. *Do you consider yourself to be a simple person? Do you get along with regular people and love your mother?*

My consultants need to help me answer these questions. I have to be careful. I can't risk offending the media. They like my being temperamental and unconventional, when I talk about myself, but only within very strict guidelines. They know what I tell them will all be according to a script.

I pretend not to be interested in publicity (and this isn't easy—it tears me up inside to lie about something so paramount to my personality). This just makes them all the more interested. The media never gives up its quarry. Nobody takes no for an answer in this country. But, then, I don't actually want them to take it. I just can't risk giving myself away.

The questionnaire seems banal on the surface, but what strikes you as banal is in actuality a series of potentially lethal traps. They want to catch you, by any means necessary. One way or the other, to expose you.

To tell the truth, nobody else they'll interview is afraid of being exposed. They love to talk about belching, farting, vomiting, shitting, pissing, being cuckolded, impotence, perversion, innumerable hidden peccadilloes and intimate defects, gastritis, tyrannical mothers, ambitious fathers, opportunistic brothers, bastard children. Smiling all the while.

> Men and women,
> gays and lesbians
> showing how they make love,
> and with whom,
> who they liked fucking most,
> what they think they're best at,
> their preferences, fetishes, perversions, flaws,
> whether they swallow or spit,
> which cunts they liked the taste of,
> how big their pricks are.
> They give their names and even their addresses.
> I don't want to be like them.*
> But I have to or I won't have my contract renewed.

---

* Of course I would! Why pretend? Everybody wants to!

249

INCREDIBLE! LA COMES BY AND PROPOSES A MURDER!

I'm suspicious. He only looks out for his own interests. What could possibly have brought the Lead Actor to my dressing room, when I've always been sure he didn't even know this wing of the studio is still standing? When I've always been sure he didn't even know I existed? Lenira showed him, of course. He must have been taken aback. The corridors and the empty dressing rooms probably seem like something out of *The Phantom of the Opera* to him. He entered Room 101 without knocking, at the very moment I was rereading an article about the Maison de Balzac, in Paris, in the Passy neighborhood—the neighborhood that was made famous in the same film that introduced the world to Maria Schneider (*Last Tango in Paris*, Bernardo Bertolucci, 1972), who became an overnight sensation. Then, in a moment's time, she was gone, vanished, thrown back again into the whirlpool (a beautiful word, a sonorous word) of anonymity. At the time, however, Maria was all anyone talked about (I have the clippings to prove it), and then, a close second, Marlon Brando's performance—and this was the old Brando, before he disappeared behind a mountain of fat—and the butter scene, of course. In the supermarket or at their dinner tables, people would look at butter and laugh. They'd get excited.

"What do you want?" I ask the LA.

"To get to know you."

"Me?"

"Lenira told me you look like me."

"No, wrong. You're the one who looks like me. I'm older."

We don't make eye contact.

We talk, each watching the other in my dressing mirror, analyzing our images. I don't bother to turn my head. I still don't believe he really came just to have a look at me. His skin is sallow, his eyes dead, his mouth weak.

Yes. A weak, sad man.

And yet, how is it possible that someone as famous and successful as him could be sad? If I were ready, if I'd had some warning, I could kill him right now, hide his body, and step out of my dressing room as the LA, with no one the wiser. How to hide the body, though? I'd deal with this problem when I came to it. I have to take this step by step, not get ahead of myself. Emergencies bring out the best in people, generate the most unlikely solutions to our problems, as we've seen in countless movies.

Killing him would close the cycle of anxiety and desire I've been living in for years. I would end a life, and step over the threshold of death. I would become him, would be famous, famous until even that began to bore me.

The anonymity that hides inside me would be stifled forever.

I would know the truth, of course, but this would hardly matter. The public would believe, and it's them who matter—what they believe is true. If they see me as a new man, I'll be a new man. I'll start with a clean slate, I'll be a man without ties, without papers, without a history. Am I married? To whom? I'm already beginning to forget who I am. I'm ready to shed my skin. Ready to rid myself of me, ready to be absorbed by the life of the Lead Actor. I'll burn my photographs, documents, birth and marriage certificates, bills. Everything, everything, everything. I will annul myself. I will forget my name.

Names hardly matter anyway. His is false too—he chose it because it sounds more exciting than what he was given at birth. And, in my new life, every time I hear his fake name, see one of his old movies or shows, I'll look proudly at his image and think, That's me! How nice I look! What good work I do!

I would exist. I would have a history.

"I came to talk about Lenira."

"Lenira?"

"We have to be careful."

"About what?"

"She's playing games with us. Playing us off against one another."

"And why would she do something like that? I'm a nobody. It doesn't make sense."

"She told me you want to take my place."

"And why would I want that?"

"She said we look alike. She said you're dangerous, that you're setting up some scheme."

"She's been watching too many movies. The history of cinema is filled with switches, twins, doppelgangers, clones. Bullshit. I just do my job, same as you. You should go get some sleep, you look tired."

(With all the drugs he does, it's a wonder he can even stand upright.)

I notice now that LA is examining his own face in my dressing mirror, not looking at me at all. He pinches his cheeks, runs his hand through his hair. Clichéd gestures, signifying self-involvement.

"It could be one of Lenira's games. She loves to play games. She has a lot of imagination."

"Games?"

"Games with people's lives."

"Sounds like a bad soap opera. By an inexperienced writer. Someone who doesn't know anything about the history of art, cinema, literature. You have a terrible fear of 'the other,' I see. An ancient theme."

Our conversation is absurd. There's no reason for LA to be here talking to me. It weakens my resolve. It's incriminating, if anyone should find out that my double visited me. I've been reading *Crime and Punishment*. In order for me to steep myself in the line of thought that allows a man to commit a crime without ever considering himself a murderer. A Crime of Necessity. Good title. Yes, nobody must know my double was here. It's the sort of thing that might trip me up later. As anyone who reads crime novels will recognize.

"I like to play, too," the LA said. "More than Lenira. And I came here to make you a proposition. I say we play against her. That Jap is dangerous. Ever since she saw *Dangerous Liaisons*,* she became fascinated with the notion that you can manipulate people, maneuver them, concoct little intrigues and stratagems . . ."

"Incredible! 'Concoct little intrigues and stratagems'!"

"Pretty, isn't it? I got it from some dialogue we shot yesterday."

"Why would Lenira want to concoct stratagems and such?"

"To feel something. Life here is cold, mechanical, emotionless, unexciting. Why don't we pool our resources, start fighting back?"

"To what end?"

"What do you think? To kill her."

"Jesus. Just like that? To kill for the sake of killing, for a game?"

"Just imagine the press we'd get! With my name involved, it'll be a sensation!"

"It would be the end of your career!"

"Oh, nonsense. You don't know the kind of world we live in. No, it'll get us months and months of free publicity, and that's all. I have fame, money, the goodwill of the public, and excellent lawyers. Don't you see? Famous people always get acquitted in these situations—governments and corporations too, while we're on the subject. We'll get off easy. And the inconvenience is a small price to pay for the exposure."

---

* Research: *Dangerous Liaisons* (*Les Liaisons Dangereuses*), 1782, is a novel by Pierre Choderlos de Laclos. In 1959, Roger Vadim, at the height of his fame, having launched Brigitte Bardot's career in *And God Created Woman*, adapted the book, intending to make Annette Stroyberg a new Brigitte. It didn't work. Vadim was definitely mediocre, but he fucked a lot of beautiful women and was world-famous, for a time. The 1988 *Dangerous Liaisons*, directed by Stephen Frears and starring Glenn Close, is a masterpiece of subtlety, and was a big hit; whereas *Valmont*, directed by Milos Forman and released the following year, was a flop, despite a script by Jean-Claude Carrière, frequent collaborator with Buñuel and screenwriter of Peter Brook's *Mahabharata*.

"And you want me involved?"

"You'll get your share of the media attention. It'll be good for both of us."

"Yes, but . . . murder?"

I fake astonishment, incredulity. I look at myself in the mirror. I'm a better actor than he is—we are not meeting on a level playing field. Still, I know he must be as familiar as I with the rules of the *Manual of Media Necessities*—with one major difference. He knows what he knows because of lived experience, whereas my information—so carefully assembled—is based on observation and analysis. I'm still only a theoretician.

"Yes, murder. Murder is a way of life. Everybody does it. Everybody *needs* to do it."

He turned to leave. Opened my door with a melodramatic flourish. I hear his golf cart hum away into the shadows. He doesn't know that he's the one who's going to die. I feel very calm.

ALWAYS KEEP YOURSELF "PLUGGED IN"

The hit of the summer are men's knee-length shorts: "highwaters" or "clam-diggers."

Body-building proteins are in.

A new eating disorder. Orthorexia: a pathological insistence on only eating foods that are considered healthy.

Foodie. Avoid canned stuff, anything packaged. Give up red meat and fried food. Only apples and tomatoes. Drink a lot of coconut milk.

A new profession: *food designer.* They put together the forms and colors that go on your plate. One day a Kandinsky, another impressionism. Never a Jackson Pollock, though. Abstract impressionism can really turn your stomach.

By the way: No one says "macaroni or spaghetti" anymore. Use the word "*pasta*," it makes a big difference.*

Thus speaks the muse of the summer: Alternative lifestyles are in, loving animals is in, film studies are very, very in. The drink of choice is the red martini: red fruit with vodka.

My Consultant on Trends and Current Events has a pocketful of wrinkled clippings from magazines, newspapers, and printouts from the internet. Why should I pay him to collect this stuff when I can do it just as well myself? Yes, I am a past-master at clipping, highlighting, circling, annotating. I'll put together a *Manual of Current Necessities (Summer Edition).* I have access to all the material in the network's archives, too. We all have our little tricks for staying ahead of the game.

---

* Reminder: Memorize the words in italics. Use them in conversation as often as possible.

YOU'RE YOUNG, YOU'RE DRUNK, YOU'RE IN BED,
YOU HAVE KNIVES; SHIT HAPPENS!

You know how it is: You're young, you're drunk, you're in bed, you have knives; shit happens!

You know how it is: You're young, you're drunk, you're in bed, you have knives; shit happens!

I adapt. I rob. I repeat the above phrase by Angelina Jolie over and over again because it seems to me to be an example of a perfect utterance—perfect in construction, in its synthesis of disparate concepts, in its execution. It ran in all the American newspapers, was translated and sent out into the world, was quoted on television. "You're young, you're drunk, you're in bed, you have knives; shit happens." Was she the one who came up with it, or was it some handler who prepared the phrase? I'd give a full fifth of my life to have made a statement like that—to have someone on my payroll who could come up with anything so wonderful! It seems to perfectly encapsulate life on this Western hemisphere: "You're young, you're drunk, you're in bed, you have knives; shit happens." Angelina, the one who supposedly used to wear a vial of her husband's blood around her neck, is one of the sensations of the new Hollywood—the daughter of Jon Voigt, still remembered for one great film (*Midnight Cowboy*, directed by John Schlesinger, 1969). (How many new Hollywoods have there been?)

I keep a notebook of these wonderful quotations. I collect them, then rewrite them, trying to make them mine, trying to make them into things I can repeat at a later date. It isn't easy—they need to be clear and evasive both. Perhaps you all can help me think, help me be a better celebrity—you should feel free to send me suggestions and helpful hints via my new e-mail address. For instance, I'd like to know what you think of the following: "Simplicity resides in the transparent darkness, in the revocation of the dispensable I, in the alteration of anachronistic structures." Pretty good, no? Something to talk about, something to be repeated. My "dispensable I" might even catch on, enter the language. When an expression you're responsible for becomes part of everyday speech, the race is over—you've become immortal. *You know how it is: You're young, you're drunk, you're in bed, you have knives; shit happens! You know how it is: You're young, you're drunk, you're in bed, you have knives; shit happens!*

Farewell to the petty! Farewell to the quotidian!

Clap clap clap clap clap clap clap clap clap clap clap.

THE POOR, THE FILTHY:
ROLL UP THE WINDOW

Life is a joke. A fraud. So why not invent my own past? There's no percentage in truth.

Everyone knows their own history best. Thus, they know how best to deviate from it when they tell their stories. The ideal thing would be if I could make people believe I was born dirt-poor, in hopeless circumstances, with no future ahead of me. Poverty is affecting. As long as it's other people's poverty. As long as it doesn't come too close. Poverty is a wonderful conversation piece when we're safely distanced from it, behind iron gates, inside locked doors, looking out the windows of our cars, enjoying the air-conditioning.

Everyone still respects the myth of the self-made man.

Everyone still loves to hear about people who dragged themselves out of the muck and made a new life for themselves.

The impotent and sentimental are heartened by such stories. Self-made men are inspirational. Role models. Winners. And everyone loves a winner. Winners get to write articles for magazines, give speeches at business conventions, preach self-confidence, and publish best-selling self-help books. I will rearrange the fragments of my life to fit this profile.

Of course, the public loves losers too. Losers make them feel better about themselves, allow them to feel sympathy, give them permission to have a nice little cry. But winners allow them to dream. I know which route I prefer.

I need a Past Consultant. Someone who can help me chart the course I should have taken, give me the proper coordinates for inventing myself a new and more appropriate back-story. For instance: rules of behavior change! What was scandalous in the '60s seems rather tame by today's standards. Leila Diniz shook up Brazil by posing in a bikini: she was pregnant at the time. Norma Bengell showed her pubic hair in *Os Cafajestes* (1962). Lines around the block. And then, more recently, in 1992, President Itamar was photographed from a very low angle alongside the model Lilian Ramos, who happened not to be wearing any underpants beneath her skirt. That caused a lot of talk back in the day. I'm not sure if it would even raise an eyebrow now.

A man must have attitudes and opinions that demonstrate the coherence of his thoughts and actions—I read this in a magazine I found at the waiting room of a lab where I went to get an ultrasound done for my prostate and liver. I was afraid of getting hepatitis—I drink a great deal, you know, due to the great burden I carry. Once in a while I go through a bad spell. And I drink cheap stuff: Cynar, vermouth, cognac made from vegetable tar. When I become a celebrity, I'll be able to drink absinth (they're making it again), like Toulouse Lautrec or Modigliani, do classy drugs like opium (do we even have opium in Brazil?), smoke hashish through a hookah.

The cheap drug here is crack, but they sell it only to inner-city children. I tried to buy some for myself, but the policemen who run the market got suspicious. They called me over and beat the shit out of me.

They hurt me very badly.

I never ever want to buy drugs from the police again. Only from real, safe, sane, professional drug-dealers!

ACE, FROUFROU, FRINGE:
RETRO

Why did I bother coming here? If Letícia saw me in the front row at the opening night of São Paulo Fashion Week, she wouldn't believe it. And yet I know she's here somewhere—she never misses a fashion show. Does she still wear that gold ring with the glittering crystal in it, and those twin bracelets of gold and turquoise manufactured by Francisca Botelho (inspired by Wonder Woman)? If she can see me, why doesn't she come over to say hello?

If I know her, she'll sit on the other side of the runway, facing me. She'll cross her legs and let her skirt slip up. That's how she wore me down in the first place. Those thighs and that smile. Her eyes, testing me. The way she spoke to me. Her lucidity.

I leave my dressing room less and less. And now this show is starting late. The photographers pass me by, they're not looking at me. Incomprehensible. My arms are full of pamphlets—each designer printed his own handout, written in a coded language, designed for one clique and one clique alone. "Trend." The word appears sixty-seven times in reference to today's show alone.

There are more fashion and entertainment magazine publishers and producers for both broadcast and cable television here than there are models on the runway. They all enter in big groups, none of them wanting to be seen entering first or last. They sit down and look at each other, check to see which of them has been given the best seat in terms of comfort and view. To entertain myself, I read the pamphlets: the models are beautiful, some of them way too thin, others looking outright unwell. Gorgeous. They don't spare me a glance! I note they didn't invite Gisele Bündchen; the organizers contend she's in decline, but I respectfully disagree, based on what I've been seeing in the foreign magazines. A very Brazilian position: that her visibility in local magazines determines the health of her career. They're already selecting another model to take her place. Yes, one ascends, one descends. Brazil is the next to last stop before hell.

I see strips of ribbon, fringe, latex—playful contrasts, uneven hems, space-age material—elongated bicycle shorts, high-laced gladiator sandals—stonewashed and form-fitting cloth, lace, retro designs, ethnic chic.

(Are these words important? Must speak to my Terminology Consultant.)

It's all beginning to wear on my nerves. I recently saw a television interview with the renowned English fashion commentator Colin McDowell. With his thin Hemingway face, he sat in the front row at a fashion show, complaining that he wished all the shows could be held in Rio, a city he finds much more charming than São Paulo. Then he went on to deliver the following words of wisdom (awkwardly translated by a voice-over recorded in the studio): "We live in an era of middle-class attitudes. We all more or less live the same life, with a certain level of taste and internationality. I know that in Brazil there exist many poor people, but they too want to have access to middle-class comfort, with a good house, a good car, and beautiful clothes. The United States is a perfect example of this way of living, with everybody wanting to look as if they stepped out of the pages of *Vogue*."

I don't know if this show is more or less glamorous than shows in past years. No one wants to talk to me. No one looks twice. I'm not even positioned for maximum exposure.

Here, I'm a non-celeb.

LA is about to die, by the way. Lenira told me. He's got some virus; the doctors can't figure it out. If he dies, and everybody knows about it—and they'll certainly know—I will disappear. I won't exist. The trick now is to keep him alive. Or else replace him before he goes.

261

Return
my
love
return!

WHO WORRIES ABOUT COMMAS WHEN THEY'RE SUFFERING?

The fashion show finally started. In the confusion of the crowd waiting around for the next presentation (by Fause Haten, who I think is really at the top of his game), Letícia snuck up to me, slipped an envelope into my hands, and left. With a man who could as easily be her new lover as just a co-worker she dragged along for company. Or was I just seeing things? Maybe she was alone, and just happened to leave at the same time as some guy she'd never seen before? Or maybe she wasn't even at the show? Maybe she sent her letter through the mail? Or did Lenira hand it to me? Sometimes, when she was angry at me, Letícia would leave her letters and notes with the doorman, in care of Lenira. Or maybe it was an e-mail? We used to write each other several times a day. Now, no longer. Even Lenira isn't talking to me anymore—too busy watching LA's decline. The well is dry. What will become of us? What will I do with my army of consultants? Start firing them? Will I have to pay unemployment?

I read the note and realize I don't know what I just read. I read it again. I don't understand a thing. I don't want to know.

> *My love,*
>
> *Yes, despite everything, I still love you. I'm going to put down the lyrics to a song by Mário Lago, sung by Carlos Galhardo. I heard it by chance, I was at my folks' house (my father just turned seventy, and we threw him a big party). They had an original cast recording from that geriatric musical,* Singers in the Shower II. *At first, the song seemed very sentimental, sugary. Then I realized that the lyrics are about us. Mário Lago was a genius! How can a fifty-year-old song say so much about a love affair that hadn't*

even begun yet, and that—let's face it—never really happened, that never will really happen, because you ran away, you couldn't handle it, couldn't take responsibility for it, refused to change? You wasted our love. You know that. How can you live with yourself, having thrown away something so important? The song is called Return. I jotted down bits and pieces. Maybe I got some of the words wrong, or have left some out. The punctuation might be wrong too, because I was crying while I was transcribing. You know how easily I cry.

"You sent back the old passionate letters / I sent you in the fever of love.

You sent back what was left of two lives, / the romance and the pain I suffered.

You sent everything back, however, / the best of what I gave you is missing. / Return all the tranquility, / all the happiness I gave you and lost. / Return all the crazy dreams, / I built up little by little and offered to you. / Return, I beg you, please, / the immense love I left in your arms. / Return it so I can still return to you / the infinite longing / I feel for you now."

Return my love! Letícia.

"Return, my love!"

The comma would signify that I'm still your love. Whereas,

"Return my love!"

Would indicate that I am being ordered to return the love she gave me and no longer wants to leave in my possession, as it were.

The comma makes all the difference in the world. But who worries about commas when they're suffering?

RESCUING THE ANONYMOUS:
THE ANABAPTISTS

History's unknowns are not always poor pitiful creatures, spurned by fate. There's also the category of those who themselves caused terrible things to happen to others, but whose identities have been protected by the shadows. Leopold Ranke, *in his* History of the Reformation in Germany, *and Karl Kautsky, in* Communism in Central Europe in the Time of the Reformation, *both cite the episode of the citizen of Münster who managed to delay a major historical process. If not for his actions, who knows what the modern world would be like? In the sixteenth century, Münster was scene of one of the earliest sustained attempts at establishing communism. Cruel and unstable, but with flashes of true egalitarianism and a legitimate attempt to establish a proportional distribution of wealth. The Anabaptists were the prime movers in this, a sect of Christians who believed that a believer must be rebaptized in adult life. Conservative forces opposed this movement, and they had the support of Bishop Waldeck, and thus the city, which had declared itself independent of both state and church, was subjected to a brutal siege. Hunger and despair reigned within the city walls. John of Leiden, who governed the community, gave his permission for anyone who wanted to abandon Münster to do so. As soon as the people left, however, they were immediately killed (or captured and raped, if they were young women) by the Bishop's troops. Nevertheless, there was a man (some say he was named "Gresbeck," and that he even tried to sell a tell-all memoir, but that hardly makes him any less a non-celebrity) who saved his life in exchange for showing the enemy troops a vulnerable place in the city walls. Thousands of people were murdered as a result of his act. And the following episode can be included in my* Notebook of Cruelties: *John of Leiden was tied to a fiery stake while his executioners tore off pieces of his flesh with heated tongs. The smell of his burning meat was so foul that the crowd—who delighted in such spectacles—finally withdrew, nauseated. Afterward, the guards cut out John's tongue, and to finish him off, stabbed him through the heart. The Anabaptists retreated and communism had to wait five hundred more years to be given a real chance. If communism had been allowed to survive, germinate, and be refined in the intervening centuries, what kind of world would we be living in now?*

WHEN I DIE

I remember my mug shots. One from the front, one from the side. Who else knows they exist? They're forgotten in some faraway police station. I don't even remember the name I was using at that stage of my life. Certainly I wasn't using my own.

I've decided that I want my friends (how many are left? I'll make a list) to throw the pages from all the soap-opera scripts I've performed in my life on top of my coffin as it's lowered down into the ground. Those pages are the poems of my life. My real life—the only one I actually lived and paid attention to—the only one I recognize. Without Letícia, I'm only happy when I'm shooting a scene, only happy outside myself, inside the characters other people have created for me to inhabit and whom I embody to perfection (read the reviews). I want to take them with me: my characters, my brothers. That way I won't feel lonely when the dirt closes in on my little coffin, and I hear the gravedigger patting down the layers of earth above this tormented body of mine.

ALWAYS KEEP YOURSELF "PLUGGED IN"

Female television announcers go out with soccer idols and get enormous coverage. Does the same go for men? Can I go out with one of the female players on our star volleyball team? I've been seeing a lot of games and often frequent the Ibirapuera Stadium. And then female pop singers manage to get pregnant by prison inmates and get enormous coverage just for that. I wonder how I could manage to sneak into a women's prison . . .

To be used, perhaps, at some party. The most recent trend in the fashion world is "Rock Zurich." It all started with this book, *Karlheinz Weinberger: Photos 1954–1995*, which published in tandem with the Zurich Museum of Design's putting up a retrospective of Weinberger's work in 2000. Weinberger took pictures of the Swiss kids who idolized Elvis Presley and James Dean, but who were less than appreciated at the time by well-behaved, square, reactionary, mainstream Swiss society. Jeans, belts with gigantic buckles showing Elvis's picture, cowboy boots, chains. I must consult my personal designer.

Old songs are very "in." I must make an appearance at the musical review *Singers in the Shower II*—quite the hit, at the moment. It came to São Paulo from the Arena Café-Theater of Rio de Janeiro, selling local audiences memories of the great days of our own Arena Theater. There's such a thing, apparently, as "gray power"— a powerful demographic made up of men and women over sixty years old. Someone had the bright idea of staging a show made up of songs by Chiquinha Gonzaga, Lamartine Babo, Noel Rosa, Herivelto Martins, Dolores Duran, and Chico Buarque. One major difference between this and other shows is that everybody in the audience already knows all the music and all the words, and they usually sing along. Music that's fifty to a hundred years old and is still being sung—it's hard to believe. Anyway, going to this show is a must. Photographers take pictures of the audience. It pays to be able to prove you've been there.

LIFE WITHOUT FEAR

My life changes when I cross the threshold of a film set and breathe in its smells. Humidity, cold concrete, wood, rope, paint, cloth, the hot metal of the lights, plastics, air-conditioning, leather, Styrofoam, the dust that collects on the backs of flats, the sweat of the crew, perfumes, deodorants, creams, blush, mascara, lipstick, lotion, lavender, cologne, chalk, and, sometimes, when they use wind or rain machines, or spray the set with mist, the sickly sweet odor of oil the filters never completely eliminate.

I begin to live when I go on the set. My blood finally starts to flow when I walk inside those thick, impermeable walls—acoustically isolated. When the outside noises are eliminated, putting real life at a distance. Real life is an abomination.

Everything that really interests me happens here, only here, in front of these façades, on these fake streets, streets that only seem real when the lights are on to form shadows, chiaroscuro, to give the impression of a certain time of day, a certain climate.

The sun isn't welcome here. The sun doesn't take orders. The sun moves and everything changes. It doesn't know when to pause, when to focus on one detail. Its light is crude, imperious. It destroys faces. Haphazard, it could never properly illuminate the corners and recesses the technicians have built into their fake city. Only the hot, overhead lights will do.

Light and shadow, tone and half-tone—black, gray, color. Here, the sun is a performer, an actor like the rest of us. It obeys the director of photography. He can manipulate and paralyze time; and, at his order, the sun—our sun—can reproduce the tenor of a single day in November, 1937. Or else, coming in the windows of a whorehouse, the sordidness proper to 1953.* It may not look

---

* Sordidness? What prejudice! I've always liked whores, I just hate paying in advance. Modern whores, now known as call girls or escorts, accept credit cards—and this is much less degrading for everyone involved. In Rio de Janeiro,

exactly as it did then, but it will look exactly as we now think it should have looked—taking on exactly the tone we imagine, or which we see in old yellowed photographs.

After all, no one who was actually around on such-and-such a day is going to show up and contradict us. Who can remember what each individual day was really like—cold or hot, rainy, cloudy—without the movies?

It's fascinating to look at the scenery when the lights are off, illuminated only by the red "SILENCE—TAPING IN PROGRESS" lights of the darkened studio. Then to see everything readied, each individual shaft of light kicked in, the camera set up at an unusual angle, a skyscraper made to tower over the viewer despite its being a miniscule plaster toy put together by the boys in the model shop (the same ones who'll be so pleased to make the bust that adorns my (his) tomb).

For me, in this false reality, life is happiness, peace. It is a life without fear, without frustration, without questions, without pressure.

Here, the light of the sun can be made to shine continuously for days and weeks from exactly the same position. Alternatively, night can be made eternal.

We ape life, but life is altered, adjusted, improved in our copy. Days, weeks, and months dissolve together. We have our own calendar—and we do whatever we like with it, as though we were a gang of Pope Gregorys, playing around with our years.

---

on Saturdays, they stage an event ("event" is a favorite catch-all term for promoters) called "The People of the Last Century." It takes place at the Pink House (550 Alice Street), which used to be one of the busiest carioca bordellos in the city, during the '50s, frequented by senators and big businessmen who arrived (and left) through a secret door between the second and third floors. One of the most notable clients was Oswaldo Aranha, right-hand man of President Getulio Vargas—minister, gray eminence, and great frequenter of cabarets and women of ill-repute, according to an article I found in the November 4, 2001 issue of *O Globo*, as reported by Daniela Name.

When scenery is torn down, pieces of it become other cities and streets. I love them all. Nothing is wasted.

It's like traveling without moving. The whole world can pass through here and I never have to leave my shelter. My haven.

I'm doing well. I am entirely at ease here in the mansions, railway and bus stations, churches, apartments, slums, hospitals, police stations, offices, stock markets, newsrooms, phone centers, bookstores, hotel lobbies, supermarkets, pharmacies, dressing rooms, castles (even though Brazil isn't really in the business of doing medieval dramas, unlike European TV), taxi stands, garages, butcher shops, bakeries, creameries, restaurants . . . to mention just a few of the different settings I've acted in.

We are the masters of time and history.

I was never happy in being myself, living my own life.

I prefer other people's lives: they seem to pass faster.

When I get bored, I simply change my character. The old one drops away, as though he's died. Though there's nothing violent about the process. It is peaceful, natural. The character ends. And I find another.

The only problem is the intervals that come between characters.

But here, in the studio, life is a dream!

NEW OPEN CLOSE DELETE INSERT PAGE DOWN

The era of the Mono Ego has finally arrived—people want happier things, want to treat themselves, declared Jean-Charles de Castelbajac (who's he?).

Pompoarist-tantric sex, the pleasure of sexual art, erotic power.

Lesbian chic, lower-class chic, radical transcendental chic, androgynous executive chic, sober minimalist chic, sensual Brazilian chic—new luxury is a typical revisitation of the classic, intimate, feminine, ludic, pop-bagatelle look!

Enormous hair. Synthetic implants.

The Polish designer Arkadius gave his new collection a simple name: *Prostitution?*—a critique of the marketing pressures that oblige designers to make their creations into brands by baptizing them with sexy names.

The '40s and the '80s are very in, and this can be seen in the return of androgyny: unisex tuxedoes made to be worn as everyday clothes, colored black, plum, beige, red, or military-green. That masculine icon, the necktie, has been inverted to capitalize on the popularity of sexual ambiguity. Leather is being mixed with the more noble textiles (a beautiful idea, a nobility of materials: counts, marquises, viscount textiles—like a deck of cards) to create a neo-punk, military-sexy, business executive's androgyny.

For the feet, high-laced boots inspired by bowling shoes are the last word.

In New York, colorful graffiti was stamped on Cavendish t-shirts—very new wave, with a hint of cowboy.

Dockers go with anything casual.

Interior design: Conceptual spaces, a Chinese junk painted in lacquer, steel furniture with a polyurethane finish (polished but not shiny).

A new fad: bringing fashionable wraps and blankets to throw over the ugly furniture they put in hotel rooms. Bringing Balinese textiles back to cover sofas and armchairs at home, hiding the mass-produced designs they came with when you brought them home from the department store.

It's indispensable to have those tiny metal Helmut Lang boxes to carry your pills around in (aspirin, Advil, vitamin C, Viagra, caffeine, Prozac, diet pills).

A new subculture of fat and hairy men have begun calling themselves "cuddly bears," and profess a great admiration for Marlon Brando. They've declared war against the Barbie dictatorship, the cult of health.

In restaurants order "Paraguay soup," which is actually a kind of cake—very in.

It is absolutely essential to listen to the highly politicized Asian Dub Foundation.

Trans-generational popularity.

There must be hordes of linguists out there inventing the proper terminology for all these fads. Philologists working in shifts studying dictionaries and the media. It's all becoming too much for me to bear. Trends flash by faster than the speed of sound, stunning me, leaving me in a permanent state of anxiety. How can I keep on top of all this? How can I be hip? It's impossible—you need antennae. Why do I bother?

How much time must I spend each day/week/month/year/decade in order to learn, assimilate so much ephemera—how much of my life must I devote to trends that are outdated before I can even memorize their names?

How many files must I open in my mind—how many new folders do I need to create, how many do I need to delete?

New, open, delete, close, cancel, insert, delete, new, open, cancel, close, cancel.

TO BE ELEGANT EVEN WHEN SLURPING UP GOOEY CONDENSED MILK

"The energy from the vacuum spontaneously bursts out of the emptiness and returns just as rapidly to nothingness." Is this somehow related to the Taoist *Classic of Perfect Emptiness*, attributed to Lie Yukou? Anyway, whatever it was that the essayist in question, Flávio Dieguez,* might have meant to say, he managed to summarize my life almost perfectly. He knows the terror of the vacuum that lies in wait for me when I can't be protected by the characters I play on television. I think this through while I set the table to have some gooey pudding from Uruguay, dripping with condensed milk, that I received as a gift. I lay down the pressed-linen tablecloth without a single crease. At the center, a crystal candlestick and a single blue candle. A plate from the Copacabana Palace, a present from Vera Ciangottini, the star of the eight o'clock soap-opera, who this year has managed to be on more magazine covers than any other Brazilian celebrity. Vera told me she bought the plate when the hotel was replacing its old china. She, nostalgic like most of us for times she didn't actually have the opportunity to live in, confessed she would have adored to have lived there during the period when Ava Gardner threw her room's furniture out the window, when Orson Welles was there taking baths in mineral water, when Jayne Mansfield—who Hollywood had invented in order to counter the influence of Marilyn Monroe—showed off her ample breasts during Carnival. The magazines still publish articles about those heady days. Those were scandals that meant something. What do we have today? Nothing. The other day, for instance, an armed man in a crowded subway car forced a woman to remove her clothing so that he could masturbate in front of her

---

* In *Gazeta Mercantil*. Unfortunately, it was dark when I clipped out the article, so I accidentally eliminated the date.

and everyone else. And nobody lifted a finger. Well, nobody wants to be shot. But the point is that nobody was particularly scandalized by witnessing this scene. They looked at the naked girl, at the guy with his dick sticking out, as though it were part of everyday life—as indeed it was.

I bring a flower and a glass of Perrier to the table. Even when eating alone, a civilized person must surround himself with the emblems of good taste, must retain a sense of style, of elegance, even when eating gooey puddings dripping with condensed milk in the middle of the afternoon. I am a sophisticate.

LOSING A FORTUNE ON THE PONIES

"You know how it is: You're young, you're drunk, you're in bed, you have knives; shit happens!" *Proposed Stratagem #1*: Go to the Jockey Club at the end of the afternoon, get close to the reporters on the horseracing beat, ask for tips, talk about breeding, betting. Go by the ticket windows, collect the receipts thrown away by the losers. Get handfuls, stuff them in your pockets. Position yourself so the press sees you. At the end of each race, look furious and tear up some of your stock of old tickets. Sit down, discouraged. Soon the news will spread that I'm addicted, that I'm losing a fortune on the ponies.

Gamblers are exciting. People like reading about them. Pauline Kael, in *Raising Kane*, devotes a lot of attention to Herman J. Mankiewicz, brother of Joseph (I forgot: I promised you we'd get back to old Joe), who co-wrote *Citizen Kane* with Orson Welles and was a terrible drunk and gambler—one of the most celebrated screenwriters of the '30s, top of the class.

Dorothy Parker also drank a lot. Vices go a long way towards helping a person become legendary. Defects, errors, peccadilloes.

Some great alcoholics on my list: Richard Burton, Ernest Hemingway. And then there's William Faulkner who said, "When I have one martini, I feel bigger, wiser, taller. When I have the second, I feel superlative. When I have more, there's no holding me." Here's a recipe: short glass, eight parts gin, two of dry white vermouth, a green olive on a toothpick, a zest of lime. "Zest"? A zest is a hint. Use a light touch. Extremely light.

On a related note—*Proposed Stratagem #2*: Go to hotels, open the mini-bottles from the mini-bar, empty everything into the toilet, and throw the empty bottles all over the place. Open beer bottles, throw the contents into the sink. Scatter the bottles all over the floor, in the bathroom, under the bed, inside the closet, as though

I had hidden them. (Once, I actually hung a bottle of scotch out my window on some rope, a trick I learned from Ray Milland in *The Lost Weekend*—directed by Billy Wilder, 1945). Bring an extra suitcase when checking in, filled with mostly empty bottles of scotch, cognac, gin, vodka, rum, grappa, tequila, moonshine, so as to be able to make it look and smell as though I've had a binge. Put bottles inside the basin of the toilet in the bathroom. Scatter cigarette ashes on the bed and carpet (collect used butts from the ashtrays on other floors).

I've discovered that yogurt thrown on bedsheets can pass in a pinch for semen. Stain the bedspreads, pillowcases, leave condoms everywhere. Who's going to double check? (Though, to tell the truth, there was this one time I came back to my room because I'd forgotten something and found the cleaning lady licking out the inside of one of these "used" condoms.) I've gotten complaints from the hotel managers, telling me to behave, but they all still make sure to sell the story of my lost weekends to the highest bidder. I couldn't be happier with the arrangement, personally. And now I'm considered some kind of superman: a one-man orgy, always drinking, fucking, shooting up. I've even found that some of the hotels I've sullied in this manner have begun charging higher rates for the rooms where I've done the most damage. Though they still won't give me a piece of the action, the sons of bitches. You're young, you're drunk, you're in bed, you have knives . . . I cause a sensation in the studio when I show up in the morning (late) with swollen, red eyes, a stuffy nose, cottonmouth, and yet still garrulous, brilliant, witty. You know how it is: shit happens!

THE GREATEST STARS OF THE CENTURY

The new century's barely begun and the newspapers and maga-zines are already featuring retrospective coverage of the last. We love to look back. To compare, to pretend we were happy, that times were good. Here's a piece on the "Hundred Greatest Stars of the Twentieth Century" in a French magazine. Their opening text is quite the oration:

Stars! The word is magical. It opens the doors of our dreams.

Let's face it: Stars have become commonplace—there are so many of them, and more every day! It doesn't take much to get your pic-ture in the papers! But this doesn't prevent the real stars, the true immortals, from shining the brightest: All the fashion models in the world can't muddy the pool so much that real star-power won't show through!

Remember: Stars aren't stars because they're beautiful or charm-ing. Stars exist to tell us stories—stories about the lives we could have lived, about the lives we were too afraid to live, about lives that can never be lived.

Stars are the embodiment of our dreams. Stars light up the night.

And their light will continue to shine even after the source has long since died out. What I want most is to appear in the *Greatest Stars* supplement that they'll put out in a few years.

I suppose you've read all those articles, essays, and books that tell us how fame doesn't make you happy, how there's always so much pain behind the smiles of our idols, such bitterness, such suffering. What bullshit. The people who write that nonsense have never been famous themselves. They don't know what they're talk-ing about. Celebrity is a permanent anesthesia, elation, joy. Like being high all day and all night. Like levitating. I leaf through the pages of my magazine. (They're all greasy from my fingering them so often.) And, guess what? There's no pain to be seen in the faces of Arletty, Gary Cooper, Dustin Hoffman, Greta Garbo, Jodie Foster, Marlene Dietrich, Fred Astaire (wearing black socks covered with tiny stars; being a star means never having to make excuses for following your every whim), Montgomery Clift, Frank Sinatra, Audrey Hepburn, Marcello Mastroianni, Clark Gable, Robert De Niro, Lauren Bacall, Erich von Stroheim, Leonardo DiCaprio, Kirk Douglas, Louise Brooks, Mel Gibson, Warren Beatty, Laurel and Hardy, Jean-Paul Belmondo, Jean Gabin, Gerard Depardieu, Isabelle Adjani, Al Pacino, Alain Delon, Steve McQueen, Brad Pitt, Jack Nicholson, Sean Connery, Gerard Philipe, Bruce Lee, Marlon Brando, Sharon Stone, etc., etc.

It's unbearable to have been left out of this list.

WEEKENDS PERFECTLY STAGED

I'm intrigued with a question that I find has been inadequately treated in serious celebrity scholarship to date. Namely, how do the famous spend their weekends? And here I'm not referring to weekends spent posing for photographers, doing publicity, etc. I mean the time off, the real weekends, assuming they actually exist. Assuming anything really exists for a celebrity. (At what point, starting from the moment that their lives are first exposed to constant media attention, does reality disappear entirely for them, replaced by the virtual (a very fashionable word right now)? Do stars ever have days that haven't been stage-managed by their PR team? Don't audiences ever get tired of reading about their idols, get tired of spying on their most intimate moments? Is the public completely insatiable?)

(Reconsider the word "consultant." I got it from a hip vocabulary list a few years back. Nowadays, people seem to prefer "guru." Is that a euphemism? Calling everything a euphemism is also very in, right now. "Guru" seems to me the more elegant term, though it smacks a little of the '60s. The Beatles, for instance, had a guru, correct? Yes, say guru, not consultant. My Aesthetics Guru, my Vocational Guru, my Cultural Guru, My Dancing Guru, my Vocabulary Guru, my Brand-Name Guru, my Guru in Charge of Places I Must Be Seen At.)

Of course, to be able to appreciate a celebrity's "normal" weekend, I'd have to know something about what a normal weekend is supposed to be like.

And yet, wasn't it Caetano Veloso who sang: "Up-close, nobody is normal"? Banal actions like waking up, stretching, brushing one's teeth, taking a bath, having breakfast (what's the breakfast of a celebrity like? organized by a guru so that you can keep your mind and body in the proper shape?), exercising, reading the papers, going out with one's family. Do celebrities go to the mall, shop for a pair of shoes or a t-shirt, go to a stationary store to buy a notebook for their children, drop their car off at a garage to have it repaired? Do they have hobbies? Cabinetmaking, photography, painting, mosaic-making, keeping a journal, scrapbooking, wasting time online, making model ships, cataloguing their stamp collections?

What do they do, unobserved, that might reveal their commonness to us? Their basic humanity, their fears, their joys?

I have a book called *Hollywood at Home: A Family Album, 1950–1965*. Photos by Sid Avery and text by Richard Schickel. It shows Humphrey Bogart and Lauren Bacall in their living room, playing with their son. Ernest Borgnine and his wife Rhoda—a fat woman reading the newspaper with her daughter on her lap. The singer Frankie Laine driving a Cadillac and saying goodbye to his family as he leaves for work. Early morning. The sun lightly illuminates the front of the house and the prosaic white picket fence of the garden. And then Paul Newman and Joanne Woodward in the kitchen of their home, her hugging the dog and he making eggs (scrambled?). Dozens of superstars frozen forever in intricately posed intimacy. My questions remain unanswered.

I've already decided how the photo shoot they'll do about my intimate home life will look. I'll need to rent some furniture, as well as special carpets, lighting, bric-a-brac. The captions will explain where to buy said items, and how much our readers ought to expect to pay. As though my house and its contents were a showroom. After the photo shoot, everything will be returned, though some of us might end up keeping a piece here and a piece there, as payment for the free advertising we're giving the stores and manufacturers.

It's a closed circle—industry and the media and celebrities (and their consultants—or gurus) helping each other out. Like the mafia. If food is served, the restaurant catering the shoot is promoted. Everybody gets their palms greased and everybody is satisfied. Unless the celebrity in question is still only aspiring to real stardom. Like one of those desperate anonymous people who the press ironically designates as "almost famous." The kind who do everything in their power to get on a reality television show to make sure they aren't forgotten. I take another look at the photos (tiny—poor guy) of the singer who recently was eliminated from one of these shows—he managed to parade with fourteen separate samba schools during Carnival this year. He hoped to get into the *Guinness Book of World Records*, to be photographed, applauded (the public had no idea who he was), to make himself believe that he really existed. It didn't work. People just made fun of him.

He killed himself on the runway of the Samba Stadium on the night of the grand victory parade of all the year's champion samba schools. This was kept secret, however, so as not to spoil the festivities—he wasn't allowed to be famous even in death.

SAINT JOAN, SAINT JEAN

I was born to be in *Breathless* (*A bout de souffle*), by Godard, 1960, which by the way recently came out in a lovely new edition on DVD. (God, I hated VHS. No depth, no sharpness, no emotion.) I've collected a ton of postcards, magazines, posters, and books all about this one movie. My dream, my one great dream, can never, I fear, come true: to play opposite Jean Seberg. Now *there* was someone who knew how to turn herself into a legend. Otto Preminger picked her from thousands to star in his *Saint Joan* (1957). And then, even when the critics panned her, he put her in his *Bonjour Tristesse* the following year. She had everything in those days—the entire Hollywood publicity machine supporting her. Nevertheless, it was a very modest French film in black and white that immortalized her, not some big American movie in CinemaScope and Technicolor. That's how destiny works. Things that are apparently unimportant become paramount, primary. Celebrities must expect the unexpected: We have to hope (pray!) that it happens to us the same way, that some minor project we condescend to participate in ends up propelling us into the stratosphere . . .

It's too bad, really, that legends like Seberg can't be around to see how they've become icons, how they've taken root in the soul of the culture. I think this would make them feel a little better about themselves, since the majority of them died under less than ideal circumstances. Seberg killed herself in a Parisian suburb. She was found in her car.

And then, another dream of mine: to be like that obstinate lawyer Gregory Peck played in *To Kill a Mockingbird* (Robert Mulligan, 1962). An idealist who believes in a cause. At the end of the film, as he leaves the court room, defeated by intolerance, by prejudice and racism, the old black reverend says to Finch's daughter, "Stand up, your father's passing." Will anyone ever have that much respect for me? Will they ever be able to say that I was a decent, upright man? Mulligan, the director, always had a preference for solitary characters. Only pure obstinacy can keep a man on his feet.

MODERNITY

"You and I are about to commune with the cosmos."

The woman has a nice face, dresses in clothes that seem simple but are made of pure silk, and wears a necklace with a bluish pendant.

"First, let's clear our minds."

She closes her eyes. I close mine too, wondering what the hell I'm doing here. "Concentrate. I see that your moon is in the ninth house. Touch those stones on the table. Without moving them."

I touch them. Cold stones. Like they just came out of the freezer.

"Bend your head to the right. Do you feel a tense spot on on your neck?"

No.

"You should. You're tense. The vibrations being emitted by your right side are making me dizzy."

She seems disappointed. I'll lie to her. Why on earth do I feel the need to please her?

"Wait," I say. "You're right . . . there's a small pain . . . no, it's getting worse."

"Contact your good spirits, be in harmony with your divinity."

Silence. I look at the blue walls, totally bare. Bare, steady, normal lighting. I think of an optometrist's office.

"You need to concentrate more on the spirit-goddess Oxum . . . I can see that you'll be applauded for something . . . you have a great work yet to complete on earth . . . but you are too indecisive . . . do you have a pet? You need to hug it more often . . . prepare yourself for stomach problems . . . Now let's look at the cards . . . this one symbolizes temperance, calmness, and tolerance . . . this one represents your rising sign . . . very good, this pattern never occurs at random, it is a sign, a clear sign . . . there's a tree heavy with fruit

deep in your mind . . . you've been blessed with intense creativity
. . . I see you working in advertising . . . no, perhaps a director for
the stage . . . more than that . . . television . . . or a painter . . . a
furniture designer . . . a promoter . . . a designer of cars . . . a florist
. . . the fruits are succulent and sweet . . . you're an actor . . . I see
now . . . more than that . . . it's a tree full of life and it always bares
fruit . . . relax, learn to breathe . . . meditate . . . calm yourself . . .
success is about to come to you . . . protect it . . . don't abandon the
sacred . . ."

A FLEETING MOMENT OF SINCERITY

I'm going to be sincere for a moment. Many times, thinking about Letícia—which I do all the time—I amaze myself by feeling so much tenderness. It's inconceivable, unreal. How did this happen? This love? Did I invent it? Is Letícia a hallucination of mine? Can hallucinations really hurt this much? Can they really cause so much joy?

This is sincerity.

I'm a man without any talent, marked for success, brilliance, fame. Life owes me for what I've suffered, for what I was forced to live through. I'm not explaining anything—it would be trite, like the clichés that get recycled every afternoon on the soaps, the one written especially for maids and less-than-hip housewives (that is, after they get back from their pottery classes, their aerobic workouts, their self-esteem courses). Let's be very clear, these programs aren't exactly made for geniuses. That's what a producer told me.

What I can do—all I can do—is come off looking good on talk shows. I am easily the equal of any host. I would say brilliant things to Letterman, to Leno, in fluent English, in whatever accent they want. I could make them listen to me, agree with me. I could speak for hours on morning talk-radio shows, keeping the audience interested despite the innumerable interruptions from the news office about traffic, the weather, violence, the stock market, current events, new art exhibitions, lectures, movies, household tips (how to repair your keychain, how to change your watch battery), and cake recipes.

And all this because I have nothing to say. I'm empty, hollow. A receptacle for trivia.

In other words, a man perfectly equipped to live in the modern day.

I know nothing worthwhile about life. I say little. I have difficulty expressing my feelings. I don't understand anything about politics, economics, sociology, behavior, style, extreme sports, music. I don't know the difference between pop, techno, funk, or rap. You probably guessed.

I'm only human. I wouldn't have the courage to take one of those monumental blondes—sculpted by weightlifting, molded by silicone: perfect statues, masterpieces that Rodin would sign, or Camille Claudel, or Bruno Giorgi—to bed. Who would?

Art in its various forms and inclinations has been given many names over the years: renaissance, classical, baroque, surrealist, expressionist, Dadaist, impressionist, op, kinetic, pop, hyper-realist, futurist, cubist, abstract, conceptual, performative, postmodern. Will the art of altering skin itself, the art of creating perfect bodies, combining flesh and bone and plastic and silicone, get a name? Will it too have its geniuses?

It's a structuralist kind of art, and yet it deconstructs what it's practiced on. "Blondsurgiplast" art? I'm no good at this. Is there a secret to making up catchy neologisms? I feel discomfortable, follied, soberish. No? I invoke the writer Guimarães Rosa. The poet Paulo Leminski. The fashion columnists who decide what to call each new style they spot being used at the clubs. I'd love to be taken into the language, to be cited by dictionaries, like them.

Well, everybody has his ambitions.

Anyway. I'm sorry not to know more about music. I actually care about music. I can listen to it, even if I don't understand it.

But they won't let me. I can only listen to what's chic.

I wish I knew if I had good taste.

ALWAYS KEEP YOURSELF "PLUGGED IN"

There are certain words that have been used to excess and are now virtually meaningless, Outmoded terms, as one says in the industry. A partial list, as of today: Fragmented, state-of-the-art, cultural imperialism, fabula, intertextual, cyberspace, globalization, multimedia, multicultural, neo-liberal, neo-conservative, connotation, hacker, efficient, self-esteem, acoustic, to read, outmoded.

Attitude, attitude, attitude.

Drink champagne at eleven in the morning, having the sun as your only witness. Or the rain.

A flute makes us happy *pour commencer le jour*.

Take up gymnastics. Exercise. Weight training. Doesn't matter if you look good so long as you can claim you're in training.

More vegetables and fruits and fewer cheeses and wines.

Get skin treatments. Russian-style massages to firm up the face and body. Pore cleansing.

Locate some safe bike paths for cycling (muggers haunt every corner). Call Weight Watchers. Invest in state-of-the-art technology to combat hair loss. And then full-body exfoliation to remove dead cells.

Also: capillary treatments to combat greasy hair and dandruff. Add softness and shine with nutritional rinses. Physiotherapy. Sessions with an osteopath to relocate vertebrae. Yoga, Tai-chi and ballet to strengthen and stretch one's muscles.

Remember: used cars (even forty-year-old models) are now referred to as "semi-new."

HATRED IS EXCITING

In *Gilda* (Charles Vidor, 1946), Ballin Mundson (George Macready), owner of the casino, notices that there's something between his wife (Rita Hayworth) and Johnny Farrell (Glenn Ford), his right-hand man—a gambler he met on the streets of Buenos Aires and hired immediately, sensing that he was astute, ambitious, and immoral. In bed, after dinner at the casino, distrustful, filled with suspicion, Mundson interrogates Gilda about Farrell. She confesses:

"I hate him!"

"And he hates you," Mundson says. "That's very apparent. But hate can be a very exciting emotion. Very exciting. Haven't you noticed that? . . . There is a heat in it that one can feel. Didn't you feel it tonight?

"No."

"I did. It warmed me. Hate is the only thing that has ever warmed me."

I've seen this film dozens of times. Nothing is explained—it's a peculiar movie. There's something between the two main characters, something indefinable that excites me, that excites the audience. We learn by watching *Gilda* that the characters we don't understand are far more fascinating than the ones we do—far more interesting than people we can relate to. We want to get closer to them.

I hate the love letters I've kept. I read and reread them. That's the last thing one should do with love letters. They need to be put away or burned forever. They hurt too much. They hurt even when we are the ones who said, It's over.

Why did I say that? Why?

What if Letícia's hatred begins to excite her?

THE TERMINAL ILLNESS THAT CONSUMES ME

I lose my strength day by day. A time will come when I will be exhausted, debilitated, nerves and muscles flaccid, neurons rotted, desires deadened.

No, I don't have AIDS. I don't take drugs. I'm not an alcoholic. I don't smoke anything. I don't stuff myself with antidepressants or diet pills. I'm clean. ("Clean" is old slang. What does one say nowadays?)

Letícia came to hate how controlled I was. She used to provoke me:

> *Yell, jump, swear, explode—say something, for God's sake!*
> *Insult me, offend me, deny me, contradict me, curse me!*
> *Kick down the doors, bang on walls, break my plates, smash some windows!*
> *You never get angry! Never react!*
> *So fucking responsible! Your goddamn invulnerable responsibility!*
> *But what about your responsibility to me?*
> *We're wasting the most rare and precious thing in the world!*
> *Where's your loyalty to love?*
> *How about some simple respect for my affections?*
> *Just once, why not do something unexpected?*
> *Surprise me, scare me, leave me thunderstruck, incredulous, bewildered, paralyzed! Frightened! Scare the shit out of me!*
> *God, I'd love to see you blow up. I'd give my life for it. I'd die happy knowing that you're human, that you suffer, cry, agonize, hurt, like me!*
> *Go on. Try and get on my nerves. Liberate yourself from your dignity a little.*
> *Cast off your chains. Dig yourself out of your little hole.*

And to think I've been so proud of being unique. Not like the others. Not having AIDS, not being a junkie, a drunk, dishonest, a son of a bitch, the kind of star who shits on everyone, a monster. I was wrong. Being so responsible, so restrained, so dignified—it's killing me, eating away at me. It's like a pair of pliers tearing out my fingernails, like acid melting the flesh off my bones.

Oh, how it hurts not to be dying from anything. I didn't realize there were worse things. Another sickness, more insidious, corrosive, and fatal, found its way inside me while I was busy looking out for the better-known diseases. I'm wasting away. I've been infected. By a plague. A plague called normality.

My mouth is weak, my teeth are loose, my hair is thinning, my eyes are burning—light bothers me, and I have to wear dark glasses all the time.

I'm imprisoned by duty.

Jailed by my commitments.

Hopelessly constrained by my obligations.

Incapable of the least infraction. Even against myself.

I was born to transgress, and yet transgression terrifies me, chokes me. I can't stand this. I can't move in any direction.

What am I gong to do about it?

Nothing, Letícia said. And she was right.

ALWAYS KEEP YOURSELF "PLUGGED IN"

More "in" words to get the hang of: recycled, colon reflorestation, interface.

Fashion: Start using strips of ribbon in your hair.

Organic bed linen, packed in recycled cardboard boxes.

Geisha is the latest perfume used by movie stars. This fragrance is a mixture of woods and teas, and the packaging is made of rice paper.

Rustic radiance.

Geometric patterns.

Art nouveau, op art.

Fried bean cakes: a new craze.

Chet Baker.

Phrase of the week. *Brazil is an exotic olive in the salad of international politics.*

Chiffon is back.

Also full skirts and pantaloons.

Pigtails.

Gold corncob braids, as created by Júnia Machado for that store Uga Uga in Rio de Janeiro. $500. Very in demand.

Also: Sneakers without shoelaces.

Polo shirts for men with a zipper instead of buttons. Snakeskin jeans for the teens.

Apparently they are working on a central computer that will run all your appliances for you. As easy to use as a frying pan.

THE MERCHANDISE AT MY FUNERAL

Unlikely as it sounds, I'm attending my own funeral. Contemplating my own coffin being carried with all due ceremony to the pink and black marble mausoleum (really, it's in extremely bad taste). The monument, by the way, was provided free of charge in exchange for a bunch of thirty-second commercials for the funeral home that commissioned it. Besides the free advertising they get because of the reruns: For three days and nights the greatest event in the sixty-year-old history of Brazilian television history will play over and again: the funeral of its most celebrated star. It happened months ago. Or was it weeks? Yesterday? Regardless, I've been virtually cataleptic since that day. LA managed to win after all: barring my way, putting an end to my future career, my dreams, my fame. If I'd only had enough time to make the substitution, he would still be alive—that is, while dead, his life would now be occupied by yours truly. But Lenira betrayed me. She'd been toying with me. The cunt rushed out the news of his death so that I wouldn't have a chance to make the switch. Lenira might as well have announced two deaths at the same time: LA's from an overdose (according to the press), and then mine by murder: to have condemned me to the shadows, to anonymity, is to kill me. The dream is over, they used to say in the '60s. And the '70s, '80s, '90s. And in '01. Well, there's always a dream dying somewhere, every decade, every year. There's LA in his casket. *Casket* is a nauseating word. We're in there together, really. When he died, he took me with him. No murder was necessary. By dying, he stopped me from being. That motherfucker. The ratings for his funeral will be massive. Death in life and resurrection on the screen. Though it's a cold afterlife: the screen cancels emotion, dissolves feeling. It's as cold as neon light.

The ceremony is imposing. Just for show. The public has to like it. They have to find it sufficiently moving, sufficiently monumental.

The masses have always been fascinated with death-rituals. Pyramids, pyres. Death must be appeased. Let's put on a show to send the Grim Reaper away. I tell you what, I'll write a *Manual for Dead Celebrities*. I've attended my own funeral, after all. I've got the inside information. No man in history has ever had this experience, had this opportunity. The cortege, the coffin, and now Lavinia, my ex-wife, the first one. What's she doing here? Did she find out about my double-work, about my plan? She's shaking her head as though warding off a cloud of bugs. I see girlfriends, many of them incidental. Over there is the woman I fucked behind the scenery of the Brazilian version of *Gone with the Wind*—the most ridiculous soap-opera we've ever produced (and yet an enormous success—they set it during the Paulista revolution of 1932). I became famous for fucking starlets behind the scenery on unused sets. Or in back of the cyclorama on Studio 9, watching the gigantic images unfold around us. There's a scene I really like in *Henry and June* (directed by the same guy who did *The Unbearable Lightness of Being*. What's his name again? My memory is dissolving. And what else have I got left, really?), when Henry fucks (Letícia hated that word) Anaïs Nin behind a screen in a nightclub with a band playing Latin music (it sounds very much like the recording of "Cumbanchero" with Ruben Gonzáles at the piano—Europe in the '30s was crazy for tangos and rumbas). And there's another starlet (an old word) who used to adore sucking my cock while she was learning her lines. And again, over there is the little dark-skinned girl who gave me her ass in the bus station while we were waiting for the bus to Aclimação, really excited because we were being watched by dozens of motorists as they drove by. Some of these women I really cared about. Did I mean anything to them, or did they just want to be seen with me—with LA, that is—to gain some press?

And then what about the stars—many of them married—who fell in love with me when we worked together? And what about

Letícia, the only one of these women who really loved me, the only one who made me feel at ease, who had anything to say to me? Why didn't I trust her? What inexplicable barrier led me to doubt her? Whatever it was, it's my fault: it was something inside me that wanted to sabotage our connection. Close-up. I think for a moment about all the tears shed through the years by that bitch who the world considered to be my real wife—and who I never touched. I couldn't. Lavinia. She's in a wheelchair, being pushed by some studio lackeys. And Lenira, of course, in full mourning— black veil and chapeau, taken from the wardrobe department. She's recreating the image of the unknown woman who brought flowers to the grave of Rudolf Valentino for years following his death. What a hypocrite—Lenira, I mean. She's just posing for the photographers. Her gestures are all just so—movie gestures, copied from gossipy movie magazines (old American ones like *Photoplay* and *Modern Screen*). Yes, here's the beautiful Dr. Lenira, author of that famous dissertation on anonymity—the most original and remarked-upon thesis ever to be approved at Dartmouth: an intriguing, almost romantic study—she got her degree *summa cum laude*—which generated seminar and lecture invitations both at home and abroad, as well as opening the doors to awards from Fulbright, Gulbenkian, DAAD, Guggenheim, Ford, and then the *Conselho Nacional de Desenvolvimento Científico e Tecnológico* fellowships (though the last one, a Brazilian award, never actually got paid out—what a surprise). Clap, clap, clap, clap, clap, clap, clap, clap. Moderate applause.

Thousands of flowers. Wreaths carried by uniformed pallbearers. An impeccable production, all in all. (And, on TV, the never-ending monotony of close-ups or photographs of those who couldn't attend but sent flowers, merging with close-ups of the people walking behind the cortege—celeb and non-celeb both. There are enormous publicity wreaths from businesses on the verge of collapse, even from stars who've been dead for years. I know the tapes by heart, I know each image. I review them over and over again here, now, in Room 101. How much longer will they let me use this space, I wonder? Will I be thrown out?)

At the reception, I took note of a name that was floating around, a name as yet unknown to the public: Elesandro. He was some jittery motorbike boy who used to make runs to the bank to cash the actors' and producers' paychecks. He even used to know trustworthy moneychangers who could give them good rates on dollars (during the time when dollars were a worthwhile investment, that is), and he would serve as a go-between for studio people who wanted to make bets on dog races or play numbers (the guards wouldn't let bookies inside the studio); he struck up friendships with drug dealers so he could bring coke, crack, heroin, and ecstasy back to the set, not to mention hiding bottles of whisky around for those with more pedestrian tastes, and arranged rendezvous between rising starlets and men who could help with their careers. He'd lie or tell the truth to reporters, as necessary, and even went so far as to do simple grocery shopping for some of the stars. He was just some greasy kid with a knack for pleasing the powerful. But then, things changed. His big break came when he was given the job of spinning the wheel of fortune on a game show when the regular spinner was out sick. What a clever little man: he made his time in the spotlight count. The audience liked him. Clap, clap, clap. The host had to ask him back the following week because he was so popular. Today, nine years later, he's had liposuction, affects an asexuality pose, has changed his name to Alex, and stars in two separate television shows, has a radio show and a chain of stores named after him, and runs a toy company, a candy company, and has his own brand of jeans. He knows all the tricks. He bought a wreath for my (his) funeral. Immense: typical of a megalomaniac. Envied for his cleverness, his ability to make things turn out his way. He is everything I admire: Uninhibited, remorseless, conscienceless, wholly unethical. A man with the perfect qualities for our day and age. God how I envy him. He has hundreds of fan clubs. The faces of his admirers would make perfect subjects for a sequel to Lenira's dissertation on the identity of the anonymous. I mean, the non-identity of the anonymous.

Traditional bands are playing funereal marches alternating with joyous and noisy pop music. The brass band from the school I attended (he attended) marches past, and then a horde of middle-age women (he/I was adored by them), representatives from various charitable and business organizations (the ones I did commercials for), publicity agents, sportscasters (I endorsed hundreds of brands of sneakers, exercise machines, and antifungal sprays), metallurgists (grateful for my performance of Lula, the fellow metallurgist and union leader who went on to be President of Brazil), and manicurists (Letícia always rubbed her fingers on the soles of my feet and complained: it's gross, you need to have a pedicure, don't worry so much about your hands). Photographers are jumping around like frogs, flashbulbs are popping (a rainy day, just like I always wanted for my funeral), professional and amateur videotapers (what a wonderful home movie!), politicians encroaching amidst protests into the cordoned-off press box. Close-ups of Clarissa, my second wife—of Francine, the third—of Camilla, a brief interlude. I think I have their names right. And close-ups of Lenira, Lenira the inscrutable, who set everything up with me. Really, it's all almost as perfect as the last scene of Douglas Sirk's *Imitation of Life* (1959). (Sirk's last major film. Fassbinder loved Sirk and referenced him all the time in his own work. And, let me tell you, *that* crazy bastard drives me crazy with envy too . . . look how spectacularly he fucked up his life! No one will ever forget Fassbinder.) Lenira and I plotted out the perfect funeral, after all. We analyzed the historic funerals of national and international figures (John Kennedy's being a particular favorite) and made our plans accordingly. I was also thinking of a different film funeral, one from a movie I saw as an adolescent: *Dr. Zhivago* (David Lean, 1965, with Omar Shariff and Julie Christie). On the Russian steppe, in the middle of winter, Zhivago's mother is being buried. When everybody leaves the cemetery, the boy looks back and calls to mind an image of his mother in her coffin, her hands folded as though in prayer.

My/his cortège moves forward through the crowded streets. Stores close their doors in respect, honoring the agreement they made previously with my consultants (who, by the way, never paid up. The shopkeepers complained to the press, but who was going to believe such a ridiculous story?). The masses press themselves up against the ropes keeping them on the sidewalks, away from the procession—extras paid to scream and cry, faint and throw flowers and pieces of clothing. Their behavior was considered outrageous by many commentators. So much for supposedly living in permissive times. Still, the real outrage—according to some hostile newspapers—comes when the women begin to take off their panties in the middle of the street, throwing them on top of the coffin as it passes by them, attended by soldiers in formal dress. On the one-month anniversary of the funeral, a beautiful photograph graces the cover of one of our weekly magazines: It shows a translucent pair of panties, stained with lipstick, hovering in the air above the casket like a bird looking for a place to land. One soldier claimed with absolute assurance that the bird in question fell right over my dead heart—though a competing magazine preferred to think that my cock was the intended target. The panty-throwers had been hired, of course—they brought extra pairs in their purses. (The production crew made some money on the side by collecting the scattered panties and selling them later.) But legitimate, spontaneous panty-throwers soon followed suit, flashing the crowd, whether out of fun, nastiness, or sheer emotion, the trajectory of the cortège became littered with panties—which will be traded on the black market between fetishists and necrophiles for years to come. (Funerals have their charming sides: there are little comedies going on all the time. A man like myself ought to be satisfied that his send-off will be remembered as a festival of humor, delirium, and sadness. Naturally I'd prepared a list of songs to be played and sung on the occasion, which helped avoid confusion by encouraging people to feel the correct things at the correct times. In fact, the entire funeral was stage-managed, blocked out, and decided in advance: the only sincerity came from the audience.)

By killing him, I annihilated myself. That's right. Did you believe the overdose story? No, it was I. It's hard to admit that I ruined my own plan. I never did figure out how to hide the body in time.

I can still see LA's baffled look when I began to shoot. Six bullets. It was Lenira who gave me the gun. "You don't have the nerve!" she'd said. I didn't miss—not even once—despite never having fired a gun before. All six bullets struck home. I blame the movies.

It's really not so difficult to kill someone when you've cultivated so much hatred for them over so long a time, when you've been fantasizing about putting them in the ground for as long as you can remember. But why did LA come down to this remote, isolated corner of the studio—this barren island in the ocean that is television? Just to pester me, as he liked to do? To say, if not in so many words, "I exist—I'm me. And you? You're nothing. You'll never be anything. Not while I'm alive." And yet, he knew I wanted to kill him. Lenira, the traitor, had warned him, and he came anyway. Why? Did he want to die? He must have. Was he sick, tired, depressed, disillusioned? He was calm. He knew what was going to happen. He was in decline, after all—I read it in the tabloids.

He made fun of me, deliberately insulted me, because he knew it would be the end of us both. "Do you want my place? Take it! It's yours! What are you waiting for? Reach out and grab it!"

Now he's in that coffin.

I know what it means.

I'm diving into emptiness, into the deep blue ocean, into the endless abyss.

I'm a man who isn't.

Two dead. And yet only one is a celebrity.

The other is anonymous. A non-celeb.

Me.

RESCUING THE ANONYMOUS:
THAT SEXY LADY IN THE MOVIE THEATER

One Thursday, I went to the monumental Piratininga movie theater to see a double feature. They were showing This Gun for Hire *(directed by Frank Tuttle, 1942, based on a novel by Graham Greene) with Alan Ladd and Veronica Lake, and* Rumba Caliente, *directed by Gilberto Martinez Solares, a Mexican director who seems to have been left out of my dictionary of filmmakers, which I keep here in my dressing room. The shows were sparsely attended. It was a dry, hot night—people wanted beer, not Veronica Lake. I was going to turn sixteen the next day, already sick to death of hearing my father ask, And what exactly are you going to do with your life? When's the last time you did any studying? Have you found a job? All you do is go to the movies. Every night. You eat and drink movies. I'm not going to pay your way forever. And it's true, I was scared, I didn't know what I was going to do with myself, sitting there waiting for the gong to strike and the curtain to open, the usual routine before the projector started up. (A ritual. And they went through it every time, no matter how empty the theater was.) I used to sit in a different place in the orchestra seats every night; I wanted to see if a different vantage point affected one's opinion of the movie. (This was a hypothesis I planned to develop in the future.) I also used to pick my seat based on the proximity of unaccompanied women, waiting for them to cross their legs, waiting to see a bit of their thighs or maybe a nice, smooth knee. Smooth unblemished knees just drive me crazy. And if the place was nearly empty, as it was on the night in question, and the usher was outside, smoking or feeling up the ticket lady, a real slut, I'd go sit near some of the older women and whip out my dick. I'm an exhibitionist, remember: putting myself on display is a pleasure I've had since infancy: my beaming mother used to grab my penis and tell me: Son, by showing this thing off, you're going to make a lot of people very happy. In the movie theater, when I flashed them, some women would get furious, would stand up and rush out—but not one of them ever reported me, which led me to the conclusion that they must have liked it. I'd just made them nervous. (At the time, however—and it wasn't really so long ago—if a woman complained about such things, she would be accused of being a whore.) Some of my other victims would just frown and pretend to go on watching the movie, but I caught them sneaking looks at me as often as they thought they could get away with it. And then there were the ones who just smiled and looked straight at me—and then the game would lose its thrill. My dream was to whip out my dick on the Chá Viaduct when I grew up, at Luz Station or in Rio de Janeiro, on Sugar Loaf Mountain, on the beach at Leblon—on the street outside the Bracarense Bar; I don't know why the Bracarense in particular stuck in my head—it was just one of my fantasies, an unrealized dream. Or maybe the Candelária Cathedral would be better. Waiting for the religious ladies to come to early-morning mass. (Are those women still out there?) But on this night, the night of rumbas and Veronica Lake, there was a woman in the center aisle, around twenty-eight, or thirty-two, or forty years old (what did I know about age?). She was a brunette, with big breasts, and was cooling herself with a fan while her mouth hung open, like a breathless athlete's. I sat near her, trying to come off as innocent, my eyes on the screen. (I had an angelic face, I'm told.) Her fan sent breaths of air my way scented with the perfume called* Tabu—*very popular at the time. For some reason, I didn't undo my fly. Slowly, very slowly, I moved my left leg until it was pressing against her hot thigh. I can still feel the heat of it. I waited for her reaction. She was silent, panting. The movements of her fan revealed her anxiety; as they accelerated, her perfume enveloped me. Tiny drops of perspiration appeared on her forehead; they dripped down past her eyelids, ran down her cheeks. From time to time, she'd close her eyes, sigh, wipe the sweat off with a handkerchief* she'd been keeping crushed in her hand. I went on pushing my leg into hers. Besides the perfume, there was also the smell of floor wax coming off the wooden, worm-eaten planks beneath us, and the must of old cigarette smoke hanging in the humid air—someone was always smoking somewhere—and then traces of the odors of all the people who had ever seen a movie there. I was fascinated, contemplating the miniscule droplets of salt water that blossomed from the woman's skin and covered her forehead, dripping, reflecting back the light of the screen. The film turned bright, going from a night scene to a day scene, and I used this transition as an excuse to abandon all pretense to subtlety, pushing my thigh firmly against hers. Her consent left me paralyzed. I fought desperately against the old feeling (old? I was only sixteen) of disappointment that always made me lose interest when I saw that a woman wasn't alarmed at my advances. I pressed even harder, and found she was pressing back. I leaned my arm against hers—no reaction. Just more fanning. I tried to lean my face over to kiss her, just like Alan Ladd, but she withdrew, giving out a muted snort. Better not to force the situation. I can't say if she was ugly or beautiful—the perspiration on her forehead hypnotized me. Afterwards, I wished I had paid closer attention to her, so I could recognize her later on the street if we ran into each other. After all, I could hardly help but run into her if I canvassed the area, and I wouldn't have minded knowing who she was, if she was married, widowed, single, a student, a railroad employee, a shop girl. I passed my fingers over her hands: I thought I felt a wedding ring, but I couldn't be sure. Her fingers clung to mine, for an instant, excitedly. The film was ending. The last feature of the last show of the evening. I had to be bold. I put my hand on her thigh and squeezed. She immediately uncrossed her legs. I was frightened by her brusque reaction and my mouth went dry. I took out a breath mint and offered her one, but she didn't seem to understand. She wasn't even looking at me. I kept my hand on her. Moved to her *smooth naked knee. Her dress had ridden up a little. Her legs were white and thin. I kept my hand still while Alan Ladd tried to make his getaway. I moved my hand upwards, now, and inside her dress, upwards towards her vagina, yes, that's the word I used in my head, repeating it over and over again, vagina, vagina, vagina, a very sexy word, full of promise. My hand reached the magical intersection and I felt her pubic hair through her coarse cotton panties. (This was before synthetics or silk or thongs, mind you.) Inexperienced, I searched with my fingers until I found what might plausibly be the spot. I knew there was a spot, but that's all I knew. I knew I had to be careful not to pull her hair or hurt her: she would get up and leave. I slowed down and noticed that, with an imperceptible movement of her ass, she was trying to make things easier for me. I stuck my index finger between her skin and the seam of her wet panties and pressed on. I encountered what felt like a sticky puddle, and it disgusted me at first. Nobody ever told me how these things worked—I wondered if she'd pissed on herself. Her fan was moving slowly again now, and as it waved back and forth, that wetness began changing into something pleasant, exciting. Sitting back with her legs entirely open now, she adjusted my finger with one of her hands. Then she began to tremble, her fan dropping onto the floor, and she leaned back even further, moaning. I moved my finger faster, smelling the acrid odor that was coming from inside her, and I wanted to tear her panties off, I felt maddened, happy—it was the greatest moment of my life (to date). She raised her legs higher, panting, sucking in air, breathing in the scent of Tabu, the theater, my breath mint, and her cunt. She groaned and I thought she was going to die, but she was smiling, and her eyes were wide, shining in the dark. Then her body jumped, she grabbed my arm, closed her legs, and pointed to her fan. I picked it up and gave it to her, my hand wet on its handle. She felt it when she took the fan from me and smiled again. She had white teeth. I felt like sticking my tongue into them, but she started fanning herself again rapidly.*

Then she stood up and ran out of the theater. I lingered for a little while longer, still happy, not really believing what had just happened. Finally I went after her. The usher was smoking, stretched out on the sofa they kept in the lobby. Which way did she go? He took a slow drag (must have seen too many movies) and looked at me with a dirty little grin. Where'd she go? Who knows! I went outside, but there wasn't anybody on the street. I looked at my hand—it shone, smelling of salt. I stuck my finger in my mouth—I needed to taste it—and I closed my eyes. I went back to that theater many more times, before we moved to another neighborhood, but I never saw that woman again. I still think about her, that anonymous woman who climaxed in my hands, captivating me forever, leaving me with a desperate desire to repeat the experience somehow, with someone. Is she still alive? It's been a few years—not too many, but then not too few. Does she still think about our encounter during This Gun for Hire? Did she like it? Well, of course she did. She must have. She let it happen. But she never even looked at my face. Could it be that I was only one of many strangers who ended up with their hand between her legs at the movies? I wonder who's fucking her right now, now as I reminisce inside my icy dressing room, waiting to be called on set? She could well be a person like me, a lonely and solitary person condemned to hunt for contact in the dark, in the suffocating isolation of those hot nights. Is she married, do you think? I've often thought of her fleeing the theater and running home to her husband, boyfriend, or lover—excited, ready! Does she ever go back to that theater? No, no, they don't show movies there anymore. Now probably it's a church for some cult, now. And if she did go back, would she look for that same seat? Listening to some conman preaching salvation and thinking that real salvation is only to be found in pleasure, in the wetness of her cunt, in her muted moaning? If she's alive, does she ever see me on television? Does she have any idea that the man she's contemplating on the small screen secretly admires, loves, and desires her—as Brazilian women desire me—that he once had his fingers inside her? How would she react if she found out that this man, this star, whom she idolizes (it's only natural), sitting in his dressing room, naked, honors her by fantasizing about the drops of perspiration that adorned her forehead, about having his hand between her legs? I've been looking for a bottle of Tabu *for years. Her perfume would make the scene complete. It's strange to think that, for her, I'm still an anonymous boy who disappeared in the dark of some old movie theater. I'm still that boy who, on the eve of turning sixteen, touched what for her is simply mundane, everyday, but for him became the polestar of his entire life, his steady compass.*

A BLOW TO THE HEART

Please excuse me.

Since I can no longer excuse myself.

There's always something, always some little problem. A little thing, an accident. I know you have nothing to do with it. I'm sorry to complain. But there's always something left hanging. Because you're in a hurry, because you have some previous commitment . . .

Or you name it.

(Pause)

My body is trembling.
I'm trembling.
I've taken a blow to the heart.
I'm so tired of saying, "Stop this nonsense, you're going to fall apart," etc., to myself.
Well, I was right. I fell apart.
It happened. For real.

ENOUGH!

ENOUGH! ENOUGH! ENOUGH! ENOUGH!

ENOUGH! ENOUGH! ENOUGH! ENOUGH! ENOUGH!

ENOUGH! ENOUGH! ENOUGH! ENOUGH! ENOUGH! ENOUGH!

ENOUGH! ENOUGH! ENOUGH! ENOUGH! ENOUGH!

ENOUGH! ENOUGH! ENOUGH! ENOUGH!

ENOUGH! ENOUGH! ENOUGH!

ENOUGH! ENOUGH!

ENOUGH!

(Pause)

I've had it. I've had enough.

I'm frustrated. Full of hatred. For myself. For having put myself at your disposal again.

I took a very long bath. Spread cream all over my body. Perfumed myself all over. Put on my special red panties. Straightened up the house. Spent the day at home, just to wait for you. Sorry, but go fuck yourself. Forget me.

Think about me, about my feelings, just this once, just a little. Think of the frustration, the deception, the pain, the impossibility of this situation. Think of me before calling me, before writing to me. Think of me before you do anything that might bring us back together. Let's end this story! I don't believe in it anymore. I don't believe in your words, your gaze, your love. It's a lie. All lies.

Enough! I implore you, Letícia.

EAT SHIT

It's going to be a painful day. The first of many. My nutritionist, a very caring individual, has been here for a whole week now, consulting books and telephoning departments of biology and entomology at universities. Selecting beetles, ants, larvae, snails, roaches, ladybugs, caterpillars. Doing research. Planning menus. All intended to accustom my palate so that I can adapt, be acclimatized, and not become nauseated at whatever it is I'm going to be asked to eat when I make my appearance on the popular Saturday-night game show *Brazil, You're Going to Have to Eat Me*. I may be able to win up to a million dollars, not to mention all the publicity I'll get. The thing is, it's a talent in itself to swallow what the show hands you, smiling all the while, as though you're really enjoying yourself. The camera zooms in for close-ups to show your face as you chew on roaches, worms, and dung-beetles. Speaking of dung, just as an emergency measure, my nutritionist actually wants to train me to eat human excrement. Then, no matter what they feed me, I'll be more or less in the clear. Game shows that humiliate and torture their contestants have an undeniable attraction. The ratings are through the roof, and advertisers are lining up, fighting each other off, even bribing network execs to try and get themselves some ad-space during *Eat Me*'s timeslot. October 12 is the big day, and it seems like all of Brazil is already preparing: drunks are shitting on street corners in record numbers, and no one is bothering to clean up the mess—São Paulo is more and more disgusting, and people vomit just seeing it. It's wonderful practice: most of us are already experts in eating shit, one way or another. The lines to register for the show stretch for blocks, starting from the ticket window installed at Cathedral Square. Thousands of people want the money. Whoever eats the most shit is going to be famous for a long, long time. Who knows, maybe even world-famous. The problem is, if the winner goes on to have a lucrative acting career—and really, isn't that what's always at stake?—all the other stars are already making public statements refusing to ever play a love-scene with the guy. They'll never kiss him. They'll never allow the winner to put his tongue—the tongue that tasted shit—anywhere near their own. They probably won't even face him, in case his breath still smells of victory.

Le temps d'apprendre à vivre il est déjà trop tard*

---

* "By the time we learn how to live, it's already too late." Louis Aragon, popularized in a song by George Brassens. It comes from Montaigne, originally (in his *Essais*): "They teach us how to live when life is already over." Kundera says more or less the same thing in *The Unbearable Lightness of Being* when he declares that life is a rehearsal.

THE FIRST IMAGINARY AUTOBIOGRAPHY IN THE WORLD

We live in a time of biographies and autobiographies.

In books, films, videos, documentaries. John Updike criticized the genre rather harshly, saying that biographies are too long and serve little purpose. Michael Holroyd, writing in *The Threepenny Review* (I don't know where it's published, somewhere in the States), declared that biographers "exploit our own weaknesses, our prurience, our snobbery. . . . Nor are they proper writers, only journalists . . . who, in the words of Joseph Addison (the founder of the *Spectator* magazine in the early eighteenth century), 'watch for the death of a great man, like so many undertakers, on purpose to make a penny of him . . .' They overlook Marlowe's mighty line, and tell us with immense scholarship and at tedious length what Byron had for breakfast. . . Flaubert was born, Flaubert wrote his novel, Flaubert died. It is his work, which is unique, that matters, not the ordinary experience he shared with so many others."

Bios (bios! abbreviation is always cool!) celebrate the famous: from L. F. Céline, Van Gogh, Nijinsky, Charles Bukowski, Althusser and Zelda Fitzgerald, to Terry Southern (a forgotten genius!), Larry Flint, Nero, Lee Harvey Oswald, Mayakovsky, Dorothy Parker, Ezra Pound, Goya, Camille Claudel, Antonin Artaud, Malcolm Lowry, and Hemingway. From Gene Tierney, Lou Andreas-Salomé, Marilyn Monroe, Al Capone and Peter the Cruel, to Frances Farmer, Ludwig II of Bavaria, and Busby Berkeley.

From Gala, the singer, to Louise Labé and Paulo Leminski. Or to Balzac (ugly, fat, and toothless, yet with so many mistresses!). The book about his house in Passy is so beautiful. I collect books and magazines showing the houses of the rich and famous: it makes me feel better.

Ah, biographies. Thanks to the Soul Watchers! How could anyone hate them? They're wonderful! They bring me books, leaflets, pamphlets, newspapers, and magazines for me to read, copy, take notes on, study, research in the solitude of my dressing room. Because it's been some time now since they've called on me to do any scenes in the Lead Actor's place for the soap opera he never finished. (Even though he's dead, I refuse to say his name. I'll hint at it: MM. So prosaic. M&M, like the candy. How can anyone with a name like his be so famous?)

Since it's only natural that my own biography will need to be written some day, I've decided to do a little planning ahead and collect useful turns of phrase or bits of history to help give some structure to my life. For instance, I'm going to use a quote from Alistair Cooke's *Memories of the Great and the Good* describing General George C. Marshall, which I find suits me wonderfully: "[He was] a man whose inner strength and secret humor only slowly dripped through the surfaces of life, as a stalactite hangs stiff and granity for centuries before one sees beneath it a pool of still water of marvelous purity."

Of all my talents, my greatest has proven to be this: to be self-created, self-creating.

A perfect construction. It's not even necessary to hit my knee with a chisel, shouting: *Speak!* Because I speak!

I created myself through solid thinking (another of my accomplishments: the solidity of my thinking, hard as marble) in order to destroy the prosaic, quotidian life that normal people cultivate, made up as it is by a series of mediocre and trivial instants, of countless banalities—arid, scurrilous, petty. "Scurrilous" is a great word.

Creation and dissipation. "Dissipation" is another good one. A word with many connotations. You can dissipate your health through drugs, orgies, alcoholism—hedonism. Or else, in perfect tranquility and with an untroubled conscience, you can dissipate your talent. Wasteful expenditure.

313

I used these and other words quite often in my imaginary auto-biography (a genre I've invented myself, and which I hope secures me a place in the history of literature).

My trajectory is complete. I've worked it all out in advance. How I'd like to end up. How posterity will come to judge me. An ideal life. Everything in its place. Really, I am a prodigy. Who else could imagine so wonderful a life, down to its finest details?

How I envy myself.

The well-informed, those who read (they're rare), the most cultivated (I'm not saying erudite) of citizens, those who consult real books from time to time, not just magazines like *Vogue*, will know that my bedside reading matter includes such learned articles as "Transgressing the Boundaries: Towards a Transformative Hermeneutics of Quantum Gravity," by Alan D. Sokal, published in 1996 in *Social Text* #46/47. Yes, my real audience will be able to figure out that this piece is the key to my approach.

You needn't bother running out to the library to read my imaginary autobiography. The finished version, ready and edited, stays safe in my mind. I thought about writing it out, but decided this would only sully its perfection. An imaginary autobiography has to be transmitted by telepathy. If somebody were able to mentalize the inside of my mind (surely "mentalize" is a word that will catch on), he or she would be able to access the entire text. No, it's not really a text. It's a series of perfect images. Thoughts aren't sentences, or not always. How do we think? We think in sequences, segments, blocks, flashes. Like video-clips.

I know how to edit my thoughts. Another uncommon talent. In my isolated dressing room, at the end of an endless hallway, I have trained myself to think perfect thoughts—sequences constructed with loving care and then saved, frozen in special compartments of my memory set aside for just this purpose. I stage a scene and then redo and correct it, change details, adjust its contours, colors, details. I bridge gaps, cut together the final print.

And yet, a thought is never really final. It's always incomplete. I just reach a point where I have no more time for research, no more time to tinker. I leave the scene and move on to the next. I am the writer, director, editor, performers, and audience. I am omnipotent, whole, and ideal in my imaginary autobiography.

(*But what about me?* Letícia said, crying. *Where do I fit in?*)

MEASURING THE SPEED OF THOUGHT

To put it another way: I can replay this invented life of mine in the space of a unit of time that can't be measured in any conventional way. Nothing is swifter than thought, and science has yet to develop the equipment necessary to measure such an impossible speed. Space-travel is nothing compared to measuring the speed of thought.

I construct a scene as needed and review every detail. Eventually I select the perfect place for my new scene to fit in with the narrative of my life as a whole. Just as the editor and director decide in an editing room where to insert shots into a film to improve its rhythm.

Thanks to my exceptional memory, every moment, every circumstance, each thing, nuance, and detail have been fixed, have been recorded with the greatest fidelity. Sometimes I remove an element from one scene and pop it into another. As simple as clicking "paste."

Most people can't do this sort of thing. Thought isn't an easy medium to sculpt in. Memories are unstable. They change. They don't hold the shape you put them in. A good imaginary autobiographer has to be comfortable starting from scratch every once and a while if his sculpture begins to fall apart. At least thoughts don't hurt when they collapse on top of you. (Except, of course, when they do.)

This is a new science—there's no body of work describing how it's done. I created it and I'm also the guinea-pig. Like all pioneers, I assume I'm going to suffer from a little misunderstanding, rejection, isolation. Story of my life. But everything that's new causes problems. *My* only problem is that I have nobody to run to with my doubts concerning my invention. Sometimes the speed of a particular scene seems beyond my control, for instance. Why? Or, again, I find that some moments seem to have merged together, becoming confused. Images and facts have dissolved into one another, losing their meanings. And then, is it possible to think one whole thought within the space of another? I managed to do it once, when I had complete quiet. The real challenge would be to think a complete thought inside of an ongoing thought already devoted to thinking about thinking. I can only try.

Another big problem is sequencing. Since thoughts are fluid, there's no way to keep them in order indefinitely: they trickle, slip, float away (they're extremely light: the next step will be to work out a way to determine the weight of individual thoughts). They used to glue pieces of filmstrip together when the editing was done. If you're dealing with solid matter, it's easy. Thoughts, however, are insubstantial. What are they made out of? What shapes do they take? How does one pin them down, make sure they don't move around while your back is turned? Soon as I finish my autobiography, I will devote myself to research. I have a lot of work to do.

Let me be clear: I believe in what I think.

The only truth is the truth of my thinking.

I was created from thought.[*]

Created from what I was and what I want to be.

I think, therefore I am.

Though thoughts dissolve.

---

[*] I found a thin paperback at a newsstand, a pop-philosophy book ripping off Nietzsche pretty shamelessly (make sure I haven't switched the Z and the S again), with a sentence that I've decided to appropriate: "There's always a bit of madness in love. But there's always a bit of reason in madness." I'll rewrite this gem and take credit for it, like so: "There's already a bit of madness in life, but there's always a bit of madness in reason." Much better, don't you think? Perhaps the *Reader's Digest* people will buy it from me. It's been a long time since I've earned any money using my own name.

PRESERVING THOUGHTS AFTER DEATH

No, I didn't write down a single one of my thoughts. I lived inside them, that's enough. Don't think it was easy. Sleepless nights, constant agitation, anxieties, doubts, self-scrutiny. All this suffering to create the perfect modern man, with all the ideal qualities necessary for the lifestyles of today. An enviable biography. Not entirely in my favor, not entirely damning. I'm only human, after all. I didn't hide my faults. I am possessed of the necessary humility to recognize my negative side. I contain both angels and demons. (Nice, no?)

Here's a question, though: Is it possible to extract the raw stuff of another man's thoughts from his mind? I'm thinking of the dead, now. Are thoughts conserved somehow in our brains after we're dead? I think they must be. Don't pretend you've never wondered.

I imagine a kind of cubicle in our minds (careful, "cubicle" is already smelling a little musty) that contains records of all our thoughts—an archive. Something that might outlive us, like our hair.

My hope is that, some day, a scientist comes to me—by chance, of course—and offers to use me as a guinea pig in his experiment. He'll twist some knobs and pull some levers, or maybe just tap some keys, and upload my unique and wonderfully arranged thoughts into his computer (if they can already analyze million-year-old DNA, this procedure ought to be child's play in a few years), where they can live forever.

Am I giving myself away too much?

The researchers, readers, journalists, and other necrophiles of the future are going to have a ball. My mind will be quite the treasure trove for anthropologists of private life and human behavior, and historians of popular entertainment during the first few decades of the twenty-first century.

How marvelous it would be to have one's own thoughts and memories available, easily accessible, like files on a computer. A little digging around and I could find my way to the last day the red digits cast me out of paradise. Or perhaps I could delete that memory once and for all. Why can't I forget? Lenira only let me leave the studio because she knew I would always come back, faithful to our plans. I had her permission to meet Letícia, my salvation. But only for a little while.

This dressing room is my prison.

Where will I go when they fire me? Now that there's no more LA to double?

I believe in each scene of this Autobiography, I'm proud to say. I'm happy with the results. It was an interesting life. As interesting as people think a movie star's life should be. A busy life, happy. Sure, I broke the rules by revealing some of my suffering and anxieties. But the times we live in demand a little pathos. I had to make myself seem believable.

Letícia ruins the picture, though. She doesn't fit. She doesn't fit, because I didn't invent her.

She's real. Or anyway, what you'd consider real.

Letícia is the truth. Concrete.

She tried to pull me down to earth.

Your earth.

Have you ever heard of Gerald Murphy? He looms large in American literature. He was a painter, never wrote anything, but he was friend and a patron to writers, musicians, other artists. Parasites, in other words, who took advantage of him. Murphy bought brilliant people in order to have them around him, forming a golden circle. He had a hand in creating a number of legends: Picasso, Gertrude Stein, F. Scott Fitzgerald, John dos Passos. He had a knack for knowing work that would last. Like me!

Once, Murphy, talking to Fitzgerald—who used him as a model in *Tender Is the Night*—have you seen the film version with Jason Robards and Jennifer Jones? directed by . . . by . . . the name escapes me—I should just make something up, but my mind is a blank—Murphy, that is, told F. Scott, "For me, only the invented part of the life is satisfying, the unrealistic part. Things happened to you—sickness, birth, Zelda in Lausanne, Patrick in the sanatorium, Father Wiborg's death—these thing were realistic, and you couldn't do anything about them . . . The *invented* part, for me, is what has meaning."* Gerald may have failed in his painting, in his life, and sexually, but he knew where truth was to be found. That is, in mendacity.

There's nothing more odious than terra firma. The clouds above us, insubstantial, wispy, comforting, silly—that's where I belong. I'm amorphous, just like them. I take on whatever form is necessary, depending upon the situation. Because, you know, I only exist when I'm in character. When I'm not, I am nothing but vapor.

Except when Letícia forced me to exist. I was never able to break her down, make her as unreal as the rest of my life.

And if I loved her, it was exactly because of that.

And if I left her, it was because she wouldn't accept me as I am.

Why did she scare me so much?

I've found out that not even an imaginary life can bring you peace.

I want to refute existence.

I'm not interested in the life, the lives, that are available to me.

I used to be happy with what I had. Now I'm not.

LA left me without prospects, dreams. I don't have anything to look forward to anymore. No ideal to aspire to. No hope.

Letícia put me face to face with myself. The real me. Believe me, I have no interest in that person. But Letícia is the truth, wants the truth. For me, the truth is unbearable. It hurts.

---

* *Everybody Was So Young*, by Amanda Vaill. Random House, 1999.

"The desolate beaches go on waiting for the two of us," as the song says. (Pretty sure it's by Antonio Carlos Jobim. See, I still have my memory.)

Letícia always wanted me to be honest, but the only "I" that interests me is the false one.

This "I" that I've refined for years, like a sculptor,

That I molded with the chisel of my thoughts

(I repudiate that last sentence, but find I don't have the strength to delete it).

Why should other people get to tell me what is and isn't fake? I don't agree with their terminology.

When I'm gone, they'll find my papers, notes, plans, manuals. Silly observations, meaningless designs (meaninglessness is intriguing), unfinished sentences, absurd texts, great and incoherent piles of words from the days and night when my thoughts were out of control, yes, and invented letters, strips of film, photographs of people I never knew (taken at little open-air markets and second-hand stores), labeled "Cousin Elisa," "Grand-Uncle Eliseu," "my meddling cousin Fábio Aurélio."

They'll call me a fraud. But what's a fraud?

Or, rather, what's real life?

I don't know the first thing about it.

MÁRIO PEIXOTO'S FORMULA:
BE INACCESSIBLE

I read an article the other day by Silvana Arantes about Mário Peixoto and his silent movie *Limite*, quite possibly the most lauded film in the history of Brazilian cinema. The article mentions that Mário told everyone that he'd received a letter from Eisenstein himself, praising his film—a twenty-two-year-old director thus entering the ranks of the great luminaries of international cinema. But the letter was a fake, or it didn't exist— though Mário seemed to believe his story. Thus, he was one of the first great self-promoters of modern cinema. Inventing himself, as we all must.

But it's this particular detail that caught my eye: Mário *believed* the letter had come. He believed in it, therefore it was real. Everything that he, Mário, wanted to see written about himself—what he thought he deserved—was contained in Eisenstein's letter. Silvana Arantes: "Mário Peixoto (1908–1992) only completed one film in his lifetime (*Limite*, 1931), but with this one film he guaranteed his status as a national legend. Curiosity about his other, unfilmed projects will be satisfied next month when his screenplay *Autumn/ The Petrified Garden* will finally see publication."

Inaccessible. That's the word. By being inaccessible, Peixoto became a legend.

Like Dalton Trevisan, Samuel Beckett, Rubem Fonseca, J. D. Salinger. Or T. S. Eliot's relationship with his wife. Difficult. That's what I need to be.

I'll only let people know things about myself that are incoherent, paradoxical, confusing, unintelligible, suspicious, implausible.

But which will nonetheless be true. Which will nonetheless be me.

NOTHINGNESS IS THE ONLY TRUE PERFECTION

For instance: pages from novels I read and memorized, poems, short stories, quotes from here and there, out of context and incoherent, passages of condensed pop-philosophy from magazines found in doctors' offices, dialog from films, and the books and leaflets dropped off by the generous (because they recognized my sensitivity) Soul Watcher organization (what a ridiculous name for a charity). And then garbage collected from behind editorial offices, middle-class homes, remainder bins, secondhand bookstores. I changed sentences around. Put together a real monstrosity. Nobody will ever decipher anything. It's going to take centuries for them to figure me out. And by then, I'll be of no interest to anybody—an anonymous savage.

Still, I'm happy to leave to history an inaccessible man. Difficulty arouses interest, makes your name stick in people's minds. All the better if you're a bit of a mystery into the bargain. Like Shakespeare, whose true identity is still being argued about. Perhaps he was really Francis Bacon, or Christopher Marlowe, or Edward de Vere, the Seventeenth Earl of Oxford, according to J. Thomas Looney's theory, published in 1920. Other mysteries: Was de Vere gay? Was he actually the son of Queen Elizabeth (1533–1603)? Did he commit suicide? Mysteries. Another enigma was Thelonious Monk, the pianist who had a penchant for mumbling incoherently and wearing extravagant hats. Also on the list of great, difficult, mysterious, and immortal icons are Erich von Stroheim, Dashiell Hammett, H. P. Lovecraft, the revolutionary singer Geraldo Vandré (why did he sell out?), André Malraux (hero or liar?), Lawrence of Arabia (a skeletal masochist), Carmen Miranda (and the circumstances of her death), Schumann (did he have syphilis? Personal tragedies are absolutely necessary to make one into a genius, you know), Leonardo da Vinci, Sylvia Plath (a cult figure thanks to her suicide), Marlene Dietrich, Miles Davis (he had a heroin period we don't know too much about, I think), Clarice Lispector (was her writing inspired by supernatural visions?), Sviatoslav Richter, Glenn Gould, Howard Hughes, J. D. Salinger, Guilherme Gaensley, the postcard photographer without a face, François Villon, Rimbaud, Gilles de Rais (intrepid, perverse, monstrous), Caravaggio (a visionary, half angel and half ogre, "who carried within him the agony of the world and the euphoria of the flesh,"* dying under mysterious circumstances), Pope Pius XI, Chet Baker—and then the fictional enigmas, who have entire books written about their impenetrable motives, like Gatsby, Ahab, or Kurtz (from Conrad's *Heart of Darkness*, or else Coppola's *Apocalypse Now* or *Apocalypse Now Redux*). Impenetrable mysteries! They might as well be Etruscans. They might as well have lived during the last days of Pompeii.

One of the Soul Watchers left me a monumental and difficult but dazzling book entitled *The Ribs of the Real* by Marilena Chauí, 941 pages long! Given its thickness, one might mistake it for a religious book. This Watcher understood that I'm a digital-age ascetic. What is an ascetic if not someone who seeks ecstasy? Chauí discusses Spinoza quite a bit. The first chapter is titled "Deciphering a Hieroglyphic." Who was Spinoza, she asks? An inconsistent man, a man without a unified identity: an atheist, a philosopher who wanted to love God intellectually, the anti-Christ, a loner excluded from a world that couldn't abide his presence, a fatalist, a lunatic, a sublime ascetic, a superstar. And what am I?

I'd give anything for there to be a book like that written about me. A thousand pages addressing my thoughts on contemporary life. In my simplicity, profundity. In my emptiness, an entire world.

What I've thought, what I've created, will go to my grave with me—but I trust that science will be able to recover it all, and then

---

* So says Christopher Liger, author of *Il Se Mit à Courir lê Long du Rivage*, Laffont, 2001.

specialists will rake through my notes and other earthly belongings. By leaving an inextricable enigma, my obscurity will manage to cancel my anonymity. I will live on forever, as a mystery.

Like that fossil found in the Alps, the one of the man frozen in ice that was studied by Professor Konrad Spindler of the University of Innsbruck. A five-thousand-year-old cadaver, with tattoos on its skin. What do the designs mean?

In a million years, the graffiti on our walls and buildings and the trendy tattoos on our shoulders, bellies, and legs will be just as inscrutable.

Enigmas last for millennia. They become legends. I'll have to keep my fingers crossed.

In Fellini's *8½*, at the end, Daumier, the guy who serves as a kind of critical conscience (a pedant, a pseudo-intellectual, a pain in the neck—an academic with diarrhea of the mouth), says to Guido, the director who can't make his film, "*Se non si può avere il tutto, il nulla è la vera perfezione.*"

Please imagine that this is the epigraph to my imaginary autobiography.

THE MOST BEAUTIFUL SOUND IN THE WORLD

Clap clap clap clap clap clap clap clap clap clap clap clap clap clap clap clap I have hundreds of CDs of live performances by great singers. Some I bought, some I copied, some I stole. I listen to them over and again. Not the voices or the songs: These don't interest me. What I listen to them for is the most beautiful sound a human being can produce, the most beautiful sound in the world: applause. Clapping, and then the attendant yelling, whistling, howling, shouting. A hysterical crowd, beside itself, delirious, standing, the palms of their hands stinging from the effort of their own interminable praise. Praise for me. I play these CDs in my dressing room every day. Just to listen to the applause. I deserve this fanatical admiration. For the admirable work that is my life.

I listen, trembling. The sound of applause is like a sort of pure adrenaline. As a sound I rate it as more vibrant and moving than all the music ever composed by Beethoven, Gluck, Brahms, Chopin, Tchaikovsky, Mahler, Handel, Schumann, Wagner, Respighi, Rameau, Hayden, Bach, Cherubini, Mussorgsky, Rimsky-Korsakov, Mozart, Albinoni, Górecki, Schubert, Berlioz, Bizet, Mendelssohn, Liszt, Gounod, or Bartók.*

---

* These are all the names I managed to dig up in Jean and Brigitte Massin's *Histoire de la musique occidentale* before the electricity went out again (conservation of energy). Christ, just when I thought this country couldn't get any darker.

ERRATA:
NEITHER ASSES, A SISTER, NOR MURDER

A little while back, during one of my "spells," feeling a little disoriented, I thought that a few extra touches of sex and violence might make this otherwise bald and unembroidered narrative a little spicier. A dirty trick, a vulgar ploy, a nauseating act, an unspeakable crime—suddenly confessed—would be good material. All great success stories start at this point. Still, I've reconsidered. I'd like to remove any and all references to LA's death or my sister's ass, and then that entire section with the list of women along with their telephone numbers. I don't even like the names of the women I invented. I took them from old files in the network's archives, from films I saw on the late movie. If I have a sister, I've never met her. My mother was dead by the time I was born. She was pregnant and got herself run over. The doctors had just enough time to get me out of her belly. Plus, I worry that some of the telephone numbers I gave out are close enough to real ones and that my readers (that is, those minds out there who have tuned telepathically onto the wavelength of my work-in-progress) might get it into their heads to call. And what if they reach a woman who resembles one of the ones I actually described? Life is full of improbabilities. (A good line for my Pithy Quotes Consultant—if such a person exists.) Also, I never had a police record. Why would I? But then having one makes you suspect, and therefore fascinating—a little ominous. Jane Fonda, Al Pacino, Mickey Rourke, Larry King, Keanu Reeves. Drugs, guns, drinking, assault, money laundering. If only I'd had the guts.

BEQUEATHING PERPLEXITIES TO THE FUTURE

"I don't pretend that I, or the letters, can explain him. Papa was lots of people. Some of them show in his fiction . . . But if you tried to read his life from his work you'd get it wrong." Josephine Marshall, daughter of Dashiell Hammett.* You'll have noticed that I tend to repeat myself. (I reiterate my main points! That sounds nicely scholarly.) Experienced television writers know that key bits of information must always be repeated several times if the audience is really meant to pick up on them. Your average TV-viewer (like many a reader) is distracted: sometimes he's paying attention, and then sometimes chatting on the phone, flipping through a newspaper, eating, arguing with his kids, running to the bathroom, adding some vermouth to his too-dry martini, paying bills, ruminating over the problems he's having at work, fantasizing about his mistress, picking lottery numbers and planning out what he'll do with all the money he's going to win. In other words, he's often somewhere else. Repetition is not filler: it's a necessity, an established means of transmitting information.

So, yes. I repeat myself. Reiterate. Insist. Also? Mislead. Give out some data in order to obscure my main points. I fabricate things. Set up impossible situations that only develop inside my head.

I contradict myself. Confuse my own chronology.

The more paradoxical, incoherent, ambiguous, inconsistent, disconnected the life-story, the more curiosity it's going to arouse, and the more books are going to be written about it. I want to keep battalions of perplexed researchers working in shifts.

It wasn't easy for me to invent all those documents, make up the letters and statements and excerpts (the only real ones are the

---

* Introduction to *Selected Letters of Dashiell Hammett*, 1921–1960. Counterpoint, 2001.

ones from Letícia, and which I've read and reread so many times, in moments of tenderness and despair, that the pages are disintegrating); to collect so many preposterous photos, rescued from boxes at small antique stores; to rifle out appropriate stories and interviews from the newspapers.

The telepathic archeologists who'll write the history of Brazilian television will be dumbfounded by all this material—these diaries, notebooks, clippings, letters.

I will leave an enigma for the future. Only questions. A mystery. Like the death of Walter Benjamin.

I remember one photograph in particular that Letícia took one afternoon and that she alleged got misplaced. It will be found. It will become an emblem of my unknowability. My gift to the ages will be my anonymity. It will last for years, since this autobiography of mine is going to circulate, confusing everybody. Eventually someone will manage to figure out how I composed it, of what elements. Man is capable of everything. Didn't the Rosetta Stone lead to our deciphering hieroglyphics? In time, the scientists of the future will reconstitute me, in just the form I intend for posterity.

Who was this man? What was his real name? Who knew him? Delicious.

A man who lived many lives. Like Hammett.

The only solid fact you can count on is that my life is a fake. There's nothing real here. And if there was, I'd deny it.

Since there's been no happiness in my life, no pleasure, I hereby cancel it—I negate my existence.

If I hadn't been born, it would make no difference to the world whatsoever.

I've never left this dressing room. This cell. I clung to a comfortable life, a life without dangers, threats, or loud noises. Here in Room 101, where I keep my papers, files, boxes of photographs and clippings, notebooks, pens, books, magazines, CDs, videos, dictionaries, my television. Nothing can touch me here.

This is how the world should be. Calm. Without surprises or pressure.

Letícia could never understand that our being together would make me vulnerable. It would mean leaving myself exposed to the world.

Giving her up was an act of courage.

I denied everything, preferring contemplation to action. In a world that respects only force.

I had to give up worldly things like pleasure in order to be whole.

But oriental philosophies endorse the suppression of pleasure, endorse renunciation. Giving up Letícia caused enormous suffering, for both of us.

Giving her up was an act of courage, but also an act of cowardice. Fear devoured me. Devoured my heart, corroded my skin. Like some form of bacteria.

And then it replaced what it had eaten. It became my new skin. My shield.

A carapace. Enclosing me.

Why didn't I fight it?

Well, out of fear. Do you know what it's like to be really afraid?

Sure you do. But I don't know of anyone else alive who's been able to use their fear to make themselves truly exceptional. A somebody.

NOW I CAN TRULY EXPOSE MYSELF

Fear hemmed me in. Paralyzed me.

Fear of not being able to see the red panties under the dress worn by a particular body that had spent the day perfuming itself uselessly with various balms and creams.

Fear of the nondescript noises I hear in the corridor.

Of the inevitable somebody who'll come to punish me.

Of being in midair and realizing I don't have wings (though I thought I did).

Of taking a step and the sidewalk not being there.

Of somebody leaving me without an explanation.

Of somebody who's staying with me without an explanation.

Of somebody being here now and then leaving.

Of somebody who left coming back.

Of being alone in a crowd.

Of not existing.

Of losing the certainty that I am a human being.

Of being shallow.

Of meaninglessness.

Of speed and slowness, of the pace of the world, of the nonexistence of time.

Of a treacherous embrace. Of polluted water.

Of her dark, questioning eyes.

Of being assaulted and kidnapped, of making mistakes, of pain, of closed doors, of words I don't understand.

Of traffic jams on the highway, without nearby exits and with no end in sight. (Of the traffic jams in my head, the thoughts lined up and refusing to move.)

Of my suffocating myself with those enormous sobs that close my throat whenever I hear flamenco music and think of the past.

Of accidentally hitting the "delete" key on my computer and losing my words.

Of accidentally hitting my own internal delete key and losing myself.

Of the money inside my heart where my blood belongs.

Of being a hostage. Of prison riots.

Of the noose. Of climbing up to the scaffold.

Of lost, wasted time.

Of letters, teeth, magnifying glasses, and therapy.

Of myself, of light, of open windows. Of being looked at, singled out. Of not being looked at, singled out.

Of her dry cunt. Her crossed thighs.

Of missed encounters, the eternal return, cold hands, the absence of pleasure.

Of the looming viaduct, words that refuse to be said, and my own silence.

Of knives and stray bullets.

Of cancer, of emotions, of the subconscious, of heart attacks, of false nostalgia.

Of the robotic voices on the phone that offer me life insurance, new credit cards, a different long-distance plan, and oral sex, all in the same tone.

Of not being able to decide, ever, like Flitcraft, who was able to make the perfect gesture, changing his life. Letícia could have been the beginning of my own gesture. I didn't see it. I couldn't. I refused.

Of not pleasing people. Of circling vultures. Of hackers getting into my bank account. Of broken glass, crying, crowds.

Of a row of traffic lights turning red at once, and never letting me go.

Of computer viruses, unpaid bills, audits, blackouts, blindness.

Of unnecessary lies, of unsaid things, suspicion.

Of love being wasted.

Of runaway elevators. Of bad dreams.

Of being followed, of rejection. Of an overdose, of scorn, of failure. Of raw fish, extraterrestrial monsters, of exclamation points.

Of never hearing Letícia have an orgasm again.

Of curt and evasive answers on the telephone, in an ironic and aggressive tone.

Of the daily news, of tainted food.

Of questions I don't know how to answer. Of apathy.

Of taking too much Lexotan, Valium, Revotril, Prozac, Tofranil, Verotina, or Zoloft.

Of drunks in the street, of anonymous letters powdered with anthrax.

Of herpes. Of leukemia. Of choking. Of shortness of breath.

Of empty walkways, wide-angle lenses, of expired medicine, of stock market crashes, of sweet drinks that make you throw up in the morning.

Of being someone else and wishing I could be myself again.

Of never being forgiven for all the tears shed for me, the hopes I've dashed.

Of losing my shadow. Of being lost in the shadows.

Of tornados, volcanoes, getting a pencil in the eye, slipping on banana peels, cirrhosis, spitting up blood.

Of irrefutable truths, secret codes, political and economic language, computer jargon, poor people's slang, schoolyard cant, scientific and academic terminology, irony, sarcasm.

Of rats, floods, cameras without film in them, ennui, foot-and-mouth disease.

Of not knowing English, of being unfashionable, of not knowing which clothes match. Of awkwardness. Of shame.

Of unfinished things, of doubt, of indecision.

Of the infinite. Of the absence of Letícia's laugh. Of being anonymous in my own bed. Of never having solved the riddle of her gaze, her paradoxes, the little deceits and exaggerations I sometimes found her enacting in the midst of her supposed passion.

Of being forgotten.

Of her not remembering the scent of my cologne, of the smoothness of my cock in her mouth, of my light touch on her cunt.

Of the certainty that no religion or philosophy on earth really wants us to be happy.

Of the red digits.

Of hunger, empty shop windows, disappearing in the night.

Of falling through the earth's crust.

Of Letícia's heartrending cries, of the pillow soaked with her tears—that pillow which, on solitary nights, in her fantasies, was me.

Of not understanding her smiles, her gestures.

Of misery, perfidy, solitude.

Of Alzheimer's and Parkinson's.

Of gigantic hawks with iron beaks, breaking through my windows.

Of my own stupidity, which led me to throw away so much pleasure.

Of snipers and preachers.

Of doubt: did Letícia really come when she was with me?

Of unanswered e-mails.

Of knowing I'm only here because I didn't say the one little yes that would have resolved everything—or nothing at all. It could all have gotten worse, of course. But that yes would have melted the iceberg in me that has for millennia torn into the hulls of passing ships, leaving bodies in my darkened waters.

Of things without names, of the telephone not ringing, of cruel laughter.

Of the cries for help I hear at night in the corridors of the studio.

Of not being able to feel my legs.

Of my teeth that are chattering now and feel as though they're going to shatter.

Of the dying light that covers my eyes like a veil.

Of the men in blue who feed me.

Of the scripts my agent brings me to read,
And of the plays I'll never act in,
All containing so many characters whose lives I'll never live.

Of things not turning out that way I'd like them.

Of being so brilliant and lucid and still not getting what I want.

Of never having been him. Of never having been me.

Of the fact that I culled out so much of my real life that I ended up with nothing.*

Of noticing how slowly my hardened heart beats in my frozen body.

Of my shell, suffocating and defending me, like a mummy's wrappings. Of realizing that my steel armor—999 millimeters thick—can never, ever be pierced.

Of mixed metaphors.

Of realizing that I'll never see her again.

Of realizing that no therapist, psychiatrist, psychologist, analyst, neurologist, phrenologist, priest, doctor, friend, or even grand amour will ever be able to save me.

> Because my greatest fear,
> absolute and insurmountable,
> is the fear of that I won't be able to withstand my fear.

---

* Research: The sentence doesn't have anything to do with him, according to the critic and theorist Ismail Xavier. The dialog is by John Lund from the film, *The Perils of Pauline* directed by George Marshall, 1947, with Betty Hutton.

ALWAYS KEEP YOURSELF "PLUGGED IN": OMNIA MUTANTUR, NIHIL INTERIT

Wear necklaces, rings, bracelets, and talismans with three-thousand-year-old Sanskrit prayers inside them, written on rolled up parchment. Keep them level with your heart and don't let the chain get knotted, or else it'll block the positive energy. (This according to Virgilio Bahde.) Visit the "Kitsch Show" at the São Paulo Museum of Art, which has things like purple cupids, refrigerator-magnet penguins, satin flowers, shocking pink shower caps, Campari posters, and Hebe Camargo dresses on exhibit. Not to be missed! (There are photographers there every hour of the day!) Wear customized secondhand clothing: Vuitton soccer cleats, leather soles with square rubber spikes. Long shoelaces that wrap all the way around the foot are gaining adherents among the hip. Bakelite, the synthetic plastic, is coming back (again): created in the early 1900s by the Belgian chemist Leo Hendrik Baekeland, it was mostly forgotten until Andy Warhol rediscovered it, and now it has twice the retro appeal. False eyelashes are back too. As is Twiggy and Le Creuset cookware. My consultant/gurus are insisting that I have an immediate facelift, that I get hair implants, a nose job, and have those two prominent pockmarks removed from my face. (But Jack Palance had his face covered with them, and George Macready had a big scar.) New teeth. A stricter diet. I apparently have to drive an Audi A4 with a multitronic transmission. Or an SUV. Then again, the Citroën C5 is a good choice. As is the Peugeot 607.

I must pray to Our Lady, The Untier of Knots.

GAZING DOWN THE DRAIN

Burning with fever, I stuck my head into my aluminum sink, which I'd filled with ice water. I almost fainted. This is my usual routine: ice water on the face in the morning is invigorating. This time it was painful. I closed my eyes underwater. At last a sense of well-being came over me. A pleasant torpor. My head stopped throbbing. I felt the ice-cold go down my spine.

I pulled my head out and then stuck it back in, several times. The water ran down my shoulders, wet my pajamas, and I began to tremble uncontrollably. Like Letícia trembled after she came. I took an aspirin and some vitamin C. Then, a shot of strong, cheap cognac, stolen from the studio kitchen—the kind they use for scorching fancy food when they need to impress an executive.

I stuck my head again into the water, with my eyes open. The bottom of the sink shone under the electric lights. The freezing water tingled on my scalp.

I saw my face reflected in the drain. It looked like that other guy's. LA's face. But it wasn't him. Just me. One eye closed, and my drain-reflection's corresponding eye closed as well. I moved my mouth, and the other face did too. Then the image at the bottom of the sink began to dissolve.

When I pulled my head out, my fever had broken.

Catching sight of myself in my dressing room mirror, I noticed that my eyes were different. Something had changed.

It wasn't their color. It was their intensity.

I was afraid to look into my own eyes.

. . . love. Each day . . . I feel my love for you . . . growing . . . When I think of you, there's a warmth that begins between my legs, and it climbs upward . . . until it takes over my whole body . . . And I become nervous and warm all over . . . thinking of and waiting for your mouth . . . your cock . . . I save up all my desire . . . until the opportunity comes again to let it out . . . When I see you again, smell your body, kiss you and touch you. Letícia.

I read, reread. Read again and reread again. I keep the letter in the box. The paper is worn and brittle.

Oh Letícia, if only
there were a hole
in the ground above me
like the one
in your wooden shutters,
and the sun, shining through,
could bring your image down
to the depths
where I've forced myself to live!

Anonymously Anonymous

LET'S GO INSIDE DRESSING ROOM 101

The body was removed by staff who did this work with the same indifference they showed cleaning the bathrooms or stacking the cafeteria trays or taking the residents to the bathroom or giving them injections. (Though, to be sure, they seemed to enjoy this last job. They said it wasn't sadism; they just didn't see why they shouldn't enjoy one of their least monotonous tasks. They liked to hear their apathetic charges scream. It made for a nice change.)

Yes, they removed the body without pity, without remorse or regret. Without even knowing the deceased's real name, since he'd claimed to have so many over the years, and some of them quite strange. Where did he come up with them?

"Call me Ishmael," he'd insisted.

Or else, "My name is Julien Sorel,

Flem Snopes,

Hans Castorp,

Guermantes,

Hernani,

Raskolnikov (they could never pronounce the name, so they shortened it to "Rasco"),

Arsène Lupin,

Micawber,

Snàporaz,

Nemo,

Kowalski,

Peer Gynt (they couldn't pronounce this one either, they'd say "Perguintee," and finally shortened it to "Perigee"),

Clyde Griffiths or George Eastman,

Magnus Pym (they confused it with *Magnum, P.I.*),

Ivan Ilych,

Sydney Carton,

Rhett Butler,

Gregor Samsa,

Bentinho,

Jack Delaney,

Holden Caulfield,

Zhivago.

For most people he was just "the man who lives in Room 101." ("Dressing room, ha!" exclaimed the cleaning staff). His room was in the wing where they kept the silent ones, the people who had given up talking. Not that the staff minded the quiet. The less the residents spoke, the better. The staff knew that they couldn't get attached to anyone. They had to make sure they could watch the residents suffer and die without adverse reactions to the spectacle. For the silent ones in particular—without names, without voices, without visitors—they didn't have the least idea who these men and women were, what they'd wanted out of life, what their dreams had been.

Of course, if you'd dared imply that the residents might have had dreams, the staff would laugh in your face. Like winning the lottery? they'd ask. Buying a big imported car, jet-skis, taking a nice vacation to Miami, getting a condo in a nice gated community? They didn't want to admit that their patients might be human—otherwise, their jobs would be unbearable.

Truth be told, one of the staff members, Onofrio José, wanted to see every resident struck dead as soon as possible. He took great pains to record every death in the building, counting upwards (#18,978) and noting the time, day, month, and year. He made his friends sign off on his count every week as witnesses to its veracity. He wanted to get the institution listed in the *Guinness Book of World Records* as the one with the highest fatality rate. He even took his documents to a notary. He said that if they got close to the record but heard that some other place was closer, he would take it upon himself to dispatch a few residents in order to raise their total. No one cared what happened to those people anyway. They were just some nameless assholes without real lives to lose. The guy in Room 101 had spoken about the lethal injections used in U.S. prisons. José talked about trying to get some of that stuff, just in case.

Where did the residents come from? Better not to know. The more you knew, the more likely you'd start to be able to tell them apart.

It wasn't José who collected and wrapped the Room 101 corpse in its yellow sheet. We don't know who did the job. All we know is that the man is lying on a rotted plank in the morgue, without identification. Identification was unnecessary. After all, who would care that he was dead?

The body would be sold to the medical school. Useful organs would be harvested and then the remains passed along to the mortuary school for use in an exam on the best ways to remove gold dentures. Next, the carcass would be dropped off at potter's field, where the nameless and the never-born are left for the worms.

Why worry about the residents? You couldn't believe a word they said, anyway. When they deigned to speak.

Wasn't that guy once the most famous actor in television/film/theater? A man who seduced hundreds of women? The most beloved celebrity of his day? Yeah, and which day was that? How come no one ever interviewed him, then? Why weren't there any reporters or photographers sniffing around his room?

And then what about the trash they found in Room 101? He was pretty attached to that junk. "My nest-egg," he called it. He almost had a fit when the staff tried to haul some of his shit out of there with big shovels and they ended up feeling sorry for him and leaving it alone (sure, they couldn't help having the occasional attack of pity—they were only human). No one even knows who was paying for his stay. He had two beds: a rare privilege. He kept one bed covered with papers and photos, newspaper clippings, magazines, pages from books, drawings, letters, receipts, documents, greasy old folders, almanacs, albums. He slept on the other bed, though without a mattress—he had a sheet thrown over another pile of papers. He loved paper. Notebooks, bread or vegetable wrapping, napkins, the cash-register rolls, calculator tape, printer paper, paper bags. And everything covered by his fine, miniscule handwriting. The words were so close together, they seemed to overlap. He wanted to economize, we must suppose, using all available space; he never knew when he would get more paper. Sadly, what he wrote is entirely unintelligible. Presumed sentences with every word piled up one atop the other, forming nothing more than a big black blot—or a red or green one, depending on which pen he was using that day.

What to do with these papers, yellowed photos, stills from soap operas and Brazilian, American, and Italian films, photos of actresses (Sophia Loren, Claudia Cardinale, Sandra Milo, Silvana Pampanini, Monica Bellucci), books, pages from scripts? No wonder he couldn't sleep.

Nobody understood what on earth he meant when he used to point to his head and announce: "If I become incapacitated—which admittedly is highly unlikely—please be sure to donate my brain to the University of São Paulo. They'll have the tools and the specialists who'll know how to remove all my accumulated thoughts . . . and my many *Manuals*, which will give guidance to all the anonymous people in the world who want, and quite naturally, to break away from the hell of being unknowns . . . what's most essential is the *Manual of Shortcomings to Be Corrected*. It contains fundamental information for anyone who wants to know about glory, fame, celebrity, success . . ."

Now he was on that plank, and the staff was collecting his "nest-egg" with rakes, mops, and spatulas. There were papers glued to the floor, rotting, crumbled and pulverized, damp reams warped into thick blocks, as though they were bricks, and mildewed photos, greenish, giving out a terrible smell.

A pile of books was heaped in a corner. An orderly picked one up—small, nice cover, though worn from too much use. As though someone had read it through forty times. And there were little notes in the margins. It was called *Fragments: Memories of a Wartime Childhood*, by Binjamin Wilkomirski. The orderly became curious. At the end of the book, in red letters—probably the same ink that graced all four walls, which were covered with incoherent graffiti—is the following remark: "*Almost perfect:* Wilkomirski *invented his own life. Too bad they found him out. But they'll never manage to do the same to me.*" The orderly put the book in his pocket—when it came time for his break and he went off to smoke a joint, he would flip through it. The room was like the basement of some secondhand bookstore, full of forgotten texts ready to be sold by the pound. Books like *Crime and Punishment*, by Dostoevsky; *Madame Bovary*, by Flaubert; *Moby-Dick*, by Herman Melville; *One Hundred Years of Solitude*, by Gabriel García Márquez; *The Metamorphosis*, by Kafka; *Light in August*, by William Faulkner; *A Hora e a Vez de Augusto Matraga*, by Guimarães

Rosa; *Dom Casmurro*, by Machado de Assis; *The Catcher in the Rye*, by J. D. Salinger; *An American Tragedy*, by Theodore Dreiser; *A Time to Meet*, by Fernando Sabino; *Two Weeks in Another Town*, by Irwin Shaw; *A Streetcar Named Desire*, by Tennessee Williams; *Twenty Thousand Leagues Under the Sea*, by Jules Verne; *The Hollow Needle*, by Maurice Leblanc; *The Maltese Falcon*, by Dashiell Hammett; *Doctor Zhivago*, by Boris Pasternak; *Under the Volcano*, by Malcolm Lowry; *Gone with the Wind*, by Margaret Mitchell; *Gabriela, Clove and Cinnamon*, by Jorge Amado; *The Red and the Black*, by Stendhal; *Viagem a Andara*, by Vicente Cecim; *The Leopard*, by Lampedusa; *The Magic Mountain*, by Thomas Mann; *The Guermantes Way*, by Marcel Proust; *The Death of Ivan Ilych*, by Tolstoy; *Hernani*, by Victor Hugo; *Asfalto Selvagem*, by Nelson Rodrigues; and *The Apple in the Dark*, by Clarice Lispector.

And then there were books whose covers were stained, their titles indecipherable. "We can't even sell most of this stuff," another orderly said. "Even in death he's cheating us. Just think what we had to endure from that son of a bitch. We should get *some* kind of compensation." And their supervisor, a man who worked with all types of residents for over forty years, said, "He wasn't the first of his kind we had here. He lived in his own little world. He loved being asked for autographs. That was how you got on his good side. For years I used to ask him for one every day, saying it was for my family, for some friends, for the crowd of fans who were waiting for him at the main gate. Did you know he had a special pen for autographs? He'd give me all kinds of excuses: 'The marketing department hasn't sent me any new photographs to sign! You know how it is: by the time they get here, there's been so much demand that they're all already claimed!' I knew all about how he used leave every day and then come back before five. Where did he go? What did he do? When he came back, he was always a changed man. If I've ever seen happiness, that was it. I couldn't understand it.

And then once, when he'd just come back, he let slip a little clue: 'I was with Letícia,' he said. Who? I asked him to explain, but he clammed up. So maybe there's a woman somewhere out in São Paulo who could actually explain Mr. 101 to us, who could tell us his name, what he used to be, how he ended up here."

A photo got stuck under a bedpost as they went on clearing out the room. It showed a scene from an old, famous soap opera—during its final week, it managed the feat of earning a 100% ratings share—that is, every single set in the country was tuned to it—an extraordinary statistic duly noted in the *Guinness Book*. One of the greatest Brazilian television actors was a regular in that show (he's been dead for years now). He was so popular that no scandal could topple him. They used to say that he had the gift of ubiquity: he could be everywhere at once. He would be spotted at a cocktail party celebrating the opening of a new car dealership, a mass, and in a motel all at the same time.

The photo found in Dressing Room 101 (everybody laughs about this) was of a scene taking place in a theater. In one of the orchestra seats one could see, amongst the various extras, a man who could have been this famous actor's double, stuntman, or stand-in. His face was the same—an exact duplicate copy, almost as though it had been made from a plaster mold.

And this extra could well have been the resident of Room 101— the silent wing.

A famous man's face placed like a mask on the corpse lying in the mortuary.

Waiting for the moment when his teeth would be stolen and his organs sold—standard practice in the institution.

FLY ME TO THE MOON

The eldest of the two coming into the office was carrying a yellow, faded box, tied with an old, loose crepe-paper ribbon. The younger orderly, who walked with a limp, was carrying a pile of books, as though he had just come out of a secondhand bookstore. Their uniforms were impeccable.

The director was at the window, contemplating his domain. Pavilions and pavilions. Two-thirds disused. Windows boarded up. Space that could be sold to a research corporation, a transportation company, or a church—turned into a supermarket or a black-market warehouse for stolen goods. He used to like to walk down the deserted corridors, looking at the empty units (as he called the rooms). He'd go into one or another, stretch out on an empty bed frame, and take in the smell of mildew, of abandoned things. He was at peace.

"I don't even know why I bother staying here," the director thought. Though he knew quite well that he stayed on in his position because there was almost no work required of him, and the pay was good enough to keep him comfortable. After all, being seventy-six years old he didn't have any dreams, illusions. He hadn't become rich, but then he wasn't poor either. He couldn't fuck anymore, but he did get to go down on a few of his forty-something female workers, from time to time. He could buy cheap coke from his employees, and really didn't give a shit about much of anything anymore. "I wouldn't even mind if I ended up among them, the residents. After all, I've spent my whole life in this place, as much a prisoner as they." This observation left him feeling neither burdened nor bitter.

"I'm willing to bet," he said to the two orderlies waiting to catch his attention, "that you've come to speak to me about that pain in the ass in Room 101."

"Mr. Director always sees right through us."

"This whole day's been a circus. Our business manager Martins Carneiro just left here in a flash."

"Yeah? How come?"

"What he saw down in 101 appalled him."

"Perfect. Now come and see for yourself."

"Do you think it's really necessary?"

"We've all got shit we need to take care of, Mr. Director, no matter which position we hold."

The bicycles with attached crates for baggage were standing by the door. No one dared walk the halls of the institution on foot—the corridors were endless and all looked the same. "Endless and eternal," said the director—but he's an idiot. The staff were impatient with him, but managed all in all to put up with his foolishness. The yellow box and the bundle of books were placed inside the baggage crates and tied down with leather straps so as not to fall out in transit—one of the director's rules. Once lost, nothing was ever found in those hallways.

The director and the two orderlies pedaled through the corridors. Usually the director only made quick, short runs, but now the ride went on and on. Where were they taking him? Was this the scenic route? Were they trying to teach him a lesson, protesting against his lunatic refusal to close any of the wings, even though the majority of the rooms were empty, against his insistence on pretending that the institution was still the teeming and successful hotel/casino it had been from the '50s through the '70s? Well, the director knew that this was the only way to keep the government subsidies coming, since they were estimated based on the number of occupied beds. Of course, the inspectors had to be taken care of. No one knew how he did it. But now there were offers being made, and real-estate companies were besieging them morning, noon, and night, wanting to buy or rent warehouse space, or else to put in assembly lines for foreign cars, or else to clear lots for parking.

Julie London's voice was coming from the hidden loudspeakers up in the deteriorating caves of the roof. First, "Call Me Irresponsible," then, "I'm in the Mood for Love," and, finally, "Fly Me to the Moon," programmed to repeat, since it was the limping orderly's favorite (he was pedaling with some difficulty, and sweating profusely).

Long trip or short, the director loved to pedal down his deserted corridors. He needed the exercise, really. Here and there a light behind one of the blue doors pointed to the occupancy of a resident. They biked for two hundred meters, turned to the right, fifty more meters, came to a fork, continued on for one hundred and fifty meters, up to the famous hall with the red-and-black checkerboard tiles. There began the horseshoe curve, leading to the rooms of the north wing. The view out the windows in this area looked out on an old housing community that had deteriorated into a shantytown—in the very place where the casino's old golf course had been. Yes, the place had been shut down when the Dutra government made gambling illegal. The roulette wheels continued to spin illegally for a few years afterwards, and then the casino was renovated into a luxurious brothel—with its fabulous, imported floorshows continuing until the artists finally ended up jumping ship to Punta Del Este and Juan Caballero. They say the director dated from around this period—his father had been a croupier. The three stopped in front of a blue door marked "Dressing Room 101." A tin star was pasted on the door. The two orderlies retrieved their spoils from their respective bicycle baskets.

"Room 101, Sector 9, Lot 38, third floor. Third floor! I've always wondered why we call this the third floor, since the building only has one level," said the man with the yellow box. "Doesn't that confuse people?"

The director laughed. His laugh was silent. He only showed his teeth, drawing his lips back as though he were in pain.

"Sir," the elder orderly went on, "You designed everything. Why the hell do we consider this the third floor?"

The lame guy who'd been holding the stack of books looked on expectantly.

"You guessed it already. To confuse people. It terrifies them when they're told to look for the second or third floors and discover that there are no stairs or elevators. The second floor is on the first. The third too. It wrong-foots them. If you want the advantage, you have to set people on edge."

"The man in Room 101 never got confused. He always understood that all our floors were the first floor."

"You know, this is my first time visiting 101. I always heard the man lived like a rodent. That he'd built a nest out of paper."

"It was his place. He'd come by, stay for a while, and leave. Then come back again."

"Dressing room. Can you imagine? What did he think he had to dress for? You say he wasn't always here?"

"He left every day for two or three hours. Lenira allowed it. Everybody knew. He just had to be back by five."

The director didn't understand it. Why would someone who was capable of leaving stay in the institution? Why would someone who left be willing to come back? "On the other hand," he reflected, "I hardly need to understand it. It doesn't even interest me, particularly. Or no more than anything else." They opened the door. The staff still hadn't finished the clean-up. They weren't particularly worried about finishing a job on the day they were assigned to it. They took a page from the director's book and didn't really give a shit.

The two adjoining rooms in 101 were connected by a door that had been left unlocked for the late inhabitant to give him more room. A provisionary measure had simply become routine. Cardboard boxes were piled up to the ceiling on one wall. Another was covered with newspaper clippings. Notebooks tied and stacked. Photos pinned to the walls.

"The man was clean, neat. Not a rat. Who are those photos of?"

"Television people," said the limping orderly.

The older one said, "He always told us he was this one here. Do you recognize him?"

"Sure. I watch a lot of television. It's Marcos Meira. Isn't it? A great actor. He died, what, two years ago? Less?" The director laughed again without making a sound. A little scary.

"He called this Marcos Meira the 'Lead Actor.' Or 'LA.'"

"And then sometimes he'd say this guy over here was him!"

"Or this one!"

"Or that one!"

"Was he all of them?"

"No, they were all him. And he hated those people. I didn't understand a thing. He'd say he was in the wrong place, that there had been some kind of substitution."

"And what about the boxes? What's in them?"

"Photos, letters, clippings from home decoration magazines, literary supplements. Old papers from years ago."

Where there were empty spaces on the walls, they'd been covered with red graffiti. Careful, calligraphic. Tiny lettering. Difficult to read. The director didn't pay much attention.

"That shit there scared Martins Carneiro half to death. He thought it was all written in blood."

"Blood?"

"He probably chose red ink on purpose. Everything in his life was fake."

"Didn't the guy kill himself?" the director asked.

"No. His heart stopped. The doctor said it just put itself in neutral and rolled to a stop."

"Carneiro raised the question. The suspicion. Of suicide." Martins Carneiro was serious, pensive, always dressed in perfect, tailored suits, not one hair out of place.

"He's always coming up with stuff like that," said the elder orderly. "He loves tragedy. He says it's the boredom of working here. White corridors, blue doors, empty heads. Not that the outside world is much different. A philosopher, our Martins."

"Is it blood?" asked the director. "If it is, it can get us all into a lot of trouble."

"No, sir. It's ink. Montblanc ink. Permanent. The good kind. The Soul Watchers are rich ladies."

"Ink?"

"Mr. 101 hated pain. Wounds, bruises, cuts. No, he wasn't the type to kill himself. He used to go around saying, 'My heart beats more slowly with each passing moment.'"

Julie London was singing "My Heart Belongs to Daddy." She gives it a different kind of erotic charge than the one in Marilyn Monroe's version, the limping orderly was thinking to himself. He regretted having taken the books—here he was back where he got them. He'd carried them all the way to the director's office for nothing.

Everything is so old in this place, the senior orderly reflected— even the music. He preferred contemporary music, the kind his son listened to and played. He and his son were inseparable. The kid had a band that was already getting gigs on the outskirts of the city.

"Are you sure it's not blood?" the director asked again.

"Our man used red ink. For his notebooks, letters, papers."

"What was so special about this guy?"

"It's difficult to say. Anyway, women liked him."

"They did?"

"The female psychiatrists visited him every day."

"They say he never talked."

"Sometimes he'd just sit there, thinking. He didn't like people to interrupt. So as not to disorganize the rigorous order of his thinking, he said."

"The what?"

"Who knows? The volunteers would pile up in here too. When he finally got his thoughts in order, he'd go back to talking like nothing happened. He scheduled meetings, invented assistants and consultants, and used to give these long monologues damning the press to hell. And they all listened to his tall tales. How he was a stand-in for a famous actor. About how he went to so many parties. How he mistreated the reporters who followed him around. He was full of stories."

"But other times, he'd let a whole month go by without talking. He was too busy thinking, structuring his life."

"But was he really an actor?"

"Maybe he was. We don't know a thing about him, really. The other day I discovered some plans of his. Blueprints, photos, all torn out of magazines. Pictures of furniture, paintings. Back issues of home decoration magazines. And then there's a notebook labeled *My House*. It's all in the boxes."

"He kept his magazines in impeccable order. He took very good care of them, even when he'd cut out pages or pictures. And then he'd paste what he cut out in a notebook, and write his own captions."

"How many years did he live here?"

"Sir, you're the one who has all the files."

"Oh, look. Everything's a mess up there. The living and the dead are all mixed together. Who can tell the difference? I don't give a shit anymore."

"Aren't you going to straighten things out?"

"I'll tell you what I'm going to do. I'm going to retire. Or drop dead. The next director can worry about making sense of it all. Disorder is my kingdom."

"Does anyone have any idea when Mr. 101 first checked in?"

"He was already here when I took over. I remember a woman who used to come visit him in a wheelchair. Laverne . . . Lavene . . . Levine. Anyway, she was always upset with him."

"That was his wife."

"She was?"

"Lenira says so. Says she's dead too," said the elder orderly.

The director looked back at the bikes. "What were you guys carrying back at my office?"

"Old books. Papers . . . we're going to try and sell them, by the kilo."

"Papers? Anything interesting?"

"No way to tell. He used to write everything over the same line. And when someone gave him an old computer, he'd print the pages of text he'd typed into the machine onto the same page, over and over. We've got reams of black paper, sir."

"Though one of the boxes is full of letters. Legible ones. Signed by someone called Letícia."

"Letters? You want letters?" asked the director. "I have a whole closet full of them."

"You do?"

"He used to give them to me to post for him." "To post" sounded nicely continental.

"Didn't you send them?"

"Come look at them."

Another endless walk down the cold, dank corridors, which offered no protection whatsoever from the humidity outside. At that time of the year, the downpours were frequent but brief. Many of the window frames had rotted away, letting the rain in to soak the floor, and the floorboards showed blotches of slippery, dirt-blackened mildew. The director led them to a room contiguous—he liked the word "contiguous"—with the chapel and opened a greenish-gray steel armoire containing packets of letters tied with strings.

"Pick one. Any one."

The elder orderly pulled out a packet. He cut the string holding it together with the Swiss army knife every employee of the institution was made to carry.

"Read one," said the director, peremptorily. He thought, "That was rather *peremptory* of me," and felt an almost erotic thrill at the word.

The orderly read a moment. Then he turned around. "What does it mean?"

"That's what he wrote. What he gave me to put in the mail. Not a language at all, is it? Want to see the notebooks too? They're all written in that same way."

"Why did you keep them all?"

"Lenira asked me to hold on to them. She guaranteed me that they'd become valuable some day. Worth money, she said. Some university would want to buy them. To study mythomania."

"Mythomania?"

"So you found a packet of letters addressed to him from outside the institution? Are they readable?"

"Completely. They're typed."

"From this Letícia?"

"Yes, Letícia. She came here once, I think. Does it matter?"

"Why would it matter?"

"I thought you seemed a little curious."

"I was born uncurious."

"We're sure wasting a lot of time over one little stiff. We lost a resident last week too. We'll lose another one next week. What was so important about 101?"

"Is he in the morgue already?"

"Washed and ready."

"Is he going right into the ground? No funeral?"

The limping guy who'd been holding the stack of books nodded yes. Unlike his colleague, he felt somewhat inhibited in front of the director, mainly because he envied him. How wonderful to be a licensed thief, to get government grants to do absolutely nothing.

The director nodded too. "You're quite right," he said to the older of the two orderlies. "What a lot of fuss over one more dead resident. Seems like the whole institution is up in arms about him." ("Institution" was the director's preferred name for his kingdom. It gave the place an air of dignity.)

"101 was different," said the elder orderly.

"Different how?" asked the director.

"Well, Lenira spent a lot of time trying to figure that out. She said 101 seemed to be afraid of the world. Both tender and aggressive. Sweet and savage."

"Lenira," mused the director. "I wonder just how many of our residents she's fucked, alleging that it's part of their therapy . . ."

"Not a single one!" exclaimed the limping orderly.

"No one?"

"Jesus, you're a dirty old man. Probably you can't even get it up."

The limping orderly was shocked at his own impudence. His hatred had caught him by surprise. The director didn't even notice, however—the world is made up of little shits with no self-control, he thought. Nothing to get worked up about.

"She was quite a woman. Interesting. Courageous," said the elder orderly. "She was the only one who ever tried to contradict you during staff meetings."

"She says the residents can be saved with love."

"Love and pleasure is what she said, sir."

"Love and pleasure. A stimulating woman. Gets on my nerves.

Makes me think. But she understands the residents. Now tell me, what do you make of all these maps?"

"No idea. We had orders. Not to interfere with 101."

"I didn't give any order like that."

"Lenira did."

Pasted to the walls, between the blood-red letters and the photos, were maps of the Bangkok, Saint Petersburg, and Berlin subway systems, as well as tourist maps of HaZafon, Saginaw, Olavarria, Boogardie, Takamatsu, Dnipropetrovsk, and Rijeka.

"May I keep the letters?" asked the elder orderly.

"What for?"

"They're beautiful."

"You've been here eleven years, and I still don't understand you. Why do you speak so slowly? A man of few words. I rarely hear you say more than two or three at a time."

"I'm thinking. Before every word. My ideal is to eliminate verbs entirely, sir. To speak without verbs. To use only nouns. A verbless world would be wonderful, sir."

The director was incapable of surprise, or even bemusement. On certain mornings, though, walking through his corridors, he'd asked himself why he hadn't written a study on human behavior—there was ample material to be had, provided by his residents and staff. The director was incapable of surprise, but now and then a spark ignited: He'd kept 101's letters because they were a mystery to him—no more, no less. And he'd noticed, too, that his staff were slowly assuming the residents' quirks. They spoke like them, thought like them, had even assimilated their particular tics and gestures. They were all constructing their own little worlds, each with his own rules, his own cosmologies. Because of this, the staff had to be rotated from time to time—personnel would be swapped from different departments, or in extreme cases sent on vacation. Otherwise, the director worried, eventually the only difference there'd be between an orderly and a resident would be the former's nice blue uniform.

LETÍCIA. 4:00 P.M. FORGIVE ME.

The man in Room 101 had always been a real challenge. Silent, impassive, almost catatonic. Or else a one-man Pentecost, a million voices in interminable flux. He'd usually have a crying fit at 4:00 P.M. And he wasn't allowed to have a clock. He just knew. What on earth had happened to him one 4:00 P.M. that it still could make him cry?

"So keep the letters if you're so attached to them."

"And what if they complain?"

"Who?"

"The family. His ex-wife. That Letícia. The Soul Watchers."

"He was brought here by the volunteers, and some cigarette company paid his way. He didn't have any family, or if he did, they didn't know he was here."

"I'd always assumed that he was rich. He had . . . privileges."

The director noted that elder orderly's nouns were still holding their own.

"Nothing like that. The company supported him and a bunch of other residents as a package deal. Philanthropy, you know. I hate it when one of their boys die. It means less money."

"Strange. He didn't seem the type. To have a sponsorship, I mean. He only seemed to care about culture. Theater. The cinema. Books."

There was no logic to the punctuation in the functionary's speech, the director decided. Like everything else in his world, it was completely inconsistent.

"Don't be silly. He didn't even smoke. The company does it because it's a good tax dodge. We have a nice arrangement: I sign the receipt for double what they actually fork over, since technically we aren't even entitled to what little they give. It's all a façade. Helps with public opinion too. You know the sign out front: *This Institution is Supported by Generous Grants from the TR, Egyptian, and Hampshire Cigarette Companies.* Speaking of which, do you think we could get away with hushing up 101's death for a little while?"

"Hush?"

"Which doctor signed the death certificate?"

"It was Zé Renato. A serious man. Incorruptible."

"Not that I was suggesting any kind of cover-up."

"We know as much about honesty as we do about health care."

"I only want to know how he died! And then, depending, I might put another guy in his room. Who would know the difference? Who would we be hurting?"

"Sounds like an old film. No one ever gets away with that kind of thing. The cigarette men would catch on right away."

"Their auditor comes every six months. If that. He'll never notice. Residents don't register. They're anonymous. No identities. Just bodies in beds."

The lame orderly thought: "This is my chance. I'll kill this old fucker. Bury him along with Mr. 101."

"And what about his identity badge?"

"We'll change the picture. Put a guy with a beard in. Beards confuse people. I'll just say he stopped letting us shave him. No one would know the difference."

"Oh, never. He shaved himself religiously. Wouldn't let anyone do it for him."

"Is that so?" asked the director. "And what if he'd slit his throat with the razor? Or broke his mirror and slit his wrists? We have regulations about residents shaving themselves!" The director was trembling. The residents were his bread and butter. He would have to be less cavalier. And even a single investigation by the Parliamentary Commission would finish him, and close the institution forever.

"He shaved himself for Letícia. That's what he said. His beard was too rough for her. It hurt her skin. Her face burned. Went red. Got irritated."

The director wished he could fire the elder orderly, just because of this new vendetta against complete sentences. Unfortunately, he had a degree from an American university. The director, by contrast, loved to talk—verbs and all. Words, after all, were meant to be spoken, to fill one's mouth, to spill over. Everything came easy to him.

"Look, we'll just forge a new badge for our man. We'll say the old one got damaged. Who cares?"

"We should finish cleaning up first."

"Yes, yes. Clean out the papers, the books, the files, the clippings. Whitewash the walls. What does the graffiti actually say, by the way? I never bothered to read it."

"Mostly it says '*Letícia. 4:00 P.M. Forgive me.*'"

"Just that?"

"Over and over. Hundreds of times."

"Or thousands. Somebody could count them."

"Why bother?"

"It's about as helpful as anything else we do here."

"There's also a sentence written in gothic script somewhere in here. Beautiful. The son of a bitch knew his stuff."

"I don't see it. What does it say?"

"Here it is. I copied it down when I found it. I figured I probably wouldn't be able to track it down a second time in all this mess. I thought maybe I could use it in a love letter some day. Maybe fuck one of the volunteers."

"What does it say, goddamn it?"

"'The love that began on that day was greater than all the love from any other place or time, and all the poetry in the world cannot encompass it.' From a letter by Dashiell Hammett. Written to Lillian Hellman."

"Hellman. Like the mayonnaise?"

"It must have been a monumental job to write all this. Years of work."

"Like the Marquis de Sade in his cell, scribbling away. Though what 101 produced is a hell of a lot less interesting."

"There he goes again, damn it!" said the limping orderly.

They were getting too far away from the matter at hand: the orderly who'd been carrying the box wanted to guarantee his ownership of its contents.

"Are the letters mine or not?" he asked.

"Shove them up your ass," the director answered amiably.

"He mistreated her very badly," the older orderly said.

"When are the letters from?"

"No date. Though the papers are turning yellow."

"It's the humidity. Are they signed?"

"No, sir."

"So how do we know he didn't write them all himself?"

"They were printed on a nice new printer. Not like what we've got."

"What did this woman do for a living?"

"How should I know?"

"It's all too unlikely. I bet he made up this woman."

"She was his obsession. I think she may have been the only thing in his life that was real."

"I may be a cynic," said the director, "But even I don't believe love can make you lose your mind. It's lack of love that does that."

"He wasn't crazy," said the limping orderly. "Strange, yes. Crazy, no. He knew things. He was heartsick over his own mediocrity. Anyway, that's what Lenira says."

"Something held him back. He was blocked. Paralyzed. Desperate. For her. But it was something else that did it. Drove him nuts. It was about celebrity. He wanted to be famous. He told me, 'I'm the most famous anonymous man alive. I'm an invisible celebrity.' I think that's what did him in."

"What do you know about it, anyway?"

"Intuition. I used to look into his eyes. I know."

"Oh, gazing lovingly into a man's eyes, eh? Tell me: Is there dirty stuff in those letters you're so desperate to hold on to?"

"They're erotic, if that's what you mean."

"Erotic, dirty. It's all the same thing."

"Not at all, sir! They're beautiful! Poetic!"

"I see. The plot thickens. So you're in love with this Letícia too, I suppose. She must be quite the woman. I wouldn't be surprised if you killed 101 to have her to yourself."

"You don't understand. Anything."

"I understand a lot, thanks. More than you glorified janitors. More than Lenira."

"Their relationship. It must have been beautiful. Letícia adored him. The man in 101."

"Who'd have thought you people would turn into romantics, working where you do, living where you live? Cleaning up after our residents. We don't even have electricity at night anymore in this country. What's there to be romantic about?"

"That woman. A brunette. She wore a large gold ring when she visited. And blue bracelets. '*From my love,*' she said."

I'll commit him, decided the director. He loved to commit people. If I can find a sponsor, I'll make him a resident before the end of the week. I'll just have to invent a case history, drum up some false witnesses, forge some papers, but that's all child's play. "Your days are numbered, my friend. "

"Can I keep them, then?" asked the older orderly again.

"Yes, damn it, take them. Whatever you like."

"I'm using them to collect material."

"For what?"

"I want to make an exhibit. Images of the subconscious. Outsider art! Like Doctor Nise da Silveira. She exhibited work by her patient. He called himself Arthur Bispo do Rosario. Bishop of the Rosary! His stuff even went to the Biennale."

"The Biennale . . . As if a moron like you ever stepped foot into the Biennale!"

"But I did. And I saw the pieces by the Bishop . . . I was stunned!"

"And what did Doctor Nise take in from displaying her patient's work like that?"

"What do you mean 'take in'?"

"As in money."

"She didn't. Not a cent. She was studying him."

"Then why bother?"

The limping orderly spoke up again: "And can I keep the books, then?"

"Keep whatever you want. Clean everything out and stick another resident in here. Bury Mr. 101 under another name. The end."

"What name should we use?"

"Doesn't matter. Make something up. I don't care."

The limping orderly suggested "Victor Hugo."

"I think that was the last name he gave us. I kind of like it."

"Sounds like a soccer player," said the director.

IN THE SNAKE PIT

To irritate Lenira, the director was smoking marijuana. The odor made her nauseous, but she didn't complain—she knew it was provocation. She hated the director, but he still ran the place. There would be two hundred residents out on the streets if the director wasn't the greedy bastard he was. Lenira was ready to retire, despite her youth. She'd started early, after all, had practically grown up in various asylums—her mother had died in a straitjacket. And for all she knew, one of the superannuated residents of the institution could be her father, incognito. Since she considered herself to be on the way out, she'd been lightening her caseload progressively over the last few months. Now, with the death of 101, she didn't even feel like making her abridged rounds. She'd liked him—he had crazy eyes. A real presence. And that's what she used to call him. The man with the crazy eyes. Crazy and forlorn. He'd made himself a private world—rich and well equipped, and with a juicy character role for her in it, which she'd appreciated, had even come to enjoy. At times, he'd narrate passages from his imagined life to her. He'd enjoyed the isolation of Room 101, so far away from the main part of the building. He'd chosen the room himself. Lenira allowed her patients a certain amount of freedom. They were even allowed to leave the building for a few hours a day, so long as they were back by a prearranged time. They had to relearn responsibility. That was Lenira's method.

"So, I heard your little heartthrob decided to leave us." the director said. "How did he go, by the way? No one seems to know?"

"He was found in that big empty room he called Studio 9."

"I've been speaking to the guys who used to take care of him. They need to get their stories straight."

"Nobody knew him."

"Except you. He liked you, no?"

The director thought he was being subtle.

"There was only one woman for him. Letícia."

"Yeah? Did it work out between them?"

"Nope."

"What a fuck-up. He never did get a break, did he?"

"Look, we already came to an agreement. It's in my contract. No obscene language in front of me. And, since you ask, he was the most complicated resident we've ever had here."

"Old and impotent, that's what you think of me."

"Careful with your language!"

"What does it matter? You know we don't accomplish a thing in this shit-hole."

"Sir, you didn't even know 101 existed until he died. You don't know a thing about any of the residents. You're always on drugs! You've got no self-control."

"Who has self-control in Brazil?"

"101 did. He never took a single risk. If you didn't know better, he'd seem like the most boring man you'd ever met."

"So self-control ruined his life?"

"His real life was in his mind. I have no idea if he considered himself a failure."

"Doesn't matter. He's dead, he's buried, and his room is free. We need all the vacancies we can get . . ."

"We have two hundred unoccupied rooms. And the money comes from private donors and the government, not the residents. And besides, I happen to know you've also been taking money selling lots on the institution grounds."

"They want to build a series of overpasses here to connect this part of town with the highway. A maze of ramps right above our cemetery! Highway robbery, literally. They're not even half-done paying."

"Despite everything, I'm still not eager to see this place shut down. I like it here. I've learned a lot."

"Oh, go fuck yourself . . ."

"Watch your language!"

"Fuck you and your ridiculous objection to obscenity. Do you know what I'm going to do?"

"I have no idea. It hardly matters anyway. You never do what you say."

"I'm going to take my dough and invest in a mound of heroin, dear. I don't give a good goddamn about one dead resident. I only wanted to know about that guy because he managed to get himself all sorts of privileges without my knowing it."

"He was hiding from something. I'm not sure what."

"We're living in terrible times, Lenira. Really insane people don't end up here anymore. They stay at home, or live on the streets. Under bridges, in the park."

The director could still surprise Lenira from time to time with some little insight like this one.

"101 committed himself, remember. He brought the paperwork proving he had a corporate sponsor. I never figured out how he managed that. Nothing about him made sense."

"The orderlies told me some volunteers brought him in off the street."

"I heard he won the lottery."

"And used his money to get himself stuck in this place?"

"He felt protected here."

"Didn't he have some woman trying to get him out of here?"

"Letícia."

"Who was she?"

"She tried everything. He wouldn't leave. There wasn't really any good reason for him to be here at all. He was as good as normal, most of the time."

"There's no such thing as normal, my dear. We're born dead. He probably went nuts because he figured this out. He became conscious of his own mediocrity. Not everyone can handle it as well as us. We only make it worse when we force lost causes like him to submit to analysis."

It was nauseating to hear him say "my dear." But, again, the director had his moments of lucidity—he hadn't gotten where he was for being stupid. He'd even been a respected psychiatrist, once.

"His egotism irritated me," Lenira said. "He really wasn't able to care about anything outside his own head."

"Do you know if he ever held down a real job?"

"He was an archivist at a television network." She laughed pensively. Remembering. Looking at the director—the spitting image of an Old Republic senator: corrupt, a mass of double chins.

"It's strange how he started out. He was studying at the university at the time. He just needed rent money. They gave him little jobs. He was in charge of synchronizing all the actors' wristwatches during taping, so they wouldn't have any excuses for being late. That's how he got a taste for that world. And that's where he got obsessed with time."

"What was he studying at school?"

"Sociology, but he never got a degree. He tried history too, but didn't stick with it. He almost got a communications degree, but he wasn't able to sit and study. It felt too much like wasting time to him. All those hours passing by with nothing to show for them."

"He must have been doing something right to fascinate you so much."

Irony. He'd always wanted Lenira. Really, the only female employees he didn't want to fuck were the Soul Watchers. They were powerful women: the wives of executives exorcizing their bourgeois guilt. The corporate sponsors loved them. Everyone else was fair game, however. Most of them left without even complaining. And if, on occasion, one did, they quickly learned that no one was going to lift a finger on their behalf.

"Was he ever an actor?" the director asked.

"An actor without a face. They let him play the corpse inside the coffin. The man waiting behind a door. The man seen from behind. The face at the window, masked by curtains. The hands on a pool cue. The horseman riding in the distance . . . And then, once, in a soap called *Cataclysms of Passion*, he was allowed to stand-in for the lead. I think it was Marcos Meira."

"I remember that soap. Did very well."

"He'd do stunts, anything that required movement—always from a distance. Marcos could barely walk—too many drugs. 101 was certain he ought to be the lead. He decided it was necessary to eliminate Marcos Meira. He was sure Meira was nothing without him—that Meira was coasting on *his* talent."

"Did he kill him?"

"Of course not. Marcos was already dead by the time he came up with that idea."

"I just don't get it."

"He was more or less lucid."

"Nonsense. He was raving. I'm glad we've put the fucker behind us."

"Please. Watch your mouth."

"Prick! Cunt! Shit! How's that? Have you diagnosed me yet? Am I more or less lucid?"

"My diagnosis is that you need to dry out."

"You're a pain in the ass."

"He was more or less lucid, but might have had hallucinations."

"You can give whatever name to 101's problems you like. You didn't cure him. I don't think you've ever cured anyone. You're just hypothesizing. Writing your next seminar presentation. What good is this post-mortem? You'll never get your own TV call-in show working on cases like this."

"Sir, you're disgusting . . ."

"I'm a man of the world, honey. Besides, I've got nothing to lose by offending you. You're on your way out. At least, I don't lie. I don't pretend."

"For the love of Saint Apollonia!"

"Sure thing. Go on with your analysis. I won't interrupt again."

"At times he showed an unusual amount of courage for such a timid man. Even arrogance. At other times, wouldn't ask for the least thing. Wouldn't complain no matter how he was treated. He didn't feel he had the right to complain—he accepted everything. Was afraid of showing any opposition whatever. He agreed with you even when he thought you were wrong. He thought the world would crumble around him if he showed his real opinions. He was a fake. A true fake. I didn't know how to save him."

"He was a bore. And I think you hated him."

"Every day, he'd tell me: 'I was born today. There's no tomorrow and no yesterday.' Every day after he was sure that Letícia wasn't coming back, anyway."

"What was she like?"

"I only saw her photo. And only once."

"I thought you knew her."

"And I'm not even sure the picture was really of her."

"What do you mean?"

"He had so many pictures. None of them were of him, or even related to him, though he tried to convince me some dated back to his university days. No, he got them at thrift stores. One time in Porto Alegre he bought a whole box of them, and then proceeded to turn all those strange faces into relatives, friends, and even himself. He used to do some touch-up work with the studio's computers. Then he got the finished products framed and put them in his dressing room."

"I don't know why he bothered."

"So the Letícia he showed me may have been a photo he took from one of his files. If it was the real Letícia, she was around thirty-seven years old. Very nice looking. Interesting eyes. She really got to him, he said. Incited him."

"Incited. I like that. You've got a way with words."

"Well . . . she inspired him to do crazy things, to ignore his schedule, break his promises, ignore his responsibilities. She represented freedom to him."

"He can't have known much about freedom."

"She was his ideal. She was necessary to him. He loved her too much—she was the only person he loved, and was probably the only one who'd ever loved him. He didn't have the courage to be with her, though. Between that and not being able to get rid of his nemesis, the Lead Actor, he was in a bad way."

"And what about his real wife?"

"He told me a story once—said he'd put her in a wheelchair. They were out for a drive. The sun reflecting off another car's fender blinded him—or something like that—and he lost control of his car. They went right off the embankment. His wife lost the use of her legs, while he walked away without a scratch. She didn't take it well, as you can imagine. Blamed him for everything. Soon he wanted her out of his life almost as much as LA. He used to close his eyes and take his hands off the wheel when they went out in the car together—her chair folded up in the backseat. He'd step on the brakes and try to flip them over, but when he was *trying* to get into an accident, everything always turned out all right."

"By now she must be dead. Shame he didn't live to enjoy it."

"I'm not really sure what happened to her. I knew he put her in a nursing home. He certainly *considered* her dead. Which isn't to say he ever got over his guilt about her accident. Or even his old fondness for her. 'Memories can devour you,' he told me once. And then he quickly told me that he was paraphrasing something from a Bing Crosby movie called *Little Boy Lost*. He would visit her in her room—they would stare at each other for hours, seething, silent. She'd bitten through her tongue, he told me, but he could still hear her call him a murderer, and swear that he'd never be free of her. As though she were telling him, 'No matter what you do, you'll still be here, sitting with me, stuck with me every day, sitting until the end of the afternoon, when the clock will let you make one more futile, temporary escape.'"

"Until the end of the afternoon?"

"Four o'clock."

"He told you all that?"

"In bits and pieces."

"Wasn't four o'clock when he had to leave Letícia? When you made him come back to his room?"

"Yes."

"How could he visit them both at the same time?"

The director was just making polite conversation now. Passing the time. His momentary spark of interest had subsided now, after so many awkward inconsistencies and contradictions, back into his usual and seamless incuriosity. He just adored having such a wonderful excuse to be with Lenira, who looked so good in her short, tight uniform. Room 101 was the only subject she seemed capable of warming to.

"A little while later he started writing on his walls. *Letícia, forgive me*. Each day, a few more words. She'd disappeared. He lost all concept of time. Withdrew. Sat and reread her letters for years. He memorized all of them. It must have been devastating to know that there weren't any more coming."

"So, she dumped him?"

"She wanted him to come back to earth. He wouldn't. Or couldn't."

"It's hard to keep track of who wanted who to do what in this story. Or am I still just a little high?"

"When aren't you high? You're a scary old man, sir."

The director laughed. His teeth were yellow. "His breath must stink," Lenira thought. She remembered a letter 101 had written to Letícia: "I love the smell of your mouth. It excites me, gives me strength."

"I'll say it again: there's nothing worth understanding about all this. Let life go on—or not, in this case. We have nothing to learn from Mr. 101."

"He was unhappy."

"He made his choice. He lived like he wanted to live. He was lucky, really."

"It wasn't a choice."

"Now you're just contradicting me for the fun of it."

"It's never easy talking with you. I get confused."

"That goes for both of us."

"Did we already get to Marcos Meira and the murder?" Lenira asked.

"Murder?"

"He started insisting, a little while back, that he had murdered Meira. He was always waiting for the call to come for him to substitute for him in the soaps. That's when he asked the orderlies to write 'Dressing Room' on his door. I had to pull strings to get him the star—it's made of tin."

"You mean he killed the guy to take his place?"

"No. He didn't kill anybody. He just decided that he must have.

He used to tell me there'd be a real scandal when someone finally deciphered his codes and figured out what all his black pages mean. 'That's when they'll learn about the real me—not him.'"

"Not him? Him who?"

"I asked him the same thing. That's when we'd return to the subject of the so-called murder. He'd say, 'Look, Lenira, we have to have our stories straight—you're the only one who can help me.' Marcos Meira died under mysterious circumstances, apparently. Overdose, AIDS, cancer, pneumonia, leukemia, multiple sclerosis. People can say whatever they want about celebrities. Personally, I don't watch television at all, except for religious and family programming. I don't have the time. He confessed to murdering Meira at least twice a day. And then he started complaining that his chance to be Marcos Meira had been buried. I didn't understand. Marcos had been dead for years. I think he only started pretending that he'd killed him about the time that Letícia finally told him *enough*."

"Did he kill himself, Lenira?"

"Zé Renato doesn't think so. If it was suicide, it was a very unusual form of it. His heart had been getting smaller and smaller, apparently. Zé called him *The Incredible Shrinking Man*. It's a good movie, really. Have you seen it?"

"I only have time for porn," the director said.

She let that go. After all, she was on her way out.

"At the end, his heart was the size of a chicken's. He couldn't get out of bed, barely had the strength to hold a spoon. All he had were his thoughts. And he was content with that. 'I want to be able to think,' he'd say to me, 'thinking is all that really matters.'"

"Let's sell his corpse to a university if he was such a human oddity. Please tell me we haven't already sold his heart. Get Zé Renato up here!"

"He's in Rio. Once a Carioca, always a Carioca."

"And 101's papers—should we hold on to them?"

"He told me, 'A restorer of frescos could do the job—remove one layer of text at a time and you'll be able to read my notes, to find out who I am, how I lived and worked, and what I learned.' He kept on writing even after his ink ran out. He didn't even notice. He was certain that his biography was finished—completely thought out. Sometimes he wrote on that old computer—and he didn't notice when it stopped working, when the monitor went blue. In the middle of the screen, who knows why, there was a luminous little dot—and he spent hours staring at it. 'It's the sun, Lenira, the false sun of the studio, a projection. Only false things can bring happiness in this country, now that the real Brazil has extinguished itself. If we hop on Kurosawa's Crane, we can ascend to the sun and climb inside it. Come with me inside the sun.' He made me sit on the bed with him and put his face up to the screen—I was worried that he might be going blind. This was when he'd started taking an unhealthy interest in me, personally. He'd added me to his story. He started asking me impertinent questions. 'What turns you on, tell me.' Which made me pretty uncomfortable, as you can imagine. I'm a Catholic, happily married—you probably remember my husband: he used to be a doctor here. 101 had a real reputation with the nurses: a wanna-be seducer. He might have managed it, too, if he wasn't so timid and didn't hate himself so much. But if he'd succeeded, it would have been a real experience, and he didn't actually want those. He preferred his imaginary world of television and fame. He called it a snake pit,* but he was comfortable in that pit. He often told me, '*You know how it is: You're young, you're drunk, you're in bed, you have knives; shit happens!*' I still don't know what he meant by that."

---

* Research: What Lenira doesn't know is that *The Snake Pit* was a film directed by Anatole Litvak, released in 1948 by Twentieth Century Fox, with Olivia de Havilland, Mark Stevens, Leo Genn, and Minna Gombell. Olivia played Virginia Cunningham, a fragile young woman in an institution—nervous, an insomniac, always mixing up dates and names, shouting that she's incapable of loving anyone. *The Snake Pit* was one of the first films to address the life of the institutionalized, at least according to Jacques Lourcelles's *Dictionnaire du Cinéma* (Lafont, 1992).

"Did you ever fuck him?"

"How can you suggest such a thing?"

"Did you or did you not fuck him?"

"You're repulsive."

"So leave, Doctor."

"You are an odious, abominable, sacrilegious man . . ."

"Yeah, I'm a goddamn scoundrel. But I'm no hypocrite."

Lenira knew that the director was right, in a way. With him, you always knew where you stood. He might be the most honest man she knew.

"Good thing I'm quitting," she said.

"Never. I'll fire you instead. Put a nice black mark on your record."

"Fire me?"

"And I have just cause, too."

"What?"

"Yes, my adorable Japanese phony. You're a crook. You've raided our pharmacy. Stolen anti-depressants. Taken home boxes of condoms for your orgies. Plus, you've sexually abused the residents."

"You're out of your mind," Lenira sobbed. They'd played this game for years, her and the director. He threatening and cursing, she playing the shrinking violet. No one else had ever spoken to her like he did. She almost liked it. If only she hadn't been assigned to Room 101. If only she'd managed to poison her little celebrity, as she'd often fantasized. He'd ruined her career. She was old before her time. Used up. And now that he was dead—of frustratingly natural causes—she'd never know if he was just wasting her time. Had he been a unique pathology, or just an unfathomable idiot?

"You may look exotic, my dear, but you're still just a hick from Botucatu. A sex maniac. You seduced all the residents, including 101. Now answer his question for me: Tell me what turns you on."

Lenira couldn't breathe. A wave of heat rose from her feet up to her neck. She didn't know if it was indignation or excitement. Her mouth was dry.

Not identified
Not identified
Not identified
Not identified
Not identified
Not identified
Not identified
Not identified
Not identified

Not
identified

WHAT DO YOU CALL SOMEBODY
WHO HAS NO NAME?

One of the orderlies suggested the following:

"What if we burned the body? Put Mr. 101 on top of a bonfire? I hear that's what they do with their gurus in India."

"The smell of roasting flesh would carry for miles. It'd turn people's stomachs."

"Just my little joke. We bury so many of these bastards. It'd be nice to liven things up a little here."

"Nobody came to claim the body?"

"Nobody even remembers his name."

"And what about his documents? The ones from when he was committed?"

"Lost."

"And then there was that mysterious fire in the main office, back when we were being audited that time."

"He used so many names. He probably couldn't even remember the one he was born with."

"The one he liked the most was Raskolnikov. Sounds Russian. Like Smirnoff."

"And a Turkish one: Ahab. Anyway, it sounds Turkish to me."

"Maybe it's Afghani?"

"Captain Ahab, he said. When Ahab lost his temper, he'd complain that Ishmael wanted to kill him."

"I wonder how he came up with that shit."

"Who knows! He read too much, that's for sure. Visitors brought newspapers, old books."

"His ex-wife came a few times, in that wheelchair. She didn't seem much saner than he was. There were the television people."

"Is that so? Did he used to be on television?"

"I bet he just worked in the office."

"What he really wanted was to be an artist. All he seemed to do was read. He'd read, read, read, clip out articles, and save them in a folder that woman brought. Letícia."

"Who was she? His wife?"

"No idea. She could also have been one of those volunteers. Rich people who go slumming in hospitals and asylums. She did everything he wanted—she brought magazines, books, some beautiful books of photos . . ."

"Which you stole."

"They're for my daughter. She's in school. Studying communications and film. She's not going to be like her father, an orderly in a nut house. Why should we leave such beautiful things here to rot? But I didn't take everything—there's a lot still sitting in the basement."

"A whole library. Food for the rats."

"Though the books are all torn up. He used to stash loose pages under his bed."

"He was quiet. Always huddled up. The doctor said he was going to end up with a curvature of the spine."

"But his eyes . . . Lenira, that psychiatrist with the big ass—she should be on TV herself with an ass like that—she said she was afraid of his eyes. She said they were like a cougar's eyes. Like he was about to jump you—a look that almost obliterates you, a wild look . . ."

"So you're a poet now? Don't go queer on me."

"I'm quoting Lenira."

"You're in love with her. You haven't been the same since that morning when she woke up and found him sitting in her bedroom in the doctors' wing. She opened her eyes and saw him there, sitting quietly, crying. Usually she would wake up when the sun came through the hole in her shutters, but that morning it was overcast. He must have been watching her for a long time before she noticed him there. He said, 'I've come to wake you up, so we can make love now, in the morning, as you always liked. I've come to see you dance for me.' He didn't try to do anything, though. Just spoke to her."

"She told you all that? I didn't know you two were so close."

"We're not."

"She told me that she was both afraid of and attracted to 101. She never thought he was really crazy."

"So what was he then?"

"She thought he died of a broken heart. I guess Lenira was a little crazy herself, wasn't she?"

"It's harder and harder to tell the living from the dead in this place."

They dropped the coffin on the dry, rocky ground. They were sweating heavily. The sky was filled with a mass of black clouds and the air was oppressive and thick. The flowers on the graves were all dried up—they only got replaced when families would come by on visiting day. The orderlies wiped their faces with the bottom of their filthy T-shirts, each bearing the insignia of the institution.

"Remember when there were three of us on gravedigger duty?" one of them asked. "Cheap bastards."

"We don't have to dig anything. All we have to do is leave him at the edge of the grave. Big Richard will come out later and bury him. He went to town to register to be in some game show."

385

"Right now I could use a nice cold beer. If Lenira was still working here, I'd invite her along."

"She was a gorgeous piece of ass, I'll give you that. But I think the only person she ever loved was the guy in this coffin."

"He called her Letícia."

"Letícia?"

"He wrote letters to her. Demanded answers in return. This was mainly in the beginning. Later, he calmed down."

"Did she write him back? He was in love with her, of course. Everyone fell in love with Lenira. That laugh of hers, the way she sat and crossed her legs . . ."

"No, she didn't write back. He wrote her responses for her. This was when she started telling everyone she was going to retire. Not that she had any intention of going."

"How do you know all this?"

"I went through his things."

"When?"

"Didn't you know he used to go out during the day?"

"How could she call it retiring, anyway. She wasn't old enough."

"She claimed that ever year she spent here, under these conditions, counted for two."

"This goddamn heat is getting to us. Where's the grave? They better fill it in soon—it's going to rain."

"They said to put him in the corner. Alone, way in the back."

"He was accustomed to being alone."

"It doesn't matter. They're just going to put a new overpass here anyway."

"What name do we bury him with?"

"None. There's no cross anyway. Our carpenter disappeared. I heard he got a job in the city."

"What do you call somebody who has no name?"

"Isn't his name on the card Lenira gave you?"

"I didn't even look. It's in the envelope. She said we should nail it to the cross."

"There's no cross."

"And there's no name. Here, read it."

"Actors are people who take every advantage of their profession in order to live forever, to make themselves immortal. A true actor is timeless."

"What the hell does that mean?"

"What kind of epitaph is this?"

"Just put it in the ground with him. The rain would ruin it anyway."

"Let's get out of here. It's Saturday—I need to buy my lottery tickets."

"And I still haven't had my rum and eggs."

They stuck the card into a slot between two boards of the coffin, and left the box at the edge of the open grave. They walked away then, spitting on the tombstones as they went, and wiping their faces with their shirtsleeves.

Se non
Si può avere
il tutto,
il nulla
è la vera
perfezione

Daumier, the critic in *8½*, by Fellini, 1963

What good is the horizon if I'm in some dark alley?

Letícia, paraphrasing Manuel Bandeira

The gravedigger won't come. It's night. Some last thoughts of the man whose coffin waits to be interred while this colossal rainstorm soaks everything, makes the cemetery into a mud hole. Don't ask how these thoughts can be recorded. It's enough to know that they exist. The card with the Gianni Ratto quotation (himself already dead and buried) got wet—the ink dissolved and ran into the ground. The wet corpse and its soggy clothes are rather repulsive, but there's nothing to be done. You can hear loudspeakers at a bingo game in the nearby town. Frank Sinatra singing "My Way."

IGNÁCIO DE LOYOLA BRANDÃO began his career writing film reviews and went on to work for one of the principal newspapers in São Paulo. Initially banned in Brazil, his novel *Zero* went on to win the prestigious Brasilia Prize and become a controversial bestseller. Brandão is the author of more than a half-dozen works of fiction, including *Zero*, *Teeth Under the Sun*, and *The Good-bye Angel*, all of which are available or forthcoming from Dalkey Archive.

A native of Massachusetts, NELSON H. VIEIRA has studied in Brazil and Portugal. He is a Professor of Portuguese & Brazilian Studies and Judaic Studies at Brown University.

SELECTED DALKEY ARCHIVE PAPERBACKS

FOR A FULL LIST OF PUBLICATIONS, VISIT:
www.dalkeyarchive.com

SELECTED DALKEY ARCHIVE PAPERBACKS

FOR A FULL LIST OF PUBLICATIONS, VISIT:
www.dalkeyarchive.com